ALL ENCOMPASSING TRIP

Nicole Del Sesto

Afterbirth Books
Seattle, Washington

Afterbirth Books
P O Box 6068
Lynnwood, WA 98036

email: editor@afterbirthbooks.com
website: www.afterbirthbooks.com

ISBN 0-933929-12-X

To those who inspire me

Introduction

This story is a fable. It's somewhat autobiographical, a little bit fantasy and a lot of pop-culture, (not a little bit country, but definitely some rock and roll).

Be forewarned, nothing is sacred. Except Oprah. Oprah is sacred, but she earned it. Everything else is fair game.

Welcome to my microcosm. The wonderful world of Nikki.

In the Beginning ....

Somewhere in Milpitas, Chuckie Rightwing invites Jesus Christ to live in his heart. He does this every day. Thus far J.C. has been extended 8,132 invitations to live in Chuckie's heart. We're not sure if Christ hasn't received Chuckie's request, or if he just hasn't RSVP'd yet. Regardless, the invitation stands, and Christ has his own bedroom with a portico, a down comforter and a twelve-inch replica of himself hanging on the cross.

In Berkeley, Devi Demi Dai, a vegan, sits down to a meal of tofu with organic flower petals. She burps, loudly, and thanks the Goddess for the opportunity to purge the toxins from her body. Later, the tofu will give her another kind of gas. She'll be equally grateful for the cleansing flatulence.

In downtown San Francisco, Kassen Kyle, a medically certified commitment-phobe, considers his options for the evening. As usual he has three events to choose from, and three times as many women slated to accompany him. There will be several disappointments.

In Chicago, Oprah films her show. In the woods, a coyote sleeps. In Jamaica, a 7-½ foot tall bald black man is having his entire body covered in tattoos. On television, a Leprechaun dances around his cereal bowl. It's magically delicious.

A normal day.

1.

By the Time We Get to Normal

Head in her hands, swinging back and forth in the chair of her home office, Nikki Nasco considered her dilemma. Despite the fact that her desk was covered with dust and debris, and she had a "things to do" list a mile long, she could not focus on anything other than what currently consumed her mind. Mentally she ran though the CD list again, which reminded her of the other list, which reminded her that she needed to make a bikini wax appointment, which got added to the list. If she could only make a list of when she would tackle the growing list, she would be in good shape.

> Call doc for anti-depressant refill (ONLY TWO PILLS LEFT!)
> Add final bullets to PowerPoint presentation due MONDAY!!!!!
> Call insurance company about bill (WTF, $700.00 increase??)
> Buy coffee and tampons
> Clean house
> Call Human Resources about diversity training
> Add trash bags to Target shopping list
> Clean desk
> Make list of things to advise Landlord of
> Pay Bills
> Check Marriott points balance
> Call Pottery Barn to get removed from mailing list
> Make bikini wax appointment

Guilt *almost* consumed her for not working on her PowerPoint, but that was on her list for the weekend. After all, she had no other plans. Living in a small Northern California college town did little for her social life. If it weren't for going to the gym, she would probably never get dressed. 20-year-old college boys could only be fantasized about for so long before reality kicked in. Reality was an aging college professor, who claimed to be equally comfortable in jeans or a tuxedo, invariably had rampant, unruly facial hair and horribly bad professor halitosis.

Oprah's voice blared from the television in the living room. "Animal medicine, on the next Oprah!"

Not to be derailed by her own wandering mind, Nikki returned her focus to the *other* list, her real dilemma. A project to which she had given way more thought than it justifiably deserved. Gathering her notebook, cordless phone and American Spirit cigarettes, she went out to the back patio to smoke and dial. A ruling was required and so she sought counsel.

Nikki and Amber met at Boot Camp (the exercise class, not the military training). In the true spirit of Boot Camp, Amber (the instructor) yelled at the class, Nikki yelled back, and they had been friends ever since.

While waiting for Amber to answer the phone, she perused the list again.

Her bold printing in hot pink Sharpie glared out at her.
THE 5 CD'S I WOULD BRING IF I WERE STRANDED ON A DESERT ISLAND
    1. Joni Mitchell — *Court and Spark*
    2. Sublime — *40oz to Freedom*
    3. Doors — *The Best Of* ....
    4. Pearl Jam —
    5.

"Hello?" Amber answered.

"Hey," Nikki replied. "Where are you?"

"Driving home from school. What's up?"

Nikki blew her smoke out very quietly so Amber couldn't hear, suspecting that her aerobics teacher wouldn't condone the smoking, even if they were "all natural" cigarettes.

"OK, so do you know the Desert Island CD game?"

"What?"

"You know, where you pick the 5 CD's that you would take with you if you were stranded on a desert island?"

"Is there such a thing as a desert island? I think that's an oxymoron."

"I don't know Amber. It might not be grammatically correct, but that's what the game is called. OK, so … Let's just say that hypothetically you knew about the Desert Island CD game, which means you got to pick 5 CD's that would be the last CD's you would ever listen to, unless you got rescued. Could you bring a 4 CD box set as one of the choices, or is that cheating?"

"Is there a CD player on the island?" Amber asked playfully.

"Am-BER, that's not the point. Listen, *Court and Spark* is easy. It's my all time favorite. Sublime, *40oz to Freedom* has a lot of songs and a good variety. Doors, *Best of ...* is Classic! It's two discs but I decided that you can have at least one 'best of.' After that I'm stuck. I need a Pearl Jam, but I don't know which Pearl Jam, and then my fifth choice. I'm thinking Bob Marley Box set but it's four discs and I think that's cheating."

"Nik?" said Amber with a hint of both patience and condescension.

"You aren't going to play with me are you?" Nikki whined.

"Nope."

"What time is it?"

"4:10, and I have to hurry because I teach Boot Camp in 20 minutes."

"Shit, I have to hurry as well."

Nikki quietly crushed out her cigarette, the paranoia of discovery outweighing the logic that even if a sound could be heard over the telephone line, it could not be identified as a cigarette being crushed out.

Cradling the phone between her ear and chin, she walked into the bathroom, washed her hands and arms and put on scented lotion to cover any lingering smell.

"OK," Nikki said into the phone line that had gone quiet, "I need to brush my teeth. I'll see you there soon."

While she was putting her hair back she noticed the grays were making their monthly appearance. Forty years since her birth date didn't change the fact that Nikki looked and felt early thirties, some days younger. With dark reddish brown hair, big brown eyes, olive skin, and well proportioned nose and lips, she was attractive. 5'3", 119 pounds, and in the best shape of her life, the knowledge of which did nothing to lessen the abiding obsession she had with her weight.

Quickly changing into her adidas bike shorts, matching top, and her favorite Reeboks, she ran to the mirror for a final check. Biceps flexed were somewhat pleasing, but when she loosened up and jiggled her arm flab, not so much.

"Damn, triceps," she said aloud.

In addition to only getting dressed on gym days, working from home also meant that she talked to herself a lot. It might seem sad, but it wasn't really. She talked to people on the phone a lot too. Sometimes.

A bottle of Crystal Geyser water and a peanut butter Balance bar in hand, she checked the mirror one last time. Her shorts didn't cover her cellulite. She scrutinized her Quads, they were fine. She posed in the one position she knew showed good hamstring, and momentarily enjoyed that, but when it came to her hip and glute area, Elvis would *not* leave the building. Realizing it was too late to change her clothes she accepted her appearance as it was.

A quick stop into her office to add "Make hair appointment" to her things to do list and she was out the door.

A normal day.

2.
More Over Than Over

Amber Lawson rushed into to her apartment, threw her law school books on the bed, and quickly stripped out of her school clothes. In dire need of a shower, but completely out of time, she donned her workout attire, put the CD's for her class into her gym bag and headed for the door. Amber enjoyed a quick chuckle over Nikki's phone call. Amber didn't have her 5 desert island CD's picked out; she didn't worry about stuff like that. The fact that Nikki did was a quality that Amber found endearing. Neurotic, but endearing.

Like the Tasmanian Devil (the Warner Brothers cartoon one, not the real Southern Hemisphere one) she hastily flew back out her apartment door, and hopped into her convertible white Rabbit. The radio came blaring on when she started the ignition. It was playing 'their song.' She screamed 'FUCK', put her head on the steering wheel and started to cry. Four weeks had passed since her lover left her.

Amber defied all stereotypes. There was nothing about her that "screamed" lesbian, though people were never surprised to hear that was her sexual orientation. At 35 years old, she easily passed for 25. Her thin blonde hair was shoulder length and worn in a flip. Her hazel eyes were almond shaped and almost disappeared completely when she smiled. She always sported a tan, and was in phenomenal shape.

~~~

Boot Camp, as always, kicked ass.

~~~

After class, Nikki got into her car and checked her cell phone. One missed call.

The missed call log revealed no new numbers. Her stomach

dropped, she assumed it must be Kassen and quickly accessed her voice mail. It wasn't Kassen, nor should it have been, they hadn't spoken in months. The voice mail was from her mother, with panic in her voice, "Call me as soon as you get this message."

Even though she was permanently angry at Kassen, and even though her mother's message sounded urgent, she hung up the phone and immediately dialed his work number which went straight to voice mail.

"Guess what?" she said, "I finally figured out who moved my cheese." They had the kind of relationship where that kind of thing was hilariously funny.

Instantly regretting leaving the message, she pressed the option for cancel and re-record, made fake cell phone crackling noises and hung up. She'd done that before. Another bullet dodged. She dialed her mother.

"I got your message, what's up?" Nikki wasn't all that nice to her mom, but mostly because her mom did annoying things.

"I just remembered, that a couple of weeks ago when I was there I made some steamed vegetables and I had leftovers and I put them in a Cool Whip container, and left them in your fridge." This was a perfect example of the aforementioned annoying things.

"That would explain the smell," Nikki replied.

"So, you should throw them away."

"Yeah, I got that mom. I wasn't going to eat two week old steamed vegetables out of a Cool Whip container, and by the way, can you please call the phone company and get your phone number unblocked? I hate when you call my cell phone. It says Private Caller, and I think it's Kassen and –"

"Are you talking to Kassen again?" interrupted her mother.

The "relationship" between Nikki and Kassen was over. It was a called a quote "relationship" unquote vs. just a plain no quote relationship because it never really was one. Kassen, in her mind, was a misogynistic sycophant. She wasn't really sure what sycophant meant, but she referred to him that way anyway because she liked the sound of it. She was pretty certain it had a negative connotation and that it applied, but made a mental note to add "look up sycophant" to her things to do list.

Sometimes she mis-pronounced it on purpose and called him psycho-fuck, or just fuckerhead. There's no correlation between sycophant and fuckerhead, but she made it anyway. It made her feel better, if only momentarily. She wished she hated him.

For ten years they had carried on what could best be

described as a bipolar, long-distance, relationship. In the good times, the mania, he would call her six times a day. He would treat her as though she were the only woman in the world, with lavish attention and affection. They would get together and have romantic comedy caliber weekends. A screenplay could have been written based on their up times, which generally lasted about three months, or until Nikki finally felt confident that things would work out for once. Then the depressive part of the cycle would begin. He would stop calling, or promise to call right back and instead take his phone off the hook. She would get neurotic and leave him incessant voice mails, and they would wear each other down with the behaviors that each of them knew pushed the other's buttons. Over was not a strong enough word. They were more over than over. Over-er? They had been over (really, they meant it this time, they were done done done) more times than could reasonably be believed. But this time, Nikki really meant it. They were over. She was moving on. Really. Over-est.

"No, I am not talking to Fuckerhead again, but I'm afraid he might call and even though I feel really strong with regard to him right now, when he calls I tend to turn to mush and I just can't do it again. I can't."

"I'd like to get my hands on him," Nikki's mother said.

Once in a while Nikki's mom ceased being self-absorbed for long enough to feel protective of her daughter. It never lasted long, and by the time Nikki arrived at home, her mother had moved on to the topic of the varying degrees of health of her eleven cats.

During the detailed description (and in between uh-huhs) of Moon-doggykitty's molar abscess, Nikki sat down at her computer and decided to check her Match.com account. Every day she was hopeful that she would receive *one* intelligent, funny, e-mail from a man in a neighboring town who did *not* sport a mustache in the style of Jeff Kent formerly of the San Francisco Giants. She didn't realize when she moved from Southern California to Northern California that she was changing decades as well as area codes. Sometimes she called her town, "the prairie" because half the people dressed like *Little House on the Prairie*. Any day, she expected Michael Landon to return from beyond to issue fashion citations to the rare style conscious resident or to teach a butter making class.

"Hey, Mom," she said interrupting the recap of Pat's (the androgynous cat) very stubborn hairball. "Do you know about the desert island CD game?" Self-absorption was in the genes.

"No, what is that?"

"Where you pick the 5 CD's you would want with you if you were ever shipwrecked? I have Joni Mitchell, The Doors, Sublime and Pearl Jam on the list, but I'm trying to figure out if it's fair if I put a 4 disc Bob Marley box set on, I mean there has to be some integrity in the game, right?"

"What about Frank? You have to have a Frank Sinatra on there."

"Well, *I* don't Mom. You can have Frank on your list, but I need to figure out a Pearl Jam and if I can bring a box set."

"Everybody loves Frank. You would be happy you had it, Nicole, you should add it to your list."

"I have to go now, mom." Nikki disconnected and walked into the living room to plop on the couch and flip through her 270 television channels.

After going through all the channels twice, she was torn between a re-run of *The Bachelor* season 2, and a new episode of *Queer Eye for the Straight Guy*.

"Lame," she said to herself, turned off the television and decided to read instead.

When she entered her bedroom she tripped over the CD collection that was strewn on the floor. She took Joni Mitchell, Sublime and the Doors and tossed them up onto the bed. Having an attack of conscience she put away her Bob Marley box set. She decided in that moment, it *was* cheating. Instead she selected Alanis Morissette *Supposed Former Infatuation Junkie* for her fourth pick. She wasn't thrilled with the choice and could have gone with *Jagged Little Pill*, but it was overplayed. Alanis went onto the bed and she faced her Pearl Jam collection.

Ten was decided against. If she needed to hear *Even Flow* or *Jeremy* she could sing them in her head. *Vs., Vitalogy, No Code* and *Yield* were left on the floor. She committed to making a list the next day of the compelling songs on each disc and making a decision from there. This was a relief, she was always better with a plan.

Donning her evening apparel, which consisted of her favorite Calvin Klein heather gray boxers and light blue Old Navy tank with built in bra, she stood in front of the mirror. She admired her obliques, but scowled at her lower abdomen. Then she pinched an inch of fat, and finally pulled down her shirt in disgust. She brushed her teeth, flossed with Glide, took her second to last anti-depressant (mental noted to herself '*Must* call the doctor tomorrow'), and crawled into bed.

Her well-worn copy of Tom Robbins' *Jitterbug Perfume*, which she was reading for the fourth time, was perched on the pillow next to her. Seattle, she yawned, beets, the lesbian bartender, perfume bottle .... She read for a couple of hours. Her last conscious thought before she dozed off was accompanied by a flutter of excitement; in just nine hours she would have her first sip of her beloved morning coffee.

~~~

Amber cried herself to sleep. She didn't realize that her car keys were in bed with her and that she would wake up in the morning with a big VW imprinted on her face. She wore a camouflage tank top and a pair of Wonder Woman underwear that Nikki had given to her. They were supposed to make her feel invincible.

Her Hello Kitty pillowcase was covered in mascara stains, and her bed littered with law books and used Kleenex. Instead of counting sheep, she counted teardrops and finally fell into a fitful sleep.

~~~

In Livermore a fat psychic speaks with the voices in her head; in Oakland a teen gives birth to a fatherless child, and a married couple suffers a miscarriage. In Golden Gate Park a homeless Irish man with no legs wheels around in his wheelchair screaming the meaning of life, unintelligibly, to all who cross his path. In Sacramento a couple falls in love, in San Jose a gay man succumbs to AIDS.

A normal night.

And then the darkness came.

3.
The Day the Coffee Died

Nikki wouldn't know for several days, but while she slept, everything changed. There was no Armageddon, the world didn't end; but suddenly everything was different, simultaneously more and less than it ever had been.

That morning, Nikki woke up and immediately started laughing. She had a dream that she was stranded on a deserted island with Eddie Vedder and he was angry with her for not having a better CD collection. "Jesus Christ," she laughed to herself, "I need to drop this insane CD project."

Outside the sky was very dark; inside her bedroom she could barely see. Unaware of the time, she pawed through her sheets in an attempt to locate her cell phone so she could check the clock. According to Nokia, it was 7:45AM.

"Huh," she said aloud, "it's going to pour rain today." She plopped her head back into her pillow and thought about calling in sick to work. 'What day is it?' she wondered and got out of bed to peer through her louvers at the street. 'It's windy, blustery windy, it must be Wednesday.' The windstorms always came on trash day. Every Wednesday morning all the neighbors eagerly disposed of their weekly waste, and did their civic duty by recycling their segregated cans, glass and paper products. By 4:00PM every Wednesday afternoon, the street was littered with Crystal Geyer bottles, Pepsi One cans, scrap paper, and trash can lids. It was somewhat humiliating to be caught picking up the remains of the remains, but it had to be done.

Determining that it was in fact Wednesday, she left the window to turn on the bedroom light. She flipped the switch; light did not appear. The only thing that happened when the switch was flipped was that her expectations of light dissipated. She was suddenly struck with a very clear idea that light wasn't going to come forth, and that was OK.

Once her eyes adjusted to the darkness, she made her way into the kitchen, and removed the bag of coffee from the freezer. It was almost empty. Coffee was already on her list. She managed to scrape two scoops together and poured four cups of water into the pot. When she turned on the coffee maker it had a strange response. It disappeared. "What the fuck?" she screamed, realizing that she had been talking to herself far more than normal.

Her head started pounding immediately, a psychological coffee withdrawal symptom which would soon become real enough. She almost cried.

Flustered and unable to reconcile the events of her morning without the clarifying effects of caffeine, Nikki gathered her trash and recycling to take to the curb. She knew that once on the curb, the cans and plastic bottles would take to the streets like P.E.T.A. protesters storming a mink coat factory, but she kind of liked it because it seemed to really irritate the neighbors.

When she opened her front door the other events of her day seemed rational – normal – by comparison. Sitting on her front porch was a coyote. Not just any coyote, but a coyote wearing a do-rag. She dropped the trash, screamed, slammed the door and got back into her bed.

With her pillow pulled over her head and she spent the better part of an hour calming herself down. She was dreaming—still asleep—that was the only rational explanation. A lucid dream. She would wake up, there would be coffee and light and a complete absence of wild animals in urban gear sitting on her doorstep.

Somehow, she drifted back to sleep.

~~~

When she awoke the sky was still dark. Her cell phone said 11:11AM. She took a step stool to the door and looked out the peephole; gazing up at her were two large brown eyes. There was the coyote in the do-rag. He tentatively wagged his tail.

Rushing to her cell phone she dialed 911 and pressed send, nothing happened. The phone did not dial. She picked up her bedroom landline – no dial tone. In a panic she threw open her closet door to grab some jeans and leave the house. Her closet was empty and all her clothes were gone. Not a skirt, not a Franco Sarto shoe, not a stick of Trident gum covered in tobacco stuck to the bottom of a purse she would never use again, remained.

She went into her office, attempted to turn on her computer and was greeted by a black screen. Her things to do list was half-covered by the notebook boasting, "THE 5 CD'S I WOULD BRING

IF I WERE STRANDED ON A DESERT ISLAND." It was then she remembered the Pearl Jam CD's, which were no longer strewn on her bedroom floor.

Her heart raced, blood pounded in her head, and she started to hyperventilate. She'd been robbed. That was it, and she was lucky to be alive. "Deep breath, Nikki," she coaxed herself. "You were robbed, everything's fine. You're fine. They cut the power and the phone lines and stole your clothes and CD's." She was in such a state that logic didn't enter the picture. What kinds of burglars take clothes and CD's, and leave behind computers and televisions? Was the Salvation Army having a rough donation season? More than anything she wanted to call 911. Instead she sprinted back to bed.

With her pillow firmly back on her head, she said to herself, "I love my bed, I still have my bed. And my sheets, I love my sheets. And apparently, I love talking to myself." She laughed at herself, and rolled onto her side. She landed smack dab on the power button of her television remote control, and instantly, the television came to life. Oprah was on. "Huh, power must be back," she said as she crawled out of bed and tried her light switch. No light. Tried the phone, no dial tone. Went to the computer, black screen. She re-checked the front door, coyote in place looking plaintive.

Though clad only in her boxers and tank, she concluded that she was beyond freaked out and needed to leave immediately. She opened the door to the garage, and was astounded to see the garage door open, and not even an oil stain to indicate that her BMW had ever been parked there.

She slammed the door, locked it and ran to the kitchen where she grabbed the biggest knife she could find. The knife was as dull as a Rubbermaid spatula. She needed to add "get knives sharpened" to her things to do list, closely followed by "find car."

Methodically, Nikki began in the kitchen and checked every cupboard, cabinet and closet large enough to house a small child to make sure the intruders were not still in her house. She even checked the silverware drawer. Cut her a break, she had no caffeine.

Walking into the living room she opened the blinds of the sliding glass door to look in her backyard and make sure the door was locked. That fact that it was pitch black outside made it difficult to see. She pressed her face to the glass and squinted her eyes. In the far corner of her backyard, next to a tree, was a man. A bald, faintly glowing, green-skinned man. Wearing a loincloth. Head bowed, kneeling in what looked like a prayer position.

"Mother fuck. Mother fucking fuck fucker mother fuck. What the fuck?" She paused to breathe. "Fuck."

4.
Left, Right, Lefty

"Mother fucking fuck."

Making a thorough check of the rest of the house, inside, she avoided further windows. She could only hope that they were all locked and secure. Nothing was found except a stale marshmallow in the shape of a green clover from a box of Lucky Charms.

Just for kicks, she looked out the peephole again. The coyote's presence actually had become reassuring. It was, thus far, the only constant in her day.

Back in her room, the television was still blaring. It appeared there was a *Survivor* marathon and they were re-running the whole first season in back to back episodes. Nikki checked the time on her cell phone and tried dialing 911 again. Nothing happened. She powered the phone off to conserve the battery, and settled in for *Survivor*, watching until Stacey got voted off, and then she became bored. After calculating what she thought the time would be, she got up to look in the mirror.

When she stepped onto her digital scale, she was surprised to find it didn't disappear. 119.5, "How did I gain a half a pound yesterday?" she asked herself in the mirror. It was at that point it occurred to her that she had not peed, eaten, drunk anything or even felt cravings for food or beverage and that quite possibly her intense need for caffeine was psychosomatic. Suddenly the thought of a cigarette popped into her mind (if one can't drink coffee, one can at least smoke). Just as quickly she realized that there was probably a green guy in her backyard, and certainly a coyote in her front yard, and she had nowhere to smoke. (It never occurred to her to smoke in the house, come on, that's gross.)

She had to lose the coyote so she could get out of the house. There was a payphone less than a mile away and certainly some news and maybe even, dare she hope for it, coffee. Psychosomatic or not, it was one craving she would maintain. She checked the peephole for the coyote, and when he sensed her he began to whimper. "Don't be pathetic," she yelled out to him. "I don't have any food, go away."

Standing in her front hallway, she banged on the front door several times from the inside, hoping the noise would scare him away. He tapped his paw. As if *he* were the one who was irritated. She threw caution to the wind and opened the door.

"*What?*" The coyote felt that "what." That was an exasperated "what." It had air.

He looked her square in the eye and said, "Ahem." (He really did, he said the word 'Ahem,' it was not strategically placed by the author to imply throat clearing.) In the most proper British accent she'd ever heard from a coyote in a do-rag (a la Tony Blair) he recited the following rap, "Left, Left, Left, Left, left right left. Get on out, get on up, get it done, right left."

She slammed the door and returned to her bedroom, where on the television, Greg and Gretchen were discussing relocation of the shelter.

Nikki picked up her remote, and with more enthusiasm than was required of the task she powered the TV off and yelled, "Survive this."

This was *not* a normal fucking day.

5.
Lefty Sings the Clues

The rest of the first week

Her days passed slowly. Nikki, an extremely analytical person, entertained every possible scenario for the events that were occurring, including the thought that perhaps she just flat out flipped her lid. The coyote remained on her doorstep, reality TV and Oprah remained on her television set, and her weight remained at 119.5 (and she was pissed, come on, no food, no drink, no weight loss? What kind of lame alter-reality was this?) The green guy may have remained, but she remained freaked out enough not to check for him. She found herself laughing at *Survivor*. She had her basic necessity. Shelter. Food and drink were not an issue, nor the need for a toilet, which she had should it be required. There were no dangers except light depravation and total isolation.

Completely sequestered with her creature comforts met … this was a reality television show in the making. *A woman, a dark house and a coyote. Find out what happens when she stops being sane, on the next Alter-World 6.*

On day three she opened the door to the coyote. He greeted her as always, with a tentative tail wag and a very proud, "Left, Left, Left, Left, left right left. Get on out, get on up, get it done, right left."

"Look," she said calmly, "this isn't *Fight Club*. If you stay out here for three days you are not allowed to enter and be initiated, now go away so I can leave my house."

"Left, Left, Left, Left, left right left. Get on out, get on up, get it done, right left."

She shut the door, and yelled through the closed door. "You are stubborn!"

It was Friday night. *The Bachelor* was on, the first *Bachelor* with Alex and the girl with the fake boobs. The really cool thing about this Friday night for Nikki, was that it would be exactly the same as all her other Friday nights. The sky was still black, it never did rain, but she was accustomed to the darkness and the lambent glow of her television. It reassured her.

On Sunday afternoon she lost the battle of the wills with the coyote. She opened the front door and sat beside him on the front porch. He lifted his paw in greeting, and gave her a "high five."

"I'm Nikki," she said, "Do you have a name?"

He panted in response.

"You can talk right? You can understand me?"

"Left, Left, Left, Left, left right left. Get on out, get on up, get it done, right left."

"You've mentioned that, is it significant? Am I supposed to know what it means?"

The coyote shrugged. Seeing a British coyote in a do-rag shrug is really something that everybody should experience at least once.

"Can you do me a favor? Will you run around to the backyard and let me know if there is a mostly naked green dude?"

The coyote ran to the backyard and back in record time. She didn't even consider making a run for it. She had a chance at freedom and didn't feel compelled to take it. He returned and looked her in the face with a blank expression.

"Was he there?" she asked.

Silence.

"Raise your paw if he wasn't there." Nothing.

"Oh, well, hmmm ... OK, raise your paw if he was there." The coyote raised his paw.

"OK, so you understand me. Do you know who this man is? Raise a paw for yes." Paw raised.

"Well, there you go," as if that explained anything. "Let's take a walk. Unless you tell me your name, I guess I'll call you 'Lefty.'"

The newly dubbed Lefty said nothing.

For the first time in days, she was out of the darkness of her house and into the darkness of her neighborhood. It could have been 4:00AM, but it was around 5:00PM. She was surprised to see her neighbors setting up for a block party. There was no talking, no laughter, no children playing. They were just going through the motions. Bringing out the lawn chairs, setting up the barbecues. She called out to say hello, but nobody looked up. Nikki and Lefty stood watching the procession until all the tasks were complete. Then one by one each neighbor took their appointed chair and sat, staring at the grass.

Nikki looked at Lefty and said, "That was almost a normal block party." She cracked herself up, but the humor was obviously lost on her wild companion.

"So, Lefty, what's up? Why are you here? Why am I here? What am I supposed to do?"

"Left, Left, Left, Left, left right left. Get on out, get on up, get it done, right left."

"Yeah, I don't know what that means."

"Left, Left, Left, Left, left right left. Get on out, get on up, get it done, right left."

"Dude, I get it OK, left left left left right left, blah blah blah. What's with the cadence? Does this have something to do with the military?" Lefty wagged his tail exuberantly. She was finally catching on.

That night the coyote slept on the floor by her bed.

~~~

On Monday she dug the notebook out of the pile of crap on her bed and   made a list of all the military installations she knew of in the area. Once the list was complete she had no idea what to do with it. She showed it to Lefty, but he merely gave her a dismissive head nod. She was frustrated. Mostly by the fact that she had the world's only British talking coyote in a do-rag, and all he could say was "Left, Left, Left, Left, left right left. Get on out, get on up, get it done, right left."

She paced, and chanted, "Left, Left, Left, Left, left right left. Get on out, get on up, get it done, right left."

On Tuesday morning she played word association with herself. Cadence/ military/*Taps*/*Top Gun*/Tom Cruise/Nicole Kidman/Divorce. Stop. Again, Cadence/military/*Officer and a Gentleman*/Richard Gere/gerbil. STOP. Again, Cadence/*Taps*/ Timothy Hutton. STOP. Again, Cadence/military/*Officer and a Gentlemen*/Debra Winger/new recruits .... BOOT CAMP!

"Boot Camp, Lefty? I need to go to the gym?"

Lefty almost wagged his tail off of his little coyote ass.

6.
Hey Jeez!

Meanwhile ....

In a studio apartment in Dublin, California, on that same Tuesday afternoon, Luke, a 3-foot tall Irish man napped on his small round bed. He dreamed of yellow moons, pink hearts, blue diamonds, and orange alerts – no, wait that's George Bush's microcosm. He danced around a pot of gold at the end of a magnificent rainbow. Suddenly, darkness fell, the rainbow was gone, the yellow moon crumbled, the pink hearts broke, and the blue diamonds were crushed. A raven landed on the pot of gold and proclaimed, "It is time."

The Leprechaun woke with a start. He sat up and looked at the raven perched on his toe.

"Jasus, Mary and Joseph, Ray," he yelled with his strong Irish brogue, "do ya have to be so dramatic?"

The raven cawed loudly, sprinted up into the air and did a loop-the-loop landing right next to Luke's ear. Mustering his best Darth Vader impression, he breathed loudly and said, "Luke, I am your –" but he thought he was so funny, he couldn't finish and instead burst into a fit of laughter, which sounded way more like Michael Jackson than James Earl Jones. He flew up again, did a pirouette mid-air, and landed back on the Leprechaun's pillow.

"It's that what ya woke me up for ya scrawny little bird?"

"No, No," cried the Michael Jackson voice, which was quite difficult to take terribly seriously, "It really is time. The new Light Seeker is ready to join her Waker."

"Well, that took a fair bit of time, then. But I'm ready to begin me mischief, so off with ya while I prepare."

The Raven lifted one wing, pointed it to corner window and screeched, "8 Ball in the corner pocket," and flew straight for the window. Which he missed. "Shit," he mumbled, corrected his direction, and somewhat dizzily, left the room.

"Jasus, Mary, and Joseph," said Luke, "I'll end up boilin' that bird for me stew before all is said and done."

~~~

Luke gathered the props he needed for the first leg of his journey and placed them in a small bag. He pushed the shamrock shaped button next to his bed and a giant rainbow appeared. It started in Dublin, and ended in Milpitas. He hated the stereotypical Leprechaun shit, but did what he had to do to keep up appearances. He thoroughly enjoyed mischief making, and eagerly anticipated his next few days.

He hopped on the rainbow and within minutes was sliding into a housing tract in Milpitas. He donned his costume, put a crown of thorns around his head, and knocked on the door of Chuckie Rightwing.

Chuckie was 32, tall, thin, thinning blonde hair, light brown eyes, and utterly unremarkable. He was also, not surprisingly, single, a virgin, and currently lived alone. He dedicated his life to God, and waited eagerly for the Rapture. He knew he was chosen. He was right. He just didn't know what he had been chosen for.

"Who is it?" Chuckie called.

"It's Jasus Christ," said Luke in a sing-song manner, "Come to live in your heart."

Chuckie opened the door with a mix of excitement and trepidation, unsure of what to expect. He was surprised to see a 3-foot tall mini-Jesus with a roller bag. Luke didn't wait for an invitation. He walked into the house, rolled his suitcase to the coffee table and plopped himself down on Chuckie's couch.

"The Sleepers shall inherit the earth," proclaimed Luke with smug satisfaction.

Chuckie cleared his throat, "Um, sir, isn't it the meek?"

"That's what I said," Luke replied irritably.

"Are you Irish?" asked Chuckie, "I always thought Christ would have a different accent, perhaps, something Arabic…and … I thought he'd be … well, taller."

"Ah, ye of little fate," Luke said.

"Faith? Don't you mean?"

"Well if you're going ta be constantly correcting me, I can't see as how you want me livin' in your heart. Perhaps I'll just go. I thought you were a chosen, but I must have got me wires crossed. "

"No, No …" pleaded Chuckie nervously, "Please stay. Can I get you anything, some water, wine? Can I wash your feet? Can I get you a Band-Aid, you seem to be bleeding a little at your temple?"

"Well, you can start by gettin' down on your knees and invitin' me to live in your heart, that's what you can get for me."

So Chuckie did. He closed his eyes, and got down on his knees and began his prayer.

Dear God,

Thank you for thy divine miracle.

Luke rolled his eyes heavenward and shook his fist. 'Oye,' he thought, 'this is going to be a long one.' Quietly he got up and looked in the mirror to check his temple. There was a trickle of blood. 'Damn thorns.'

He sat back down and checked his watch, the fool would be praying for days.

For bringing your son into my life and showing me indeed that I am among your chosen.

For sending your son to die for my sins, that I may be saved and live in heaven for eternity.

Lord, I invite your son Jesus Christ to live in my heart.

That was Luke's cue. At that moment, he seized Chuckie's heart and made it his own.

~~~

With a click of his rainbow remote Luke was on his way to Berkeley. He knocked on the commune door. The sound of jingling coming toward the door could be heard from the outside, as Demi Devi Dai thanked the Goddess for the wood her door was made out of before she called out, "Who is it?"

"It's the Goddess," Luke cried out in a voice five octaves higher than his own.

Demi Devi Dai opened the door as quickly as she could, threw herself prostrate to the ground (and in so doing hit herself in the eye with one of the bells that was woven into her skirt,) and awaited the command of the Goddess.

Luke shook his head in wonder. He knew these people were extreme, which was the whole point. It was the extremeness of their extremity that never failed to surprise him.

Lying before him was a woman in her late twenties. Her long dirty blonde hair had an occasional silver streak. Oddly placed braids adorned her crown, and she wore several layers of clothing in multiple shades of purple, including her flowing skirt with the bells woven into it. Clearly tears were streaming out of at least one of her eyes.

"Justine, Mary, and Josephine," muttered Luke. "Rise, daughter, let us embrace and make sure you didn't poke an eye out. You'll need those."

When Demi Devi Dai rose, Luke saw that in fact tears were coming out of both of her big brown eyes, but the left one was red and puffy. What Demi Devi Dai saw was a 3-foot tall, very masculine looking woman, with greenish-tinged skin, and a long white robe.

"Goddess, Mother," Demi Devi Dai said post embrace, "You honor me, how can I serve you?"

"I've come to you to perform a ritual of initiation. You aren't truly servin' the Goddess until you have dedicated your life to my service."

At that moment a smell hit Luke's nostrils that almost knocked him out cold. Demi flushed slightly red and said, "Sorry, Mother, it's the Tofu. But I thank you for the – "

Luke cut her off, "Let's start the ritual then, take my hands –"

"Oh, Mother, please, I must prepare, I must honor you as is your due. Please, let me gather the instruments of the initiation."

While Demi ran around her home gathering paraphernalia, she tried to make small talk with the Goddess. "So, you're Irish, then?" Demi had suddenly slipped into her own brand of brogue.

"Yes," Luke answered with disdain.

"I thought you'd be taller," he heard as Demi fumbled through her box of incense.

Luke put his head in his hands and mumbled to himself, "One Mississippi, Two Mississippi, Three Mississippi." By twenty-two Mississippi she was back. Sweat trickled down her face as she laid out the accessories for the ritual. Luke had never seen so much crap in his life.

There was a silver chalice, a scrying mirror (which she didn't need, he knew her future without it), seven candles (Chakra colors), an alter cloth, two sage sticks, some patchouli (why?), an incense burner with three different types of incense, a Celtic cross in silver, more sage, a Greenpeace calendar from 1987, a rose quartz, a smoky quartz, a quartz quartz and a quart of Maalox. He was ready to fight her for the Maalox.

She created a circle on the hardwood floor with the loose sage and invited the "Goddess" to step into the circle.

Luke, completely aggravated by the hoopla, took her hands and said, "Repeat after me. I dedicate my life to you."

Demi Devi Dai solemnly repeated, "I dedicate my life to you." That was all he needed. Two down, one to go.

~~~

Luke put on some street clothes and took BART to San Francisco. It was late. Kassen would just be getting in.

Kassen was very successful, and dressed the part. Armani suits, expensive ties. He was short. He told people he was five-foot-seven, but that was at least a modest exaggeration. He had thinning hair, which was not quite salt and pepper, but the brown was definitely going into remission. He had spectacular piercing green eyes, a strong perfect nose and thin lips.

When he opened his garage door, Luke was sitting inside on the step waiting for him. When Kassen got out of the car, Luke stood up to greet him.

"Who are you?" Kassen asked impatiently.

"I'm fate."

"I've been waiting for you," Kassen said sardonically.

"No ya haven't."

"Uh, yes, I have."

"No you haven't."

"This is crazy; I'm not having this conversation."

"That's what ya always say, and laddie, that's the problem."

Kassen gave Luke the once over. "Huh."

"I know, you thought I'd be taller."

"Yeah, and femaler," Kassen replied.

"Ya think they'd send *you* female fate?"

"Well, if they wanted my attention they would."

"Oh … you're a bright one Mr. Kyle and I'm relieved ta find ya. But, Fate visited you numerous times, lad, and you ignored her every time."

"Well, fate is fate. If it's out there, it'll find me."

"Right, Mr. K. But, don't be forgettin' what I tell ya now; Fate can be derailed by free will. You chose never to fall in love; Fate had it all ready for you."

"Really, who?"

"Tsk, tsk, t'isn't time for regrets, there's a new fate now. Ya ignored your old fate, and new Fate is here. In the form of me. "

"And … ?" Kassen grew impatient again.

"And, Kassen, you'll now be usin' your seduction skills for *my* purpose."

"Whatever," Kassen inadvertently consented, and that was all Luke needed. Rainbow remote, and whoosh, he was gone.

~~~

In Chicago, Oprah is deified. In college town, a singing Coyote drops clues. Having left Jamaica, a 7-½ foot tall bald tattooed black man is sailing, seasick, on a ship close to San Francisco Bay. On television, Aaron and Helene of *The Bachelor's* second season say "hello."

In Livermore a fat psychic isn't speaking to the voices in her head, they pissed her off. In Golden Gate Park a homeless Irish man with no legs wheels around in his wheelchair screaming the meaning of life, intelligibly, but no one crosses his path. In Sacramento a couple breaks up. Everybody else is asleep.

Normal? Normal doesn't live here anymore.

7.
Dinner at the Dump?

Nikki prepared for her four-mile walk to the gym. She was nervous about walking in the dark, but determined no other options. It wasn't like she could call a taxi, and she had Lefty for protection.

Unsure of whether or not she would return to her home, she packed the only things that seem to have retained any substance in her life, the items that were on her bed the night of the change and her notebook. Into a pillowcase went her cell phone, the television remote, her worn copy of Jitterbug Perfume, and her flat sheet (fitted sheets were always a pain).

As she stripped her bed she came across the four CD's she'd put aside for her "Desert Island" event. "No friggin' Pearl Jam, Lefty," she told the coyote. But at least she had *Court and Spark*. She tossed a couple of used Kleenex to the ground, and discovered a pair of unmatched socks tucked way down in the bottom of her bed and her American Spirit cigarettes. There were 14 in the box. She was elated about the socks and the smokes, though quickly realized she didn't have a light. Literally, not one little spark of light or fire anywhere. She didn't care and packed away her precious smokes. With no caffeine or anti-depressants, she was reassured by at a least the promise of one of her vices.

Checking the room for a final inventory, she donned her newly found socks (one Winnie the Pooh slipper sock, and one white gym sock) and decided to weigh herself one last time. 119.5. Whatever.

As she and Lefty left the house, they saw the neighbors gathering for what had become their nightly block party. She was thrilled to be getting away from it.

~~~

After the first mile they reached the local strip mall. A mini-van or SUV sat in every parking space. She approached Safeway (which had its own Starbucks) and told Lefty to stay. "I'm going for coffee, Lefty. Wish me luck!"

Though she had no money, not even a wayward quarter had landed on her bed, she felt compelled to at least *try* for a caffeine-fix. She walked up to the counter, in the pitch-black store, and saw the green Starbucks apron. It comforted her. She could smell the coffee, almost taste it ... a tear of joy sprung into her eye. Boldly walking up to the counter she ordered a Venti coffee. No sooner did the words escape her mouth then Starbucks disappeared without a trace.

"God damn it!"

Lefty had an almost 'I told you so' look on his face, and she was irritated. Irrationally irritated. She was going through Prozac withdrawal.

"Whatever, dude," she said, "You didn't tell me so, so wipe that smug look off of your do-rag wearing face."

As they continued their journey, Nikki's allergies kicked in. Fifteen minutes in the open air did it every time. While her eyes watered and nose itched, her socks collected burrs. She had no idea what to expect at the gym, but hoped that they still had t-shirts for sale because by the time she arrived, she had wiped her nose on her Old Navy tank twenty-two times.

It took them an hour and a half to get there. When they entered the parking lot, she saw Amber's car. She was both elated and petrified. Her only hope was that Amber knew a little of what was going on. The fact that her car was there could mean that she was just as zombied-out as everybody else in town.

Leaving Lefty outside, she walked into the gym. It was strange to see it in the dark. She checked a clock on the wall, 5:00PM. It would be the middle of Boot Camp. She looked around and saw that every elliptical machine was occupied. "Left, left, left, left, left, right left," went through her head. Neither an exerted breath could be heard, nor a bead of sweat be seen on any of the exercisers.

She walked to the back of the gym toward the Aerobics room and saw Amber standing outside of the room with her face pressed against a window, looking in. Amber was dressed as ridiculously as Nikki. The camouflage tank-top with a pink Hello Kitty pillowcase around her waist as a skirt assured Nikki that Amber was as deeply involved in the weirdness as she was.

"Amber," she said.

Amber screamed. She was startled; she hadn't heard another person's voice in six days. Nikki was relieved; she also hadn't heard another *person's* voice in the last six days.

"Jesus Christ, Nik." Amber rushed to Nikki and gave her

a bear hug. They were both afraid to let go in case the other disappeared.

They finally let go and looked at each other, "Amber, is that a key print on your face?" Nikki asked.

"Nik, is the key print on my face the strangest thing you've seen in the last week?"

"Uh, no. Good point. But it is pretty remarkable, I mean, you could make a duplicate key from that, and the VW is kinda cute."

"Focus, Nik. I've had time to get used to it. It's been there since the event."

"*What* event?"

"I don't know but look at my class. Something is really friggin' wrong."

Nikki looked in the window. What was normally a group of very aggressive, determined, sweaty exercisers, were instead thirty women going up and down on a step, in what closely resembled slow motion.

"They're not even sweating, Nik, they are a big bunch of sissy-la-las."

"Is that the strangest thing *you've* seen in the last week, Am?"

"Unfortunately, no."

"We need to get caught up. Not here, though. This place is giving me the creeps. Why are you here?"

"I've been coming here every day. I kept thinking either I was in a coma, having a really bad acid trip, or I was suddenly the only conscious person on the planet. Then I noticed that you weren't coming to class, so I thought maybe you were like me and maybe you'd end up here eventually."

"Do you have any money, Amber?"

"Cunning is our only currency now, Nik."

"You've been saving that one up for just the right moment, haven't you?"

"Sorta," Amber replied sheepishly.

"So your car runs?"

"Yeah."

"That's strange, mine was stolen, or something. How much gas do you have?"

"A little under a half a tank."

"Have you tried to *get* gas?"

"Nik, I haven't tried anything. Remember the leg press

machine that was over there by the Spinning room? I sat down on it and it disappeared. Bruised my ass."

"Yeah, I walked into Starbucks on my way here. Ordered a Venti and Starbucks was gone. Have you had coffee?"

"No, and I don't want to talk about it."

"Let's go outside, I have something to introduce you to. It's the second weirdest thing that I've seen in the last six days, though I've gotten sort of used to him."

As they headed out the door, Nikki stopped and gave Amber the once over. "Nice outfit. You're wearing your Wonder Woman undies under that, aren't you?"

"Yeah. I like your outfit too. Especially the socks."

~~~

When they got outside Lefty was waiting in the darkness. His eyes glowed and his white do-rag showed against the dark sky.

"You got a dog, Nik?"

"Not a dog, it's a coyote, and there's more. He—"

"Is that a do-rag, Nik?" Amber interrupted.

"Uh, yeah, but there's m—"

This time Lefty interrupted. "Ahem." He said, and then launched into some beat box noises, followed by a very disconcerting rap. "Yo, Yo. Yo rock star deaths, yo plane crashes, yo natural disasters. No time to waste, don't hesitate, you better work it faster. Yo."

"Is that rap, Nik?"

Before Nikki could answer two things happened. First, the sky lightened just a shade. Second, across the street from the gym, standing on the railroad tracks was the bald-green-loincloth guy formerly of Nikki's backyard. When he had the attention of Nikki, Amber and Lefty, he bowed his head, and extended out his arms in a welcome greeting. Then he was gone.

Amber began to hyperventilate.

When she was calm enough, Nikki ventured a comment, "The green dude was the first weirdest thing that I've seen, by the way. I guess I should have warned you.

"Look," Nikki continued, "we need to get our heads together and figure out what's been happening. Before just now, I didn't know that Lefty could say anything other than 'left right left.'"

"Before just now, I didn't know animals could talk. Or rap," Amber said.

"Does anything work at your house? Lights, television, phones, computer, Coffee maker?" Nikki became melancholy at her own mention of coffee.

"Nothing at all, just my car."

"OK, let's go to my house then. I have television, although, there isn't any news. Nothing's on but reality TV and Oprah. Does your car radio work?"

"Yeah, it works, but there's nothing on but re-broadcasts of reality TV, Oprah, and Dr. Laura."

The mention of Dr. Laura made Nikki's stomach turn. In the back of her mind she heard, "I'm Dr. Laura and I am my kids mom." It made her want to vomit.

"Let's make sure we don't accidentally hear Dr. Laura, OK? How about CD's? Anything?"

"None, they were all in my apartment. The only stuff I have is what was on my bed that night. What are we going to do?"

Lefty took that moment to chime in with his latest tune. "Yo, Yo. Yo rock star deaths, yo plane crashes, yo natural disasters. No time to waste, don't hesitate, you better work it faster. Yo."

"Not now, Lefty." Nikki admonished, "Let's go to my house, then, I've got 4 CD's by the way. Joni Mitchell, Sublime, Alanis Morissette and the Doors."

"No Pearl Jam?"

"Shut-up Amber."

They piled into her white VW Rabbit (Lefty was particularly excited to have his first car ride ever.) Sans headlights they left the parking lot toward Nikki's house. Shortly thereafter, they encountered hundreds of people walking toward them.

"Dinner at the Dump," Amber casually mentioned as if somehow that served as an explanation of anything. "It's been going on every night since the event. It seems like the entire population shows up there. They get cheap red wine in plastic cups. I went a few times, but nobody talked to me, and when I picked up a wine cup it disappeared, so I gave up."

"Well, whatever 'Dinner at the Dump' is, doesn't really seem like something that's up your alley."

Lefty confirmed his assent in the usual manner, "Yo, Yo. Yo rock star deaths, yo plane crashes, yo natural disasters. No time to waste, don't hesitate, you better work it faster. Yo."

~~~

Once they arrived at Nikki's house, they turned on the television and put it on mute so they could have a little bit of light. The stars of the *World Wrestling Federation* were on *Celebrity Fear Factor*. Nikki and Amber sat on Nikki's bed, since it seemed the safest place to be. All their worldly possessions were piled in a corner at the end of the bed. Lefty made a bold move, and hopped up to join the women. He sheepishly looked at Nikki and started, "Yo—"

"Yo not Lefty. Get down!"

Lefty left the room, but they could still hear him mumbling his little verse quietly under his breath.

"We're going to have to figure out what he's trying to tell us with that song, because I'm getting pretty sick of hearing it," Nikki told Amber.

"Why do you think it means something?"

Nikki spent the next couple of hours explaining to Amber everything that she had experienced over the past week. From the disappearance of the coffee maker, to finally ending up at Boot Camp. She explained the outcome of the Desert Island CD game, and how she had tried to scrub the mascara smudge off of her left cheek but that it wouldn't go away. Amber decided to wait until morning to recant her own recent experiences.

Nikki yawned, "What if his clue means the apocalypse? Plane crashes and rock star deaths? God, I hope Eddie Vedder doesn't die. And what if we have a time limit? That little rap said we need to work faster. In the morning, we can make a list of everything we know and see if can start making some sense out of everything."

Amber started to chuckle.

"How can you be laughing at me? This is serious, and I'm just trying to be organized."

"Sorry, it's just you and your lists."

"Whatever."

They decided to err on the side of caution, and both slept in Nikki's bed. It was close quarters with law school books, CD's and Tom Robbins, (the book obviously, not the author) but they couldn't risk losing what little they had, or losing each other. From the other room they heard Lefty talking in his sleep. Nothing new or earth shattering, just, you know, "Yo rock star deaths, yo plane crashes, yo natural disasters."

8.
Can You Hear Me Now?

Somebody else's Wednesday, Week 2

In Dublin, just before dawn on Wednesday morning, Luke made himself a cup of tea and booted up his computer. He had been awake all night, plotting.

He launched his internet browser and intended to go to Google to print a map of Union Square. His fat fingers missed the "G" and he ended up at oogle.com, which immediately cyber-sped him into the Hot Leather dreams website, with several pop up windows inviting him to watch live Asian cum shots. He wondered briefly about humanity's fascination with Asian porn.

After printing out the maps he needed, he checked his e-mail, and as he deleted a deluge of SPAM, a pop-up appeared on his screen. A pop-up of a raven. He hit CTRL-ALT-DEL as fast as his fingers could move, but he missed again and inadvertently launched the Raven pop-up. It was way too early for Ray's voice, but he knew it was too late.

A moment later, Ray was perched on his shoulder emulating his Darth Vader breath. "Luke –" was as far as he got, before Luke knocked him off of his shoulder. He landed directly on Luke's teacup, wherein he instantly and purposely pooped.

Michael Jackson voice, like fingernails on the chalkboard of Luke's poor head, said "Jeez, you scared the crap out of me." And he tittered with laughter at his pun.

"Top of the mornin' to ya Ray," Luke uttered in the most sarcastic voice he could muster. "What can I do for you *very early* on this Wednesday morning?"

"He's coming today."

"I'm well aware of his schedule."

"He'll want to meet them."

"I'm well aware of his agenda."

"Well, what're you gonna do?"

"Ray, you're familiar with the expression, 'don't shoot the messenger'?"

Ray nodded.

"Well, sure and I don't subscribe to that theory." Luke reached for the closest object that could be used as a weapon. It was a Sharper Image World Time Swivel Clock. He hated to lose it, but if it would get rid of Ray, he felt it worth the sacrifice, besides, for some reason Sydney time was always off by an hour.

Ray understood the message, and without his usual dramatic exit, he disappeared into thin air. Luke heard his distant voice saying, "I'll pop in later, you know, just to make sure he got in all right."

~~~

At 8:37AM Luke dialed the cell phone number of Mr. Kassen Kyle of San Francisco, CA. He knew Mr. Kyle would just be pulling out of his garage, off to his office. He knew this not because of any psychic ability, but because this is what Mr. Kyle did every weekday of his life. He stops at Starbucks and orders a short house in a tall cup, sometimes with an add-shot. He becomes aggravated by people in Starbucks talking on their cell phones about non-urgent matters. He jokes around with the people in the green aprons who reach in for his maple oat scone before he even orders it. Barring any unforeseen circumstances, he arrives at his office by 9:03AM. He was very predictable. It was one of the reasons Luke was so grateful to have him. Today he would lay the bait for the Light Seeker.

"Hello," KK answered.

"Fate here, Mr. Kyle."

"What?"

"Fate here, Mr. Kyle," Luke shouted.

"Can't hear you."

"Mr. Kyle, can you hear me now?" (Utterly overused joke, and yet …)

"I'm in a bad area," Kassen ranted, "this whole town is a bad area. I swear I'm taking this phone back. Hold on, almost clear. OK, four bars…. Hello?"

Luke was beyond irritated, he'd be less irritated if he had invented cell-phone-irritation-factor, but he didn't and thus was as adversely affected by it as the humans. "Yes, Mr. Kyle, this is Fate calling."

"And?"

"How's Nikki?"

"WHAT?"

"How is Nikki, have you spoken to her lately?"

"I don't have time for this, Nikki is fine."

"She'll be coming to the city. I'll tell you when to meet her."

"I have plans."

"I haven't even told you when yet, Mr. K."

"I'm busy. I get it now. This is one of her elaborate schemes. You can tell Nikki –"

"Call her."

"What?"

"Call her, I'll hold."

"I have to wait until I get to my office."

"You can use the phone at Starbucks, they know you there."

Kassen pulled into a parking spot in front of Starbucks. He got out of his car and looked around, wondering how the voice on the phone knew his location. Inside, there was a long line but no leprechaun. Four women were talking on their cell phones.

He walked toward the counter, and asked to use the phone. After immediately being handed a Maple Oat scone and a short house in a tall cup, he silently thanked the Starbucks Gods and asked to use the phone again. He dialed Nikki's cell phone number and was alarmed when he heard an annoying beep followed by "The number you have reached is not in service at this time and there is no new number."

Three more dialing attempts met with the same message. He threw a $5.00 bill on the counter and walked back to his car, nauseous. He picked up his cell phone and told the waiting Luke, "It's disconnected."

"Her number is disconnected?" Luke asked with a false concern. "Has that ever happened in the time that you've known her?"

"Never, I'll track her down once I get into my office. Where can I call you back?"

"No need to call me back, I'll be at your apartment at 9:30 this evening. There'll be five of us total. Snacks and soft drinks are fine. One of us is a Vegan. Good day Mr. K."

Kassen Kyle spent the entire day trying to locate Nikki Nasco. The fact that he could not reach her suddenly made him frantic with the need to speak with her. He called every phone number, sent a fax, sent e-mail and even prepared a letter to get to her via Federal Express. He was utterly panicked at the thought that perhaps he had lost her for good.

~~~

45

Luke hit the "Compose Email" box on his computer screen and addressed a message to lovejesusguy@jesus.net and wiccanpriestess@blessedbe.com, Chuckie and Demi Devi Dai, respectively.

> *Dear Loyal Follower:*
> *Your presence is requested this evening. Please arrive at 620 W. K Street, San Francisco no later than 9:30PM. Snacks will be provided.*
> *Love,*
> *Jesus and Goddess*

~~~

Luke checked his still in tact swivel clock. It was 10:14AM. He had just enough time to get to Sausalito to meet the Big Man's boat.

9.
Makin' a List and Checkin' it Twice

Nikki and Amber's Wednesday, Week 2

Nikki woke up crabby. Really really crabby. PMS times fifty crabby. It was officially one week since she had caffeine, an anti-depressant, or a phone call. Nobody should have to live like that. To further her irritation, she stepped on the scale. 119.5. This was followed by a feeble attempt at wiping the mascara off her cheek. Zero success.

She walked to the living room and was greeted by Lefty. "Don't *even* start with me this morning, Left. If I hear that song one more time, I'll scream."

"What is it? We don't have news, so we won't even know if the apocalypse has started."

She sat down on the floor next to the coyote.

"It does make sense that the apocalypse would begin with the elimination of coffee."

Saying the word coffee sent a little shiver down her back.

"I mean, it couldn't be anything other than something apocalyptic right?"

She looked to Lefty who merely looked blank back.

"Can you talk?" she asked accusingly.

It was like he was in a coma.

"Are we in danger, Lefty?" she was starting to feel a little panicky.

"How does it go again?" she asked.

"Yo, Yo. Yo rock star deaths, yo plane crashes, yo natural disasters. No time to waste, don't hesitate, you better work it faster. Yo."

"I'm not fucking around with you, Lefty. If you can talk, you'd better tell me now because I am starting to wig."

He padded out of the living room and into the kitchen, where he very likely took on an indignant air.

Nikki began to pace the living room floor. Her carpet really needed to be cleaned. Somewhere out there a list was begging for that to be added.

Nikki thought she'd go the word association route again.

"Rock star deaths, plane crashes and natural disasters.

"Rock star deaths, plane crashes and natural disasters.

"Rock star deaths, plane crashes and natural disasters, oh my.

"Lions and tigers and bears; past, present and future. Father, son and holy ghost. Peter, Paul and Mary. Triangle. Rock star deaths, plane crashes. Earthquakes. Floods. Rock star deaths? Rock star deaths come in threes. And plane crashes come in threes, and natural disasters come in threes."

Nikki went to the kitchen. "Everything happens in threes," she told Lefty as if he didn't already know. "Are there supposed to be three of us?"

Lefty lifted his paw in the affirmative. Nikki was grateful; at least communicating with him was getting a little easier if not less irritating.

"Do we need to find another person?"

Lefty didn't move.

"Are we the three? You and Amber and I?"

He raised his paw.

"So now what? Do you have another song?"

Paw raise.

"Well? Do I suddenly need to issue you an invitation?"

Lefty motioned to the bedroom with his nose.

"Amber's sleeping. You can't just tell me anymore? You need Amber now too?"

Lefty padded into Nikki's bedroom, jumped up onto the bathroom counter, and located an old prescription bottle. Picking it up with his teeth, he tossed it at Nikki with a look of disdain. It was her last Prozac.

"Very very funny. Hilarious. You've got that wicked British humor I see. Whatever Lefty, you try having your whole world change overnight ..." As she continued to whine, Lefty took his front paws and covered his ears. He made it very clear he wasn't going to listen anymore.

Amber woke up disoriented. The key print on her face looked fresh and more inflamed than it had the evening prior. In spite of Nikki's pissy mood, it made her laugh.

"Lefty's aggravated with me, and he won't sing me the next song until you're awake to listen to it. Apparently, I'm not good enough for him anymore. And can I just tell you that I can't wait to burn these boxers? I've been wearing them for seven days. I hate them. If my cellulite wasn't so bad I'd take them off and walk around in my underwear."

Amber got out of bed, and gave Nikki one of her famous bear hugs. "Nik, I spend most of my day in a pillowcase. We'll figure all this out, let's just make the most of it, OK?"

"Wanna go in the kitchen and smell the empty Starbucks bag?" Nikki suggested.

"Sure!"

The girls walked into the kitchen and picked the discarded bag up off of the counter. Each took a big whiff and then they closed their eyes and imagined a cup of their favorite morning beverage. Amber had a happy, peaceful look on her face. Nikki had tears in her eyes.

"This sucks."

Lefty entered the kitchen and started with the now familiar, "Ahem. And you may find somebody kind to help and understand you. Someone who is just like you and needs a gentle hand to, guide them along. So maybe I'll see you there, we can forget all our troubles, forget all our cares, so go downtown, things'll be great when you're downtown — don't wait a minute for downtown — everything's waiting for you." This time, though, instead just singing the song, he also danced. A little Bassanova, just enough so that his light mood became contagious.

"Oh," said Nikki, "He sings too. That was my favorite song when I was like four. Petula Clark, *Downtown*! Woo hoo." Nikki started to feel better.

"Sing it again, Lefty," Amber encouraged the coyote. She joined in both the singing and dancing, and soon the three of them were singing and dancing around in the kitchen. Sliding around on the hardwood floor like children at play.

"This is like that scene in *Almost Famous* … you know, on the bus where everybody is mad at everybody else, and then somebody starts singing *Tiny Dancer*, and then everybody starts singing and they all make up. Remember that scene?" Nikki asked the now breathless Amber.

"Yeah," Amber replied, "Music is powerful."

"They knew all the lyrics though, we only know this one part … maybe we should sing *Tiny Dancer*."

Nikki started to sing, off key, and off base with the lyrics … "Pretty eyes, Paris mile, marry a music man." She got the hold me closer bit right, but then went completely unintelligible with something that sounded like: "maybe darlin' she's so frinnin', you house a few from day to day."

Amber laughed, there were some songs that no matter how many times you heard them, you didn't understand the lyrics, and Nikki had thirty years of botched *Tiny Dancer* lyrics stuck in her brain.

"One more time, Lefty," yelled Amber, and he began another of the same chorus of *Downtown*. After which, the mood in the house significantly changed for the better. Nikki thanked them both with a hug for Amber, and a back scratch for Lefty.

"OK," Nikki pronounced, "Let's figure this shit out."

Nikki and Amber returned to Nikki's bed, where they turned on the television for light. *American Idol* was on. Season one. It was down to Justin and Kelly, but at least there was a little music in the background. Lefty curled up next to the bed to take a nap. Amber told Nikki of her adventures prior to their meeting. Nikki took notes for their list.

My time hasn't been as exciting as yours, Nik. Like you, I tried to make coffee and it disappeared. My cell phone wouldn't even turn on, and I opened my drawers and found I had no clothing. Pretty quickly I realized that the only objects available to me were the things that had been in my bed that night. Fortunately, I was so upset when I got home that I didn't bother to straighten up, and ended up falling asleep with my keys in my hand, and eventually, I guess I used them as a pillow.

My initial reaction was to try to get to my loved ones, but as I got ready to go to see them, I felt like that was exactly the opposite of what I should do. Somehow I knew that they were all right, and the best thing that I could do for anybody was to try to find somebody else in the same condition I was in.

I didn't meet any talking animals, or see any green men. I went to the gym everyday, but nobody could ever see me. They didn't know I was there. I would try to touch somebody's arm, and for a second it seemed like they would react, but then they would just go on about their business.

I haven't eaten, showered, or brushed my teeth, and yet I don't feel grungy. It's like everything physical stopped that morning when I woke up. I walked around downtown and couldn't find one person who displayed any degree of consciousness. It's like they are all asleep. I feel this great need to wake everybody up. It borders on obsessive.

I told you I went to that Dinner at the Dump a couple of times. I stood on top of a table and screamed as loud as I could "Wake up!" Nobody even looked up from their cheap red wine and baked beans. But, Nik, the more I think about it, the more I think that they are asleep. They aren't zombies. This isn't some **Night of the Living Dead** *thing; the people just need to be woken up.*

"I had that same feeling about my family," Nikki interjected, "it was strange. Like whatever I needed to do didn't really involve them, but that my getting involved would ultimately help them. I wonder if this all has something to do with the light, or lack thereof. Maybe we went into perpetual nighttime, and they *are* all asleep. You know what I was thinking? I was thinking that we should try to get a Clapper and install it on my light, and then sit on the bed and clap and see if we can get the light to turn on."

Amber laughed. "Where are we going to get a clapper?"

"Yeah, OK ... So, we need to figure out what we're going to do. Clapper notwithstanding, I think we need to get to a city. Do you think the Downtown clue could be that obvious? Or do you think it's something to do with my childhood. That is the first song I ever remember."

"Should we take a drive to Sacramento?"

"I don't think Sac is the place. We'll ask Lefty when he wakes up. Think about it Amber, why us? If everybody is asleep, why are we awake, and where are we most likely to find more people like us? This was a sleepy town before all of this happened, so it doesn't surprise me that they are non-responsive here, but somewhere ... I'm thinking Berkeley, Marin or San Francisco."

"I don't know 'why us'. Maybe because we're smart, we're deep, we're caring and compassionate."

"Yeah, but a lot of people are. I think we need to figure out what is less on the surface."

"I don't know, Nik. Anyway, Lefty said, downtown, so wouldn't you think downtown should be San Francisco?"

"We can talk about it in the car. Let's pack up our pillowcases, and get ready to go."

Nikki turned on her cell phone; it was 11:11AM, again. In the background Kelly Clarkson was singing. Everybody needed a moment like this, right?

~~~

At exactly 11:11AM the Big Man arrived into Sausalito on a speedboat. Luke spotted him immediately; he was hard to miss. 7 ½ feet tall, with skin so dark it was like all of the colors of the spectrum in a really big dog pile. Luke noticed two dramatic changes, the first being that the Big Man had cut off his dreadlocks and shaved his head bald. The second was that his entire body seemed to be covered in brightly colored art. He wore shorts and a tank top, thus most of his body was exposed. Luke was bundled up in a green wool suit. He experienced a little shiver of cold just looking at the Big Man.

Luke rushed to meet his boss. "Top 'O the Mornin' to ya, Biy-em. Welcome, welcome." Luke noticed irritably that Ray was perched on the Big Man's shoulder, and thought to himself, 'Damn rodent.'

Ray squawked, "Did you hear that Biy-Em? He called me a rodent."

"I heard him mon, but off with you, bird. We've business to discuss."

The Big Man picked Luke up and gave him a hearty hug. "Long time, mon," he said with his lilting Caribbean accent, and borderline patois language, "Wha happen?" Luke was busy having the air crushed out of him, and couldn't reply.

Biy-Em was woozy and lost his balance. Both of them went toppling to the ground. Somehow Luke ended up on top, otherwise he was sure to have been crushed by the man who was more than twice his size. They were quite a sight, the little green man and the huge black giant.

"Haen't gotten your land legs, yet I see, Biy-Em. Well, they'll come back soon enough. Ya need a whisky."

"What me need, is for you to get your little green ass off of me arm."

As Luke struggled to remove himself from his employers left shoulder, he noticed the detail of the tattoo. "Is that Van Gogh's Starry Night on your shoulder, sir?"

"Yah, mon. Me have all of Van Gogh's famous paintings tattooed on me body. Me show you da favorite later, right now me need food, a Mojito, and a stationary surface."

Biy-Em was one of the nicest, most easy going, gregarious, affable evil forces in the world. Everybody loved him. To look at him one would never suspect that he was the author and executor of a plan in which the final outcome was world domination. It was the Rasta in him. A roots man, cool runnings, Irie, Bob Marley, ganja, and all that jazz. The peaceful energy he exuded lulled people into a false sense of security and trust, which always worked to his benefit.

~~~

Lefty ended up sleeping most of the afternoon, while Nikki and Amber packed up the contents of the bed. They decided it best to gather all the bedding and find a way to construct some kind of clothing out of it. The flat sheet easily became a toga, but the pillowcases were more functional. One Nikki used as a suitcase, the other she was determined to make into a shift of sorts. While Nikki mourned the loss of her 280-thread count Calvin Klein pillowcase, Amber went back to her apartment to get the last of her supplies. A lone tear slid down Nikki's cheek as she slit armholes and a neck hole in the pillowcase with her dull knife. She paused a moment to ponder just why the knife was still functional, when everything else disappeared.

It took Amber longer than she had expected to get across town and back. By the time she returned, the bulk of Nikki's house was empty. Sitting in the middle of the living room, as Lefty looked on with incredulous chagrin, was Nikki and a pile of worthless bric-a-brac.

"What happened here?" Amber asked, more than a little concerned about her friend's mental health.

"Everything doesn't disappear."

"What?"

"Everything doesn't disappear. I ran around the house touching things and some of it disappeared, and some of it stayed. This is a pile of all the stuff that stayed."

Amber looked at push pins, a *Nightmare Before Christmas* coffee mug, some old Hallmark cards, a family photo, a can of Raid, a cassette tape, a Sharper Image World Time Swivel clock (currently set to Moscow), a Fed Ex envelope, a 1983 *The Lion, The Witch and The Wardrobe* calendar, a blue plastic domino with four on one half and five on the other, the six Pottery Barn catalogs that Nikki had received in the last two weeks, a Freesia scented candle, and a half-melted plastic plate with the Rugrats on it. And of course, the empty Starbucks bag.

It was a junk drawer, come to life. A plethora of useless garbage suddenly turned to treasure because it was still there. It was in solid form.

"So, what are we supposed to do with this stuff, Nik?"

"Nothing, I mean, well, I want the domino and the photo, but the rest of it doesn't matter. Well, we should take the candle, just in case. I'm just saying we can touch things. Things that aren't important, but still, maybe we *can* get a clapper.

"Also, if you look at the stuff that's missing, it's mostly things that we thought were important a week ago. Or things that we were unnecessarily dependant on, although I don't understand why we still have reality TV, but I think that's important too. It all plays in somehow. All the pieces fit, none of this is random.

"Plus, I made a chronological list of everything that's happened to us since last Wednesday since we woke up. And, most important, I wrote down the lyrics to Lefty's songs. I think there are more than the obvious clues. Like the cadence, says 'get on up', right, well if people are sleeping they need to get up, right? And the three rap, well everything comes in threes yes, but good things come in threes too. So I think there is real danger, otherwise why issue such a scary clue? But *Downtown* talks about the lights being much brighter there, and that there is someone who can help and understand us, and maybe we can help them too. Do you see? There's more to all of this. So, I made a list of people we know in the city. Kassen, and your friend Melia and —"

Amber finally interrupted, "Dude, you're overanalyzing it. Did you ask Lefty about going to the city yet?"

"Um, no, I forgot. I was busy."

In her best moments Nikki was intense and neurotic, obviously the stress of the situation was affecting her more than Amber had realized. Amber knew she needed to help her friend move some of this manic energy before they could make any progress. Nikki needed focus to plan, and she was all over the board.

Amber asked Lefty, "Should we go to San Francisco?"

Paw raise.

"Today?"

No paw raise.

"OK, tomorrow. We'll go tomorrow. Let's go for a walk, you need to relax a little."

Nikki's neighbors were gathering for their nightly block party, and somehow, this had become normal.

10.
Champagne Budget, Cheez-It Reality

Wednesday Evening, Week 2

At 9:15PM Kassen pulled into his driveway. He had to cut his dinner date short, but it worked out well for him, because his next date was meeting him at his place at 10:00PM. He hoped Fate would be gone by then.

He opened his refrigerator and was somewhat surprised by the stark contents that greeted him. Four water bottles and some Del Monte fruit cups. Oh, and a bottle of Tattinger, but that was for later. He placed the water and fruit cups on the coffee table, and found an open box of Cheez-its in the cupboard and put them on the table as well. They were only slightly stale.

His answering machine message light was blinking. He had four new messages, and three missed calls on his cell phone from during dinner. He wondered, briefly, if Nikki had called him, but put the thought out of his mind. She'd turn up eventually, she always did. That's what they all do. They leave, they come back. Just the way he liked it.

There was a knock at the door. He walked down the stairs to his front door, opened it and stood facing a young, thin man. Chuckie said a bit nervously, "Jesus sent me."

"I don't have time for a Jehovah's Witness right now, so another time."

He shut the door, walked back up the stairs and into his entertainment room where he put Bob Marley in the CD player and turned it on. That helped to lighten his mood a bit. He checked his watch. 9:29PM. There was another knock on the door. He walked back down the stairs, opened the door again and was hit with the stench that resembled a frat house bathroom the morning after a big tequila bash. He also detected undertones of body odor and patchouli. The stench appeared to be emanating from a wildly dressed hippie woman. Over her shoulder he saw the rejected Jehovah's Witness sitting on the top outside stair.

"The Goddess sent me," she said.

He closed the door in her face without comment.

He was halfway back up the stairs when there was a third knock. Already frustrated with the evening's events, he yanked open the door in irritation. This time it was his expected guest surrounded by four people who looked eager to be invited in. Fate, a very large black man, the Jehovah's Witness, and the hippie chick.

"Top 'o the evening to you Mr. Kyle, we're all here so we'll be getting started. Please, everybody, come in, make yourselves comfortable, Mr. K has been expectin' us."

Kassen was mystified that Fate had taken over, but who was he to argue with fate? They all gathered in his living room. A room he never used.

"Sit down, sit down," Luke continued. "We'll not have much time this evening so we'll be gettin' to business. Our Kassen here is a very busy man, Eh, Mr. K?" "Fate" nudged Kassen conspiratorially. Kassen was dismayed.

"Lovely refreshment, Mr. K, sure and we hope you didn't go to too much trouble," Luke commented with mildly masked sarcasm. "Let me make the introductions, our kind host is Mr. Kassen Kyle. Womanizer. This is Mr. Chuckie Rightwing, Jesus Freak and virgin. This is Demi Devi Dai, our odorous, free spirit, sprite, and Wiccan priestess.

"Lastly, may I present the Big Man, direct from Negril, Jamaica, my mentor, my boss, Biy-Em. And you may call me, Luke."

While Luke had been introducing Biy-Em by way of his best Ed McMahon impression, Biy-Em had walked to Kassen's bare refrigerator and removed the bottle of Tattinger. Back in the living room, he popped the cork, took a huge sip out of the bottle, belched loudly, sat in Kassen's chair, and said "Irie."

It was at this point that Demi removed a huge root from the inside of her bag, and started chomping on it. Kassen and Luke exchanged glances of putrid disgust and both gave Demi a look of pure shock.

"It's daikon," she said. "Good for the bowels."

Kassen commented under his breath, "It smells like the bowels."

It was 9:40PM. They hadn't even begun. The cordless phone that sat on the coffee table began to ring. Biy-Em looked at the device and it was instantly silenced.

"D'ya think it was Nikki?" Luke asked shooting Biy-Em a 'let me handle this look.'

"Well," said Kassen, "it if was, she'll call my cell phone once or twice, leave three voice mails at my office, and then call the house until I answer. Nikki doesn't give up."

"Right. The three of you will be workin' together for the Big Man and meself. You'll be takin' your direction from me, but ya have to answer to him if ye fail. We've got tasks for each of ye, and you've been chosen for your skill and devotion to your primary function in life. Demi, ye serve the Goddess. We ask you to do no more than that. Chuckie, ye serve the Lord Jesus Christ, and in serving us, you serve Him as well. And Kassen, well, you're a ladies man and always will be. Your powers of seduction serve you well.

"Through your special gifts, you will help us to keep the world in a peaceful slumber. Sex and religion are the lullaby of our time. They comfort humanity and provide reassurance, pleasure and an outlet to escape the horrors of the world. Ye have received the gift of the lullaby by the Big Man and meself selectin' you for your tasks. You'll help protect humanity from the nightmares they would be havin' if me and Biy-Em weren't such compassionate folks. The universal slumber is about to turn to chaos; you will aid our efforts to keep structure and calm."

"Let me get this straight," Kassen chimed in, "You're telling us that through sex and religion we can keep universal peace? That seems a little contrary to the way the world works. And why just sex and religion, what about politics?"

Luke cast a glance at Biy-Em, "Told ya he was a smart one."

To Kassen, he said, "Ah, Mr. K, we've no need to worry for the politicians. Nothing could wake them. They've slept peacefully through wars, famine, prejudice, world hunger, hate crimes, poor health care, terrorism and every financial crisis possible. Nay, they are none to worry for. They sleep the sleep of the dead. Nary a rapid eye movement to show the world they are the slightest bit conscious.

"So, from tomorrow on, you two preach" he indicated Chuckie and Devi, "and you will seduce." He gave Kassen a lewd glance which made Kassen uncomfortable and slightly nauseous.

The phone rang again. Biy-Em cut it off again. Luke shot him another look. Biy-Em burped again, and said, "What mon, me enjoyin' me champagne, we don' need phones ringin' all de time."

"This meetin' is adjourned. Don't expect you'll all be meetin' again, so say your goodbyes, and remember that ye are powerful, and part of a powerful team, and ye are working to the greatest cause of all. Peace."

At the door Luke looked to Demi, he pressed his hands together as if in prayer and bowed to her, "Namaste," he said,

"Blessed Be." She burped. It smelled like poop.

"Blessed Be," she responded as she jingled all the way down the stairs.

"Aye, Chuckie, let's us have a little prayer before you leave. Kneel with me will you." Chuckie knelt, Luke stayed standing. They were eye level. With eyes closed, Luke began his prayer. "Our Father, which art in heaven. How loud be thy name? Yeah though I walk through the valley of the shadow of debt. Peace be with you. Amen."

"Sir," Chuckie said, "I wonder if you may have some of your bible passages mixed up. You see, the Lord's Prayer says –"

Luke interrupted, "Who d'ya think knows the word of the Lord? Huh? The humans who translated it, or someone who was there when it was originally spoken? That's right. Now the Lord likes his name spoken loud, so you go and tell that to your people. Jesus loves you, this I know. For the bible … well you know. Now, Lad, have you yet received the gift of tongues?"

"No, Sir, I have not been so blessed."

"Well, here ye go."

Chuckie started blathering, "Mulakasi, mulakasa, adah shuna." He positively glowed with excitement, and eagerly left to share his good news with the world. The Lord had gifted him with tongues, he truly was *chosen*!

Luke covered his mouth to hide a wry smile. 'That'll teach the boy to keep correcting me bible passages,' he thought, 'now that I've bestowed upon him nothin' but a wee bit o'Blarney.'

He reached into his pocket and pulled out something small. He winked at Kassen as he tossed him a condom in a shamrock shaped wrapper. Biy-Em left with the half-drunk bottle of Tattinger in his hand. Kassen had suddenly lost his appetite for seduction and quickly dialed the cell-phone number of the woman he knew to be en route to his house to postpone their date.

His home phone rang again but he decided not to answer it. Once message number five had been left on his machine, he took his phone off the hook and crawled into bed. From the living room he could hear Bob Marley singing and when it hit him, he felt no pain.

~~~

That night Kassen dreams he is on a houseboat. Nikki is with him and they are making love. Biy-Em walks in, but Kassen doesn't recognize him as anyone he's met. He's just very large and scary and is covered in bright tattoos. He approaches the bed and pushes Kassen aside, and tells him,

"I'm going to have your woman." As the man begins to rape Nikki, Kassen *just lies idly by doing nothing. Not helping her, not calling for help.*

Suddenly there is a room full of people who come in to save Nikki. They brought ham sandwiches. He wishes they brought turkey. Then he woke up.

For a brief moment he felt guilty. He knew that in his waking life he'd have at least tried to save her. He wondered briefly why saving others from nightmares didn't apply to himself.

He later dreamed of a flight attendant named Claudia then woke up happy.

11.

Downtown

In Milpitas Chuckie Rightwing doesn't sleep. He spends the evening on his knees speaking in tongues thanking the Lord for his new gift, and the illumination of his life's purpose. His eyes are bloodshot, and he looks even more thin and pallid than normal. In spite of that, adrenaline courses through him forcefully; he believes the Holy Spirit has possessed his body. He plans to spend the day in Golden Gate Park. There is a Gay and Lesbian awareness rally; he dreams of converting the sinners.

In Berkeley Demi Devi Dai is awakened early by a loud noise. It is her flatulence. She has a massive bowel movement, and notices that she has begun her monthly cycle. She pops a moon rag into her organic cotton panties and thanks the Goddess for her release. She lights a Nag Champa incense stick and makes some Miso soup and a cup of Chakra balancing tea for her morning breakfast.

In Chicago, Oprah drinks a Latte. She doesn't sleep anymore. She finds herself more awake than she's ever been.

In Dublin, Luke has a pillow over his head and is trying to catch a last few minutes of sleep after a fitful night. Between Biy-Em's snoring, his nightmares about Darth Vader and the fly buzzing around his head all night, he knows that he will be very crabby. He also knows when the Big Man is in town, there is no time for napping.

Just as he is about to drift off again the fly swoops by his head. He lets out a frustrated scream and throws his pillow into the air. He looks up and sees that Ray the Raven is in the middle of a nose dive, and headed straight for Luke's ear. "Ye mangy air rodent, you've been buzzing me all night long." Luke grabs his pillow and is intent on a little game he's fantasized about for years. Othello. Raven style. If he could just get the bird under the pillow long enough to suffocate him.

~~~

All Encompassing Trip

Nikki woke up on Thursday morning with her intensity level dialed back to normal, which for her was still quite intense, but manageable for her and those around her. In fact, it was even somewhat endearing.

They sniffed the Starbucks bag, loaded up Amber's car, and began the next leg of their journey. Nikki didn't even flinch when they rolled her 280-thread count Calvin Klein duvet into a ball so it could fit in Amber's trunk.

Nikki and Amber were both light-hearted and filled with excitement about their trip. There was a certain innocence and freedom in having no responsibility, no solid agenda. There was no slavery to bodily functions. They had no idea what their current purpose was; they were happy with the journey though the destination was ambiguous as the dark sky. All the normal things that generally propelled their thoughts had been removed from consciousness; no thoughts of paying bills, of meeting deadlines, no PowerPoint presentations, figuring out what to wear, and eventually, even their mutual obsession with weight went away … they weighed what they weighed, and those thoughts could no longer distract them. In fact, that was the overriding sentiment. There were no distractions; their minds were open to following the path they'd unexpectedly been placed on. To what purpose they couldn't worry over, because they quickly came to accept that all would be revealed in time, and that it was truly pointless to focus energy on any type of projections into their future.

They listened to the Doors and Joni Mitchell *Court and Spark* – the most perfect Road Trip music ever. Why else would it have been on the desert island?

Ordinarily the drive to the city was just over an hour, but the lack of light slowed down their pace tremendously. Two hours into the drive, they finally crossed the Carquinez Bridge. It was at this point that they began singing campfire songs. Loudly. Even Lefty joined in, though Nikki suspected it might have been against the rules.

John Jacob Jingle Heimer Schmidt was sung verse after verse getting softer and softer except for the last line, La da da da da da da, which they would yell, and then giggle, and start again.   They sang *K-K-K-Katy*, and *This Old Man, Old Dan Tucker* and some songs from Nikki's old church days which she had to teach to Amber who had fortunately been spared experiencing her own "church days." It was really the only part of church Nikki ever liked. A lot of times they didn't know all the words, so they made them up. Once they finished singing *Pass it On* Nikki was in a more mellow and reflective mood.

"I think the reason why we are together is because we're powerful. That's what we have in common. We're powerful, and self-aware, and we are leaders. Of course, we have no one to lead right now, but my guess is by the time this is over, that will be our role. Leaders. Think of what you've already taught me, Amber. You have this amazing gift of helping people see the best in themselves and loving what isn't all that great in spite of it not being perfect."

"You're thinking again, Nikki!"

"I know, but I can think of a couple hours a day, can't I? I mean, I haven't asked you one time where we're going once we get to the city. You have to give me credit for that."

"You're right. Good job. And of course, we need to figure some things out, but I loved what we just did too. Singing and acting like kids. That was more fun than most adult things I've done in a long time."

"I know, this whole situation is strange and weird and a little bit scary, and I *miss* light! But there seems to be a greater internal light in all of this that makes it bearable. Anyway, the other thing I was thinking is that we both tend to be caretakers, and we have this goal of 'healing.' We don't like to see other people suffer, you know? And you, well, you make people feel invincible, and empowered to take on the world. I think that's why straight women always fall in love with you."

Amber laughed, "Don't remind me."

"Well, there is most certainly something about you. You're magical. People want to be around you, and if I had to pick somebody to go through 'this' with, it would be you."

"If I wasn't driving, I'd hug you. I'm happy to be with you too, Nik."

And they kept driving through the darkness. Closer to the city, closer to the promise or possibility of light or even enlightenment. On the adventure of all adventures they were ready to face it with strength and a little ballsiness.

When they finally reached the Bay Bridge, they pulled into the toll lane, and waited to be able to pass even though they didn't have the three dollars cash it cost to cross. Amber rolled down her window to explain to the toll-taker our current financial situation. When they both looked up and saw the green bald dude waving them past, the sky lightened just a twinge.

"We should name him," said Nikki. "He's a good guy, he seems to bring the light back. Should we call him Greenie?"

"You already named the dog, Lefty." From the back seat Lefty snorted. He didn't mind being called Lefty, he *did* mind be called a dog. "Sorry, Lefty, Coyote, coyote. Anyway, Nik, for someone as creative as you are you don't seem to be too good with names. Why don't we just give him a name like Clarence, or Roland or Howard, or Ralph?"

"Ok," said Nikki, "Howard."

~~~

Chuckie arrived at Golden Gate Park very early in the morning to set up his area. He was methodical in his site selection. He had a map of the day's events and wanted to strategically place himself where he would have the most exposure. He chose a spot between the Chai Tea seller, and the port-a-potties. Either way he knew there would be lines, and he would have a captive audience.

He brought a step stool to elevate him above the crowd, and every bible he could find in his house. He also had a big white poster board with the letters, 'W.W.J.D.?' painted in bold blue letters. That always caught people's attention. As he finished setting up and placed his "What Would Jesus Do" sign in plain view, a legless man in a wheelchair rolled by and said, "The Sleepers shan't inherit the earth." Chuckie ignored him. As Christian as he was, he was uncomfortable with men with no legs. And lepers, and sick people, the poor, and Muslims, and small children.

Demi Devi Dai also headed toward Golden Gate Park. She would spend the day working the high colonic booth that a couple of her gay friends owned, so that they could participate in the rally. One of them was giving a lecture called, "Change Your Colon, Change Your Life." Demi took it upon herself to create a banner for the booth. She'd hand weaved some hemp fabric, made dye from organic herbs and her moon blood, and painted a sign that said "Coln Cleansing." She'd forgotten the second O in colon, but didn't have time to fix it.

She was excited about her day. She was fascinated by colons and bowels, and the cleansing of such. Plus, she knew there would be ample opportunity to discuss the Goddess with the audience who couldn't escape because they had tubes up their butts.

Biy-Em was still sleeping it off, and Luke was still chasing the bird around with a pillow.

Oprah put together a plan to launch a new line of O Coffee; her producer staged an intervention. He started to suspect she might have a problem with caffeine.

~~~

When Amber and Nikki finally arrived in the city they had no idea where they should go. The only contribution Lefty made was his *Downtown* refrain, and an occasional verse of *California Here I Come*, which was leftover from their earlier sing-along.

"Is there an actual 'downtown' in San Francisco?" Nikki asked Amber. "I mean, there's the Tenderloin, and the Castro, Union Square, the Haight, the Richmond, SOMA, North Beach, Fillmore, Twin Peaks, blah blah blah, but I don't know exactly where 'downtown' would be."

"You forgot Pacific Heights."

"I know, I got bored. I also left out the Mission, the Marina —" Amber cut her off. "Nik, do you know where downtown is?"

"No, but I think Macy's and Nordstrom are downtown, which is near Union Square, Moscone Center, and the Tenderloin."

"Thanks, Rand McNally."

"I hardly would consider myself well-versed in mapness. I have no sense of direction. The fact that we got here with no U-turns is only because you drove. I only know how to get to two places in San Francisco. The 5th and Mission parking garage and Kassen's apartment. I think I can get to Kassen's apartment. I always get confused on whether I'm supposed to go east or west, and there's invariably a U—"

"We'll go to Melia's. I think it's a good place to start, she can give us an idea about downtown, and maybe she knows something of what's going on. She lives in the Haight. I can get us to her house."

"The Haight's not downtown. That I know for sure. I think. I wish we had appetites; we could go to this great place I know in the Mission. Then we could have nightlife in the Castro. We could traverse all the neighborhoods?"

As Amber navigated her way to Haight-Ashbury she noticed a sign advertising the Gay and Lesbian rally in Golden Gate Park. She made a quick U-turn.

"See, you can't get anywhere in San Fran without making a U-Turn." Amber made no comment.

"Amber, where are we going?"

"Golden Gate Park."

Lefty wagged in agreement, while Amber looked for parking. Nikki thought it best not to ask any more questions.

Amber wedged her way into a spot between a Hummer and a Suburban and the three of them walked toward the park.

In the total darkness, the odd trio made their way down a street lined with homes and a couple of neighborhood bars. The only available light came from the glow of televisions. Every television was set to the same show, *The Amazing Race II*. They passed an open door of a bar, and Nikki stepped inside for a peek.

In front of a 70-inch screen were 25-30 men and 5 women cheering as though they were watching a sporting event. However, on the TV screen was the same episode of the *Amazing Race*. The teams were in Thailand. Alex and Chris were the last to leave the pit stop. Loud wagers were being placed on who was going to be eliminated from the race that week. Mary and Peach were the first to leave the pit stop, but Nikki knew that this was the episode when they were eliminated.

She went back to the door and called Amber into the bar. "Stay out here, Lefty, OK?"

"Check this out, Am. They're making bets even though this episode aired years ago. Do you think they can see us?"

Amber clad in her pillowcase walked in front of the big screen and stood there while Blake and Paige planned strategy at the airport. Nobody seemed to notice. Nikki leaned over to the man closest to her and said, "Mary and Peach get eliminated this episode." He scratched his ear.

While Amber stood in front of the screen, Nikki approached the bar and ordered a coffee. It had the usual effect, and the bar vanished. Amber shot her a look, "You ordered a coffee didn't you."

Nikki sheepishly replied, "Yeah, sorry. What do you think happens to them?"

"I don't know."

"There's one more bar down the street. Let's check it out."

"OK, but please don't try to order coffee. I'm feeling sort of bad about zapping people out of existence."

"I won't. This time you try to talk to somebody. I feel like maybe people hear you better."

"Well, not that I've seen. Come on, Lefty. Nikki's caffeine addiction demolished another building."

"Right, but give me some credit for not complaining about not being able to smoke the last 14 cigarettes I own."

"Nik, remember that I never knew you smoked."

They arrived at the bar next to the gas station which was kitty corner to one of the entrances of Golden Gate Park. Inside, the scene was essentially the same, only there were more women. Again, bets were made on the outcome of the episode. Most had their money on Wil and Tara.

"Amber, tell somebody that Mary and Peach are going to be eliminated."

Amber looked around the room, and spotted a woman sitting toward the back of the bar, looking bored. She approached her, and said hello. The woman didn't respond. "You should bet on Mary and Peach," she told the woman.

Though the woman didn't appear to have heard Amber, she did make her way toward the betting throng and put five dollars on Mary and Peach. She was the only one with money on them. It was then that the betting was announced as closed.

"Did she hear you?"

"I don't know, she must have heard me on some level, but it certainly didn't seem like it."

"Let's wait and see what happens, OK? It's not like we have to be anywhere."

So they waited. For fun, they each found someone they felt an attraction to and sat on their laps. Nikki chose a short, dark haired man, with olive skin and penetrating green eyes (yeah, she had a type). Amber chose the woman from the back of the bar. She was thin and fit, shoulder length blonde hair and deep blue eyes. She appeared to feel some of Amber's weight on her; she shifted uncomfortably several times, but didn't leave her spot.

When the episode ended and Amber's gal won her prize, a couple of the woman's friends gathered around to find out her betting strategy. "They were in first place, how did you know?" "I can't believe it Trini, you've never bet before." And, "The boys are so jealous, was there something that gave it away?"

Amber stood behind her, with her hands on her shoulders. She leaned in to the woman's ear, and whispered softly, "Can you hear me?" The woman looked around, confused. Amber tried again, "Wake up!"

Looking around her at the empty space, Amber spotted Nikki and fixed a glare on her. "Did you order coffee?"

"No, I swear to God, I didn't. I was standing right here. Ask Lefty."

Lefty shrugged.

The odd thing about the vaporizing of that particular establishment was that the blonde woman still stood in Amber's grasp. She was pale and unable to speak. Before any further conversation could occur, Nikki screamed excitedly, "I see a light, I see a light."

12.
Not That There's Anything Wrong With It

Thursday afternoon, Week 2

Kassen left his office and went to the Hallmark store to search for a card to send Nikki. This was an event. Nikki always seemed to have the perfect card for him, and though he'd never ventured a look at Hallmark himself, he was under the impression that it must be a simple task to walk into a store and find the perfect card. He had, on occasion, bought his mother a birthday card at Safeway, but that was the extent of his card buying experience.

The first shock he experienced upon entering the store was that it was decorated like a Winter Wonderland. It was September. Plastic Christmas trees were covered with Keepsake ornaments, and the shelves were packed with boxed Holiday cards. *It's the Most Wonderful Time of the Year* played merrily over the stores speaker system, offering a final smack of holiday cheer.

"Huh!" he muttered to himself.

"Help the next person in line," a girl behind the counter yelled. He looked around, he was the only person in the store.

"Merry Christmas," Kassen offered by way of greeting. No response. "Um, yeah, I'm looking for a card."

"Birthday, Christmas, Wedding, Baby, Divorce, Chanukah, Easter, Get Well, Cope, Kwanzaa, Mahogany, Maxine, Earth Day, Bosses Day, New home?" the terse Hallmark gal with no discernible personality asked.

"Something funny, I guess."

"What occasion?"

"No occasion in particular, just you know, hi, or it's been a while. Something clever. I'm always getting clever cards, is there a clever card section?" Kassen's charm was wasted.

"Love, Friend, New Relationship, Break Up, Cope, Adult, Workplace, Congratulations, Just For Fun, Sorry, Thinking of You, Keep in Touch? Sir, we have thousands of cards."

"How about Just for Fun?"

She led him to the Just for Fun section.

Two hours and thirty-seven minutes later he left the store

with the perfect card. (Though, in fairness, he had spent twenty minutes in the bathroom. Something about the store made him need to do a number two. It happened in bookstores and libraries too. He sensed it was a paper thing.) The outside of the card said, "He was so afraid of commitment that he wouldn't even open an e-mail if it had an attachment." Inside it said, "Men...can't live with them, can't delete them." Sure, it was a card for a woman to send to another woman, but he felt it apropos of the current state of affairs with Nikki to try a little self-deprecating humor. Besides, she'd be so blown away that he bought her a card, that what it said would be irrelevant.

He rushed back to his office in order to make the mail pick up, and didn't have time to put effort into writing of it. He scrawled a quick, "Nikki, Did you delete me? Call me, KK" and popped it into the post. He felt an overwhelming sense of accomplishment; Nikki would call in no time. Oh, he'd need to grovel and fawn, make false promises about it being different this time, but she'd be back.

~~~

Biy-Em finally awoke in the mid-afternoon. Luke, every nerve fiber on end from the snoring, had decided to wear earmuffs around the house to block the sound. He ended up having a rather peaceful afternoon.

The peace was shattered when Biy-Em tapped him on the shoulder.

"Jasus, Mary, and Joseph, Biy-Em, ya nearly scared the Irish outta me."

The Big Man removed the earmuffs. "Been tryin' to get your attention, mon. What you still doin' here?"

"What d'ya mean?"

"Ya can't leave dem at the rally on they own, ya need to point out the Waker, and look for the Seeker."

"I really hadn't planned to go down there, ya know? Sure and Mr. K hasn't heard from her, or I'd know it. That means they can't yet be in the city."

"Go to the rally, mon. And order me some Pizza. None of that gourmet crap, I want Dominos."

And that was how Luke came to be at the Rally.

~~~

Nikki took off running at soon as she saw the light, with Lefty in hot pursuit. Amber felt rude just abandoning the woman from the bar without explanation, but there was no explanation to offer. The bar was there, and then it wasn't. No point trying to conjure answers where there were only questions.

When Amber finally caught up with her crew, Nikki was completely out of breath and in an absolute frenzy.

"I don't see the light," Amber remarked.

"It's right there, to the right of those Porta-potty looking things. Can't you see it? It's not too bright, just a flicker, like a candle."

"I don't see it."

"Well, Amber, I'm not hallucinating, the light is there."

"I'm just saying that I don't see it, Nicole. You don't have to get snippy about it."

"Lefty, do you see the light?" Amber asked the Coyote who also seemed curiously out of breath.

"Jesus Christ Amber, the light is there, you know the dog doesn't talk."

"Coyote," Amber corrected, "Are we having our first fight, Nik?"

"Ha ha."

To cut the tension, Lefty broke into a winded chorus of *Downtown*, but it was a different part of the song than he'd sung before, "The lights are much brighter there, you can forget all your troubles, forget all your cares."

"Ha," Nikki said to Amber, and they managed a laugh.

When they finally got into the park, Nikki follows the flicker of light, like a mosquito followed a bare arm on a summer evening. (OK, she also followed it like a moth to a flame, but that was *so* obvious.) Amber and Lefty were close behind, and Amber still didn't see any light. She saw a lot of people, and a lot of Porta-potties. She saw a sign that said "Coln Cleansing" written in what looked like blood, but she did not see any light.

When Nikki burst into the Coln Cleansing area, Amber didn't know what to think. But sure enough, when Nikki entered the tent, she saw a large orange candle burning in the corner, giving off just the faintest bit of light. Now that she was in the room, she could hardly believe that small amount light had drawn her from so far away.

Amber and Lefty entered the tent just behind her. The three of them gazed upon Demi Devi Dai in her full regalia. Today she wore seven layers of clothing in various shades of brown. Earthy

71

colors, or poopie, depending on how you wanted to look at it. She wore a colon cleansing tube around her neck, and was reading a book called *Divining Your Inner Goddess*.

"Welcome sisters," she said, enveloping first Nikki then Amber in a hug. Nikki and Amber who had not even been noticed by, let alone hugged by, another human being in two weeks stood in mute shock. "The dog will need to wait outside."

Lefty was uncharacteristically growling at Demi, and Nikki and Amber said in unison, "He's a coyote."

"Regardless," Demi said, "He'll need to wait outside, this is a sterile environment."

"Wait for us outside, Lefty," Amber encouraged the still aggravated coyote. "We'll be out there shortly."

Then she leaned into Nikki's ear and whispered, "I don't see any light, Nik."

"Sisters," Demi interrupted, "I'm so glad you've come today. We can set you up with your colonic now, and you'll still have time to catch the proprietor's lecture on healthy colons. I try to get a colonic every couple of moon cycles. I find that I can stay much more in harmony with the Goddess when my bowels are free from toxic obstruction." She looked to Amber, "Would you or your partner like to get started first?"

Amber ignored Demi and continued to try to talk to Nikki. Nikki was lost in a gaze of the candle's flickering light. "Nik, what are you staring at?" Amber followed Nikki's line of vision, and all she saw was a large orange candle. Unlit.

Demi, not one to be ignored, put her hand on Nikki's arm and said, "Come sister, we'll do your partner later." Something about the touch of Demi's hand on her bare arm sent a chill down Nikki's back. She shuddered, and then screamed. Her gaze finally broke from the candle's flame, and she looked to Amber and said, "We need to leave here, now."

As they rushed out of the opening of the tent, they almost tripped over Lefty who was watching over them protectively, and fiercely. They heard the crazy colon woman yelling after them, "If you can prove that you share a residence, I can give you a couple's discount." The girls didn't look back and Lefty turned around and snarled at Demi, which was sufficient enough cause for her to return to her tent. When they got to the center of the line of Porta-potties, Nikki dropped to the ground and started crying. Sobbing, actually.

Though Amber couldn't imagine what might be wrong with her, she sat on the ground next to her friend, and held her and comforted her until the crying jag subsided. Even Lefty offered his support, and nudged his way in between Nikki and Amber, and rested his head on Nikki's thigh. Today marked the day he began to feel true affection for his charges. He'd felt danger for them, and with that a sense of loyalty that went far beyond his duty to protect them.

Amber stroked Nikki's hair and chanted soothing things in her ear, until at last Nikki was able to speak again. First she blew her nose in the pillowcase that was wrapped around her shoulders, and then she looked at Amber. "I know you're straight, Nik, but you didn't have to flip out just because she thought we are a couple." They laughed briefly.

"That woman saw us, Amber, she saw us and spoke to us."

"I know."

"Did she give you the creeps?"

"She was a little weird, but I didn't feel threatened by her or anything. I would have liked to spoken to her a little more and tried to understand how it was she acknowledged us when nobody else has for days. But, she was trying to stick a tube up my ass and she stunk," Amber said.

"Dude! She reeked. I almost gagged. We need to come out with Goddess endorsed deodorant; we'd make a fortune. I think I can still smell her."

"We're sitting in front of the Porta-potties."

They both laughed again. Not that it was very funny, but laughter was such a welcome relief after the tense half-hour they had just experienced. Not to mention that they had obliterated two bars, and left a poor woman alone and disoriented with no explanation.

Amber stood up and held an arm out to Nikki to help her up. They hugged and Nikki gave Lefty a pat on the top of his head. As they started walking towards the Chai Tea stand, they began to talk.

"You couldn't see that the candle was lit?"

"No, it was just as dark in there as anywhere else."

"Amber, I saw images in the flame. I saw Kassen's face, and I think maybe my ex-husband's face. But he was bald and seemed taller."

"The black guy?"

"Yeah. And there was a leprechaun, but he was a mean leprechaun and he seemed really familiar to me, but I don't know if it was from a movie, or a book or a dream. I know that he was trying to take something from me. Something that was core to my being, but I can't say what it was. I kept seeing flashes of their faces, and it was sort of hypnotic, and I couldn't look away. And then that woman touched me, and I felt this chill go through my whole body, and I was afraid of her. I felt like she was evil, that she could betray me."

"Lefty didn't seem to like her either, he was growling at her which I've never seen him do, but I didn't really get any kind of scary vibe from her."

"That's because you see the good in everybody. I don't know how you do it. Sometimes I wish I could be more like you, but other times I'm pretty sure that I don't *want* to see the good in everybody."

They walked along, through a crowd that most assuredly was not acknowledging them. After every couple of people that passed, Amber would jump in front of somebody to see if they would notice her. Invariably, she was either ignored or unseen. They chatted a bit about their day, and tried to determine a pattern based on events. It had been a long day. It felt like they'd been in San Francisco for years instead of an afternoon. They knew they must be in the right place. They'd followed Lefty's clue, and he seemed to be in agreement with their destination. Howard welcomed them to the city and lightened the sky on their arrival. All signs we're pointing to this being the right destination. But, they were more confused than ever by the events of the day and Nikki felt a great need to get to her journal and chronicle so she could study her notes later with a clearer head.

Finding a small table just in front of the Chai Tea stand, they took a seat to relax a bit, and do some people watching. Nikki checked her cell phone for the time, it was 5:15PM. Not too far away they could hear a preacher talking of salvation and repentance. It seemed incongruous with the environment they were in, though the rally had drawn far more types of people than just the Gay and Lesbian community. There were extremists of all kinds. Hippies, Animal Rights Activists, Vegetarians (mostly Vegans,) of course protesters of the event and, apparently, those who thought to clean the colons and save the souls of the condemned. Whoever they may be.

Nikki had led a somewhat sheltered life. Though she had always known gay people, she'd never truly felt a close friendship with any of them before Amber. It wasn't a homophobia, but rather felt more like a lack of common interests. She'd certainly never been in a circumstance where there were so many same sex couples in one place. The stereotypical butch lesbians mingled with the stereotypical flamboyant gay men. There were the people who took every opportunity to mention that they had a partner in case you had any doubt that they were lesbians. 'How are you?' 'Oh, my partner and I are fine.' 'What part of town do you live in?' 'My partner and I have a loft in the Presidio.' 'Do you have any spare change?' 'My partner and I give at the office.' As if a woman with a shaved head, dressed in men's pants and tie left any room for doubt as to sexual orientation.

Then there are the really *gay* gay men, who somehow always think that straight woman are after them. They manage to add into every conversation, 'but you don't understand, I like men.' You know what? We understand. We understand in spades. They only way we could understand any more would be to catch you in the act. You cook, you decorate, and you live with a man. We get it!

More often than not, the stereotypes were the flavor of the day. But there were plenty of couples who just looked "normal." Really great looking men, completely comfortable with who they were. Absolutely at ease with their sexual orientation with nothing to prove by dressing up or running around like interior decorators or wedding planners at every event they attend. There were couples of women who could have been Amber and Nikki. No gender-bender styles, no shaved heads. Just two individuals with a lot in common who enjoyed being together. It seemed to Nikki, that being gay or anything else for that matter, should be about making a choice for your life, and not needing to shove your choice down the throat of the world. But then, the world has a poor gag reflex, so it's probably why people try so hard to prove their supposed individuality. It's too bad it all gets lost in a stereotype.

Nikki had been ruminating on all of this for a while before Amber placed her hand on Nikki's and asked, "You OK?"

"Yeah, I'm fine. I think I'm on people watching overload. "

"We can leave if you're uncomfortable. I think you're probably more homophobic than you realize."

"I may have tendencies, but I try to look at individuals vs. the mass. People who don't really understand how to be themselves flock into these extreme masses and end up becoming a stereotype, which is totally ironic because it achieves the exact opposite of what they hope it will achieve. I don't have problems with gay people as individuals, I mean, I adore *you*. I'd say that I'm definitely stereotypiphobic. All stereotypes. Not just gay ones."

Two couples walked up to the Chai Tea line. Two women covered head to toe in tattoos, and two men in leather chaps, with their bare bums hanging out and piercings in places that Nikki had never seen piercings. Just in front of the Porta-potties two men were kissing.

"I think I'm more conservative than I give myself credit for. I don't see why people need to flaunt their sexuality. I like it doggie style, but you don't see me attending a rally about it."

"Nik, you don't understand, and that's OK because you're straight and white and because of that life is easier for you."

"I wouldn't exactly characterize my life as 'easy.'"

"Well, imagine all the difficulty of your life, all your struggles, and then add something to it that society doesn't accept."

"I know, I guess I just don't understand why it even matters. To society, I mean."

"Do you think people choose to be gay?"

"No, I don't, not at all. I think people are born with sexual orientation programming. But, I also believe that it can be very individual. I mean, I'm straight and there were times I could have seen myself falling in love with you. However, since that's been done again and again there'd be nothing shocking about it. All the straight girls want you."

"Yeah, but it's never the right straight girls and never for the right reasons."

"But that just proves my point. Though I think people are biologically programmed, free will definitely enters the scene. I don't think you can choose to be something other than what you are, but you can definitely add to it. Anyway, you are the cult leader of self-esteem, only people don't realize that how they feel is coming from within and not from you."

Nikki continued, "So, what's sex like between two women? What do you do?"

Before Amber had the opportunity to skirt the topic like she always did when Nikki asked that question, Chuckie Rightwing approached their table. Lefty immediately began to growl.

"Sisters," greeted Chuckie, who was holding a copy of the book, *Divining Your Inner Jesus*. "Have you invited the Lord Jesus Christ to live in your hearts?"

Nikki chose to answer, even though she wasn't convinced he was talking to them. "Yeah, I invited him in when I was about 12. I evicted him about a year later. Bad tenant."

Chuckie was startled, and wasn't sure how to respond. He didn't have much of a sense of humor, and sarcasm was generally lost on him. "Well, sister, Christ should always be invited back in."

"Amber, how come we're suddenly the female siblings of every whack job in Golden Gate Park?"

Lefty inserted himself between the girls and Chuckie

Rightwing, becoming even more fierce than he had been earlier in the day.

"Should we head out, Nik?"

"Please."

They left Chuckie standing there quickly flipping through the pages of his book, trying to find something that would help the lesbian couple divine their inner Jesuses. By the time he found something appropriate, they were long gone, the coyote trotting behind them.

As Nikki and Amber headed back to the car, Amber looked at Nikki and said, "You were kind of hard on that guy."

"I don't do Christianity."

When they were close to the exit of Golden Gate Park, a legless Irish man wheeled by them and called out. To Nikki he shouted, "Greetings, Seeker." To Amber, "Good Evening, Waker!" Then to Lefty, "Hello to you old friend."

Nikki and Amber both looked to Lefty for an explanation, but the man wheeled himself away, and Lefty had nothing to say except to sing another chorus of *Downtown*, "And you may find somebody kind to help and understand you. Someone who is just like you and needs a gentle hand to, guide them along."

But if they were to receive help from the legless man, it wasn't to be imminent. He was gone and in the darkness, nobody could see which direction he went.

"Dude, I swear to God, this day has been like a David Lynch movie. I'm just waiting for the dancing midget to complete the ensemble. I'm freezing."

Amber looked at Nikki with a bit of shock on her face. "You're freezing?"

"Yeah, I don't see why that's so remarkable, this is San Francisco."

"Yeah, but Nik, when was the last time you felt hot, cold, hungry, thirsty, or anything like that?"

"Oh yeah, I'd say 'that's strange' but it's all relative, so I'm going to just go with ... Huh!"

By the time they got to the car Nikki was shivering.

~~~

Domino's took over thirty minutes to deliver the pizza and Biy-Em refused to eat it when it arrived. They had to order another pizza and wait another twenty-nine minutes for the delivery. The

Big Man was surly and Luke couldn't wait to get away from him.

Because of the Pizza delay Luke got to Golden Gate Park much later than he intended. He followed his nose, and knew he would either end at Demi or the Porta-potties. Either way, he knew she would be nearby. When he arrived at her booth, she was just being hooked up to the colonic machine for her own procedure. Luke conjured a face mask for himself and sat down beside her.

"Ms. Dai," he said formally, "Greetings to you on this fine Thursday afternoon. How went the teachings of the Goddess today?"

"Well, Mr. Luke Goddess, it was a wonderful day. I spent most of my day in that chair right there where you sit, sharing the spirit of the Goddess with all who experienced the ultimate physical cleansing."

"And did ya see anything unusual today?"

"Oh, sir, there were many strange and wonderful things here. I saw a lovely necklace woven from dove feathers; there was a brilliant old man who had a live iguana on his shoulder, and so many lovely couples celebrating the mother with their feminine love. In fact, one couple shared their picnic lunch with me and we had home made plain yogurt with miso and raw peanuts for protein, and — "

"Ms. Dai," Luke cut her off, "Did ya happen to see a woman with dark hair, and big brown eyes, who was not celebrating the mother with her feminine love? Just an average woman, perhaps with another woman? Who may not have required a cleansing?"

"Well, yes, there was one couple who was a little *different*. I offered them a couple's discount, but they seemed very anxious to get away. Their dog didn't like me very much. He growled at me. Normally I'm very in tune with animal energy, but there was something about this dog. Perhaps he was abused. I should have given them the name of my friend the animal psychic. Darn it, don't you hate it when you think of the perfect thing only after it's too late to do anything about it?"

Demi bowed her head, closed her eyes and began mouthing words. Luke waited impatiently.

"Excuse me, Ms. Dai, could you –"

"I was asking for the Goddess's divine intervention on behalf of the dog."

"Could ya please describe the dog?"

"Well, he was brown. Medium-sized, and had a lovely white scarf tied around his head. Oh, and they said he was a coyote."

Luke sighed. "How long ago was this?"

"Oh, a few hours now."

Luke produced a cell phone and handed it to Demi. "If ya happen to see them again, press one on this phone and it'll dial me."

"Oh, I don't use cellular phones, Mr. Luke. There's radioactive waves that can get into the brain and cause not only terminal diseases but a disruption of energy."

Luke handed her a headset and walked away. "Aye, the extremists are a wearisome group," he muttered to himself as he walked toward the Chai Tea stand. He then picked up his own cell phone. "Evenin' Mr. K."

Mr. K was silent. Waiting.

"Nikki's in the city."

"OK," Kassen responded, failing to understand the relevance.

"I suggest you find her."

"It's a big city, Luke. How would you suggest I locate her?"

"Check her favorite places, her friends. She was at Golden Gate Park a few hours ago."

"At the Gay and Lesbian rally?"

"The very same."

"Huh!" He was quiet for a moment, "I'll do what I can. I sent her something in the mail today. She'll call after she gets it."

A gay couple approached Luke. The taller of the two said, "Excuse me, but cellular phones are prohibited here." Luke shot him a withering look and continued more ostentatiously than before.

"She *won't* get it, Kassen, you need to find her."

"Thanks for the call." Kassen ended the call abruptly.

Luke had made his way to Chuckie's installation. He sucked it up and approached the makeshift pulpit. "Top of the evenin' to ya Mr. Rightwing. How goes the saving of souls today?"

"A little slow, sir, but edifying."

"Well, never forget the lesson we all learned when Jehoshaphat begat Joram."

"Right," said Chuckie. He'd learned to ignore his mentor's biblical references.

"Did ya see anything unusual today?"

"Well, sir, no disrespect, but this is a Gay and Lesbian rally."

"True."

"And this *is* San Francisco."

"True, again."

"I guess what I'm trying to say is, unusual is relative. I saw many things today that I haven't seen before. I took it in stride and knew that I was here for the Lord's purpose, but I was uncomfortable from time to time."

"Did you see a couple of women, with a dog wearing some kind of head attire?"

"Yes, I did see them. The dog growled at me, though I think it was a coyote. The dark-haired woman was fairly rude to me."

"How long since you've seen them?"

"Hour, hour and a half. Not long ago. They left the park after that. I'd just found an excellent passage for back-sliders, which the dark-haired girl was, but they'd gone before I was able to minister to them."

Luke handed Chuckie a cell phone with the same instructions and bid him a good evening. Though Kassen was his favorite of the three, Chuckie was far preferable to the Goddess woman. He was relieved to be heading back to his home, though unsure of how the Big Man would take the news of the close brush with Nikki. He decided to have a quick pop at his favorite nearby sports bar before heading back to Dublin. However, when he got there he found the bar was gone, with no trace of it left behind except a bewildered woman sitting on the curb. He touched her shoulder and said "Sleep." And she was comforted.

~~~

When Nikki and Amber got to the car, Amber got Nikki's down comforter out of the back seat and wrapped her friend up in it.

Through chattering teeth Nikki asked Amber, "Do I have a fever?"

Amber felt her head, Nikki was burning up.

"Hang in there, Nik, we'll be at Melia's soon and you can rest."

"What if she can't see us?"

"I don't know, but we'll figure it out. OK? Don't worry."

"Am," Nikki yawned, "How much gas do we have?"

"A little under half a tank."

"So, we drove 100 miles, and the gas gauge hasn't changed?"

"Yeah."

"Well, I've had my cell phone on for two days and the battery hasn't gone down at all. Just another oddity to add to the day's notes."

They were quiet the rest of the drive.

When they pulled up in front of Melia's Haight-Ashbury apartment, Amber was able to find a parking space right away, which was a Haight-Ashbury miracle. The building was light pink with dark gray trim. A typical San Francisco building. Tall and skinny, charming and inviting. Nikki knew there would be hardwood floors, and old-fashioned bathroom fixtures. Maybe even an Avocado green refrigerator or a bright pink bathtub. All she really cared about, though, was a bed.

Wrapped in her comforter, she helped Amber gather their limited belongings to schlep them up the stairs. Lefty followed closely behind Nikki. His presence was as comforting to her as Amber's. She was definitely feeling the physical stress of the last week, and it hit her like a ton of bricks.

When they got to the top of the stairs, they didn't even have to knock and the door opened. Jake, Melia's husband, stepped out on the stoop and hugged Amber. "We've been waiting for you," he said.

Nikki felt a huge sense of relief to be seen, recognized, and welcomed. Lefty wagged his tail, but Amber felt alarm.

"Jake, you remember Nikki. She's not feeling too well. Can we stay here tonight?"

"I made up the guest room for you, but before we go in, I need to tell you about Melia. It's a really long story, but she's lost her eyes, Amber. She's blind."

Amber rushed in the house and went straight to Melia's bedroom.

Jake took Nikki to the extra room, and loaded their belongings onto the bed. "You had visions today?"

Nikki's shivering had almost reached a convulsive state. "Yes, sort of. I saw light for the first time in days."

"I know, it's normal. You're fine. It'll pass. Melia went through it as well."

Nikki scoffed, "Normal."

"Well, normal for who you are and what happened to you. The light won't affect you as much the more exposed you become."

"Jake?"

"Yeah?"

"I don't have the mental capacity for any of this right now."

"I know," he said and tucked her into the bed. She was now covered in two down comforters, but was still cold.

"Where's Lefty?"

"He's with Pilar, I'll send him in if you like."

"mm'K ..." Nikki yawned "Who's Pilar?"

"In the morning."

"K ... Can you give me my book please?"

Jake handed her *Jitterbug Perfume* and left the room. Had there been light, he would have turned it off and Nikki would have felt comforted. She clung onto her Tom Robbins book like it was a stuffed animal, and drifted off to sleep.

Amber came in shortly after Nikki fell asleep and crawled into the bed next to her. She moved the book to the bottom of the bed, and settled herself in. She had been crying.

"Amber," Nikki said sleepily, "I think I would pick *No Code*."

"What, Nik?"

"No Code, for my Pearl Jam CD."

"Good night, Nik."

"Nite."

13.
A Whale of a Belly

Kassen Kyle awoke with a hard-on.
Luke awoke with a hangover.
Demi Devi Dai awoke with crippling gas pains.
Chuckie Rightwing awoke with the joy, joy, joy, joy, down in his heart.

~~~

Nikki awoke with a comfortable body temperature and whole new world of surprises. She quietly took her notebook from the edge of the bed and began to chronicle the experiences of the day prior. It was an eventful day and there was a lot to consider. She sat on the hardwood floor, leaning against the double bed so she didn't wake Amber. By the time she was finished writing it all down, she could barely process all the information they'd received. What happened after their arrival at Melia and Jake's was a little fuzzy, but she had some recollection that Melia wasn't well.

Lefty wasn't in their room, so she decided to venture out into the living room. She checked her cell phone, which she now relished for its supercharged battery power, and discovered that it was only 7:15AM. She was sick of darkness.

She padded quietly across the hardwood floor and discovered Lefty asleep in front of the couch. "Good Morning," she heard a whisper behind her in a voice that sounded an awful lot like Penelope Cruz.

Nikki turned around to discover a gorgeous, sleek black panther with a pink lace shawl tied around her neck, covering her back, and dangling slightly above her legs. It was very pretty, and somehow suited her. She was the most beautiful animal Nikki had ever seen. Her eyes, big, round, dark and expressive, her coat shiny and bright, and body lean and graceful.

"Good Morning," Nikki whispered in return, "You can speak?"

"Oh yes, does Quentin not speak to you?"

"Quentin?"

"Your protector, the coyote. You call him, Lefty."

"Oh, no, he sort of raps. His name is Quentin?"

"Yes, but he does not mind the nickname you have given him. I am Pilar, and am the protector of Melia and Jake." Her Spanish accent was hypnotic. Different than the Mexican Spanish Nikki was used to. It had a more romantic, more French sound to it. Nikki thought she detected a hint of sadness in the panther's tone. "I was unable to protect Melia. That is the sadness you feel."

Jake passed through the living room from his bedroom, and walked automatically to the kitchen. "It wasn't Pilar who let Melia down, it was me." He yawned. "Every morning I go to the kitchen to make coffee, every morning I go through the motions. It's just something you don't really adjust too."

"How long have you been without coffee?" Nikki asks.

"Five weeks. Five weeks with no light and no coffee. Melia lost her eyes last Wednesday."

"I'm not entirely up to speed on what's gone on here."

Nikki and Jake were sitting on the couch, Amber sleepily joined them. "Melia had her eyes stolen. God I need some fucking coffee."

Nikki leaned her head onto Amber's shoulder, and gave her a hug. "You, OK?"

Amber started to cry again, she hated crying. "I'm frustrated, and crying makes me more frustrated. My best friend lost her eyes, and the world as I knew it changed overnight. I normally have such a firm control of my life. Everything regimented, and structured. I studied law. I need that order and balance, not because I can't handle the chaos, but because I thrive on keeping order. Now I don't know what to do, and I can't plan anything because we never know what's going to happen next." Nikki wiped Amber's tears away.

"I'll be getting Melia up soon," Jake interjected, "After Oprah, we can explain what we know of what's been happening. It might help clear some things up for you."

"After Oprah?" Nikki didn't understand the correlation.

"Yes," said Jake, "She's the Supreme Waker."

"OK, I have no idea what that means."

At that point Lefty woke up, stretched and yawned. Nikki looked over at him, and gave him a very evil glare, "I *knew* you could talk."

Lefty raised his right paw in answer.

"Well, why don't you then? For God's sake, you let me ramble on about the apocalypse."

Pilar answered for him, "We all choose to communicate in the way we feel most effective. For your journey, it is important for *you* to determine your way. Quentin provides suggestions. It's best for you."

They all heard Melia call from the bedroom, "Jake, I'm awake, can you come and get me please?"

Jake led Melia out into the living room to join the group. She had a strip of sheet or pillowcase tied around her eyes. Her pale skin appeared more pale than usual, her freckles a little bit darker. Her medium brown hair was pulled back and tied with another piece of sheet. Amber got up to hug her friend, and Nikki followed. Even though they had only met once, Nikki felt very connected to Melia. Once all the greetings were done, Jake led her to a chair facing the couch and turned on the television. Kelly Clarkson was singing *A Moment Like This*, again, as season one of *American Idol* came to another momentous close.

"Do you guys know what's up with reality TV?" Nikki asked. "It's like all that's ever on. We saw some people in a bar betting on *Amazing Race* yesterday."

"That's something we haven't quite figured out yet, but *American Idol* is on all the time," answered Melia. "At least we have *some* music."

"I ended up with four CD's on my bed the night of the incident."

"Any Pearl Jam?" asked Jake hopefully.

"Don't ask," Amber answered, "It's kind of a sore subject with her."

Just then the Oprah music started playing. Pilar, Lefty, Jake and Melia reacted as if the Pope had just entered the room and was preparing to answer life's burning questions. They were glued to the television as if Oprah was the most important person in the world. "Today is about the animals," began Oprah. "There has been a recent rash of performance animal related injuries. White Tigers and Killer Whales apparently lashing out at their trainers. Apes escaping from zoos, maiming children and other innocent bystanders. Today on Oprah we'll talk about why we expect this trend to continue, and what the significance is. We'll speak to Animal Psychic Xui Shu of Berkeley, California; P.E.T.A. leader Mimsy Gardenia; and world famous animal trainer Jacques Eray. We'll be back."

Since commercials had gone the way of light, coffee *and* the dinosaurs, Oprah was literally right back. Nikki left the room to get her notebook, rather than trying to remember each day's events, she thought she'd better start writing things down as they happened.

After forty-three minutes of Oprah, the world was enlightened to the facts about using animals as a form of entertainment. Mimsy Gardenia was against the horrific exploitation of the animals, naturally. P.E.T.A. and Greenpeace were working closely together to liberate all exploited animals and return them to their natural environments. Jacques Eray pontificated about how loved the animals were, and how well they were treated, and how if they were able to communicate verbally, they would tell the world that they love what they do. The fact of the matter was that they communicated non-verbally and have delivered these messages to all those who were willing to listen. Xui Shu disagreed with both of them.

Xui Shu was Asian, with very very narrow eyes. In fact, it wasn't until Oprah mentioned it, that they all realized, he didn't have eyes at all. His eyelids covered empty sockets. This bit of information captured the attention of all current inhabitants of the pink apartment building in Haight-Ashbury.

Oprah's interview went something like this:

Oprah: Now, you lost your eyes, tell us how that happened.
Xui: (heavily accented) Well, Oplah. It long stoly. My eyes stolen. But dat not impoltant. What happen after, bely bely impoltant. Because when my eyes go, I find inner light. I find the healing the animals.
Oprah: So after you lost your eyes you had a gift to heal animals?
Xui: No, not heal. Heal, Heal. (He pointed to his ears.)
Oprah: Oh, so you could hear the animals. What did they tell you, is there a message they are trying to deliver?
Xui: Yes, Yes, Oplah. Bely impoltant message. They say they have a message. The people need to wake up. The animals have to fight back to get the attention of the people. People don't listen. So the animal have to bite them. You undastand?
Oprah: I'm not sure we all understand (she does a sweeping hand wave including her audience) how the mauling of a man by a white tiger acts as an alarm clock.
Xui: The animal wild. It not nomal for them to live in glass or cage, to be given food without hunting, to be the acting in the show oh the cilcus. It upset the balance. In the biting they sending the message, you need to let me go. You need to figure out how you live without me. I not for this job no more. You need to wake up the people. The

animal biting wake up the people. They see it wlong. The more they see wlong, Oplah, the more they wake up. Undastand?

Oprah: Fascinating. You know that for weeks our shows have been dedicated to waking up those parts of ourselves that may be asleep. About watching and listening and applying what we see to our own awakening. Is Xui Shu right? We'll check in with our panel of experts when we return.

Oprah: And we're back. Xui, you said that these animals need to be wild, that zoos, circuses and circus-like shows, and marine parks are upsetting the balance of nature. Does that mean then, that you support the efforts of Mimsy and P.E.T.A. to release all these animals back into the wild?

Xui: No, Oplah, no. The Greenpeace and the P.E.T.A. too extleme. They no have balance. They sleeping too. The animals will follow they instinct if the trainer leave the animal to make they own decision.

It was at that point that Oprah lost control of the show. Mimsy began to pontificate about her awareness and expound upon what she believed were the truths about animal liberation. Jacques, who was surprisingly not French, began to rant about the trainer's deep level connection with the animals, and about the supposed choice the animals have made with their careers. Xui was standing on an audience chair chanting "You find the light, you know the tluth," over and over again.

Oprah lost her patience when a chair went flying past her and a woman in the audience lifted her shirt to expose bare breasts. Oprah screamed into her microphone, "Enough! This isn't the Jerry Springer Show."

All the noise and commotion suddenly stopped. Time was up. "We're out of time for today, this is Oprah Winfrey saying good day and peaceful awakenings."

(For a transcript of today's show send $4.00 to Harpo Productions, Chicago, IL)

~~~

Kassen spent his morning combing every Starbucks in the SOMA area for Nikki, though he soon realized that looking for Nikki in a San Francisco Starbucks was like searching for a gay marriage in a red state. He laughed at his own joke even though he was frustrated by the search, and way over stimulated by the six short houses in tall cups he had consumed along the way.

There were 107 Starbucks in San Francisco (not counting the ones in the airport,) though he suspected by the time the day was through there would be 108. They appeared to breed like Alabamans.

He stopped into the W Hotel at Third and Howard to pee and check to see if Nikki was registered there. It was one of her favorite San Francisco hotels and her most frequently visited. He walked through XYZ restaurant looking around for her, and was sidetracked by their beautiful French Toast. He wished he hadn't eaten scones. He hit the bathroom, and visited the black clad "cast member" at the front desk. "Can you please tell me if Nikki Nasco is registered?"

"Certainly, sir. No, I'm sorry sir. She is one of our VIP guests though, and was here with us just last month, but isn't here now."

"Thanks."

"Huh," remarked Kassen, and then to himself he thought, 'That's two trips to the city without contacting me. She might be serious this time.'

He hopped back into his car, which had earned a parking ticket because of his double parking. "Fuck," he said as he threw the ticket onto the floor of his car which was littered with empty coffee cups and scone bags. He directed his car toward Golden Gate Park for a scope of their Starbucks, but he wasn't holding out much hope. He dialed her number again.

Same recording. He threw his phone in frustration and it ended up in the back seat, where it immediately began to ring. Incessantly. By the time he got to Golden Gate Park he had seven missed calls. No new numbers. No Nikki.

~~~

The mood was quiet after Oprah ended. There was so much to say, and nothing to break the monotony of the constant analysis and evaluation of the things they saw and did. No meals to make, no jobs to go to, no school, no exercising. Everything that had defined their daily lives prior to the change was gone. As everybody does, they adjusted. Like Oklahoma City adjusted to the bombing, like a small Colorado town went on with life post Columbine, like the world survived September 11. Once September 11 was just a day, now it's a noun. And now it is normal for us to live with terrorism. To remove our shoes in airport security, to toss our lighters in the trash pre-boarding and to fear hairspray bottles and turbaned seat mates.

Their eyes had adjusted to the darkness, their bodies to the absence of hunger, their minds to new stimulants they were being fed. Their souls had adjusted to the new purpose, or discovered the purpose that had been lurking all along. Each day normal was redefined. A survival mechanism that was almost frightening in its ability to obliterate the emotion from the past, to make the present bearable, livable.

"I swear to God, I want a fucking cigarette," said Nikki.

"Do you have any?" Jake asks, "I have a lighter, and it works."

"Well, this day's taking a turn for the better," Nikki exclaimed.

Amber wished Nikki didn't want to smoke, and in any previous version of normal she would have tried to talk her out of it. But today, today was a different day.

Jake took Nikki and her precious 14 cigarettes out to the back patio. She put two in her mouth, and Jake told her to close her eyes. "It's better if you don't see the flame today." He lit them both, and once they had gotten going, she handed him one. The taste was awful. It was funny how cigarette smoke tasted so horrendous when it had been a while since you'd smoked, but the feeling of the smoke hitting her lungs was reassuring. They smoked in silence. Both enjoying, and at the same time repulsed by, every puff.

Once they were done they went back into the house and regrouped on the couch. Nikki and Jake stunk, and Amber and Melia kept their distance.

"Who should start?" Jake asked.

"I think they should start, Hon," Melia answered, "that way we can fill in the blanks for them. Our short time is best spent giving them new information so they can get out of the city. It won't be safe for them much longer."

"Uh, I'm not leaving you," Amber told Melia. "Nik, you understand right? I have to stay here until she's better."

"You can't, Amber," said Jake, "Though we really appreciate the offer, you, Nikki and Lefty are only safe if the three of you are together. That's where Melia and I went wrong. But, we'll get to that. Why don't you let us know what's happened to you thus far."

"Whatever you need to do, Amber. I'm not worried about me," Nikki said. She opened her notebook to day one and began to read her notes to the group. Lefty napped, Pilar listened intently, and Amber looked astonished. She put her hand on Nikki's knee and said, "We've done really well for ourselves. We've been through a lot and we should be proud."

Outside they heard somebody coming up the stairs. There was a noise at the front door, and three pieces of mail dropped through the slot in the front door. Amber was closest to the door, so she got up to get the mail. She tossed it on the coffee table.

"Pottery Barn catalog?" asked Melia.

"Yeah, some pizza coupons and your PG&E bill. That's a joke seeing as there's no electricity."

"We get Pottery Barn catalogs every other day," Jake chimed in.

Nikki continued relaying their experiences through her notes. She updated them on all the events from the zombie block parties, to the man in the wheelchair in Golden Gate Park. Very little of the information seemed to surprise them.

When she finished their recount Nikki asked, "Have you tried to get a clapper?" Nikki launched into her clapper from the bed theory while everybody had a good laugh. Not *with* her, but not exactly *at* her, either. It was something to break the tension.

"Nik has a very busy mind," Amber explained with a strange mix of pride and apology.

It was one-o'clock in the afternoon and they'd been talking all day, with the exception of the Oprah hour. Everybody seemed a little low energy, so Melia suggested they all take a rest before hearing the Melia/Jake version of the story. All agreed it was a good idea.

~~~

Jake and Melia took a nap in their room, the animals slept in the living room, and Nikki and Amber meandered to the guest room.

"It's weird spending this much time together, huh?" Nikki asked Amber.

"I think it's great."

"Well, if you get sick of me, let me know, I feel like I am a lot for people to take in large doses."

"Don't even worry about it, Nik. I love spending time with you. It's great; we've never really had a lot of time together. Now it seems like we have an indefinite amount."

"Yeah, it's a little scary, huh?"

"I won't desert you, you know that right?"

"Amber, whatever you feel is best for you. I know that's hard for you to do because you care so much for other people, but really you need to follow your own path."

The conversation died off after that. Amber lay down on top of the bed, and Nikki sat propped up next to her. She decided to read *Jitterbug Perfume*. Take her mind off of her world of seeming fiction, and focus on somebody else's version of fiction.

When Amber woke up, Nikki was seated on the floor Indian style, very still, with her head bowed over, apparently observing a body part.

"Nik," Amber whispered, "What are you doing?"

"Practicing omphaloskepsis. Alobar does it in *Jitterbug Perfume* and he's really enlightened, so I thought maybe I could learn from it too."

"It looks like you're staring at your belly button."

"I am. I guess it's some eastern thing. Contemplation of the navel as an aid to meditation."

Amber hadn't been sure if there were any more of Nikki's ideas that she would find odd. She thought she'd developed immunity. Like the Clapper was the highlight of weird ideas and nothing could top that. This did. "Did you learn anything?"

"Yes. My stomach is flabby and I need to do more sit-ups."

Almost as an afterthought she added, "Oh, and light emanates from my navel."

~~~

Kassen spent the afternoon calling all of Nikki's favorite restaurants to see if she had a dinner reservation at any of them. At 3:33PM his cell phone rang. He knew who it was, and answered the phone accordingly. "You know, when you first called me you said you'd tell me when and where to meet her. I drove all over the city this morning looking for her, and spent my entire afternoon calling her favorite restaurants to see if she has a dinner reservation for tonight. Not to mention the two and a half hours I spent at the Hallmark store yesterday. I can't even be sure she's still in the city."

"She's in the Haight."

"Well, if you know where she is, why can't *you* find her?"

"You have the connection with her, Mr. K. You're the one who knows what she will say before she says it. You're the one who has the sense of knowing with her."

"Am I looking for her for you or for me?"

"Find her Mr. Kyle."

"Whatever." Kassen replied typically non-committal.

~~~

When Nikki and Amber walked into the living room they could hear muffled voices coming from Jake and Melia's bedroom.

"You don't know that Lia, if he is looking for Nikki too then she may be able to get to them. I don't understand why we can't at least ask them."

"Because," Melia answered, "It's too dangerous for her. I'm sure he wants her eyes too, or perhaps worse."

"I'm just saying that if they use Nikki to lure him out, then Amber could get into his place and maybe get them back."

"We don't even know if it would work, Jake. Besides, we know he took my eyes because I am a Seeker, but we don't know what he might have done to you if we were together. I'm not willing to risk either one of them. We'll go to Berkeley and find that Xui Shu character and see what information we can gather. At the very least, we can get more information from him and maybe we could all work together."

They opened the door and walked into the living room and looked guiltily at the girls sitting on the couch. It was late in the afternoon, and they knew they had a long night ahead.

Amber spoke first, "No holds barred, guys, you need to tell us everything."

14.
Jake and Melia's Story

Still Friday, Week 2

Melia speaks:

At the beginning of August Jake and I went to Chicago see a Giants/Cubs game. While we were there, we got tickets to sit in the audience at Oprah's show. Jake didn't want to go with me, but I made him. Iyanla VanZant was on and the show was about seeking enlightenment in non-traditional ways. After the show was over, Oprah approached Jake and whispered to him, 'You have a gift, Waker. Use it.' And that was it. We thought it was odd, but forgot about it until other things started going awry.

We left late that night, and got into San Francisco around midnight. It was a really dark night. We both fell asleep in our clothes with our carry-on bag at the end of the bed. Like you, in the morning we woke up and everything was darkness. A lot of really odd things were missing from the house, and the coffee pot bleeped into another dimension when Jake went to the kitchen to brew a pot. He still goes in there everyday to try to make coffee; did he tell you that? Anyway, we figured out all the same things you did. The only things we had were the things on our bed, and light didn't work for us, but seemed to appear as normal for most of the rest of the world.

Pilar showed up that day shortly after the arrival of the Pottery Barn catalog de jour. We went through an adjustment period as well. But Pilar is very soothing, and she made us feel comfortable and protected.

We didn't have clues to follow, per se, but Pilar would lead us places and we began to understand that what we were doing was like putting together a puzzle. Early on, none of the pieces matched at all, so it was more like gathering a piece and bringing it home, and just staring at it willing it to make some kind of sense. You know how much information you get every day, and processing it, like you do Nikki, is constant. It's hard not to get stuck in your mind, and it's really important to bring yourself out of it sometimes and just let your mind rest.

One day, or night, we didn't know which, we were out walking. We ended up down by Golden Gate Park, and like Nikki I saw a flicker of light from a distance. I ran until I found it and it was this one Tiki torch that was all by itself in the middle of the park with just the faintest glow of light coming from it. Jake didn't see it at all. I too had visions while staring at the light, and afterwards I felt the deep cold that nothing can take away but time. On our way out of the park a man in a wheelchair came up to us and said, 'Greetings, Seeker. Greetings, Waker. Hello Pilar.'

The next day, when my shivering stopped, Jake reminded me what Oprah said to him. Two people had called him Waker, and we couldn't ignore it. We decided to go back to Chicago and see if we could get on the show. Nikki, I know you must be wondering how we got there and how we paid for it with no money, etc. and I promise you, we'll tell you all about it, but for now try to just listen to the story and don't focus on the details.

Nikki was rightfully admonished; she was just about to ask.

We ended up in the audience on a day scheduled for audience appreciation. The whole episode focused on people in the audience, and Oprah said that if you were there that day, you had been brought for a higher purpose. Jake and I were in a lot of the show; there were cameras on us constantly. Pilar was under our feet, but nobody but Oprah was able to see her.

Nikki wanted to ask about bringing Pilar on the plane. She refrained.

Oprah kept asking us questions that led us to believe that she had experienced, or was currently experiencing exactly what we were. After the show she kept us behind. She gave us the biggest piece of the puzzle. She said to me, 'Melia, you are always questing, always thirsting for knowledge. You see and understand the problems of others, and can help bring their issues to light. Even in the darkness you can find illumination. You are a Light Seeker.'

She said to Jake, 'You have the ability to help people recognize the best in themselves, and see the best in others. You open eyes to possibilities; you feed people's dreams and help them see that the impossible is truly possible. You awaken within them what they have forgotten. You are a Waker.'

'I am a Waker, Gayle is my Seeker. My protector is a toucan named Annabella.' Of course this didn't make a lot of sense to Jake and me at the time.

She told us, the world is sleeping but it doesn't know it. It is the purpose of the Waker to bring as many people out of sleep as possible. The Seeker feeds the Waker. Helping to find those close to enlightenment so they may be released from slumber. The Waker and the Seeker only have power together. If they are separated, the balance is lost and it opens the door for evil, which is how I lost my eyes. She couldn't tell us more than that; she is still on her path.

What we've discovered is that we have to work through our issues and tasks before we can help others. Jake has been able to wake some people up, but there are things we still have to do with our own information before we can achieve our full power. Does that make sense? To be melodramatic and cliché about it, we can't save the world unless we first save ourselves.

Jake takes his turn with the story:

The most important thing is not to doubt yourself or your tasks. Don't look for opportunities to awaken, the opportunities will find you when it's right. If you want to categorize the world as we understand it now, it would be something like this: Sleepers, The Awakened, Seekers, Wakers, the Extremists, and the force that we don't quite understand just yet, but it includes our enemy, Mr. Lucky Charm, the eye-stealer.

After we came back from Chicago we went back to the park and spoke with the man in the wheelchair. His name is Riley, by the way. Riley sort of sketched it all out for us. For the Sleepers and the Awakened, life is still normal. They have coffee and light. The Awakened struggle with feeling out of place, that they are somehow different, but don't have the understanding of why. They are more individualistic, not stereotypical. The Sleepers are the people you see and you sort of wonder how they get through life. They're often religious, or political. They live their lives without great passion or great tragedy. They merely exist.

You know as much as we do about the Seekers and the Wakers. The people you need to be wary of are the Extremists. Like your Goddess lady from the colonic booth, or the preacher. There aren't a lot of them, yet. Though we really don't know who they are, but they are people like Jim Jones, or Pat Robertson. Even George Bush, who people follow blindly, which keeps their individual consciousness locked onto these superpowers. And the reason they are superpowers is because they are feeding on the energy given to them by the masses. When the ratio of Awakened outnumbers the Sleepers then all of humanity will turn and there will be mass awakening. Light, and coffee, for all.

The Extremists are threatened by the Awakened, and are

out to thwart the efforts of the Seekers and Wakers. And it doesn't have to be religious or political, anything extreme, doctors who over-prescribe anti-depressants, Alcoholics Anonymous, the pornography industry. Reality television. Anything that keeps people from their own thought systems.

We believe that these Extremist groups are controlled by an even more elite group who want to keep humanity asleep. But we don't know enough about them to give you any solid information; all we know is that they stole Melia's eyes.

Melia takes up the tale again:
The day I lost my eyes, was the day that you became part of the darkness. I wonder if, when a Seeker is taken out, another is brought in. Jake and Pilar were sleeping and I decided to take a walk outside. I walked further than I'd planned, and again saw a light. Over the course of the weeks, I'd found that the more light I saw, the less reaction I had afterwards, so I took every opportunity to experience light that I could. The light lured me into a particularly dark part of the park.

As usual, I got lost in the vision that the light brought. It was always the same vision. I should have known it was a warning, but I didn't, I mean, so much has happened, I didn't really understand that the sense of danger I felt was real. This vision was stronger than the others. With nobody there to pull me out of it, I had no idea how long I stood there transfixed. All I know is that the vision ceased being a vision and became reality. There was this little leprechaun looking guy, and he just oozed evil. I was knocked flat, and before I knew it he had his fingers in my right eye, and just popped it right out of the socket. Like popping a zit. It didn't even bleed. He took the left one and he was gone. I passed out.
Nikki's stomach turned. She hated eye shit.

Jake starts again:
Riley happened by her and understood what had happened. He spent a great deal of time trying to pull her up onto his chair so he could wheel her closer to where we might be able to find her, but he couldn't muster the strength. She was deadweight.

Though he was worried to leave her behind, he decided it was best to do so and try to find some way to get the attention of Pilar or myself. He got as close to the edge of Golden Gate Park as he could and he began yelling for me. Apparently, he can't leave the park. We never really did get any clarity on that issue. Pilar woke me up and told me that Melia was in danger, and we rushed out of the house and started running toward the park. It wasn't long before we heard Riley's voice and once we found him he led us to Melia.

Since then we've been here, mainly waiting for you to arrive. Melia's healed exceptionally well, from my perspective. Now we are just waiting for our next puzzle piece to arrive. Since Pilar told us of your arrival, we're assuming it's to come from you.

~~~

When they were done speaking Nikki and Amber sat quietly, looking at each other, trying to take it all in. They'd considered many things since the start of their adventure, but imminent danger wasn't one of them.

Nikki finally asked a question, "Do you know who the green dude is? The one we call Howard."

Pilar answered, "Green is the color of the heart Chakra, representative of love. It is also a color of healing. Howard is your icon, Nikki. He's there, in love, to show you that your decisions are correct and that you are following the proper course. He plays no role other than to confirm for you that the healing is in process."

"Can we watch television? I need some mindless entertainment. Maybe *Temptation Island* will be on," Nikki offered.

Temptation Island wasn't on, but the first season of *The Mole* was, and Nikki hadn't seen it so it was the perfect method of escape.

"You know," Amber volunteered, "Before last week I'd never seen one reality television show."

"Jake, do you think the Sleepers and The Awakened still get *Sex in the City* and *David Letterman*?"

"Yeah, I think so Nikki. But, I think the Sleepers watch Jay Leno, and the Awakened watch *David Letterman*. That's why his ratings are lower. Because he appeals to the more select group of people."

After a few episodes of *The Mole* they all lumbered off to bed. Another dark night, to face another dark day.

15.
Illumination, (Sort of)

Saturday morning Nikki was back at her journal analyzing the information from the day before. She was up first again, which was sort of starting to piss her off because she had never been a morning person.

Jake was the next to roll out of bed, with Melia and Amber closely behind. After their daily dose of Oprah, Nikki began to pelt them with her current assertions. She was having one of her intense days.

"So, after what you said yesterday, I sort of worked it out that Seekers are more inward. Always searching for truth or light, looking for ways to make sense out of things that don't necessarily make sense? Right? Like mind-fucking everything to death?"

"Well," answered Melia, "I wouldn't say we mind-fuck everything, but certainly search for greater truths, illuminations."

"Lia, you could give Nikki a run for her money in the mind-fuck arena," Jake cautiously added.

"If it wasn't for mind-fucking, I wouldn't see *any* action, so I'm OK with it." Nikki jumped in. Nobody got the joke, or nobody thought the joke was funny. "OK, sorry to digress," she continued. "If the Seekers are inward, then the Wakers are more outward. Right? They look outside themselves, see the light in people and bring it out."

"That's makes sense to me," Amber interjected.

"Yesterday Jake said that the Seeker supports the Waker? But, how can that be? If the Seeker is so inward, seems like they'd be a little narcissistic and focused entirely on what they think needs to be brought to light. At least, that's what my self-deprecating opinion would be."

"You illuminate the truth in me," Amber answered. "I know it's there, but you make it brighter for me to see. You help me see that the things I do are unique and that I really can help people, and that I really do care for people. It's something I take for granted about myself. And if I didn't, I'd have a huge ego and I'd probably lose it all. A little humility does me a lot of good."

"Oh, I'm glad."

"And," Melia added, "Amber awakens the truth in you. Once you really believed in your ability to have that same kind of effect on people, but you let that part of yourself rest for a really long time. She is helping to bring that part of you back into your consciousness."

"That's how you sustain each other," Jake interjected, "There are many who would just take from Amber without giving any of the goodness back. People want to be around her, even though she does have that gruff exterior, because she makes them feel good about themselves, and they are so intoxicated by their own self love in her presence, that they don't manage to convey it back to her. In that way, Amber often feels lacking." Jake looked to Amber, "I'm right, right?"

Amber nodded, "Yes, you are right. Right. But I rarely see it that way. Mostly I feel like I don't do enough."

"But you always do," said Nikki. "And thus, we have completed the cycle. Cool. See, I didn't over-analyze it. I articulated it. Go me." Nikki gestured a victory fist into the air.

Lefty apparently decided that Nikki needed something new to ponder and approached the group with his now familiar, "Ahem."

"This is the part where the dog sings," said Amber.

In unison, Nikki, Melia, Jake and Pilar all said, "Coyote."

"I know, but that comment called for a one syllable noun."

"Ahem," ventured Lefty, a little more aggressively and launched into the chorus of *It's A Small World*.

"Dude," said Amber.

"Sometimes he dances," offered Nikki. For some reason the singing Lefty was embarrassing compared to the sophisticated and sultry Penelope Cruz voiced Pilar. "Left, we know you can talk, why don't you just tell us the next clue? I mean, is it Disneyland?" Lefty wagged his tail sheepishly. "It wasn't a very challenging clue. It just seems like it would be easier just to have you give us direction."

Pilar spoke on Lefty's behalf, "If Quentin just told you flat out, you need to go to Disneyland, you'd ask him why, and then why some more, and you'd gather all the information and pick it all apart and find flaws and draw your own conclusions which may be wrong, and then you'd still have to go back to find the answer you really needed before you could move on. Quentin is saving you some unnecessary and time-consuming steps. Plus, he's helping you learn to trust him, and I guarantee you will be grateful for that trust when the time is right. We don't all speak. We all choose to communicate in whatever way best facilitates success. You like signs, Quentin gives you signs. Does that help you?"

"Yeah, I understand. Sorry Lefty. But, why *are* we going to Disneyland? And how are we going to get there? I hope to God we're not driving, because that is just not fun in the dark. But since you guys flew then we can fly too, that's cool. Except for that plane crash thing from the first clue. Do we need to worry about the plane crash thing, Lefty? We need to figure out how we're going to pack all our stuff, where we're going to stay when we get there, and ....."

Nikki continued as the others left the room. She started to make a list of things they would need to do before departure.

~~~

On Saturday afternoon Kassen went to his office. There were a few others there, but the receptionist who sorted the mail was off on Saturdays. He picked up the large pile of mail off of the floor, and tossed it on her desk. A familiar white envelope with purple squiggly lines fell to the side of the pile. He recognized his scrawl on the envelope and picked it up.

The door opened behind him and the spry little Luke entered the office. Kassen shook his head, and handed the envelope to Luke. The envelope which now read, *return to sender, addressee unknown.*

"She doesn't even get on an airplane for a day trip without letting me know where she's going. How could she have moved and changed her phone number without telling me?" Kassen asked Luke.

"It's all different now, Kassen. Everything has changed."

"But Nikki is the constant. She's always been the constant."

"Ya need to put some effort into finding her."

"I don't know what else you expect that I can do, I've tried everything."

"Well, I don't think she's sittin' on your desk. So ya haven't really tried everything, now, have ya?"

"I have a life. I have things to do. Nikki will show up when she's ready, you need to leave me alone. I can't keep having these conversations and confrontations with you. There's nothing else I can do at this point. Don't push it. When it happens it'll happen."

"I've got a 7 ½ foot tall man with Van Gogh's Sunflowers tattooed on his ass. I have to answer to him. I'm three feet tall. Given a confrontation with you or him, I choose you. No offence, Mr. Kyle. "

101

"I see your point, but I have nothing else to offer you. It's that simple. You haven't told me why I need to find her. You haven't told me why you are looking for her. Maybe it's better for her if I don't find her. I don't know you, for all I know she's hiding from you and not me."

"Drive me to the Haight."

"What?" Kassen was flabbergasted by the gall of him.

"Drive me to the Haight. Now."

Kassen felt powerless. They got into his black BMW strewn with Starbucks litter and drove to Haight-Ashbury. Traffic was terrible. Protestors were out in force which always affected traffic. This week's protesters actually appeared to be protesting protestors, if that was in any way possible.

~~~

In Milpitas, Chuckie spends his day attending on-line bible studies and preaching in AOL's pornographic chat rooms.

In Berkeley, Demi Devi Dai drinks hemp tea and prays to the Goddess for relief from her gas pains.

16.
Hold, Please

And on the seventh day he rested?

Nothing of note happened today. Nothing. Oh, there was the usual bickering between Luke and Ray; the prima donna rants of Biy-Em. Oprah was a re-run, and Chuckie spent the day at church. Demi felt better, and enjoyed the day outdoors communing with nature. Nikki, Amber, Melia and Jake took it easy. And for the one day, everything felt sorta ... well ... Normal.

17.
Taxi!

On Monday morning after Oprah, the Seeker/Waker clan of Haight-Ashbury put their plans in motion. The logistics of travel were explained to Nikki and Amber. As a group they decided that Jake and Melia would drive the three of them to the airport so that Jake and Melia could keep Amber's car to facilitate a visit to Berkeley in search of Xui Shu, the eyeless animal guy.

Since they had no way of checking flight schedules, they planned to depart for the airport by 10:00AM to ensure that a flight could be made that day. All their belongings were packed away into pillowcases, which left their "clothing" in a state of disarray. Melia donated her jeans to Nikki, and Jake gave Amber the sweatshirt he had been wearing. It wasn't fashionable, but at least it was something different. They felt like new women.

Shortly before departure, Nikki took Melia by the hand and led her to the guest room. They sat together on the bed Indian style, facing each other. Nikki held Melia's hands and softly told her, "I think I know how you can find light."

If Melia had eyes, there would have been tears in them. She missed her vision; she missed seeing Jake's face, and the trees in the park, and even Pilar's shiny coat. Most of all, she missed light.

"Bend your head forward, and focus your attention on your belly-button area." Nikki whispered quietly, solemnly, un-Nikki-ly. It made Melia laugh.

"I'm serious, Lia, it worked for me the other day, I really feel like it could work for you."

"I'm sorry," Melia whispered back solemnly. This time Nikki burst out laughing.

After several attempts to be serious met with mirth, they finally were able to quiet their minds, and their senses of humor, and begin the omphaloskepsis experiment. Nikki stared not at her own navel, but at Melia's. Their breathing was synchronized and as they both fell into a truly meditative state, almost hypnotic, Nikki was able to see light. Light emanating from Melia's navel, which immediately facilitated similar visions to the ones she had before. She recognized now that the black man wasn't her ex-husband. The leprechaun was running around the Matterhorn (the ride not the mountain,) which was different. There was a scene change and she was interrupted by Melia's excited cry. "Nikki, I can see light. I mean, I don't guess that I can literally see it, but I sense it, I feel the warmth from my belly, and the visions are there, but they are different now."

"Strange, huh?" Nikki said.

"How did you know?" She asked.

"I didn't know, I just tried it the other day and it worked for me, so I thought it might work for you. I read about it in *Jitterbug Perfume*. I'm going to leave the book with you and Jake. He can read it to you. There may be more to learn there. Tom Robbins is probably a Seeker, also. I'm guessing that's why it worked. Anyway, I feel like you should tell that Oprah animal guy about it as well. Whatever's going on, the more Seekers seeking, the better. I think."

"I agree. Nikki, I have to tell you something. In the short vision I had, I saw the leprechaun at Disneyland, at the Matterhorn."

"I know, I saw him too. We'll be fine, OK? Don't worry, and we'll be back soon to catch up. I paid four thousand dollars for LASIK surgery, I don't plan to lose my eyes."

They hugged and went back into the living room. Amber, Jake and the animals were ready to leave. More hugs, and a few tears were shed as the final goodbyes were said. There was comfort in the pink apartment, and Amber and Nikki knew they were about to leave any semblance of comfort behind.

Nikki handed Jake her copy of *Jitterbug Perfume*, and her last twelve American Spirit cigarettes, "Save two for us, OK? To celebrate when this is all over?"

"You got it," Jake answered.

"I wrote my cell phone number on the front page of the book. If by some chance normalcy is restored before we get back, please call us. Of course, if normalcy returns my cell phone battery will be dead, but you can leave a voice mail."

They lumbered down to the car, and shoved the pillowcase luggage into the trunk. Amber drove, Jake sat in the front, and Nikki, Melia and the animals squeezed into the back seat. Lefty began a rousing chorus of *It's a Small World*, and the others, even Pilar, joined in.

"I know this is a little lame," said Nikki, "But I'm kind of excited about going to Disneyland."

~~~

Nothing says consistency like an airport. Life got you down? Feeling like people are moving *and* eating your cheese? Need a little sense of static? Go to the airport.

Granted, it's not the most pleasing place to be, what with the angry travelers (their flights have been delayed, their luggage is lost, and some pissy gate agent just told they they'd be happy to refund their ticket and the traveler could forgo the flight all together). The bitter airline employees, who really don't care if you don't fly them again, because their flights are going out full. The inept, and now government run, airport security (is inepter a word?) But we all enjoy a little game of box-cutter hide and seek, right?

Bad food, expensive prices, long lines, and the taunting, teasing, tantalizing aroma of Cinnabon wafting up your nostrils and directly onto thighs with their 730 calories and 26 grams of fat. No offense, but you'd think the people actually eating the Cinnabon would notice the correlation between their girth and the calorie count in this "snack."

There are two things you can see at the airport that you can never see anywhere else. Vasa Water, and people. Did you ever notice? Vasa Water? When do you ever see that at the grocery store? Never. They may as well call it airport water, because that's what it is. And the people ... Where did they come from? You know they must live somewhere near you. But you've never seen them at the grocery or the doctor, or the car wash. They are from another time and place. Sometimes they're even Amish. They come from different decades; they wear overalls or bike shorts. You swear they can't be from California, but they are. You overhear them. They tell business travelers insignificant travel facts like, "You know if the airline overbooks you they have to compensate you. It's called, 'getting bumped.'" And the business traveler can only blame himself, he knows better. He knows you can't go to San Francisco airport on a Monday morning without an iPod and some Bose noise reduction headphones and not expect to get the 'bumping' speech by a once-a-year flyer.

~~~

Nikki and Amber hauled their cumbersome and lumpy "luggage" into the terminal and looked at the monitor. They selected United flight 437 departing San Francisco at 1:36PM arriving into Orange County at 3:01PM. There were two flights after that if they needed alternatives.

Jake and Melia told them to walk through security and board the aircraft; it was very unlikely that anybody at the airport would be able to see them. With Lefty in tow, they did just that. They stood in the long security line with the rest of the proletariat and waited as laptop after laptop were removed from their cases and put into plastic trays that looked like they were purchased from Target during dollar days. Coats, shoes, belts, sunglasses, cell phones and spare change went into a second plastic container and half-dressed people waited to be "wanded."

"I had my underwire verified once," Nikki told Amber matter-of-factly.

"What does that mean?"

"A big butch security woman put her hand under my breasts and said, 'I'm just going to verify your underwire.' I loved it. How many people can say they've had their underwire verified?"

There was a ruckus at security, a drama unfolded right in front of their eyes. First, an old woman had her knitting needles taken away and then a three year old child pitched an absolute conniption while the parents tried to remove his shoes so he could get through security.

"All this," commented Amber, "and people are still getting box cutters on airplanes. Look, see that woman with the big hair to the left, they just confiscated her hairspray."

"I wonder when the class action suit for airport epidemic athlete's foot will be filed."

It was their turn. Nikki, Amber and Lefty, pillow cases in hand, all walked through the metal detector together. It beeped. This threw the TSA for a loop as they could not see anybody walking through security.

Just for fun, Nikki grabbed her case and went back through. It beeped again. Several TSA began to congregate at security stall seven. Nikki slid back through, and the final beep caused them to shut down the apparently malfunctioning detector. Unfortunately, Nikki's little prank caused a complete security shut down, resulting in not only the delay of United flight 437 to Orange County, but for all United Airlines flights that afternoon and well into the evening.

Every passenger in the boarding area was herded back to security and made to clear again, and subjected to individual "wanding." Many an underwire was verified. Flights were delayed by three hours.

"Cute," said Amber. "That was a lot of fun, Nik. And think, a three hour delay and that poor old woman couldn't even do her knitting."

"Sorry, I should have known it would end up being a huge friggin' ordeal."

Over the PA they heard, "This is a security announcement. Unattended baggage may be subject to search, inspection and removal. Please do not accept items from anyone unknown to you."

"Whatever. What time are we boarding now, did it say on the monitor?"

"Yeah, 4:13PM. We should be in before 6:00PM. What are we going to do when we get there?" Amber asked.

"Well, I've been thinking."

"Of course you have," replied Amber.

"I don't think the small world is just Disneyland's small world, I think there's more to it than that. I grew up near there. It *was* my small world, my microcosm. I don't think this trip is about Space Mountain."

"Did you think it was going to be?"

"Sorta hoped so. I used to love Disneyland. It was so magical. We'd get candy and souvenirs and a day out of school…all the make believe and the characters. I loved the Island in the middle. I can't remember the name of it; I don't think it's there anymore. But, we'd go and run around for hours. My parents would pay all that money to get in, and my sisters and I would spend time on that Island. I think it was Tom Sawyer's. We'd watch the fireworks, and leave really late, and we'd be tired and sick to our stomachs, and I remember I'd always want a big glass of milk.

"They used to have ticket books, and Matterhorn was an 'E' ticket ride, and it was really the only roller coaster, everything else was like Mr. Toad's Wild Ride, and Dumbo, and the teacups (Barf!) I actually did barf on teacups once, but it was at Knott's Berry Farm.

"Disneyland changed, though. Or, I changed, and Disneyland lost its magic. As I got older I guess I really began to notice that spending forty-five minutes in line for a 3-minute ride wasn't a particularly 'magical' investment in time. It's kinda sad.

"Las Vegas is my Disneyland now. That's where I feel magic."

"United Airlines would like to announce pre-boarding for delayed flight 437 to Orange County's John Wayne Airport."

"Shall we pre-board?" Amber asked.

"We certainly shall." Nikki answered.

~~~

Once aboard the aircraft Nikki and Amber went to the back of the plane and waited while the visible, paying passengers took their seats. There was an all woman flight crew, including the pilot and co-pilot.

"This sucks," Nikki whispered to Amber as they huddled in the galley with Lefty, their "luggage" and the drink cart.

"What sucks?"

"I don't like women pilots. I like men pilots. Older men, with graying temples."

"Nik, you know that's ridiculous, right?"

"Yes," she paused, "Doesn't change how I feel though."

The doors closed, and the girls selected seats just a couple of rows from the galley. Lefty wedged himself uncomfortably underneath the seats in front of them, and their pillowcase luggage took up way more overhead bin space than technically allowed for stowaways.

Once they were seated, Amber looked at Nikki sternly and said, "Don't order anything."

"OK."

"I'm serious, Nik. I don't want this airplane evaporating over the Pacific Ocean."

"I won't, don't worry."

The flight attendant speeches had started, emergency exits, blah, blah, blah, flotation device, blah blah blah, seat belt fastening instructions (???), sudden change in cabin pressure, blah blah blah, tampering with or disabling smoke detectors, carefully review the safety information card, the end. Nikki looked around, several people were reviewing their safety information cards. That was new.

"Should I turn off my cell phone?"

Amber shrugged, "I would think so. I don't know. Yeah, wouldn't hurt."

Nikki turned off her phone as they began to taxi. And taxi they did. They taxied out of the airport and onto the 101 South. They taxied here, they taxied there, they taxied 'til they had gray hair; they taxied left, they taxied right, the end of taxi nowhere in sight. They taxied so long, Nikki thought they were driving to Southern California.

After a thirty-minute taxi, on the freeway, in traffic, which none of the car drivers seemed to find odd, they took off. For just a few minutes. Then the plane landed at San Jose Airport where they picked up a whole new load of travelers.

Once the new travelers were seated, the 'aftmost' flight attendant bolted up the aisle screaming, "My turn to fly, my turn to fly!"

Nikki looked at Amber, "No wonder we're taxiing forever, these people don't know how to fly. Maybe we should get off. They didn't even check ID's. Maybe I should check ID's. Why are flight attendants flying? They should be attending, not flighting."

"Nik, you're wigging. And flighting isn't a word."

"I know, but it made the sentence funnier, don't you think?"

"You're awfully enamored of your neuroses aren't you?"

"Well, I do think it's funny."

"Yeah, but the thing is that you sort of hide behind it. Even in the name of humor, all this self-deprecation keeps you from really showing people that you are in fact, powerful, strong, and capable."

"You hide behind your tough boot-camp instructor personality with the exact same effect, you know that, right?"

"In a way, yes, I do. But, my 'boot camp' personality as you call it, also empowers people to be the best that they can be."

"No matter what the cost to yourself?"

"How did you turn this back to me?" Amber asked, incredulous.

"I do that," Nikki replied. "But you know I heard you, and I'll neurose about it for a while, and you know eventually I'll listen. And yes, I know, neurose is not a verb."

Their brief but deep conversation almost caused them to miss the hullabaloo brewing outside the cockpit. The two aspiring-pilot flight attendants were arguing about whose turn it was to fly the plane. Though the verbal argument seemed to be over, and a physical altercation had begun. It couldn't even be considered air rage, as the plane was still on the ground, firmly attached to the Jetway. Several men in the first few rows were enraptured by the commotion. They only thing missing from their "chick fight" fantasies was some Victoria's Secret lingerie and down feather pillows.

"This is fucking insane, Amber. I'm about 12 seconds from getting off this plane."

After a few more minutes of hair pulling, biting and graphic name-calling, the flight attendant formerly known as 'aftmost' backed her way into the cockpit, slammed the door, and securely locked it. Her breathless voice came immediately over the P.A. system, "Ladies and Gentlemen, this is Captain Morgan your pilot speaking," (she sounded proud), "In just a few moments we'll begin taxiing so that our delayed flight 437 to Orange County may resume. Flight attendants," in her most cocky voice possible, "prepare your doors."

The flight attendant formerly known as pilot and soon to be 'aftmost' slammed overhead bins all the way down the aircraft and took a jump seat in the rear of the plane. Nikki and Amber could hear her muttering under her breath.

Taxi part II began. The plane drove west and west. It drove until it reached the ocean, and then it drove some more. Amber glanced out the window and saw a flat, calm sea. Deep turquoise and green water like one would expect to see in Tahiti. "Nik, look how beautiful the water is."

Nikki looked out the window. "Spectacular," she said flatly because obviously she could see nothing but blackness, "Are we going to sail to Orange County, because I don't have any Dramamine?"

The plane drove down what appeared to be a very long runway built out over the ocean. It picked up no speed, and gave no indication that the taxi was anywhere near over. The beauty of the water mesmerized Amber, but Nikki had her head hung in impatience and frustration.

"This is a friggin' nightmare," she remarked, but Amber had decided not to acknowledge her again until they arrived. Lefty emitted a snore. Nikki shook her head, incredulous.

Ten minutes later they were still driving. Nikki became convinced that they were in fact driving, and once she gave up the expectation of flight she relaxed a bit. For Amber it was entirely an entirely magical journey. The water had gotten more and more beautiful, more translucent. Whales became visible out of the port side of the aircraft. It was the closest she'd ever been to them, and they performed for her, as if only for her and she was forever touched by their dance. Lefty yawned loudly, which broke the moment for both of them.

At that point the aircraft came to a complete stop. It wasn't a smooth stop either, it was as if the pilot had been approaching a yellow light, and right as she was about to enter the intersection the light turned red and she noticed that it had one of those little camera things on top and she was afraid of getting a ticket. That kind of stop.

Once everybody finished rubbing their necks, the "pilot" emerged from the cockpit and headed aft toward her disgruntled counterpart. Nikki and Amber could hear them arguing in loud whispers.

"Um, I ran out of runway," said current pilot.

"Well, you shouldn't have been flying anyway," said former pilot.

"Can you please take off for me?" Said current pilot.

"Why should I?" Said former pilot.

"Because we're late, and we're going to get in trouble, and Captain Marmut is going to be awake soon, and he's going to be pissed."

"It wasn't your turn to fly," said former pilot.

"I know, but I missed my turn last time because I got my period and I didn't think it was fair and now we're at the end of runway and I can't take off. Please."

"OK, fine, but I get to fly your next two turns and you have to make up the story to tell Captain Marmut."

"That's not fair," whined current pilot lobbying to return to 'aftmost' flight attendant.

"Don't care." Former pilot crossed her arms, closed her eyes, and tapped her foot.

"Fine," yelled (not whispered) current pilot returning to 'aftmost' flight attendant, "but believe you me, I'll find a way to get even."

Aftmost flight attendant, suddenly hungry because of the stress of the situation, began to eat out of the passenger nut cups.

Former pilot became current pilot, and skipped up to the cockpit where she promptly threw the plane into reverse, backed up, put it in drive, and at an alarming rate of speed the plane finally got into the air. And it stayed there, for a good thirty minutes before it began its descent.

Nikki didn't say a word.

~~~

It was dark when they landed in Orange County, which was really no surprise considering that the flight was seven hours late. Not that they had been expecting light no matter when they landed, but they held out some hope that, perhaps, the lack of light was a *Northern* California thing.

"This airport used to be one terminal. It was run-down, reminded me of Montego Bay. There was a big statue of John Wayne in the front. I guess that's around somewhere," Nikki narrated as they walked through the terminal. "Now it's this big beautiful airport with two terminals, great parking and tons of food! They finished construction on it the year I moved. I seem to have that airport luck."

Nikki was always fascinated by all the airport details, comparing airport to airport, always searching for the perfect terminal. There is no perfect terminal. The United terminal at Denver International Airport almost made the cut for its fine assortment of shops and various food choices, but after an extensive layover at said airport (blizzard), Nikki found that they were lacking in anything a stranded traveler may find remotely useful in a circumstance where luggage is in one city, and traveler is in another.

"Orange County makes me uncomfortable. I always feel like I'm going to get run over by a Suburban or a Range Rover, with a Jesus fish and a Bush/Cheney sticker on the back. It's amazing how quickly a place stops feeling like home. Now I don't feel like I have a home really. No comforting location to go back to. I don't feel 'from' anywhere, anymore, because I don't feel like I belong here."

They continued through the airport and out into the airport parking lot, which looked more like a Sport Utility Vehicle sales lot. Hummers, Suburbans, Land Cruisers, Range Rovers, all the big ones. Nothing but the biggest, gas-guzzling-est, most impossible to park vehicles for the Irvine soccer mom set.

"Amber, you're quiet, you haven't said a word since we took off. Is everything all right?"

The words broke Amber's spell. "It was the whales, Nik. They were so beautiful and powerful. They affected me like nothing ever has before. I'm sorry, I haven't really been paying attention. Do we have a plan that I missed?"

There was no plan. Though the trio was walking briskly through the parking lot, seemingly following Lefty, nothing, outside of getting to Disneyland eventually, had been thought through.

"Jesus, we don't have a plan!" Nikki panicked. Lefty stopped in front of a blue 1978 Datsun B210 Hatchback, and plopped himself down next to the passenger side door. "Jesus, this is my old car!" Nikki announced with the exact same inflection she'd used on the "we don't have a plan" comment.

"What do you mean this is your car?" Amber asked.

"It's my first car. Well, technically my second car, but it's the first car I bought. Check the license plate, 538PQG, right?"

"Yep, it is. Looks like we have a plan," Amber replied.

"Well, I wouldn't say we have a plan … we have a 25 year old car. That's mine. Well, it used to be mine. This car brings back memories."

"What memories? Maybe the plan has to do with the memories?" Amber had really begun to understand that Nikki's thought process was much more productive when she was brainstorming.

"Let's see ... High school. My second boyfriend who kicked that huge dent in the driver's side door, getting drunk and puking out the driver's side door, the song *Strawberry Fields Forever*, and the band Rush. To name a few. Oh, and I have a picture of it in front of my dad's old apartment in Corona del Mar when the street was completely flooded. I think it was the first El Nino, or at least my first El Nino experience. I drove it to Oregon; my friend stole it and drove it to Oregon, all kinds of stuff, Amber. I bought it from my dad, and paid $88.00 per month for it. I don't see how that helps us figure out where we should go."

"Which place is closest?"

"Corona del Mar."

"Let's go there then." Amber was being practical, "Hopefully there'll be a place to sleep and then we can figure out a plan in the morning. At any rate, it's way too late in the day to start a Disneyland adventure, agreed?"

"Agreed."

The doors of the Datsun were unlocked, and the keys hung in the ignition. Nikki recognized the KLOS 95.5 key chain she got at a Pretender's concert. The driver's door was hard to open and made a familiar squeak. The car had that old car smell, like the smell of cracked leather in the heat, even though the interior was definitely vinyl. The ashtray was filled with Virginia Slims lights cigarette butts.

"This is gross," said Nikki. "Why couldn't they give me my family's old Mercedes, or my dad's Ferrari?"

"Who's *they*, Nik?"

"Whatever."

Nikki tried to start the car a couple of times, with no luck, before she remembered that it was a stick shift. "Even my BMW," she muttered, "it could have been my missing BMW. Would that have been such a stretch?"

Finally succeeding with the intricacies of the clutch, Nikki got the car moving. Without hesitation she knew exactly how to get where they were going ... the early eighties. Just a right turn on MacArthur Blvd. and a left on Coast Highway... OK, so maybe not exactly, but a few U-turns were always good for the thought process.

As soon as Nikki saw the light shining over the ocean, she knew they were going in the right direction. She didn't even bother to ask Amber if she saw the light, and they made the short drive in silence. By the time they arrived at the apartment on Dahlia Street, Nikki was shivering thus confirming for Amber, too, that they were in the right place. Lefty slept through it all, comfortably balled up under the hatchback.

~~~

Meanwhile, in Dublin … Biy-Em was sitting at Luke's computer looking at internet porn while waiting for a report on the whereabouts of the Seeker/Waker/Protector trio. Entering the room tentatively, Luke nervously cleared his throat.

"They went to Southern California," he said quietly.

The Big Man, of course, knew this already. He nodded to Ray who was perched eagerly at the edge of the computer monitor. At a glance from Biy-Em, Ray flew to Luke's shoulder and in his best radio announcer voice, complete with pantomimed microphone, he queried the Leprechaun, "Luke, you've just lost a very important Seeker and Waker, what are you going to do?"

Luke's eye-roll was cut short by a glare from Biy-Em. "Uh, I'm going to Disneyland?" he replied.

Biy-Em pulled up the United Airlines website, and gestured for Luke to have a seat before he and Ray left the room. Luke grumbled as he selected the flight and booked 4 one-way reservations to Orange County for the next day.

He composed an e-mail to his motley crew.

Mr. Kyle, Mr. Rightwing, and Ms. Dai,
Join me for a sojourn to the happiest place on earth. We'll meet at San Francisco International airport at 11:00AM for our 1:36PM departure on United Airlines. Don't forget your photo ID, and carry on luggage only. No need to RSVP, your attendance is required.
Luke

He shut down his computer, took two Advil and a shot of Bushmill's, stuck earplugs in his ears and crawled into his bed. His best hope for the week was a sweet dream, though a speedy resolution to the Seeker issue would be quite nice as well, and as he drifted to sleep he entertained the fantasy of her capture followed by a nice quick jaunt through Mr. Toad's Wild Ride.

18.
Starry, Starry, Night

He awoke at dawn with an intense throbbing in his ear. As he came to his senses a bit, it was less like throbbing and more like a flutter. Sound then silence, "Jasus, Mary and Joseph," he yelled, though what he heard was, "Jay .... Mar .... And .... Seph." He put his hands to his ears, but rather than feeling ear on his left side, he felt feather. "Rayyyyyyyyyyyyyyyyyyyyyyyyyyyyyyyyyyyy," he screamed. The bird dropped the earplug, and flew quickly from the room onto the shoulder of Biy-Em.

Luke removed the second earplug, and ambled into his bathroom. He stepped up onto the bathroom stool and took a good look in the mirror and noticed that his left ear was bright red, and had been plucked of all hair.

"Lovely," he said to himself, "just lovely." With a splash of cold water on his face, and a quick brush of his teeth, he went to the kitchen for a cup of tea before packing. Though he was anxious about the trip ahead, he was more than eager to be away from Biy-Em and Ray for a few days, even if it meant being in the company of the extremists.

By 8:00AM he was packed and ready to go, and despite the early hour, he left his apartment in search of the solace of the airport. Rolling his luggage to the front door, he was just about to leave when Biy-Em caught sight of him from the kitchen. His deep laugh stopped Luke from turning the handle.

"Sure and you aren't laughin' at me, Biy-Em?"

"Sure and I am, mon. You crazy? You look like dem Iowa tourists. De extremists gonna be wearing matching shirts?"

It was true. Luke did look ridiculous. Though he proudly wore his Mickey Mouse ears, the Hawaiian shirt, fanny pack and white shoes with black socks painted him as tourist extraordinaire.

"I'm trying to blend, besides, the shirt is Tommy Bahama," he answered weakly.

"Well, I never met a man in Nassau with a shirt like dat. Dat Seeker gonna run for miles when she see you, mon. You one scary tourist."

"See you in a few days, Boss," Luke said as he walked out the door and let it slam behind him.

~~~

Nikki sat straight up in bed and yelled, "Fuck!" The whole room seemed to move around her, and she lay back down, willing the room to stop moving.

"Amber," she moaned.

Amber came into the room, with Lefty on her heels. He jumped up on the bed, and the room swirled even more. "Yeah, Nik, I'm right here," Amber's voice answered reassuringly.

"I think I'm really sick," Nikki whimpered. "Everything's moving, and I feel really dizzy and nauseated, like I'm seasick or something."

With only the mildest of chuckles, Amber walked to the right side of the bed, and pulled Nikki up so that she was standing on solid ground. Lefty, still on the bed, remained in motion.

"Water bed," Amber pronounced. "And not the more modern kind, the really old school kind that are really watery."

"Holy Shit, it's my dad's old bed. What happened last night, I don't really remember much. I mean, I remember the light, and I had a dream I think, but I don't remember getting here."

They walked out into the kitchen and Nikki got her first conscious look at the place. "I've had recurring nightmares about this apartment for as long as I can remember. My sisters too. We have no idea why, none of us remember anything bad happening here, but it was never a good dream." She took Amber to the back bedroom and showed her the alley behind the house. "That alley is always a part of it too, and the garage."

The apartment was the top half of a duplex. The wooden stairs leading up to it ended at a small patio with a sliding glass door, and a warped wooden front door. On the patio two empty flowerpots sat atop a bright orange door (unhinged), which lay flat on white plastic tubing and currently functioned as a table. The name of the 1960's tennis legend Rod Laver was painted in bold white letters. It used to be a dressing room door when Nikki's father had owned a pro-shop at the Sunny Hills Racquet Club. Nikki shared the "not being able to throw things away" gene with her father. It meshed nicely with her "cling to the past" gene.

Most of the apartment was bereft of furniture, with the exception of a large black piano, with several broken keys, which rested against the dining room wall. The small kitchen, also empty, backed against the first bathroom which was across the hall from the master bed and bath. The second bedroom was at the very back of the house overlooking the alley. That had been Nikki's room when she lived there.

They walked back out into the dining area, and sat on the piano bench. Nikki turned to play the one tune she knew. A basic little Mozart number that had stuck with her since childhood lessons.

"My dad always used to play. Beethoven's Fifth or Claire d'Lune. It was awesome, I loved to watch him when he got to the part of Beethoven's Fifth where his hands would start at the bottom and work his way up. Piano is brilliant. Anyway, what happened? Did I black out from the light?"

Amber put her hand tenderly on Nikki's head and smoothed down her hair a little bit. She tried, unsuccessfully, to remove the now permanent mascara smudge. "It was really pretty uneventful. You sort of tranced out. We left the airport, and you saw the light over the water, and we drove here. By the time we got here, you were shivering, but it didn't seem like you were having any visions and the shivering was much more mild than the last time."

"How did we get in here?"

"The second key on your key chain. You just walked right up, opened the door and crawled into the waterbed and fell asleep."

"Wow. I'm sorry. Were you bored?"

"No, it was fine. I hung out with Lefty for a while, and then came in and went to sleep."

Nikki quickly jumped to a conclusion, "Did Lefty talk to you?"

"Don't be paranoid, Nik. Of course not. Oh, you did say something kind of funny in your sleep. You were talking about kissing, and about lips not fitting."

"I can't kiss anybody but you, because my lips only fit yours … I was dreaming about Kassen. Made me miss him a little bit."

"NO KASSEN!" Amber, as versed as any in their roller coaster romance, was consigned to ensure that Nikki stayed strong in her resolve to extricate him from her life.

"Even if I wanted to call him, Amber, I couldn't. Remember?"

"I know, knee jerk response. Forget him anyway. What should we do today?"

"Don't laugh, OK?" Nikki pleaded, "I want to just get our thoughts together. Try to make a plan, write down what happened yesterday, and make a list of the things I think we should take a look at while we're down here. Is that all right with you? And later this afternoon, maybe we can catch the sunset down at the beach?"

"That's funny. You're very funny, Nik."

"We'll go at sunset time, and imagine a sunset ... how does that sound? And we'll conjure an imaginary Venti, low-fat, two Splenda latte to go with it."

~~~

Luke arrived at the airport with ample time to spare. He hated the domestic terminal, though that really was relative since he hated most human things as he did most humans. It wasn't really a hot hate, more the way humans feel about insects. They are a bother and should be exterminated.

The international terminal was so much calmer, with ambient lighting and civilized security. It housed interesting passengers with passports, eye masks and sleeping aids. If the Seeker had chosen Sydney as her destination, then he'd be on a night flight with six movies and three full meals. He sighed and succumbed to the smell of Cinnabon. When in domestic, do as the domesticates do. He chuckled at himself. He thought his last sentence was really funny.

By 10:00AM he was through security and held a boarding pass with seat 14C. With any luck the rest of his crew would be scattered throughout the rear of the aircraft and he wouldn't have to see any of them. When he arrived at the gate, however, Chuckie Rightwing was already there, sitting in the lounge, reading his bible. If possible, he looked paler and thinner than Luke had ever seen him. He, too, wore a fanny pack, only he was serious about it. His luggage consisted of a hard case cosmetic bag like flight attendants used to carry in the early days of flying. Luke almost felt sorry for him.

"I took the liberty of speaking with the gate agent and asking for all of our seats to be assigned together, Mr. Luke. I don't fly very well, and I thought perhaps we could pray together as we are taking off."

"Lovely," Luke said sarcastically, knowing full well that the sarcasm was lost on Chuckie. "I'll just be over here, Mr. Rightwing. I'm needin' a little time to compose a parable before we go."

Ten minutes later, Kassen Kyle joined them in the gate area. Ever the ladies man he looked the part, and succeeded in charming the gate agent into a free First Class upgrade. He wore dark Gap jeans, a tan t-shirt, and a green suede Wilkes Bashford coat. His black

Hartford luggage perfectly complimented his ensemble, and with the just the briefest acknowledgements to Luke and Chuckie, he sat down and pulled out his copy of Paulo Coelho's *The Alchemist* and began to read.

Demi Devi Dai was the last, and loudest, to arrive. With several layers of metal woven into her skirt, and several necklaces around her neck, she ran into a bit of difficulty in security. She was clothed in various shades of yellow and gold, which made her skin look a little bit on the green side. She carried three bags, none of which were actual luggage, all of which were hemp. Kassen smelled her before he saw her. An overabundance of Patchouli mingled with body odor and the familiar outhouse smell that always clung to her. She saw Chuckie first and called out to him, waving her arm dramatically, "Chuckie, oh Chuckie."

Kassen looked up just in time to see that her armpit hair was beaded.

He shook his head, sunk into his chair, and began to read again, pretending he didn't see her.

"Oh My Goddess, it was quite an ordeal getting in here," she said to Chuckie in particular, but loud enough for all the neighboring gates to hear. "I had to take off all my jewelry. And then my skirt kept making the alarm go off, and I had to take off my shoes, and …" she stopped herself, "Kassen," she yelled, "You're reading *The Alchemist*? I love that book. My Goddess, how far have you gotten?" She dropped her bags by Chuckie and plopped herself down in the seat next to Kassen.

"Hello Demi," he said, and tried to go back to his book.

She rested her chin on his shoulder, and began to read along with him. Demi was not immune to Kassen's natural charm. He was however, quite immune to hers. "Oh, I love this part … wait until you find out what happens, it will change your life, it will." He sneezed. Perhaps he was not so much immune to her, as allergic to her.

"Oh dear, Kassen, are you getting a cold? I have some herbs for that. They may make you a little gassy, but they keep away the cold. I take them every day. Let me go get them out of my bag."

Kassen looked at Luke and they shared an eye roll.

While Demi was riffling through her "luggage" boarding was called. "Oh no," she exclaimed, "wait, Kassen, Chuckie, Luke, please come here. I have a safety ritual for us." She went back into her bag and pulled out a large sage wand and a Bic lighter, and lit it up. She chanted as she waved the wand in front of her fellow travelers. Kassen first, of course, then Luke, Chuckie backed away with his hand on the bible and yelled to Demi, "The devil is in you woman, you will burn in hell for eternity if you don't accept Jesus Christ as your savior." As he began to pray, First Class passengers were called to board, and security approached Demi, seized her sage wand and the lighter that was supposed to be disposed of before security, and told her that there was no smoking in the terminal.

As Kassen readied to board the plane, he looked at Luke and they shared yet another eye roll.

~~~

Kassen was seated in 2C with a Mimosa in his hand and some warm nuts on his tray table when the rest of group boarded. Luke "accidentally" bumped his arm, spilling the drink on Kassen's $1400.00 suede jacket. "So sorry, Mr. Kyle," he said with mock innocence.

"No worries, Luke, it's waterproof," said with a gracious smile.

In coach, only the most minor incident occurred when Demi and Chuckie began the Jesus/Goddess/Devil argument. Luke quickly dealt this with by switching seats with Demi, and sitting quietly sandwiched between the two religion enthusiasts. After that, it was a remarkably relaxing journey and before they all knew it the pilot was on the horn advising the passengers of their *early* arrival into Orange County's John Wayne Airport.

Early arrival. Seven minutes early. That's a big deal to those airline folk. The pilot was inordinately proud.

Once deplaned, and de-full-bladdered, the group assembled in front of the ground transportation sign for a debriefing. Four cyber green Volkswagen New Beetle's awaited, complete with plastic yellow daisies in the flower holders and women drivers in matching cyber green and daisy outfits.

"We meet at the main gates of Disneyland tomorrow morning at 9:00AM sharp. Don't be late; you can take the monorail in from the Disneyland hotel where you all have single accommodations booked under your own names. Until then, the lassies will take you wherever you wish to go. Keep your cell phones on. Enjoy!"

Luke tossed his bag into the trunk of the first VW, quickly (and comfortably) hopped into the backseat, and was gone before anybody had an opportunity to blink. Chuckie ventured toward the next waiting vehicle, and asked the driver to take him to the

Crystal Cathedral in Garden Grove. His tall lanky body got into the Beetle with slightly more difficulty. Demi, hampered by the many accoutrements hanging from the various and bulky parts of her, struggled into the third car, and asked the driver to take her to the Self Realization Fellowship in Encinitas.

Kassen hailed a cab and headed for Balboa Island. He didn't "do" the Beetle thing.

~~~

Amber was restless. She did Yoga in the empty living room, though she'd rarely done Yoga before. It helped her pass the time. Most of the day Nikki had spent writing notes and compiling lists.

"You know those whales you saw yesterday?" Nikki asked, trying to fill the gaps in her notes.

"Yes?"

"Do you know what kind they were?"

"Um, no, Nik ... I didn't take Marine Biology."

"But it was dark though, how did you know they were whales?"

"I don't know if I saw light or just felt it, but they were very clear to me."

"Have you ever known whales to be in Northern California in late September?"

"What difference does it make? They were beautiful and they gave me peace, do you have to over-analyze them?"

"Kinda. I just think they weren't supposed to be there, and if they were there they were there for you only, and maybe that makes them important, so we should pay attention to them."

"Okay ... note time is over. We're going out!"

Amber closed Nikki's notebook, grabbed the car keys and the cell phone, motioned for Lefty to follow and they left the apartment in silence. Amber headed for the car, while Nikki walked down Dahlia Street, and prepared to cross to Fernleaf and Goldenrod where she knew there was a cross-over bridge that led to the beach. Lefty stood looking between the two as if watching a ping-pong match. Lefty began to follow after Nikki, which led Amber to about face and join them and soon the three of them were walking together toward the smell and sounds of the ocean.

"I'm bored too, you know," Nikki was the first to break the silence.

"I know, but at least you have your journal. That's

something to do. I can't contribute anything locked in a house all day."

"What time is it anyway?"

Amber checked Nikki's cell phone, "5:15 ... at night."

"I'm sorry, I really didn't realize how late it was. Tomorrow we'll be at Disneyland and hit sensory overload. It'll be great."

"Yeah," Amber replied, "and maybe we'll get some answers. And a new song. Lefty's been clueless ever since small world."

Lefty growled in indignation, but Nikki enjoyed Amber's play on words.

~~~

Corona del Mar beach can be accessed one of three ways; down a steep driveway, down steep stairs, or down a steep rock climb into a small cove called Pirate's. In the darkness Nikki was reluctant to try the rocks. Between the steep stairs and the steep driveway is a grassy area with benches, trees and sunset seekers with blankets and picnics. Nikki and Amber had no blanket, no picnic and no sunset, but they stayed on the grass anyway.

Settling down on the mildly damp grass, Nikki sat Indian style and began to focus on her navel. Lefty curled up into a ball next to her knee, and Amber lay stomach down, up on her elbows, eyes closed, smelling the ocean and listening to the waves crash.

"Paint the sky with me," Nikki whispered quietly.

The odd trio sat in strange meditation as Nikki conjured a sunset. *Catalina Island is off in the distance to the right. Focus there. The sun is a great yellow ball, impossible to look at, even for a moment. The Santa Ana conditions have created the optimal circumstance for a dazzling sunset, the sky is scattered with thin wispy cirrus clouds. The changes in the sky are perceptible to the attuned, like watching liquid color being poured onto a canvas. First, orange, deep red-orange, colors the entire sky with the clouds turning to dark red. The waves are large, and the whitecaps appear light orange and the whitewater turns pink. The sky darkens and the colors deepen. Two whales appear in the distance, their blowholes blow before they leap out of the water, high enough to be framed against the multi-colored sky, leaving their silhouettes etched into the vision. The edges of the clouds turn purple, the red-orange turns pink in spots so the sky is a mix of pink, purple, orange and red. Subtly, carefully, the colors blend as the sky darkens further, it is all one color, but the color is impossible to describe. It has never been seen before, and will never be seen again. The whales bid goodnight. Against the horizon the sun sets, and the magical green flash makes its brief appearance. To the naked eye the sun is down, though the sky remains illuminated for a last few final moments of surreal beauty.*

Lefty and Amber luxuriated in the vision Nikki created for them, and stayed with the imaginary sunset after Nikki stopped speaking. For Nikki, the sunset turned into an omphaloskepstic nightmare. The sky flickered, turning to full daylight just long enough to see that the water was emerald green. A wave built and grew larger until it covered the entire horizon, light shining through it before it reached its full height and crashed to the shore. The clouds filled in and turned black, and the sky dimmed to somehow ominous shades of deep orange, purple and red. Then there was complete darkness again.

When the sky returned to sunset colors, a rock shower was pelting down on Corona del Mar beach from Pirate's Cove. When the assault stopped, the rocks grew like seedlings into huge obelisk shaped stones of varying colors, sticking sharply out of the water. Nikki knew the ocean to be forever changed, and felt immediate danger.

A loud noise like a rocket filled the air, and once again there was an emergence from Pirate's Cove. Seven very large metal beings landed on top of the shimmering obelisks and scouted the ocean and the shore for their victims. Nikki could sense danger, not only for the people around her, but for the whales as well. She looked over to a woman on a picnic bench, and said, "Aren't you worried?"

She looked back to Nikki and said with indifference, "There's only seven of them."

Nikki felt a chill run down her back. The brief interaction with the woman felt incongruous with what she knew to be her current reality. Somehow she was trapped in the sunset, and she knew she needed to pull herself out.

Standing abruptly, startling both Amber and Lefty, Nikki yelled, "I've got to catch a boat."

~~~

In Anaheim, comfortably settled into the Goofy Suite at the Disneyland Hotel, Luke orders a grilled cheese sandwich and a Foster's Lager from room service. After a bubble bath in Minnie Mouse bubbles, he crawls into bed and orders 'Disney porn' on pay-per-view.

In Garden Grove, Chuckie thinks he's died and gone to heaven. As he enters the Crystal Cathedral he bumps into none other than *the* Dr. Robert Schuller. The minister. From television! In a moment that could have been nothing less than divinely guided, Dr. S. invites Chuckie to stay and study with him to become an apprentice minister. Chuckie doesn't feel badly about disappointing Luke.

In North County San Diego, the VW Beetle carrying Demi Devi Dai, makes its VW Beetle noises down Pacific Coast Highway. Past the AM/PM, past the 7/11, past Leucadia Pizzeria and on to the meditation gardens at the Self Realization Fellowship. Demi is so blissed out by the whole event she forgets to fart for the entire duration of the drive.

On Balboa Island, Kassen Kyle orders a lovely sea bass dinner at Amelia's and a glass of J Pinot Noir (one Nikki's favorites). He silently toasts her as he reminisces about the weekend they spent in Orange County and the fun day they had visiting Balboa Island.

~~~

Lefty and Amber didn't have time to properly respond to the lunacy of Nikki's need to catch a boat. Before Amber could even drop a sarcastic, "But she gets seasick on a waterbed," Nikki was more than halfway down the steep staircase running toward the beach. Amber squinted out to the ocean to see if she could catch a glimpse of any boats near the shore. However, being that it was pitch black, and that her eyes were squeezed into a squint, she saw virtually nothing.

By the conclusion of Amber's squinting, Nikki had hit the bottom stair and had gone in the direction of the abandoned snack bar. Amber yelled, "Shit, Lefty, run down to the water and see if there are any boats, I'm going to chase after her. Meet me by the lifeguard stand if there is one and howl for me." Amber and Lefty raced down the stairs. Amber was in significantly better physical condition than Nikki so she felt confident in reaching her.

Nikki, however, had other plans. She ran to the beach parking lot, and hopped on a bus that was just about to leave. Before Amber touched the bottom step, Nikki was up the steep hill heading out of Corona del Mar. Why was the bus there at that exact moment, you might ask? Because it was Nikki's microcosm and she needed it to be.

Amber walked around the parking area of the beach sensing no sign of Nikki, and seeing no evidence of the departed bus. Lefty ran headlong into the water and ended up in a tangle with a medium sized squid.

As the bus drove up the Coast Highway in the direction of the Balboa Peninsula, Nikki finally paused to catch her breath and panic over her circumstances. The most important piece of advice given to them by Jake and Melia was to stick together. Now she had left her friends in a place they didn't know, and she was headed who knows where for who knows why, with no idea how or when she would get back. Who, where, why, how, when … something missing. What? What the fuck was she thinking? It reminded her of a New Mickey Mouse Club song, the song for Who, What, Why, Where, When and How Day. Which reminded her of Disneyland, where she was supposed to go the next day with Lefty and Amber. Instead she had gone off on a half-cocked mission. Probably not the best decision she had made thus far.

As the bus began to pass familiar territory, she knew that the boat she was to meet was near. What she didn't know was when the bus would stop. All attempts to ask those around her were met with utter silence. Afraid that she wouldn't find out in time, she crawled out of a bus window and pulled herself up to the top of the bus. You know, like they do in the movies, only with trains. She apparently left her judgment behind with her cell phone. "Crap," she said aloud, because frankly, no one could hear her, "I left my cell phone with Amber."

To her right, she saw the theatre where on eighteen Fridays during her sophomore year of high school, she watched the midnight showing of the *Rocky Horror Picture Show*. Nik did the time warp again. She knew this was her stop, but the bus kept moving. When bus slowed to make a turn, Nikki slid down the front windshield, grabbed a wiper for stability, and hopped off. She landed nicely on the corner of Main and Balboa Boulevard, where she knew the Balboa Island Ferry to be. *That*, was her boat.

Nikki tried to remember if she and Kassen had taken the ferry, surprised by the lack of recall of the details of that weekend. She remembered it being bliss, and laughing about the holiday flags that hung in every doorway. But, did they take the ferry? Did they visit the Fun Zone? She thinks they may have. She remembered him looking at baby furniture, and asking him about it, and his uncharacteristic reply, "We have to start thinking about a future sometime." One of his 'caught up in the moment' statements which were expressly forbidden to be read into.

She felt him so strongly on that corner, and knew that he must be thinking about her. That happened often, and he would always call. Maybe he had been trying to call her, she didn't know. She told him never to call again but she told him that at least twenty times, and he always called.

The sound of the ferry pulled her out of her reverie and she took off running toward the direction of the water. "Fuck Kassen," she yelled loudly. It was liberating. Upon arrival at the ferry landing, she found she had missed the boat. Faintly she could make out the bulk of another ferry moving her direction.

She took off her Pooh/gym socks and walked in the sand, squishing it in between her toes. It was cool and silky and the feeling was relaxing, despite the fact that she knew the grains of sand which would be forever stuck in her one pair of socks. There was a Carousel attached the Fun Zone, and it was the next stop. She definitely remembered being there with Kassen. She laughed. His cell phone had rung and he took the call despite her irritation, when the Carousel music started to play indicating its departure, Kassen had told his caller, "I have to go, my Carousel is ready." She thought it was really funny at the time, but in retrospect it was probably just the giddiness she felt when with him.

Nikki wiped the sand off her feet as best she could, and put her Pooh/gym socks back on. When she got back to the ferry landing, she had missed another boat. Frustrated, but restless she walked up the stairs to a restaurant that overlooked the bay. There wasn't much of a view in the darkness, but her eyes were adjusted enough that she could make out shapes. Certainly she could see the next ferry from there. Behind her was a cork bulletin board, and pinned to the board was a check. Check number 383, written by Nikki Nasco, in 1990, for $1.00.

"Oh my God," she said aloud, "That is bizarre."

Fifteen years earlier she had ordered a coke and didn't have enough cash for a tip. She could understand why it had never been cashed, but why was it there? Posted? She was mortified, skulked guiltily out of the restaurant, and tried to convince herself that it was better to write a check for a dollar, than to stiff the waitress.

The third ferry was arriving as she got back down the stairs, and she waited for the cars and passengers to disembark. She glanced back up at the restaurant still puzzled by the ancient check, when she heard a voice call "Nikki?" Her heart sank, as she turned and found herself face to face with Kassen. Kassen's presence was like a shot of adrenaline to the dormant butterflies which resided in Nikki's stomach. It was the first real feeling she had since the darkness.

"Of all the Ferry Boats, on all the peninsulas, in all the world, you had to walk off of mine?" Her attempt at being glib was betrayed by the shaking in her voice.

"Nikki," he said joyfully, grinning from ear to ear, "What are you doing here?"

"Kassen," she mimicked sarcastically, "What are *you* doing here?"

"Long story. I'll tell you later. I've been thinking about you, and trying to reach you for days. Your cell phone isn't working, my mail was returned. I thought you were trying to avoid me."

"I am," Nikki looked up as she had missed another boat. "Shit, Kassen. There's no way you are here. This is crazy. I mean, are you, you know, like me?"

"What does that mean, Nik?"

"Is it a full moon?"

Kassen looked up in the sky, "Quarter moon, right there, you can see it." He moved her head toward what she saw as a black spot in the sky. "See it, Nikki?" he asked tenderly. His touch gave her goose bumps.

"I see it," Nikki whispered quietly, knowing that Kassen was not going to shed any light on her circumstances, literal or otherwise.

He turned her face to his, and for a moment she was lost in his eyes. She loved him so much, and it would never go away. But he didn't love her, and after ten (TEN!!!) years of unrequited love she had put an end to it. Was it a little universal joke? Was the outcome of this happenstance providing dinner-party entertainment for Fate and her guests? Her heart pounded, she wanted to crawl inside his skin and never leave.

"I have to go, Kassen," she said weakly. "I left my friend behind and I need to get back. Please go away, don't call me, don't miss me … don't try to reach me, don't even think about me."

"Don't I even get a hug?" he asked.

They hugged, and then she couldn't let go. He kissed her gently, tenderly and whispered in her ear, "I've missed you."

She broke away and started walking back toward the Balboa Theatre. She would go anywhere to be away from him, her strength was ebbing and she was afraid of his power over her. He was kryptonite to her Superman.

He grabbed her arm to stop her and put his arm around her as they began to walk. He never would hold her hand. After a block they made a left turn and Nikki found herself being led up the steps of a small bed and breakfast inn. "I have to go," she whispered.

The door of his room was open; he led her in, shut the door, and took her to the bed. "I miss you," he said.

"I know," she answered, "Kassen, I miss you too, some days. But it doesn't matter."

"It matters." He was so convincing when he used that voice, she almost believed him. Of course it mattered, but the fact that it mattered didn't matter. And, it didn't change anything.

He kissed her again, softly, gently on her lips. No tongue. Just like her dream. 'My lips don't fit anybody else's,' she remembered. Pathetic.

"Can't we be friends, Nik? We had fun, right?"

"We had fun, Kassen, but there are so many other women, and every time you and I would get close you'd pull away. What would be different? Why should I put up with the flight attendant, the woman from your gym, the woman from your office, or the anorexic girl? I'm way too great to be lumped in with a bunch of other women."

"They don't hold a candle to you. I don't have what we have with anybody else."

"I know. I do know that, it would be impossible. So are you saying that you're willing to give up Kelly and Karen and Jennifer and Cindy and Barb and Leann and — ?"

"Well, no, I mean, I don't want a relationship, but you liked things the way they were."

In a bold move, Nikki rolled over on top of Kassen and kissed him several more times. They connected physically, fully in tune to the sexual reaction in each other. Though no clothing was removed, and the kisses were simple, the passion was overwhelming.

"I love you," she whispered.

"I love you, too" he whispered back. Words that she had been waiting ten years to hear, finally uttered, but too late. She'd always known he loved her, but in his fucked up way. A way that would never satisfy her, nor allow him to be only with her.

She stood up, looked at him lying in the bed, so vulnerable for such a brief moment in time. "It doesn't change anything. I know you miss me, I know you love me in your own strange way, but you can't come back."

Kissing him on the forehead before she left the room, she ran back to the ferry stop and didn't look back. In the sky above her three stars began to shine through the darkness. "Huh, that's unexpected." Her ship finally came in and she boarded it across to the Island.

~~~

Luke awoke with a start, "Dammit," he yelled. He rushed to the window and saw the starry evidence of his premonition. He picked up the phone and dialed Kassen Kyle.

Luke was beyond pleasantries, and when Kassen issued an abrupt hello, he met with an abrupt question, "Are you in the hotel, Mr. Kyle?"

"No," Kassen's reply was as loaded with "none of your business" attitude as a two letter reply could be.

"Fine, then, Mr. Kyle. Your services are no longer required."

"Really?" Kassen answered incredulous. "Well, it so happens that I found her." And then he was smug.

"And it so happens that you lost her," Luke mimicked, "Permanently."

"She'll be back, she always is."

"You really don't get it, do you Mr. K? You've lost her. She's stronger than you are. Which makes you of no further use to me. Good night then."

Luke grabbed a Bailey's Irish Crème out of the mini-bar, downed it, and crawled back into his bed. Sleep was not to come, however, as the newly released stars shone brightly into his room that night, an effulgent reminder of his failure.

19.
The Temple of Doomed Tofu

Very early Wednesday, Week 3

Nikki arrived at the Dahlia apartment just after midnight.

Lefty and Amber were perched on the Rod Laver table formerly known as a dressing room door. In the slight glow of the starlight Nikki could see worry on Amber's face, and after a double take, observed that Lefty was covered in something that looked like ink. His previously white do-rag appeared tie-died and there were large black spots on his fur. Something smelled fishy.

"What happened to you, Left?" asked Nikki, unaware of the coyote's horrible night and foul mood, which were both direct results of Nikki's abandonment.

He glared a serious coyote glare, and walked back into the empty apartment.

"What happened to him?" Nikki asked Amber, still maintaining the illusion that she had done the right thing with her night.

Amber gave her a serious human glare, and walked back into the empty apartment. It was effective. Nikki got the point.

"How could you run off and leave us? We don't know where we are. We don't know why we are here, and Jake and Melia told us that under no circumstances should we separate. Do you want to lose your eyes, or worse? It was totally fucking irresponsible." Nikki had never seen Amber this angry.

"I saw Kassen."

"Oh, of course you did. Nothing ever makes you as stupid as Kassen makes you. Is that why we came here? Did you know Kassen was here?"

"Look, Amber, you're going to need to calm down. How could I possibly know he was here? I've been with you. Without communications, without lights, remember? I haven't spoken to him in months, and I certainly haven't spoken to him since this shit started happening. Let me explain everything to you."

Nikki laid out her unexpected evening for Amber, from her visions at the sunset, to the check at the restaurant and the manifestation of the three bright stars that now provided some degree of light.

"Wow, Nik. I'm proud of you." Amber hugged her. Lefty gave Amber a good glare. "Dude, she's one of the few humans that I can interact with right now, I doubt I'm going to go long without speaking to her."

Lefty turned his head; he wasn't bothered by his lack of human companionship options.

"So, what did happen to him?" Nikki asked.

"He rushed into the ocean looking for a boat and ran into a squid. It wasn't pretty."

"Did you see it happen? It must have been kind of funny."

"No. And it's not funny. He's very sensitive. He told me."

"He told you? Like he sang a song and you guessed what happened? What did he sing, *Octopus's Garden*?"

"No he just told me. In words, in his cute little British accent."

"He spoke to you?" Nikki was dumbfounded.

"Yeah, but don't worry about it because he's not speaking to you at all."

"I'm too tired to care tonight, really, and I'm afraid of a Kassen crash tomorrow, so we had better get some sleep." Nikki hugged Amber, "I'm really sorry I worried you tonight. I didn't know at the time what the pull was, but it became clear when I saw Kassen. I never thought this day would come, you know, that I would actually feel totally free of him?"

Nikki patted Lefty on his sulking head, "I'm sorry Lefty, I promise to be more careful in the future."

As Nikki and Amber walked to the second bedroom, Nikki whispered, "Does he stink?"

Amber nodded and the girls giggled as they set up camp on the floor and drifted off to sleep.

~~~

At 8:57AM that same morning, Luke stood alone at the main entrance of Disneyland. He pondered the human psyche and tried to come to terms with the idea that Disneyland could be a symbolic force in an adult mind. It apparently was for his Seeker otherwise he would not be there.

Aside from the obvious lure of youth, the "happiest" place on earth, and perchance offering the opportunity to live, however briefly, a fantasy, he couldn't understand how an overcrowded, overpriced amusement park could remain significant to an adult. His impression was long lines, fleeting reward, more long lines. Blisters, junk food comas, and the common thread of myriad families from around the world wearing matching Hawaiian print shirts.

This Seeker was tough. Unexpected. He smiled a half smile, for truly he was delighted by the challenge.

At 9:09AM, Demi Devi Dai's driver pulled up to the entrance and Demi stumbled out of the car laden with her luggage and what appeared to be a picnic basket. Luke shook his head. His lone extremist. He needed to call for backup.

"Oh, good morning Luke. Goddess Bless! It's such a beautiful day. I haven't had any sleep, I'm afraid. I spent the evening at the Self Realization Fellowship, and well, it was divine. I just couldn't bear to leave, so I hope you don't mind that I didn't use my room."

No one had used his or her room except Luke. He minded. He could also smell that she hadn't been able to use a shower. He minded that even more.

She kept on with her prattle, "I brought sandwiches. For you and the others. Where are they? I thought I was late. There was a lovely health food store in Laguna Beach, we took the coast back, which is why I was a little late, but the ocean was so magnificent. Anyway, I stopped for an organic soy spinach okra shake at this little stand, and picked up some Tofu Eggless Salad with Nayonaise, organic sprouts and tomato on spelt pita. They are lovely. I had one in the car."

She grabbed a sandwich and shoved it into Luke's hands. He was numb, and, without thinking, he ate the sandwich. Later he would remember it tasting like sawdust with a side of dirt.

"Seaweed chips?" she asked after he finished.

"No thank you, Ms. Dai. We are on our own, you and I. T'others have finished their service for now. D'ye have your cell phone?"

"Yes, sir."

"And it's charged?"

"Yes, sir."

"And is it on, Ms. Dai?"

Demi looked at her phone, which was of course, off. She blushed slightly, turned the power on, and listened to the polytechnic sounds of Tom Petty's *American Girl* as her phone immediately made her aware of waiting voice mails.

"I want ya to stay in the area of Indiana Jones Adventure.

135

Watch for the girls, and when ya see them, call me. I'll be by to check in every hour."

Luke bought their admissions and they entered the Magic Kingdom.

~~~

At 9:10AM Nikki woke up and the first words out of her mouth were, "I'm crabby." Amber and Lefty shared a secret 'as if this is a revelation' glance, and prepared for Nikki's tirade. It would be on one of two topics. Kassen or coffee.

Nikki marched to the front of the apartment, opened the sliding glass door and stood on the Rod Laver table. "Do you think this is funny, Universe? Do you sit up there and plot on how you can fuck up Nikki's life? Am I special, or do you wreak havoc with all the 40-year-old single girls? It's bad enough that there's no coffee, no light and we don't know what the hell is going on in the world, but you have to throw Kassen into the mix? That's just great. Hey … thanks!" Nikki finished her rant with a very aggressive middle finger pointed somewhere in the direction of where the Big Dipper might be, were it visible.

"I'm going to find him." Nikki announced.

"Going to find who?" Amber asked cautiously.

"Kassen. I made a mistake."

"You didn't make a mistake … you made stars appear."

"I don't care. He needs me."

"Did he let you leave?"

"Yes, so —"

"Then he doesn't need you."

"Whatever, Amber. You don't understand, can't understand and will never understand."

Amber began to verge on crabby as well, but she knew the only thing that would help would be to be rational. "Nik, we need to get to Disneyland. That's why we're here. When we are done, I promise, I'll go look for him with you. But right now, we need to get some answers and you're the only person who can get them."

Nikki pointed at Lefty. "He has them. Maybe the two of you could find a Starbucks and chat about it. For all I know, since he talks to you, he can probably get you coffee."

"Let's just go, Nik."

~~~

At 10:15AM Luke made his first pass of the Indiana Jones ride in search of Demi and an update. He found her sitting on a rock at the entrance. She had a Sari draped over the rock, her picnic basket beside her, she was seated in lotus position, and *her eyes were closed.*

Luke cleared his throat. She didn't move.

"Ms. Dai," he ventured. She held one finger to her lips.

"Ms. Dai," he yelled.

She slowly opened her eyes, "I was meditating to pass the time."

"And how d'ya suppose you'll see the ladies we're here to find with your eyes closed?"

"Oh, I'll sense them. I was tuning into their energy. I think they will go to small world first, so I don't understand why you have me here."

"Well, Demi, because I am in charge and that is what I've told ya. Now, I'll just be to the men's room and be back to relieve you for a quick break. *Please* keep your eyes open."

Since Demi possessed no concept of time, the fact that Luke was gone for thirty minutes didn't alarm her. What did alarm her was that when he returned he was quite green. Well, greener than usual.

"Oh, Mr. Luke," she cooed, "you aren't well." She dug through her bag and pulled out a very very green beverage. She poured a small amount into a plastic cup which she took from the bag, and thrust it in his face. "Here," she said, "Wheat grass juice."

Luke bolted straight back to the men's room.

When he returned, Demi was still seated on her rock. "I'm afraid I'm a bit indisposed, could I trouble you to get me some first aid or medicine?" he petitioned.

"Well, I have all sorts of homeopath------" He cut her off. "I think the Nayonaise did me in, Ms. Dai, I'll stick to some Pepto-Bismol if it's all the same to you."

After two frantic queries for directions and one just-in-time stop at the "Prince's" room, Demi and Luke discovered that the Emporium on Main Street carried a small amount of sundries. When they entered the store, they were directed to a counter past the Mickey Mouse sweatshirts where they sold film, lip-gloss and trial sized medicine packets.

Luke made his purchase, and a Disney "cast member" left the counter to get him a bottle of water. Demi played with the lip-glosses, trying the various flavors (Goofy Grape, Minnie Melon) with the Q-Tips that sat in a jar next to the sample case. When Demi grew bored with the Pluto Plum lip-gloss, she decided to make use of the available Q-Tips for another purpose. As Luke turned to beckon her for departure, he watched in horror as she stood in the middle of the store, cleaning her ear with a Q-Tip. Removing the Q-Tip, inspecting her wax success and then inserting the other end.

Practically rendered speechless by the oddities of humanity, Luke stood dumbfounded. Demi finally noticed he was ready to leave and actually had the sense to blush when she realized she'd been observed. "I keep forgetting to buy ear cones, and well ..."

"Let's be on our way, Ms. Dai. I've enough going on intestinally without getting into detail about that."

Luke led Demi by the elbow back to the main entrance. He needed time to decompress.

~~~

At 11:11AM, Nikki and Amber were greeted at the admission booth of the happiest place on earth by the one and only Howard.

"At least we're on the right track," Nikki muttered crabbily under her breath. "Hey Howard, what's up? Do you speak, or are you going to sing for me too?"

Howard smiled at Nikki, "Voici votre passeport s'il vous plait."

"That's cute," Nikki responded. "Vous desirez un porteur madame?"

"Nik," Amber interjected, "What are you doing?"

"Playing with Howard, obviously. Those are the two French sentences I know. Voici votre passeport s'il vous plait, and vous desirez un porteur madame. I learned them on a French language tape...Your passport please, and would you like a porter, ma'am?"

Amber remained quiet. She knew it would be a long day, and sensed rather than really knew that Howard wasn't just quoting French for Travelers.

Howard issued another smile, "Voici votre passeport s'il vous plait."

Dumbfounded-ness was running rampant at the Magic Kingdom that day. Nikki stood studying Howard. He was as green as ever, but today he was clothed in Disney apparel. Navy pants, with a red golf shirt with Goofy embroidered on the pocket. A mouse ears nametag was pinned to his left side, and it read, 'Oward. Nikki issued a deep sigh and sat down on the ground right in front of Howard and put her head on her knees.

"Why would *It's a Small World* have been a clear-cut instruction to go to Disneyland? Nothing has been so direct in the weeks since the light went away. Everything in this world has a different meaning. Now I'm taking clues from a green guy with a strange and obscure sense of humor."

Nikki looked up into Howard's mischievous eyes. "Voi-ci vo-tre passé-port S'IL VOUS PLAIT." He said it very slowly and loud. The way people often do when trying to convey a message to somebody with an accent.

Amber stood back a little further, for some reason she was filled with mirth and had to suppress her laughter. Lefty, still annoyed from the night before, stood smug and somehow satisfied by Nikki's irritation.

"Ok, 'Oward," Nikki said with bad French accent and as much sarcasm as she could muster, "I get it. We're not getting in today, and I need to find my passport, which probably isn't really my passport, but in looking for my passport, I will somehow be led to discover what it really is I'm looking for. Right?" Howard was silent.

"Right?" she yelled at Lefty.

Lefty's response was fitting, "Ahem," followed by the hook from The Who's *Who Are You?*

"MOTHER FUCK," Nikki yelled so loudly that she caught the attention of a little man and a hippie woman huddled together just inside the main gate.

Luke quickly ran from inside the park to the admission booths and saw both his prey and his nemesis. "Oye Vey," Luke exclaimed.

Howard suddenly went, well, a pale lime shade. He cast a fearful glance at Lefty and Lefty was immediately agitated as well. The smile left Amber's face, and Nikki felt a sudden irrational danger. All at once Nikki, Lefty and Amber said, "We need to go." Without a look back at Howard, the three of them were running to the parking lot and the perceived safety of the Datsun B210.

They needn't have bothered. Luke was pacing near the Mad Hatter store, mouse ears and duckbills mocking the severity of his dilemma. He had no choice. He knew he was out of his depth. He got his phone to place the call that was the admission of his failure.

The phone rang four times, and his own voice answered. "Hello, you've reached the Dublin California residence of Luke, at the tone please leave a message."

Luke spoke tentatively, "Um, Biy-Em, it's Luke here. I'm with Demi, and we're at Disneyland."

The gruff Jamaican interrupted his message. "Luke, mon, you got the Seeker?"

"Your brother is here, Big Man. We're going to need reinforcements…the whole crew."

There was silence on the other end, uncomfortable silence. After two minutes Biy-Em said, "Are you sure it was my brother?"

Luke knew it wasn't a time for sarcasm, but how many seven-foot-tall green men did his boss think there were on earth? "Yes, certainly, sir. He's here, and he gave the Seeker a message."

The line went dead. Luke knew there was nothing to do but wait. Biy-Em had his personal group of extremists on reserve, however, Luke preferred to select his own. The Big Man's creeped him out. He shuddered at the thought of the arrival of the "Rasta-Fiveyins," Matthew (the flight attendant), the twins, and Old Tom and Madge. Demi thought he had a chill and offered to make him some Miso soup. Instead, he took her to spend the afternoon in the Tiki room. Where the birds sang and flowers bloomed, and he couldn't hear the big voice in his head go boom.

~~~

Once the trio arrived back at the Corona del Mar apartment, Nikki walked to the back of the house, slammed the door of the room that faced the alley and yelled out to her companions, "I think it's best if you leave me alone for the rest of the day."

~~~

In Garden Grove, Chuckie Rightwing has found his true calling, and the real Jesus Christ moves into his heart.

At San Francisco Airport, a 7½-foot tall black man, covered in Van Gogh tattoos, awaits his backup crew at the information counter in the United terminal.

At Orange County Airport, Kassen Kyle boards a flight.

In Anaheim, Luke has nightmares about tropical storms, singing birds, and the Tiki-Tiki-Tiki room refrain is constantly running through his head.

In Chicago, Oprah makes a great discovery.

20.
Seoul, Man

Thursday, Week 3

Amber popped her head into the bedroom and found that Nikki was still sleeping, though fitfully, under the window. She was talking in her sleep, and seemed disturbed by the alley behind the house. "The garage isn't safe, either," Nikki blurted somewhat incoherently.

"Nikki," Amber whispered, "It's just a dream."

Nikki was approaching lucidity, but not fully there. "This house haunts me, I don't know why. If I never know why, will it always haunt me?"

"I don't know, Nik," Amber whispered back thinking she was still having a conversation with Nikki. Until her next sentence was, "Microwave popcorn." And then, "Happening in the alley."

Then Nikki began to scream. Amber shouted, "Wake up." And they were all standing on the empty lot where the house used to be.

"Well," Nikki said with uncharacteristic lightheartedness, "I guess we don't need to worry about coming back here again." Even the alley was gone.

"Do you think this place will still haunt me, Amber?"

"I don't think so, Nik. I think it must have been time to let it go … and it's gone."

The three of them lumbered into the waiting Datsun B210 where their meager possessions waited for them intact. The confusion about this was lost in a song by Lefty. "Who? Who? Who? Who?"

"To the airport," Nikki said as she put the car in first and drove away from a place that would never require her return, in her dreams or in her reality.

~~~

Biy-Em, Ray, Luke, Demi and the "Rasta-Fiveyins" stood in line at the McDonald's in Orange County airport.

Luke felt hung over, even though he hadn't drunk the night before. His stomach was still not right from the bad eggless salad he'd eaten and the smell of McDonald's hash browns made him queasy. In a move of sheer antagonism, Ray alighted on his shoulder and sang the Tiki room song loudly, intentionally out of tune, and directly into Luke's ear. He jumped onto the counter, ended the song with a big "Hooooooo," and moon-walked across until he bumped into an Egg McMuffin, which knocked him to the floor.

Demi burped, and the twins burst into a fit of laughter.

Despite the motley look of the group, and they were motley, they were very effective. Biy-Em had a fresh cup of McDonald's coffee, and a macka spliff, which he had lit and was smoking in the middle of the airport. Even *that* smell couldn't cover the smell of a post-nayonaise and eggless salad Demi. As Luke's head reeled in the olfactory nightmare, Biy-Em called their meeting to order.

"Greetings I bring from Ma. Mata Hari. I say, she fly away home to iron, fly away home." Biy-Em was kind of a mamma's boy, and his mother still did all his laundry. Whenever he was with the Rasta-Fiveyins he brought her up.

"Yes I," he continued, "we have a Seeker who need to meet with I and I."

He first turned his attention to the twins, Arthur and Lancelot. Really, those were their real names. The twins wore their traditional Sci-fi garb, which consisted of black shirts and slacks, with gray vests (only the most imaginative think it looks like armor) and large silver plastic helmets which covered their faces. Were the helmets removed, they would look like any other Dungeons and Dragons, Star Wars, Lord of the Rings obsessed fellows. Mid-thirties, full beards, unkempt curly hair and oversized wire rimmed glasses. At 6-feet each, they were an imposing looking pair from a distance, but they were both about 30 pounds overweight, and when they bent over, butt crack inevitability ensued.

They became a part of the "Rasta-Fiveyins" because it was the closest thing to a real life role-playing game that they could find.

Both of them had tartar breath. Not tartar sauce breath, which Listerine could work wonders on, but tartar-plaque build up-haven't been to the dentist in years-breath. Middle earth was obviously lacking a good dental plan.

Luke hated them.

"Art and Lance," the big man managed with a straight face because even *he* thought their names were lame, "you go to the childhood home. This Seeker may be smart enough to start there, I and I don't think so, but we don't know what my brother had the opportunity to tell her."

He directed his comment at Luke whose obvious failure allowed the message to be delivered in the first place. Demi silently farted at that moment and almost knocked Luke out from the smell. He was shaking and sweat beads had appeared on his brow.

The Twins turned to face each other, spoke in some twin-speak that only they knew, but which sounded suspiciously like Klingon, banged their helmeted heads together, struck John Travolta *Saturday Night Fever* poses, and left the terminal.

Biy-Em next turned his attention to Matthew the flight attendant. Matthew was gay. Very very very gay. You couldn't get more gay than Matthew. That's why he was chosen, for his extreme flight attendant gayness.

Matthew always wore a flight attendant uniform, wings and a nametag that said … well … Matthew of course. He didn't actually work for any airline. He was too short and had sort of a nervous tic. He was very muscular, had a very short haircut (though a full head of hair) and very red skin. He had the most gay voice a gay man could have. (Not that there's anything wrong with that.)

Luke hated him.

"Matt," Biy-Em started.

"Uh, Big Man," Matthew started in his gay San Fernando Valley voice, "It's Math-thew both syllables please." Matthew pointed at Biy-Em as if he were showing him where the oxygen masks were going to drop from in case there was a sudden loss of cabin pressure.

"Right, mon, you go to Korean airlines."

"Oh," Matthew tittered, "I've never been to Seoul. I hope I've packed right."

And with that, Matthew took his flight attendant style rollie bag and headed toward the gate.

Truly, it was Madge and Old Tom that Luke hated most of all. They were relegated to the baggage claim area.

Biy-Em informed the group that he would be stationed at security, and that Demi and Luke were to each find a Starbucks.

Luke knew then that he was being punished. Among the very first things all new Seekers learn is that there's no point in trying to order a coffee. Both Luke and his boss knew that the women would not show up at Starbucks. Resigned to his fate for that day, he stopped by a newsstand, grabbed a Maxim magazine, and meandered to the closest Starbucks.

~~~

Nikki pulled the Datsun into the exact same spot it had been in two days earlier.

"I don't know." Nikki answered Amber's unasked question.

"I didn't say anything," Amber said.

"You were going to ask me why we're at the airport, and the answer is, I don't know. I think it makes sense that if you are looking for your passport, and you're nowhere near your home where even if you were there you wouldn't know where your passport was, that you should look at the airport."

"I think that just gave me a headache."

"Well, humor me; we're going to the airport to look for my passport."

In the event that the Datsun were to disappear while they were in the airport, they once again bundled all their worldly possessions and trudged back into the terminal.

Nikki approached the arrival/departure monitors and studied them carefully, while Amber and Lefty glanced around the airport. Amber was the first to notice Madge and Old Tom.

Madge was quite possibly the creepiest human that Amber had ever seen. From across the terminal, Amber could see that Madge was pacing back and forth in front of a kiosk, though she couldn't read which kiosk it was. Her hair was up in a Bob's Big Boy waitress bun, and Amber would have bet money that she was wearing a hair net. She had on a medium blue polyester suit, with a white blouse underneath. She had very large plastic framed glasses. What caught Amber's attention most was not the woman's attire, but her behavior. Every time somebody walked by, she would wait for them to just pass her, and then she got right up behind them (personal space considerations ignored) and said something. It was extremely intrusive behavior.

Amber's curiosity got the better of her, and she headed the direction of the woman. Once she passed her, the woman came up right behind her and practically yelled, "Free buffet, show tickets." In a manner that was very consistent with an old school Vegas tobacco girl calling out, "Cigars, cigarettes."

Amber turned around, and said, "I beg your pardon."

"Are you interested in a free buffet, and show tickets?"

Madge started to guide Amber toward the kiosk. Amber knew Nikki would be pissed, but she did the only thing she could

144

think of considering the circumstances, she yelled, "Wake up." But nothing happened. Madge grabbed her even more aggressively and practically shoved her up to the counter where she came face to face, and nostril to odor with Old Tom.

"I think my friend wanted to see a show, I'll just go and get her and we'll be right back."

Amber quickly backed away and ran back to Nikki eager to tell her friend that she'd been "seen."

When she approached, Nikki had all her belongings gathered again and seemed anxious about any delay.

"There's a Korean Airlines flight to Seoul in 25 minutes, we've got to get to the gate."

"Nik, maybe we don't need to, I just met some people who —"

"Amber, this is a domestic airport. There aren't any international flights out of here. International flights require passports. I don't have any time to waste. I've got to get on that plane."

"They saw me."

"Later, we don't have time, let's just get up there. The flight leaves in less than a half hour. If I don't find it there, we'll come back down here. OK?"

Amber started to gather her things and speak her consent, but Nikki was already on the escalator.

When they got to the gate the flight had already boarded. They walked invisibly down the Jetway and boarded the plane. The first class cabin was empty so they set their belongings down and looked around.

"I'm just going to walk around the plane. See if I see anything that gives me a clue. I mean, it is weird, right? An international flight? To Seoul? Soul? Get it? That's got to mean something."

"Nik, I'm really not comfortable with us separating again."

"We can't get separated on this plane, I promise, Amber. I'm just going to look around and I'll be back. I don't want to be on this plane when it takes off. I'm hoping Seoul is metaphorical and not a place we really need to go. I don't do Asia."

Nikki walked down the aisle of the 747, past the "Upgrade Curtain" (the flimsy piece of fabric that separates the arrogant frequent flying upgraders from the proletariat). She took great pleasure in throwing the curtain aside, despite the fact that no one could see her.

She passed through business class without incident, but

when she got to coach the first person she saw was Kassen in an aisle seat, with a newspaper in the middle seat next to him, and the window seat open. Across the aisle was an older blonde woman who looked as though she had a serious case of Parkinson's.

Kassen lifted the newspaper, and patted the seat next to him. Nikki sat down, "Did you forget we were flying together now, Nik?"

The blonde women with the head bob shook her empty miniature-sized Skyy vodka bottle at Matthew, the flight attendant, squinted at Kassen and said, "Gotta have my bloody Marys."

Nikki wondered if perhaps it wasn't Parkinson's, but just a massive case of the DT's which caused her head to constantly bobble. Nikki touched Kassen's shoulder and said, "Do you– ?" But she was cut off by bobble, who began speaking with Kassen again. "I just love talking to people on airplanes. Don't you?" Bobble. Squint. Eyelid flutter.

Kassen was aghast, but Nikki was laughing. She stood up, "I cannot imagine anything worse on a 12-hour flight, so I'll leave you to it," but as she started to walk away, the plane began to move. Kassen grabbed her arm, and pulled her back down in the seat.

"Shit!" Nikki exclaimed, "Shit. Shit. Shit. Amber is going to kill me if we end up in freaking Seoul."

The plane began another interminable taxi, as it drove down residential streets in Costa Mesa. Bobble was babbling constantly, inundating Kassen with the usual barrage of obvious travel tips. Nikki had headphones on her head, which was currently between her knees. She was half-listening to Alanis Morissette noticing that major editing had occurred. Kassen gave her an affectionate pat on the knee, and a plaintive appeal with his eyes. She was contemplating ordering a coffee to make the plane disappear, but instead gave Kassen a smirk in return.

Nikki pulled off her headset to relay the amazing *Ironic* Alanis editing to Kassen, but still couldn't manage to break into the conversation

"You see," Blondie tittered as she threw back another Bloody Mary, "Airlines overbook their flights, because very frequently people don't show up, which I think is rude. But the good thing is, when they do overbook the flights, they look for volunteers to 'bump' and if you get bumped, they have to compensate you, did you know that?"

Nikki stood again, "Do you have my passport?" she asked Kassen.

"Nikki, sit down," he admonished, "we're going to take off."

"Kas, I can't go anywhere, and I can't go with you. Do you

have my passport?"

"No," he answered, "Why would I?"

"Because you are here and you shouldn't be. Because I gave you everything I had to give, I thought maybe I'd given you my identity as well."

The plane finally took off, and was flying low just above the city. Kassen pulled Nikki to his lap, and she sat there stunned looking out the window. It was daylight. The sun was shining in full glory, the sky was brilliant blue, and fluffy white clouds drifted intermittently by. It was spectacular; and no place she had ever seen. She knew that somehow they were no longer in Orange County. The colors of the buildings and the grass and trees were more vibrant and alive then she ever imagined possible. They flew so close to a bank building that she could see the writing on the sign, but it was not English, or any other kind of Western writing for that matter. But shortly afterward, they passed a street sign that said San Francisco.

She was more confused than ever, when Kassen put his hands on her face, turned he toward him, and began to kiss her. She lost herself in the comfort of his kiss, knowing it was wrong, knowing it would set her back. She let go and let the lambent flick of his tongue take her further away.

"I like these international carriers," she heard in the background, "they give you free drinks and headsets. I'm going to ask for a couple of small vodka bottles to put in my purse ..."

And then even the drone of the passenger from hell faded, and the plane was back on the ground, and she was alone, it was dark again. Dismayed, disoriented, and disgusted, she disembarked. There wasn't another passenger in sight.

When she reached the end of the Jetway, the hubbub of activity returned, and she found herself back at Orange County Airport. On the arrival monitor, a message blinked for her, "Nikki, Amber waits in Sweden until your passport is found."

"Jesus H. Christ on a stick," Nikki exclaimed loudly, though no one could hear her. As randomly as all the decisions she had made of late, she turned in the direction of baggage claim to find a payphone and call the Swedish Embassy... Collect.

~~~

Biy-Em had a very irie buzz when he finally caught sight of Nikki walking toward him with intense purpose. He laughed deeply to himself, and thought 'Dis Seeker need ganga.'"

His seven foot bulk stepped directly in front of her, and said, "Your passport, please."

"What?" Nikki answered, both distracted and irritated.

"Your passport, please."

"This is a domestic airport, what do you need my passport for?"

"Come with me please," he said, and put his hand on her elbow to lead her away. His touch made her feel faint, and it was hard to get a breath.

It finally dawned on her that he was able to see and converse with her. "Oh," she said, "you're a part of this."

"I and I help you find your passport, young one."

Dazed, she allowed herself to be led. But in the back of her mind, she thought she could hear a coyote howling, and her name being called. She started to notice debris strewn across the airport floor. A familiar notebook, a Calvin Klein Shantung flat sheet, a 95.5 KLOS key ring. It was the blue domino that finally slapped her (figuratively) back into consciousness. She pulled away from the man helping her, and picked up the domino. Once she was far enough away from him physically, her head began to clear and she could see that Amber was standing right in front of her, screaming for her to run.

Though still somewhat weak and shaken, Nikki took off running on pure adrenaline, and she didn't stop until she reached the Datsun where she promptly passed out.

21.
If I Could Share Time in a Bottle

When Nikki woke, the Datsun was parked in front of a Starbucks, and she was wrapped in her Calvin Klein comforter. Both Amber and Lefty were staring at her expectantly.

"What happened?" she croaked, deep with morning voice.

"How far back do you remember?" Amber asked gently.

"The guy at the airport wanted my passport, and I felt really weak, and then I saw all our stuff and I just ran."

"When we got to the car, you were on the ground shivering. We got you into the car, and got the doors locked just in time. That man reached the car, and I was so scared I stalled the car twice before we took off. We drove around with the heater on, and you still had the chills so we finally stopped here and covered you up. Lefty stayed alert all night so he could warn me if we were found."

"All night?"

"Yeah, Nik, it's morning."

"I think I had another vision, only this time I went into it. I remember it like it happened, but now I remember just before we boarded the Korean flight I saw a light."

"We didn't board the Korean flight," Amber explained, "You stood there frozen for a while, and the next thing I knew our stuff was strewn everywhere. When I started to pick it up I saw the big black man, and you were being led away."

Nikki relayed her experience or "vision" of the day prior. Back to the flight with Kassen, the woman sitting next across from him, the strange flight and the clue about the Swedish Embassy.

"Jesus Christ. Did I find my passport?"

"No, no passport and Lefty's still singing the *Who Are You* song, so I guess we have to keep looking."

"Which means, back to the airport?"

"Which means, no matter where we go, we are not separating again, Nicole."

Nikki knew Amber must be serious if she was using her full name. Amber continued, "I didn't get to tell you yesterday, that when I was in baggage claim a woman saw me and talked to me. She said she had free show tickets and a buffet. I yelled 'wake up' but nothing went away, so I'm guessing she's part of this. Which means, she can either help us or hurt us. I think we should go back there, but we have to stay together."

"We slept in the car?"

"Yeah, Nik, can you focus? I think we should go back to the airport."

"Ok, but what if that man is there again? I'm freaked out by him, he made me weak. Lefty, can you protect me from him?"

Lefty just sang...

Nikki and Amber changed places without a word, basking in the aromatic sensation of Starbucks as they did. Nikki put the car in first, and they drove, with far more apprehension than the previous day, back to the airport.

~~~

Madge was deep into her daily hustling when the tremulous trio tiptoed with trepidation back into the baggage claim area. There was something particularly creepy about the way she just appeared behind people crooning, "Free buffet, show tickets."

The three watched her from behind a large column, trying to decide if she was one of the good guys or one of the bad guys and wondering if they were willing to take that chance.

Amber and Nikki quietly put their heads together. "I wonder if she's been here all night," Amber whispered. "I think those are the same clothes she had on yesterday."

When they looked up again, Madge was nowhere to been seen. Nikki panicked. She opened her mouth to speak, but she was certain that she hadn't uttered the words that she heard, "Free buffet, show tickets." Nikki screamed. Madge had snuck up behind them.

It bears remarking at this point, that not only were her glasses the largest Amber and Nikki had ever seen on a non-Elton John/Olson twins face, they were also the dirtiest. Since Madge was invading all of their personal space considerations, they could see every speckle of dust and grease on the lenses. Nikki had a strong urge to pull them off the woman's face and clean them. She could almost swear that she saw the face of Jesus, but then one of the pieces of 'dust' crawled away and the illusion disappeared.

"I remember you from yesterday," Madge said directly into Amber's face. She turned to Nikki and touched her arm, Lefty immediately growled, so she removed it and indicated with a head tic, "This your friend who likes free shows?"

Nikki shot Amber a look. Amber shrugged off her innocence. All bets were off when big-bunned-polyester-wearers invaded your personal space, the shrug seemed to say.

"Sure," said Amber with a very warm and Amber-like smile. Madge head tic-ed again, this time in the direction of the kiosk. In the direction of Old Tom, whose individual repulsiveness was boundless.

Madge urged the trio forward, and as Amber had yesterday, Nikki found herself face to face and nostril to odor with Old Tom. Tom's myriad appearance and hygiene issues were something to be chronicled, and not taken all in one glance. However, to ensure a proper painting of the picture, it's important to take a moment and elaborate about all that was soon to be discovered about Tom.

First, he was a card carrying member of the Bulbous Nose Society. On first impression one was immediately put in mind of the Wizard (picture the Hot Air Balloon scene at the end) from the Wizard of Oz, six-feet tall, easily 250 pounds. The 43 hairs that Tom had on his head were scattered, in disarray, and hadn't been washed in any kind of discernible past. They also had some kind of pomade on them, so that if one was askew (and it was) it stayed askew. There was also a peeling scalp condition which was visible in small patches. From the ears and nostrils sprouted an additional 43 hairs, all visibly crusted as well, though Nikki suspected, not with pomade.

He wore khaki colored Dockers. (If only I could stop there, wistful sigh … but it would deprive you of the full image were I to do so.) He wore khaki colored Dockers which had a fresh dribble of pee just beneath what could only be his very large and saggy testicles, (oh, they were visible). He wore a French blue oxford shirt, a green and black bow tie, and a sky blue and white striped seersucker jacket, circa 1981. There was a spot of crusted green mucus on the front of his shirt just above his bulging belly. His fingernails were ragged and unkempt, with dirt under each and every one.

But none of that—none of it—could compare to his smell. He smelled like a greasy corpse with halitosis, a tartar problem, and had coffee breath with a slight garlic undertone. On her best day, Nikki didn't enjoy being touched by strangers, and this was far from her best day, and the worst kind of stranger.

As they approached Old Tom, she could see it coming, but there was no avoiding it. He was a toucher, and a pocket-changejangler, but first and foremost a toucher.

Madge used another of her now famous head tics to introduce Nikki to Old Tom. He took her hand, shook it, raised it to his chin, and would not let go. "Hello there, my dear," he spoke directly into her face, insisting on eye contact, thus facilitating maximum smellage. "Thomas Hotaire, at your service." He bowed, still clutching Nikki's hand like it was the last life preserver on the Titanic. Lefty growled.

"Hello there, poochie," Thomas Hotaire said to Lefty, though not breaking eye contact with Nikki, "My, you are a fine looking poochie, and I'm about to make you a very happy poochie."

At this point, Nikki tried to take a step back and retrieve her hand, but she found that Madge was still right behind her and ended up stepping on her foot. It was no use. Whatever they were about to endure, they were going to have to endure it.

Tom finally released Nikki's hand, then promptly put his arm around her shoulder, and led her toward a door. Nikki looked back at Amber and could read the mirth in her eyes, "I hope you bite a hole in your cheek," she whispered sharply.

Amber, Nikki, Lefty, Old Tom, and Madge walked into a large room filled with small tables. The small tables were populated by people in varying states of obesity, who to a man, woman and very chubby child, were wearing fanny packs.

The scent of Cinnabon wafted through the air, and Nikki could see empty Cinnabon cartons littering many of the tables.

Old Tom selected an empty table, and indicated chairs for Nikki and Amber to occupy.

"What are we doing here?" Nikki asked, afraid to actually know.

"Well, my dear," Tom replied, "We are here to talk about vacation home ownership."

"Time share?" Nikki asked, incredulous.

"We don't think of it that way," Tom replied with his well-rehearsed rhetoric, "We like to think of it as an investment in you."

"Time share." Nikki echoed herself hollowly.

Tom pulled out a pen and paper and launched right into his spiel. Drawing circles on a piece of paper as he spoke, which were somehow equated to selling points. It was hauntingly familiar, and Nikki had a flashback to the time when a "friend" put similar circles on a piece of paper while trying to sell her on the Amway concept.

When the arts and crafts portion of the spiel had concluded, Tom went in for his big "get." "I bet poochie here likes a good vacation every now and then. You agree with me, right?"

"Uh, right," Nikki answered.

"And most resort hotels, they don't accept animals, you agree with that."

"I guess."

Nikki could feel Amber on the verge of bursting into laughter. She knew if she allowed her mind to wander she would be lost as well. She focused on Old Tom (and this, for your information, was the moment she discovered the dried snot on his shirt) and tried to listen.

"Well, I think you'll agree that with vacation home ownership, that's not an issue."

"I'm awfully agreeable, aren't I?" Nikki asked sarcastically.

Old Tom looked up over Nikki's shoulder, and before she had a chance to look herself, a plate of food was shoved into her face, "Cold Salmon Salad?" asked the ever-intrusive Madge.

"No, thanks," said Nikki, and then ever so nonchalantly, "I'd love some coffee though."

Madge's phony smile went away, she gave Nikki a wry wink, and said, "Nice try."

Old Tom excused himself, and Amber and Nikki realized that this wasn't a funny happenstance affair; this was a dangerous situation which they had no idea how to get out of.

"Um, Poochie," Amber said to Lefty, "This is bad, right?"

Lefty wouldn't even dignify the poochie comment with a verse from The Who.

When Tom returned (enter the pee drip), Nikki decided to try to move the nightmare in a direction that was at least somewhat related to the reason for the return to the airport.

"Mr. Hotaire," Nikki asked, "If we were to invest in a vacation home ownership, would you require a passport?"

"No, no, of course not. Nothing intrusive, my dear, we just need you to fill out some paperwork and a small deposit, and you're on your way. The whole process shouldn't take more than three or four hours."

Tom pulled out a stack of papers as thick as *War and Peace*, yanked a pen out from behind his ear (Nikki made a mental note not to use his pen) and began writing silently.

"Now, my dear, you aren't married, right?"

"Uh, no," answered Nikki, "but thanks for bringing it up."

Before Tom was allowed to elaborate on why he had asked, Nikki, entirely bereft of patience, decided to lay it out on the line for him.

"Look, Tom," she said, "I have zero intention of buying a time share today."

"Oh, my dear, it's not a time share. It's investment in YOU."

"Ok, Tom, I have zero intention of making an investment in me today. Unless, somehow, it's going to get me a passport."

"An investment in vacation home ownership is a passport to adventure."

"OK, Tom, I'm done. I'm getting up and I'm leaving here now."

And then, he touched her, again. Laid his raggety-filthy-fingernailed-just-back-from-the-bathroom-probably-wasn't-washed hand on her arm and said, "Let me just get my boss."

Before very long a woman more unpleasant than Madge, but slightly better groomed than Tom showed up at the small table. She wore the neck brace of the recently whiplashed, and the face of a sour lemon.

~~~

As quickly as his heavy testicles would allow him to travel, Old Tom got to a phone. He dialed The Big Man, and nervously relayed the situation. "I'm losing her, sir. I need back up."

"Mon, you lose this girl, and this your last gig. Matthew close, I send him over and be close behind. Doan' let dat girl outta your sight."

"Right, sir. I won't let her out of my sight." Which, of course, she presently was.

~~~

Meanwhile, back in Cinna-hell, Nikki and Amber had spent the brief time berating Old Tom's boss, who told them that they would never be given this opportunity again, lectured them on their obligations as attendees of vacation home ownership presentations, handed them complimentary fanny packs and discount coupons to Cinnabon and sent them on their way. By the time Tom returned, the trio was out the door and half-way down the hall.

They fast walked rather than ran, until Nikki looked behind her and spotted Matthew. "Amber," she said calmly, "It's the flight attendant from the Korean Air flight. We need to run." And at that Nikki bolted, and soon they were back at the Datsun, once again escaping the airport.

Unsure of her destination, Nikki's only instinct was to go north. North on the 405. North on the 55, north on the 5. It wasn't long before traffic came to a dead stop, and Nikki realized that they were at the Orange Crush, *the* definitive Orange County traffic nightmare where the 5, 22 and 57 freeways all converged. A literal cross-roads.

"This has to be some kind of joke," Nikki said mostly to herself. "Uh, we have three ways we can go here. We stay on 5 and we can go back to Disneyland, or even home. We go on the 22 and we can hit Knott's Berry Farm, or we can get on the 57 and go to Fullerton."

"What's in Fullerton?" Amber asked.

"My childhood home."

Amber shook her head, "Well, Nik, I suspect we're supposed to go to Fullerton. Seems like a good place to find your passport, right?"

"I know," said Nikki somewhat petulantly, "but I'm just not sure I'm up for it today."

"Well, Disney is dangerous for us at this point, so Knott's?"

"Knott's," Nikki answered decisively, "We can park outside the chicken dinner restaurant and drool."

"Perfect," said Amber. Three hours later, they completed the 20-mile drive, and arrived.

~~~

At Orange County Airport ...

Luke lights up a Monte Cristo cigar in a non-smoking Starbucks.

Demi Devi Dai gets a wheat grass shot at Jamba Juice.

Old Tom and Madge sneak out of the terminal, and catch a bus to the Crystal Cathedral.

Biy-Em makes a phone call and activates the twins.

Ray, the bird, flies around in the Altitunes store, searching for Michael Jackson CD's and singing *Thriller* just loud enough for customers to think it is playing in the background.

Outside of Knott's Berry Farm Chicken Dinner Restaurant, Nikki, Amber and Lefty stand watching the television in the restaurant's very crowded waiting area. Rob reappears on *For Love or Money 2*, sending Erin reeling before breaking for a commercial. Oprah's face lights up the screen "Omphaloskepsis on the next Oprah Winfrey show."

22.
Burning (Yellow) Rubber

Saturday, Week 3

The click-click-click of the Ghost Rider roller-coaster woke the trio still parked outside the chicken dinner restaurant. Despite the early hour, a line had already formed for lunch.

Nikki and Amber awoke refreshed and in remarkably good moods.

"I love Knott's rhubarb," were Nikki's first words, characteristically about something she couldn't have.

"I've never eaten here," said Amber, "but it does smell great."

"There is no better fried chicken anywhere. When this is over we have to come back. Kassen and I came here once and –"

Amber interrupted, "No more Kassen talk, OK?"

"OK."

"So," said Amber conversationally, "it looks like Jake and Melia have gotten a message to Oprah."

"Yeah," Nikki answered somewhat distractedly.

"You made a major discovery with that stomach meditation stuff."

"Why do you think people can still see Oprah?"

"What?" Amber asked somewhat shocked.

"Oprah can be seen and can interact with people but we can't."

"Nik, you made a discovery that is so important to whatever it is that's going on here, it's going to be on the next Oprah. Can you bask in that success without moving on to the next challenge?"

"I don't know. I don't know. Why is Oprah even a part of this? Or, better question, why are *we* a part of this if it's an Oprah thing? Why aren't Tom Cruise and John Travolta running around with their Seeker and Waker allies?"

"I know you want all the answers now, Nik, but they aren't available to you now. You can't skip from A to F. You have to traverse through B, C, D and E."

"I *hate* B, C, D and E, Amber," Nikki was in a full whine now.

"I know you do, but you don't have a choice, so let's pop in a little Joni, and head for the days of your youth."

"Yeah, the car of my youth doesn't have a CD player, so do you have a plan B? Or C? or D?"

Nikki pulled out of the parking lot, and not exactly knowing which direction to go went with her instinct, which was of course the wrong direction and four U-turns later they were back on the freeway barreling toward 1468 Kensington Drive... where it all began.

~~~

Luke awoke in unusually high spirits, and with a mad craving for Boysenberry Pie. The high spirits came from a deranged satisfaction he felt over a conversation that he had participated in the night before.

He replayed it in his mind, further buoying his mood. The conversation occurred in the cab while his group was on their way from the airport to the Disneyland Hotel, and it was about *Captain EO*, an attraction at Disneyland which featured Michael Jackson, Angelica Houston and various Muppets in a 3-D musical adventure.

The discussion went something like this:

Ray: Boss, remember that you promised me we could see *Captain EO* before we go home?

Biy-Em: Yah, mon. We go tomorrow, not much for us to do while we wait for the twins.

Ray: Thank you boss, thank you. It's my life-long dream to see *Captain EO*.

Luke: *Captain EO* is gone.

Ray: What?

Luke: *Captain EO* is gone, no longer there, finished.

Ray: Boss, do you see how he treats me, making up stories like that. They would never take *Captain EO* away.

Luke: Sure and they did. Was there yesterday, if you recall. *Captain EO* is gone, and in its place is a delightful show called *Honey, I Shrunk the Audience*.

Luke really thought *Honey, I Shrunk the Audience* was insipid and inferior to *Captain EO*, but he so enjoyed bursting Ray's bubble that he didn't mind the slight slur on his own taste. After that, he left Ray to his grief and quietly hummed *We Are Here to Change the World*, the EO anthem, all the way to his room.

Thus, on a beautiful Orange County Saturday morning, minus one irritating bird, he dressed and called the concierge to determine where he may locate a superb piece of Boysenberry Pie.

~~~

"I really thought I was going to marry Donny Osmond," Nikki confessed as they approached the Nutwood Drive freeway exit. "Michael Jackson too, though he came a little later in the fantasy years."

"I liked Electra-Woman and Dyna-Girl," Amber contributed. "But my real crush was on the red-haired chick from Josie and the Pussycats."

"Weren't there any girl bands, like the Osmonds or the Jacksons?

"Josie and the Pussycats was a band," Amber replied defensively.

"Yeah, but weren't they a cartoon?"

"Technicality! Besides, I didn't think I was going to marry them. How did you think you were going to meet Donny Osmond to marry him?"

"I don't know. I just knew it would happen, somehow. I used to listen to this one song over and over. It was from the *Homemade* album, which they never put out on CD by the way..."

"Tragic," Amber interrupted.

"Anyway, this song was called *Sho Would Be Nice*, not 'sure', 'sho,' and mostly the brothers are singing but there's this one part in the song where Donny gets a solo. One night I listened to that part of the song about 40 times in a row. I remember lying in bed, and having to get up and move the needle back to that part. And I just kept thinking that Donny knew I was out there, and he was singing it for me."

"How does a 12-year-old sing about romantic relationships and get away with it?" Amber asked.

"I don't know, but can you see me married to Donny Osmond? He's Mormon and has like 8 kids."

Nikki exited the freeway, and before Amber could answer the rhetorical question about Nikki in a Mormon marriage, Nikki pulled the car over to the side of the road to issue a stern disclaimer.

"I was not old enough to drive when I lived here. There will be U-turns."

Amber laughed, "You didn't need to pull over for that, my friend."

"I know," Nikki said, "But I'm nervous."

"The sooner we get to B, the sooner we'll be at F."

"OK, I think it's sad that I totally understood that."

Amber gave Nikki an affectionate squeeze on the thigh, and said, "You'll be fine Nik. Now, tell me, who else did you think you were going to marry?"

"Tony DeFranco, David Cassidy, Val Kilmer and Eddie Vedder."

"OK, Eddie Vedder's only from like ten years ago, how long—?" Amber's rhetorical question was interrupted by Lefty's contribution to the conversation, which was an imitation of Donny Osmond singing *Puppy Love*.

Amber and Nikki dissolved into a fit of giggles over the stiff-upper-lip rendition, and the car began to wind its way through the familiar yet almost surreal streets of Fullerton, California.

~~~

Biy-Em, Ray, Luke and Demi Devi Dai met in the hotel lobby for breakfast and a de-briefing. With Ray perched on his shoulder, Biy-Em ordered the Snow White and the Seven Dwarves super platter which consisted of Mickey Mouse shaped pancakes, three fried eggs, two slices of bacon, four sausages and a slice of ham. Demi ordered the Minnie-meal (Oatmeal topped with raisins in the shape of Minnie Mouse) and two cups of hot water, and Luke ordered a hot tea. He had plans for his appetite that didn't include anything named after animation.

Though Luke's spirits were not yet dampened, despite present company, he did notice that all three of his companions had spent a little extra time that morning accessorizing. Biy-Em wore a scarf tied around his neck that had a Donald Duck motif. Demi was wearing a strange yellow bracelet that appeared to be rubber, and most disturbing of all, Ray had donned a single white glove which covered his left talon.

The scarf he could attribute to the Big Man's normal eccentricity, and he assumed the glove was Ray's way of mourning the loss of *Captain EO*, but he was puzzled by the yellow bracelet.

While Demi was bent over rifling through her bag, undoubtedly to procure a vile breakfast accompaniment, Luke wrestled with the idea of asking her about it. He decided against it.

She resurfaced with two different Ziploc baggies, one was most assuredly green powder, and the other could only be described by saying it looked like powdered Poi. It turns out it was powdered Poi, and the green stuff was something called Spirulina, and before she got too far into her daily diatribe of the benefits of multiple bowel functions, Luke weighed the evil lessers and broke down and asked about the bracelet.

"Demi," he asked timidly, almost wondering if would be better to hear about the Spirulina, "What is that yellow thing around your wrist?"

"Oh," she replied far more enthusiastically than warranted, "It's in support of Lance Armstrong."

Luke looked puzzled. He didn't figure Demi Devi Dai as a bicycle racing enthusiast. In fact, he was quite surprised she knew who Lance Armstrong was.

"For his cancer," she volunteered, which perplexed him even more.

"Because he's a cancer survivor," she ventured again, as if this would put to rest any confusion about the yellow rubber on her wrist. "I got it in the gift shop for $19.95. See?" She shoved the bracelet into his face, which had the unfortunate side affect of exposing her armpits to the open air, thus spoiling all available oxygen.

"I see," Luke nodded, almost wishing he'd gone with the Spirulina demo. And as Demi slogged down a big gulp of hot previously powdered Poi, he took the opportunity to change the subject.

"I have a lead I want to check out this mornin', Big Man, another nearby park called Knott's Berry Farm. I feel the Seeker is drawn there." He got this "lead" from the concierge when he made the call about his Boysenberry Pie craving. The only feeling he had was hunger.

"Sure, mon," Biy-Em replied, "Me havin' lunch with me brother at Blue Bayou."

"You're seeing Howard?" Luke asked, alarmed.

"Ya mon, it's irie. No worries. Cool runnin's."

When the Big Man used 'irie,' 'no worries' and 'cool runnings' in the same sentence, things were never really irie. Luke was worried. Hot runnings. Forgo the Boysenberry Pie worried.

"I'll come with you then, boss."

"No, mon. Me got things to say to dat boy and me don't need your three foot ass dere interfering. The twins gonna bring in the Seeker, and me gonna leave this jah forsaken mouse trap."

"What about Matthew?" Luke suddenly realized the flight

attendant's absence.

"Me got him on special assignment."

"Bring Demi then. She'll be good for –" Luke was cut off by Biy-Em's glare and sudden outburst. He knocked Ray off of his shoulder and which sent him flying across the room.

"Ray," he bellowed, "Wha you wearing a damn glove for? There's nothing to go in the finger holes and they just brushing on my shoulder ticklin' me."

At this point, everybody's mood was dark, except Demi's. She was about to unleash the grandmommy of all dumps, and she was positively beaming.

~~~

Nikki was very focused as she drove down Nutwood, squinting to make out quasi-familiar shapes in the dark. At a corner she would have known blind, she announced, "That's Acacia Elementary, my school."

She turned right and passed the school. "That's St. Juliana's, my church."

"You were Catholic?" Amber asked, incredulous.

"Kinda," she answered, "I liked the dramatic parts, like communion and sitting and standing at the certain parts of church. But I didn't like the 'Peace be with you' part because you had to touch strangers."

Nikki made a left. "Oh my God, this is just … surreal. I haven't been here in years. Everything looks so small compared to my memory of it. I cannot believe I used to walk to school." Pointing to the right she said, "My friend Cindy lived there. She had the biggest boobs of all the sixth-graders."

They crossed an intersection, "My dog Licorice got run over by a car in that intersection. God, I've had a lot of dreams about this street."

They made another right, and started up the hill of Kensington Drive. "That was MaryJane and Sharon's house. I used to play Barbie's with them." Further up the hill, "That's Michelle's house, she was one of my best friends. And I don't know those people's names, but they did really cool stuff at Halloween, and that's Jessica and Lisa's house, and my best friend Trish, and there is my house."

Nikki pulled into the driveway. "Amber," she said in a panicked voice, "I see light." She threw the car into reverse, flipped an erratic U-turn, and drove as fast as she could down the hill. No narration, just blind terror pushing her forward until the car pulled into a parking space of the Alpha Beta on Raymond.

Her heart was racing, and a slight chill stole over her. She stalled the car, got out and stood staring at the Alpha Beta sign. "Uh, Toto," she looked to Amber, "I don't think we're in the 21st century anymore."

~~~

The duo seated in the far corner of the Blue Bayou, overlooking the water of the Pirates of the Caribbean, stretched even Disney's imagination. A 7 ½-foot- tall, very black, very bald man wearing Bermuda shorts, a muscle shirt, Converse All Stars (purple, high top) and a Donald Duck scarf around his neck; conversing with a 7-foot-tall, moderately green, also bald man wearing nothing but a loin cloth.

The gentlemen were quite a sight in their own right, but the tattoo-a-palooza was even more memorable. While Biy-Em prominently displayed Van Gogh's *Memory of the Garden at Etten* on his left forearm, (admittedly a less well-known painting, but his personal favorite), Howard had a replica of Peter Max's *LOVE* on his right shoulder. The wait staff was in the ice station playing rock-paper-scissors because nobody wanted to wait on them.

A waitress named Lucy lost the game and approached the table. Biy-Em promptly ordered a bottle of White Zinfandel. He hated White Zinfandel as any respectable wine lover does, so the beverage was ordered for the sole purpose of irritating and embarrassing his brother, who was beyond wine lover, he was a wine snob.

"Lucy," Howard pleaded after reading her name tag, "Ignore my brother's poor taste. Please bring a bottle of Lakoya Howell Mountain 1998 Cabernet." Howard didn't have a single voice, he had many voices. Today he was using his "I think I'm better than everybody else" tasting room manager voice.

Before Lucy could speak, Biy-Em had his hand on her arm (the hand with the mini self-portrait tattoo), and his gaze boring into Howard's eyes. He said, "Brudder, mon, it way too hot for dat heavy wine, we need a nice refreshing White Zin."

Howard's gaze bored into Lucy's eyes, and he said, rather sternly she thought to a person who hadn't been able to get a word in edgewise, "Bring the Cabernet."

Before Biy-Em could issue the White Zin retort she knew was coming, she boldly took a step back to extricate herself from the Big Man's grasp, and simply stated, "We don't serve wine."

In unison, the brothers said, "Then bring us a couple of Guinness." They laughed. Biy-Em said, "Jinx, buy me a coke," but Howard spoke anyway so Biy-Em punched him in the arm and Lucy just about flipped her lid.

She was PMS, had slipped on cotton candy walking into the park (which caused both a knee scrape and a sticky ass), missed four calls on her cell phone in the two minutes it took her to run into Blockbuster to return movies, and had lost at rock-paper-scissors. She was not in the mood for the "try to order alcohol at Disneyland" game.

"Gentlemen, we don't serve *any* alcohol in the Magic Kingdom. We have lemonade, iced tea, Arnold Palmers, diet Pepsi … ?" Her lip was curled, she was bitchy. (That sentence might not have sounded that bitchy, but it was. So maybe read it again, only with really bitchy thoughts in your head. I'll wait. See? Told you, bitchy.)

This sobered them up rather quickly. "Oh yeah," Biy-Em said, "I and I forgot. My bad."

"Mint Juleps," Howard said with revulsion (which was directed at his brother, not at the Mint Juleps or Lucy. He liked Mint Juleps. He liked Lucy too, he thought she'd have a great ass if it didn't have empty popcorn bag stuck to it).

Lucy returned shortly with their drinks, sans popcorn bag which a compassionate co-worker finally decided to tell her about, and managed to take the brothers' food order without incident. The mood at the table changed dramatically between the battle of the wines and the arrival of the mint juleps. There was an intensity at the table now, like the intensity of her PMS actually, that made her more apprehensive than ever about approaching the table.

"Why you so interested in this Seeker? There tousands of Seekers out there, mon, why dis one?"

"I could ask you the same question, Bartholomew."

At the use of his given name Biy-Em's skin prickled. "Doan call me that name. You know I hate that name."

"This Seeker is mine," Howard stated plainly.

"You already got that Oprah lady's Seeker, what makes you think you get all the powerful ones?"

"Because," replied Howard, "I invented the game and as such I get to pick my playing pieces, and this Seeker is mine."

The food arrived. Lucy tried to flirt with, cajole and beg

various co-workers to deliver the food to the table which now had kind of a sinister glow about it. But as the sinister glow wasn't actually a figment of her imagination and the others could clearly see it, she had no takers.

Three bites into his chicken cordon bleu Biy-Em's cell phone rang. Polyphonic *Buffalo Soldier*. A very smug Luke was on the other end of the call.

"How's lunch?" Luke asked.

"Mon, you callin' to check up on me, because me doan—"

"Where are the twins supposed to be today?" Luke interrupted the Big Man, which he rarely did, but he was so full of "I told you so" at this particular moment, he couldn't help himself.

"You know the answer to that, mon."

"Right, ya don't want to say it in front of Howard. Well then, I'll tell ya where they actually are. They are at a comic book convention outside of Knott's Berry Farm in Buena Park."

"Bumba clot," Biy-Em disconnected the call, stood and left the restaurant without a word to his brother. What fun was the game if he let his brother make all the rules and pick all the best players?

~~~

"Well," said Nikki, "There's good news and bad news. The bad news is Alpha Beta doesn't exist in the 2000's. Albertson's took it over years ago. The good news is that back when Alpha Beta was still here Carl's Jr. had their old fries. I loved those fries. I will never understand why they changed them. They were so golden and crunchy on the outside, and airy and delicious on the inside. Always perfectly salted, not too little, not too much. It's been 25 years, and I can still remember what they looked like. "

"Jesus, Nik, ten minutes ago you were burning rubber to get away from light, which would be really nice to see about now, and now you are going on and on about French fries like we have nothing else to do today."

"All I'm saying is, I'm guessing we somehow got to the early 1970's, and right around the corner is a Carl's Jr. and if they have the old fries, then we'll know that somehow we went back in time thirty years. And I'm telling you this—if we go in there and they have them, I'm ordering them. I don't care if every Carl's Jr. on the planet gets blown to complete oblivion, I have to try. I want them more than coffee."

165

"We can spend fifteen minutes on French fries and then we need to get back to your house. I don't want to spend another night in the car. Besides, I have a really strong feeling that we need to be in your house *today*."

Nikki was listening to Amber, really she was, but she was already walking toward the sidewalk, past 31 Flavors, and— "Amber, I just remembered, I had my first date at this Carl's Jr. It wasn't much of a date though, it was more like two 11-year-olds of the opposite sex rode their bikes to a restaurant, got fries and rode home. Jim Clarke. I thought I was going to marry him too, so you can add him to the list."

"You are totally manic right now," was Amber's reply as she ran to catch up with Nikki. Lefty padded along after them, continually mystified by humanity.

The smell of greasy fries hit their nostrils while they were still four shops away from the restaurant. Nikki got butterflies in her stomach. Since their visibility was hard to predict, Nikki decided against trying to order them straight away. Instead, she planned for invisibility, entered the restaurant and walked straight back toward the fryers. Unfortunately, it turned out to be a visible time and the Carl's Jr. manager stopped her.

"Shit," she muttered to herself. "Sorry," she said to the manager, "which way is the restroom?"

She was given directions, grabbed Amber's hand and went to the back of the restaurant in the general direction of the bathrooms. "Why can they see us?"

"I don't know but good thing we left Lefty outside," Amber replied. "Are you done with this now? Can we go?"

"Nooooo ..." Nikki whined. "We have to at least try. We need to at least *see* the fries."

"Well, since the 'walking right into their kitchen' plan didn't work, we have two options. Three actually. You can walk around and check out the food on the other diners' trays, you can try to order them or you can look in the trash."

"Oh, there's a trash can right there, I guess I—"

"Nik, I was kidding about the trash."

"OK, let's walk around a little bit."

There were only a few diners scattered throughout the restaurant, so it was hard to look at their food and not appear obvious. As one of the diners got up to leave, tray in hand, Amber offered to take it and throw it away for them. She knew Nikki well enough to know that this French fry thing would not die until her curiosity was satisfied. Amber casually strolled to the trash can and once the diner left the building they took the tray to a nearby table. There was one lone fry in the French fry container.

Amber picked it up and held it with her fingernails for Nikki's inspection. "That's it," Nikki screamed in delight. "It's the old fries. We're in the friggin' 70's. Come with me."

After they dumped the trash, Nikki walked up to the cash register and ordered three large orders of fries. Nothing happened. The store didn't disappear. The cashier rang her up … "$1.77," she said.

"Crap," Nikki panicked, "Money. I'll be right back. Amber stay here."

She ran back to the car, jumped in and drove it into a spot in front of Carl's Jr. She then dug through every crevice of the car until she came up with $1.29, mostly in dimes and nickels which were covered in old gum and tobacco.

Breathless she re-entered the restaurant and put the change on the counter. "How many fries can I get for $1.29?" she asked.

They ended up with two large orders of fries and eleven cents change. They took the fries outside and got into the Datsun. Nikki poured all the fries into one big bag, and divided them up three ways. "You my friends, are about to have a French fry experience that none of our contemporaries can share." And as the three of them sat with a napkin full of extinct fries in front of them, Nikki took a particularly long and golden one, and crunched right into it. Bliss. Just like she remembered. They didn't even need ketchup.

~~~

Biy-Em sat on the Monorail back to the hotel, beyond irritated that his cell phone had no reception. Why have a cell phone at all if you can't use it where you are most likely to have an emergency?

As soon as he disembarked at the hotel, he dialed Luke. He got two words out and then stepped into an elevator and lost reception again. The call dropped. He was about ready to drop kick the phone. He really hated Cingular. "Fewest dropped calls" his ass.

Once he got to the main hotel lobby, he stood in the middle of the room where he had four bars, and dialed Luke. "You get those twins, and you get back to the hotel now. 'Dis whole day wasted now and da Seeker gonna get another clue." He disconnected without waiting for a reply.

Luke, sitting in Knott's Berry Farm chicken dinner restaurant, had just finished his second piece of Boysenberry Pie. He paid his bill and left.

~~~

Nikki licked the salt off of her fingers. Amber wiped the grease off of her mouth. Lefty stared at both of them perplexed. It was two o'clock in the afternoon and the most they'd accomplished was the consumption of two large orders of fries.

"OK, Nikki," Amber said, "back to the house."

Nikki felt empowered by the whole French fry experience, put the car in first and launched into a chorus of *I Will Survive*. Within five minutes they were back on Kensington Drive, and shortly thereafter pulled into the driveway of 1468. They got out of the car and looked around.

"Do you see light again?" Amber asked.

"Yeah, I do. From my mom's bedroom, up there." Nikki pointed at the sliding glass door just behind a balcony, and then turned to the house next door. "Did I tell you that is Trish's house? My best friend?"

Amber nodded.

"And on the other side were the Ballestero's, and then the Ferguson's and Mrs. Moore's. I think I spilled over her milk cartons once and got in trouble. There's a pomegranate tree over there, and we used to pick them and eat them under that street light over there."

Nikki felt a little melancholy looking out at the cul-de-sac of her youth. A simpler time, where eating a pomegranate was a huge treat, her parents were still married, and she always had a boyfriend.

"Well," she turned back to her own home. The grey painted two story house had a balcony facing the street. There were stone steps leading up to the front door, where Nikki had once fallen, split her lip and was rushed to the hospital for stitches. The front yard was big, edged with ivy and had a magnificent dicondra grass lawn with little pansy patches strategically placed. "I can tell you that I came here once in the early 80's and the house was completely different. It was painted a different color, and the new owners had taken out the grass and put a wrought iron fence around the whole front yard. I knocked on the door and told them my name, and asked them if I could take a look inside. They let me. That was weird.

"Of course, everything was different. My hot pink carpet had been replaced, and everything was dark and weird. I'd forgotten how much I loved this house. We had to move because my parents ran out of money, and love, I guess. Back in the days when I thought I'd marry Tony Howard," she looked to Amber, "Junior High obsession ... I thought I'd buy this house and move back here and have little Tony juniors. Now I wouldn't live here if I had to. The house is great, but I'd never want to live in Southern California again, especially this part."

Nikki took another look around, "We used to play Wizard of Oz out here."

Amber was serious, quiet and mentally providing Nikki with a huge dose of moral support. Being here was huge. An important piece of the puzzle would be discovered, and the reminiscences were part of the process.

"Ready?" Amber asked.

Nikki nodded. Amber took her hand, Lefty flanked her other side and together the three of them walked the stone steps into Nikki's past. Literally.

23.
Little Nikki

Saturday Afternoon, Week 3

Meanwhile, back at the ranch ...

It was three in the afternoon and Biy-Em was in a foul temper, thus Ray, Luke, Lance and Arthur were heartily being abused. Demi was oblivious, and was busily arranging the three new colored rubber bracelets she had added to her collection. Luke was particularly out of sorts because it had been he who had discovered the twins and he should have been in the Big Man's good graces, instead he was being treated as if Luke had been the one who had driven the twins to the comic book convention.

"Me almost had lunch with Howard today. He wan this Seeker, bad. Dat means that dis no ordinary Seeker. Dat means we can't keep losin' her." He glared around at everybody for effect.

"Dat Oprah got Seekers and Wakers joining every single day, and we about to get very very busy. We spending way too much time on this Seeker, and we need to get her taken care of and move on to de next."

"Uh, sir," queried Lancelot, "Why don't we just forget this Seeker and go after another one. There's a million of them out there, and —"

"Me tell you again, Howard wan this Seeker. That mean the Big Man wan this Seeker. That mean YOU GET ME DIS SEEKER."

Lance was quiet. Arthur almost wet himself. Demi took all her bracelets off and re-arranged the colors one more time. Luke tried to remove a boysenberry seed from his teeth with his tongue. Ray sat on Biy-Em's shoulder feeling very smug and above it all.

"All of you," he glared, "meet me in the restaurant at 7:00AM."

"You," Biy-Em pointed at Luke "are not to leave the twins' sides until this Seeker got no eyes.

"You," he looked to Ray on is shoulder, "Are gonna remove that bloody glove from my shoulder before I take it and strangle you with it.

"You," he got right up in the twins faces, "are gonna do

your job, or I am gonna set fire to your entire *Star Wars* action figure collection, including the originals, just to watch it melt. Irie?"

The twins were stunned by the sacrilege, yet finally understood the gravity of the situation.

"You," he pointed at Demi, "you gonna share any of those bracelets?"

~~~

Amber opened the unlocked door of Nikki's childhood home, and the three of them entered. Every light in the house was blazing, and from the front hallway they could hear music playing. The entryway was tiled and empty. To the left was the formal living room, decorated in 70's chic. Expensive suede couches, purple felt chairs, a chrome and glass table; textured paint covered the walls and unique works of art were scattered about the room. A fireplace was central to the room, with a disconcerting black painting that hung over it, featuring a sullen girl with a lone tear sliding down her cheek. The carpet was long brown shag, and the room was restricted to use on special occasions. The exception to the rule was the dog that used the room to do his business in the long brown carpet, which meant finding *his* surprises the hard way. Behind the living room and up three small stairs was the formal dining room, even more rarely used. Nikki still had the walnut veneer table in her dining room at home. It was an eyesore, but she was sentimentally attached.

To the right of the entry way was a doorway leading into the kitchen. It was there that the noise was coming from. Just past the door was a staircase carpeted in lime green shag, and on that staircase were currently a dozen young girls posing for a picture. Nikki recognized many of them.

She spotted herself right away, wearing a long red corduroy skirt with matching vest, and a white peasant style blouse underneath. She loved to have her picture taken and was hamming it up. Big Nikki laughed at herself; she hated to have her picture taken now and goes out of her way to avoid being caught on other people's film. She recognized her best friend Trish, Kelly Burns, JoAnna Hayes, Cindy (of big boob fame), Maryanne Wyatt, Ellen Fraser, Michele, her two younger sisters, and a few others who were very familiar but she couldn't immediately recall their names.

The kitchen table was covered in different types of Mexican food, and looking into the kitchen Nikki could see her old live-in housekeeper Carmen, who had prepared the feast. Carmen made the best *sopes* Nikki had ever eaten, and to this day *sopes* remains her favorite Mexican food.

"Well," Big Nikki said to Amber, "I know what year it is. 1974. This is my 11th birthday party. You can see all this, right? You can see the light too?"

"Yeah, I can see the light. Look how cute you are Nik."

They stood before the scene watching it as if it were a television show, quietly absorbed in the simple family life in 1974 suburbia. Big Nikki looked around and noticed her father wasn't there. Of course, he had moved out by then. The girls were singing songs, Nikki opened presents, and a Snoopy ice cream cake from 31 Flavors was cut and eaten. All the while little Nikki was acting like the belle of the ball.

"You really do like to be the center of attention, don't you?"

"Yeah," she replied. "I'm not sure if I ever got over that or not."

The party moved into the backyard, and the trio moved with it. It was obvious that they couldn't be seen. Nikki's mom and Carmen fussed over all the girls as they changed into their bathing suits (one at a time in the bathroom, oh the modesty!) and headed to the backyard. Nikki walked around the kitchen while the girls were changing. She touched everything, the lamp hanging over the table, the Marimekko daisy wallpaper that covered the kitchen's main wall, the round white table, the avocado green wall-mounted dial telephone.

She walked down three steps and into the family room. It was littered with sleeping bags of various design, Nikki's was Snoopy. She recognized her pillow case, hot pink with large orange polka dots. This was the only room in the house with a television, and she knew that television only had 13 channels. There was wet bar at the back of the room. Nikki used to sit on the counter and call Mark Steinke incessantly.

"I was going to marry Mark Steinke too," Nikki casually remarked to Amber, inviting her into the conversation she was having in her head "do you think it's ironic that I never ended up being married?"

"All that husband potential, what with Donny Osmond and Eddie Vedder and all."

"Ha," Nikki said. "I still remember Mark Steinke's phone number, 879-9985. We should call him."

Nikki went to the burnt orange phone and dialed. Really dialed, no push buttons, 8799985.

"Is Mark there?"

"Who's calling, please?"

"Nikki."

Mark's mother sounded dubious, "Nikki?"

"Nikki Nasco," Nikki tried to sound more childish.

"He's grounded right now, Nikki. He'll have to speak with you at school."

Nikki hung up and said, "Burn ... Mark's grounded."

"Burn?"

"Whatever, I'm 11 here, remember?"

Crossing the family room through a minefield of sleeping bags, Nikki and Amber went to the sliding glass door that led to the backyard.

"Wow," Amber said, "You had it made. Is that a tree house *and* a jungle gym over there?" She nodded to the right.

"Yeah," Nikki replied, "We used to play 'family' in the tree house. How lame is that? Family. I guess when you don't really have a normal one you pretend that you do, only I think I remember us pretend fighting a lot."

"And there," Nikki nodded to the left, "is where we used to play mermaid." The pool was huge, flanked by lounge chairs, and featuring a Jacuzzi at the deep end.

The girls were screaming in the pool, laughing, running, splashing each other, doing cannonballs off of the diving board, and having good old-fashioned childish fun. Little Nikki was strutting down the diving board like she was a model on the catwalk. When she'd reach the end, she'd strike a ridiculous pose and then cannonball into the water, giggling all the time.

"How great was it to walk around in a bathing suit and not have to worry about cellulite?" Nikki asked aloud, and then looked at Amber who obviously couldn't relate.

The sun was out, but Amber and Nikki were so taken in but the rightness of the scene that they had initially neglected to notice. They noticed simultaneously, and smiled at each other with huge elated grins.

"Sun!" they said together, and looked at Lefty to share the moment with him, and were greeted with a very distinct, 'Jeez, took ya long enough' look.

They wandered to the lounge chairs and sat there absorbing the sun, the mood, the energy, and the celebration. As the sky grew darker, Nikki's three stars shined brightly in the sky. They waited until every last vestige of light was gone before they went back inside.

There was no moon.

The children were all dressed in baby doll pajamas. Nikki's were light blue with a small white floral print. Her wet hair hung in clumps and her sunburned cheeks glowed. Big Nikki walked up to her and gave her a kiss on the cheek. "'Nite, little Nikki," she said, "I love you." It felt weird.

As they walked quietly up the green carpeted stairs, Nikki turned around to Amber and whispered, "I used to dream about flying down these stairs. I always tried to really do it the next day. I always believed I could."

"Why are we whispering?" Amber asked.

Nikki shrugged, "Dunno, seems sorta sacred here I guess."

The giggles could still be heard below, and the stillness of the upstairs was stark contrast. A sense of peace stole over all three of them that really couldn't be attributed to any cause. They just felt peaceful.

Nikki, still in whisper mode, gave Amber a tour of the upstairs. The master bedroom, with its wall that looked like a roof, the huge king bed and the fantastic bathroom, had the same green carpet as the stairs.

"This is my baby sister's room," Nikki said quietly to Amber, who looked in to see a room with deep forest green shag carpet. The next room was that of her middle sister, and that carpet was deep purple. (Not the *Smoke on the Water*, kind.) The bedroom had its own sink with a big mirror, and a white desk built into a wall unit.

Nikki's room was a similar set up, with the sink and mirror. Hot pink carpet, with a mustard colored desk set and wall unit. The double bed was covered in a fake fur bright orange bedspread, which matched Nikki's hot pink and orange sheets. Nothing matched the mustard color, though. Viva las 70's.

They put all their belongings on the bed. Despite the current state of light they weren't taking any chances on leaving their belongings anywhere but on the bed. They wouldn't believe that much had changed.

"I hope nobody takes a very close look at the car," Nikki suddenly ventured, "It's 4 years ahead of it's time, and it looks 30 years old."

"Your brain never stops, does it?"

"Nope," she replied, and went to a glass case in her wall unit. She slid the glass back.

Amber turned on the radio, the station was set to 1190

KEZY. Nikki's favorite. Barbra Streisand's *The Way We Were* was playing. Appropriate and hard to believe it was a coincidence.

When Amber looked up Nikki was lost in her own misty watercolor memory. She was holding a little silver ring. It had a single pearl, which had a silver heart on either side. She slipped it on her pinky finger and looked at it.

"This must be before we get robbed," she said, "I lost this ring in the robbery. It's totally worthless; I don't know why they would have taken it."

For hours they laid on Nikki's bed listening to 70's music, singing along to *Billy Don't Be A Hero*, *Top of the World*, and *Midnight at the Oasis*. They told each other stories of their childhoods during the commercials, while Lefty slept on the floor at the foot of the bed. Every fifteen minutes Nikki asked what time it was, and when 9:00PM finally came, she tapped Amber's arm and motioned her to follow (careful not to disturb the sleeping coyote) and took her into the master bedroom.

She opened the sliding glass door, and they stepped out on to the balcony. Nikki pointed to a portion of the sky, and told Amber "Watch."

Within five minutes, the sky erupted in an elaborate fireworks display. They were distant but distinct. There was no sound, just the bright colors lighting up the night sky.

"Disneyland," Nikki whispered. "We used to watch them every night that we were allowed to stay up this late."

After ten minutes or so the fireworks stopped. Nikki didn't move. She just stood there, waiting. Suddenly the air around them crackled with firework sounds. "I used to think it was magical that the sound of the fireworks would come after the show was over."

"Very cool," Amber said.

They crossed back through the master bedroom. Nikki's mom was in the room getting herself ready for bed. Futile with 12 pre-pubescent girls in her family room, but she went through the motions.

"'Nite, Mommy," Nikki said.

"Goodnight, Nicoley," her mother replied.

Nikki stopped short and turned around to look at her mother, but she was still going about her nightly routine and didn't give any indication that she'd seen, or heard, her grown up daughter.

"That was weird," Nikki said.

~~~

In Chicago, Oprah stays up all night long reading *Jitterbug Perfume* from cover to cover.

At the Magic Kingdom a bitchy waitress finishes a double shift. As she walks to her car she flashes back on the large green man she waited on at lunch. She suddenly finds herself very *very* horny.

In San Francisco, Kassen Kyle makes a date. Hey, he tried.

In Fullerton, two single women in a double bed drift off to sleep with visions of the 70's doing the funky chicken in their heads.

At the Crystal Cathedral, Chuckie Rightwing sits in a prayer circle with Madge and Old Tom. The three of them pray for the salvation of Biy-Em, Demi Devi Dai, and most of all Luke. They forget about Ray.

In Anaheim, on a walk around the grounds, Luke finds a four leaf clover covered in cake frosting. 'Huh,' he exclaims to himself, 'a frosted lucky charm.'

24.
Deep Purple

Luke sleepily exited the elevator door and staggered into the restaurant. He saw Biy-Em, Ray and Demi already seated at a table and made his way their direction, stopping a waitress along the way to order coffee.

He sat down, grunted a good morning and followed the waitress with his eyes until his coffee showed up. He didn't immediately notice that both Biy-Em and Ray were wearing yellow rubber bracelets. Biy-Em's was so tight that it actually looked like a rubber band on his wrist, and Ray's was wrapped three times around the talon still sporting the white glove.

As Luke began to focus on the conversation, he realized that not only was everybody now wearing the bracelets, but they were talking about them as well. Demi had apparently gathered quite a collection since the prior afternoon, and she was walking Biy-Em through each of the meanings.

"Sky blue," she pointed to her wrist which was covered in rubber bracelets to her elbow, "Beat Bullying. White and black, Fight Racism; blue and white, Tsunami Relief; Camouflage, Support our Troops; pink, Breast Cancer Awareness; red, AIDS; multi-colored tie-dye, Anti-War; rainbow, Gay Rights; dark green, Save the Earth; dirt brown, Eat Organic and light green, Seasonal Allergies."

Luke wanted to know which was it, support our troops or anti-war, but he didn't dare ask. He also wondered how much awareness seasonal allergies really needed, but in truth the only rubber bracelet he was interested in would be one that said, "Bring Me Coffee."

The twins swaggered in fifteen minutes late, with *Star Wars* Light Sabers strapped to their sides. They both had big black circles under their eyes, though it was hard to see since the plastic helmets they wore on their heads covered most of their faces. Before they even sat down, Biy-Em looked up to them and said, "It's too bad you stay up all night movin' da action figures, boys. You gonna need your energy today."

Deflated, Art and Lance sat down at the table and ordered their breakfast with Mountain Dew instead of coffee. They exchanged glances with each other which clearly said, 'How does he *always* know?'

Once they had all eaten, drunk and peed, Biy-Em returned to serious bad guy mode. He was gesturing with his hands a lot, which made it difficult to concentrate seeing as he had a yellow rubber tourniquet on his wrist. Luke followed the yellow wrist more than the conversation.

"Now," the Big Man boomed, "we got two chances, one dat the Seeker not too bright and she goin' back to Disneyland today, or two that she in da house. If she in the house, nothin' we can do but wait for her to leave da house, and we need to grab both her and the tokens."

"What are the tokens?" Arthur asked with a yawn.

"If me know that, me would go get dem myself. Da Seeker can't move on without them, but only she know what dey are."

"Right," answered Lancelot.

"Me and Demi will go back to Disneyland, and Art, Lance and Luke go to the house in Fullerton."

At the sound of his name, Luke was jolted from his yellow reverie. "Beggin' your pardon sir, but twas thinkin' it would be best for me to get back to Buena Park, just in case she shows up there."

"Mon, you goin' wit da twins. If she dere, and if dey catch her, we need da eyes, and only you can get dem."

And so the plan was laid, and once again the evil forces were in pursuit of Nikki, Amber and Lefty.

~~~

When Nikki awoke she was alone in the bed. She checked her cell phone and discovered it was 7:30AM. The house was completely dark. She tried a switch and nothing happened.

She walked down the stairs, searching for Amber and Lefty and found them on the couch in the family room watching an episode of *The Dating Game*.

"Morning," she said.

"Good morning," Amber replied, "Let me give you a little update. The house is completely empty. No kids, no mother, no maid. I found her bedroom back there." She gestured behind the couch. "The car is still in the driveway, and all thirteen channels including UHF are showing episodes of *The Dating Game* and *The*

Newlywed Game."

Nikki sat down on the couch in a daze.

"We're back to no light, there's a bottle of Taster's Choice instant coffee in the kitchen, and the only way we're going to see Oprah tomorrow is if we are back in the correct decade by then. Did I miss anything?"

"Did you try to make the Taster's Choice?"

"No, I didn't want to deprive you of the pleasure. I have something to show you too, but I'll wait until you are a little more awake."

Nikki went into the kitchen and saw the Taster's Choice sitting on the counter. She pulled a coffee mug out of the cupboard, got a teaspoon from the silverware drawer and looked around for a microwave oven to heat water.

"No microwave," she called out to Amber, whose reply back was simply "Seventies."

Lefty padded into the kitchen, and Nikki scratched him on the head in greeting. He was quite amused by her coffee addiction and wanted to see how resourceful she could be. He watched as she turned on the faucet, and saw delight on her face as water actually issued forth. He felt her disappointment when she turned on the electric burner to see if she could heat the water, and no heat arose. In the end she put a teaspoon each of instant coffee into two cups, added cold water and took a sip. It was dreadful, but she served the second cup to Amber anyway. They sat on the couch sipping cold Taster's Choice, while Amber watched *The Dating Game*, and Nikki updated her notebook with the events of the prior day.

When Nikki finished and slammed her notebook shut, Amber looked at her and said, "That coffee is repulsive," which made them both laugh.

"Would you like to see where I got the coffee from?" Amber asked as she stood up from the couch.

Nikki nodded and followed her into the kitchen, where they stood in front of a very large two door pantry. Nikki knew the pantry well, as she had spent quite a bit of time in there as a youth. Amber opened the lower pantry door, and they both peered in.

"I'm the Lady in the Cupboard," came the voice of an even younger Nikki than the day before, "Today we are featuring this lovely jar of mushrooms from the Green Giant. Now, I don't really like mushrooms–" Amber shut the cupboard, waited thirty seconds and opened it again.

"I'm the Lady in the Cupboard, and today we have this nice

fruit cocktail from Del Monte. Now this has many uses, you can serve it as a fruit, or a dessert, and it comes in—" Shut, open.

"I'm the Lady in the Cupboard, and I'm holding a big jar of dried creamer –" Shut, open.

"I'm the Lady in the Cupboard—" This time Nikki shut the cupboard. "I get it," she said slightly blushing. "I need to check something upstairs," and she headed for the stairs hoping Amber wouldn't follow. It didn't work. Even Lefty followed.

She walked into her bedroom, toward the big walk-in closet and tentatively opened the door. She wasn't a bit surprised to hear a slightly older than 'Lady in the Cupboard' Nikki say, "Bachelor number one, if we were on a date and my mother insisted on coming along, how would you handle it so that it wouldn't be uncomfortable?"

Nikki shut the closet door and leaned back against it, "*The Dating Game.*"

"I gathered," answered Amber. "You were really quite imaginative Nik, and a bit of a dork."

"I know," Nikki answered, "but the thing was, I didn't know I was a dork until people started telling me. God, I thought I was hot shit. When my parents had company in the 'living room' they would play music and I would go in there and put on a big performance, and everybody would tell me what a great dancer I was, and I really thought I was. Modern dance, I thought I was doing. And other times we'd play Stevie Wonder's *Superstition* and I'd do the funky chicken and I just thought I was so hip. I wonder if the grown ups laughed at me? Jesus, it's humiliating in retrospect. No wonder I have no self-confidence now."

"Do you really think people telling you that you were a dork had an affect on how you felt about yourself?"

"Of course," Nikki replied, "I became so self-conscious of all of my actions. I even stopped believing that one day I would have a Lady in the Cupboard television show. I was so naïve. I didn't know anything. It was almost like I was raised without social skills."

Nikki walked over and sat down in front of the sink, which had a little two foot cupboard underneath it.

"Please don't tell me we're going to find another little Nik in there," Amber teased.

"Nope," Nikki replied, "just stuff." Amber turned on the radio. *Seasons in the Sun* was playing as Nikki started to pull papers out. One by one she pulled out drawings of Snoopy, drawings of herself on stage with her name in lights which read "Nicole the

Great." She found a piece of pink construction paper, with a colored red Mercedes 450 SEL convertible with a license plate that said NRN RED.

"What's the NRN?" Amber asked.

"My initials at the time, I didn't like my middle name so I decided to change my name to Nicole Rochelle Nasco. I planned to change my name legally when I was old enough. By the time I was old enough I didn't want the name Rochelle anymore."

Nikki pulled out a big stack of papers and giggled. "My butthole papers."

"What?"

"My butthole papers. I called my sister a butthole and my dad made me write 100 times, 'I will not call my sister a butthole,' but I kept getting in trouble and not finishing in time so he kept adding to the amount. In the end I ended up writing it 500 times. I eventually got tired of writing butthole, so I used an illustration." She showed her artist rendering "butthole" to Amber, "That probably didn't go over too well either."

There were several more "Nicole the Great" drawings, and some early poems that Nikki had written, and a lot of torn pieces of construction paper. When the cupboard was almost empty, and papers were strewn all over the floor, Lefty made his way toward the doorway and sat up on his hind quarters, as if in anticipation.

Nikki reached toward the very back of the sink, and pulled out a piece of paper that had been stuck by a glob of toothpaste to the back wall of the cupboard. As she pulled it out, several things happened at once.

Nikki screamed, "Oh my God." Lefty said, "Ahem," the radio started blaring Paper Lace's *The Night Chicago Died*, and the sky lightened.

Both of the girls were looking several different directions at once trying to decide which was best to react to. The sky lightening was always a good sign, and the "Ahem" meant a clue was solved and a new one was to come, and *The Night Chicago Died* was one of Nikki's favorite songs, but the *most* reaction worthy of the reaction worthy happenings was the little blue piece of paper in Nikki's trembling hands.

She showed it to Amber, and they marveled at it together. It had been white poster board, colored with blue crayon and folded into a 3 ½ by 5 rectangle shape. There was a yellow eagle colored in the center of it, and in bright bold yellow letters at the top was the word, "PASPORT."

Lefty said "Ahem," again, and Paper Lace continued to sing but Amber and Nikki ignored them both, and opened the little crayon passport. Inside was a self-portrait, and in block letters it said, "This is the PASPORT of Nicole the Great." Beneath that was a scrawl that Nikki recognized as her much practiced 'Nicole the Great' autograph.

They jumped up off of the floor, screamed, hugged, and grabbed each others hands (careful not to crumple the passport) and danced around the room. They fell to the bed laughing and breathless and grinning from ear to ear. While Nikki was carefully scraping the dried toothpaste off of the back of the passport, Lefty issued an aggressive "Ahem," which finally caught their attention.

"Would you like your next clue?" Lefty asked.

"Of course," Nikki answered, not entirely shocked by Lefty's actual speaking.

"It's totally anti-climatic at this point," he said in his bored British way.

"Well?" Nikki asked, and by way of a response Lefty pointed his snout toward the radio.

~~~

Luke was seated in the pomegranate tree (of 'eat a pomegranate under the streetlight' fame) when the sky changed color. He knew the tokens had been found and another clue would be issued, further complicating the apprehension of the Seeker or at a minimum the collection of her eyeballs. He was so lost in planning his next steps that he didn't hear the flapping of wings and Ray was able to get right up next to his ear and yell "Busted," before Luke even knew he was there.

The noise startled Luke so badly that he fell out of the tree, landing in a patch of dead ivy, and was hit on the head by two separate pomegranates that were loosened by his fall.

"Ouch," he yelled, "Jasus, Mary and Joseph, Ray ... If you're not goin' to be part of the solution ..."

"Then what?" Ray laughed and took off, "I'm not going to catch the worm? Going back to report this to Biy-Em," he yelled, and then stopped, did a mid-air moon walk, yelled "Hooooo" and flew away.

Luke stood, dusted himself off and looked for the twins. He could not believe he had to entrust the next part of the mission to them. He spotted them behind a bush in the Ballestero's yard. Lancelot was biting his cuticles, and Arthur appeared to be picking his nose. They were doomed.

~~~

The sky was now a deep purple (again, not the *Smoke on the Water* kind), vs. the various shades of black it had been. The color of a summer night at 9:00PM, dark but with a hint of the day just passed. With the three stars and the new sky, visibility wouldn't be great but it would be much improved. Lefty, Amber and Nikki were all kneeling on the bed, looking out at the sky and spotting a figure that appeared to be Howard swimming laps in the pool. When he approached the shallow end of the pool, he looked up and they all waved. Well, Lefty tried to wave but it threw him off balance and he fell off the bed.

"This day," he muttered quietly to himself.

"Are you going to start talking now, Lefty?" Nikki asked hopefully.

His response consisted of a brief humming of the chorus from *The Night Chicago Died.*

"Gotcha."

"OK," Nikki said, "so let's recap. I have my identity back, and I am apparently 'Nicole the Great.' We need to be at a 21st century television by tomorrow morning to watch Oprah, and it appears that we are going to Chicago. Would you agree?"

"Well, except for the fact that nothing is as it seems, and probably the identity discovery requires a little more discussion, I'd say that yes there's a good chance we need to get to Chicago."

"OK, then let's get our stuff together and go to LAX. It's an international airport, so there are always people sleeping there, and we'll be more likely to find a television and a non-stop to Chicago."

25.
One Ringy Dingy

Pillowcase luggage in tow, the dynamic trio exited Nikki's dream home eager for the next phase in the journey. Nikki finally felt like she was getting the hang of things in alter-reality. Amber popped the hatchback and started loading their possessions when she heard a strangled cry.

"Arughhhhhh," Nikki belted out and scrunched up her face like she'd just bitten into a sour lemon.

Amber panicked, threw the things in the car and ran to her side, "What?" she asked urgently grabbing Nikki's arm.

"ALLERGIES!!! They are killing me."

"Nik, don't do that. You scared the shit out of me."

"I'm sorry," Nikki said as she went to the driver's side door, "but I constantly feel like I have to sneeze but nothing ever happens, and it's so frustrating. God, everything else is gone, appetite, need to use the bathroom, need to shower, coffee … what the hell, why can't my allergies—crap, Amber, I forgot to leave my ring behind."

She turned to run back into the house, but she turned and ran right into Lancelot instead. When she tried to move and reach Amber, she found her feet were stuck solidly to the ground. She twisted her body around so that her feet were facing one direction and her head the other. Amber was all the way across the street on the edge of the Royer's hilly driveway, standing next to Arthur. The attempt to call out to Amber failed when her voice came out in slow motion.

"Aaaaaaaaaammmmmmmmmmbbbbbbbbbbbeeeeeeeeeeeeerr rrrrrrrrrrrrrrrrr."

Lancelot laughed. "We're going to play a little game called Statue, Lancelot style."

Nikki was now completely frozen into position. She wracked her brain trying to remember the rules of Statue, a game she had ironically played on the very lawn she was three feet away from. The children move around in various positions, and someone yells freeze and they have to stay in that position until … until what? She couldn't remember.

She tried to converse with Lancelot, wanting to dispatch a sarcastic comment about Lancelot being a peerless knight and overall good guy, but all she got out was a very long, "Iiiiiiiiiiiiiiiiiiiiiiiiiiiiiiiiiii iiiiiiiiiiiiiiiiiiiiiiitttttttttttttttttt-tttttttttthhhhhhhhhhhhhhhhhhhhh," then lost interest and dropped it. Clearly this wasn't the appropriate time for sarcasm anyway.

The only really good thing about being frozen was that she no longer felt like she needed to sneeze. The really bad thing about it was her position. It brought her perceived dorkiness to a new low. The upper half of her body looked like she was winding up to throw a discus in a track and field event, while her feet were waiting in line for the bathroom – in the opposite direction. Her knees were slightly bent and her fingers were curled in what could only be described as mid-fist.

Lancelot walked around her, giving her the once over, twice. From the direction of Mrs. Moore's house, and the pomegranate tree, Luke began strolling casually toward the pair. With Amber safely frozen across the street, and Lefty nowhere in sight, Luke felt the utmost confidence in walking up to the Seeker and popping out her eyeballs. He pulled out the Ziploc bag that was always on hand for just this kind of occasion. He even drooled a little in anticipation. It is not surprising that lost again in the depths of his mind he failed again to pay attention to his environment and was summarily trounced by Lefty.

The instant he was pinned to the ground with coyote ass dangerously close to his face, his cell phone rang.

"Can I answer that, Quentin?" He asked, nicely.

"I shan't think so old chap," answered Lefty.

"Thought to try."

"Always a good policy," Lefty said politely and then hunkered down a little more to secure his catch.

On Lancelot's third once over of the frozen Nikki, he finally saw the little silver ring and grew very animated. He looked over to Arthur across the street, waved his hands and yelled, "It's the one ring! It's the one ring!"

"Forged by the dark lord Sauron in the fires of Mount Doom?" Arthur yelled as he dashed across the street to join his brother. When he did so Amber's "freeze" was off and she made a break for it. From the corner of her frozen eye she thought she had been able to see Lefty and figured the best course of action would be for the two of them to join so they had better odds in their favor when trying to free Nikki.

188

She took a quick step backwards and found herself sliding down the Royer's iceplant hill.

She started running up their driveway hoping to hide in the bushes by Mrs. Moore's house before crossing into the street where she thought she saw Lefty. She was half way up the hill when the "freeze" hit her again, and there she was, mid-stride balancing precariously on her tiptoes. Arthur was back, and rather than leave her alone again he carried her frozen body up the rest of the hill and back across the street, after which time he was completely spent.

Looking around for Luke and not seeing him, the twins realized they needed to come up with a plan of their own or risk losing Kenner's Han in Hoth Gear and all 732 other action figure pals. Nikki and Amber were left facing each other while the twins conversed openly about potential strategies.

Lance: We need to whisper so they can't hear us. If we walk any further away, they'll unfreeze.

(Amber and Nikki eye rolled each other)

                Art: We need the ring.
                Lance: How can get it off her frozen finger?
                Art: You need to unfreeze her.
                Lance: But then she can get away.
                Art: Not if I hold her.
                Lance: If you hold her, she'll be frozen again dummy.
                Art: Right.

(Meanwhile, Amber and Nikki were trying to communicate a plan through their eyes. If the plan was for their eyeballs to pop out of their heads at any given moment, it would have been a good plan. As it was, somebody was destined to pop a blood vessel.)

Lance: What if I tell her I'll unfreeze her so she can have a stretch and get more comfortable, then when she does her fingers will be in a new position and we can get the ring.

                Art: Not plausible. Would Lord Vader ever allow anyone an opportunity for comfort? Would Emperor Palpatine?

(More eye rolling from the statues)

Lance: Right.

Art: What then?

Lance: OK, I'll unfreeze her. She'll try to run, you'll knock her down, she'll be frozen again, but in a different position and we can get the ring.

Art: But if I take my attention off the other one, she'll unfreeze.

Lance: It won't matter by that point because we'll have the ring and the frozen Seeker, and he didn't tell us we needed the Waker.

Art: OK.

Together: One land, One King!

(Nikki's and Amber's eyes had rolled so often they both would have had headaches if they could have felt anything. They had also gained a comprehension of dorkiness that could never be equaled. The twins made Lady in the Cupboard look as normal as Candyland.)

The evil, and remarkably inept, twins turned back to face them with baseless pride beaming from underneath their plastic masks. Lancelot touched Nikki and said, "Unfreeze." She stayed in position with the exception of her fists which were now no longer mid-fist, but full fist. Arthur, expecting her to run and not realizing she hadn't, jumped the gun and plowed right into her knocking her frozen, in discus position with clenched fists, down to the ground. This lapse in his attention freed Amber, who ran like hell until she reached Lefty in the middle of the street. All the eye-bulging had paid off.

"OK," said Arthur, "That didn't work."

"Really?" Lance asked sarcastically. As it turns out, it really *was* an appropriate time for sarcasm.

"Plan B," said Arthur, "Let's slice her hand off with our Light Sabers."

"That would be a good plan, Arthur, except the Light Sabers aren't real."

"Good point."

"Maybe we could tickle her," Arthur tried again. "That would get her to move."

"With what?"

"Light Saber?"

"OK."

Lancelot touched Nikki again and said, "Unfreeze." Arthur proceeded to shove the Light Saber up in her armpit in an attempt to tickle, which caused Nikki to yell "Ouch," reach for her pit and unclench her fists.

"Freeze," yelled Lancelot. "Or that could work."

Nikki now had one hand in her armpit, and the other hand thrust up into the air with every finger straight. Fortunately for the twins, the hand in the air was the ring bearer.

Lancelot slipped the ring off of Nikki's finger. He and Arthur each held on to it together, which was quite a trick owing to the fact that it was a very small ring. They got down on their knees, held the ring up over their heads, and Arthur said, "One ring to glue them all."

Lance answered, "One ring to bind them."

"One ring to fling them all," Art answered.

"And in the darkness to —"

Once their attention was diverted, Nikki was unfrozen. Lefty and Amber were almost to the driveway when Nikki took her foot and kicked as hard as she could into Lancelot's kidney area. "Take that you stupid Lord of the Rings Motherfucker!" she yelled.

Amber and Lefty were able to pin Arthur down with much less drama, and while Lefty acted as the dead weight, Nikki and Amber tied the twins up with their own black coats. It wouldn't hold them long, but the trio didn't need long to get away.

"Have a Steven Seagal moment there?" Amber asked.

"Little bit," Nikki replied sheepishly.

Lefty maintained watch over the squirming twins, while the girls combed the dicondra for the ring. Light would have helped substantially, but as it was it didn't take too long before Nikki had it back on her finger.

Getting right up into Lancelot's face, Nikki said, "Now we're going to play a little game called Hide and Go Seek, Nikki style," and she kicked him one more time for good measure, which really hurt her toe more than anything since the only thing on her foot was a very worn Winnie the Pooh sock.

They piled into the Datsun and Amber looked at her and said, "You *are* weird."

"I know."

~~~

Ray was flying circles around Luke, whose hands had also been bound by his coat.

"Ray, please," he pleaded, "please help me get free. Sure and your not helpin' our cause any by flyin' around when ya could be gettin' me loose."

"Who's bad?" Ray crooned.

"You're bad, now please."

"If I help you get free, then you need to do something for me."

"What?" asked Luke suspiciously.

"You can never call me a rodent again, it hurts my feelings."

"Fine," Luke replied.

"And you need to get me a Captain EO video."

"I'll try, now will you please loosen this thing. My phone has rung twenty times and I need to update the Big Man."

"Oh, he's updated," Ray said and flew down and worked on Luke's coat with his beak.

Finally free, Luke stretched his arms out in front of him and noticed a white powder all over his hands. He looked at his coat, which also had a few spots of powder. Then he looked at Ray more closely and saw that he was covered in white powder as well.

"What's this?" he asked, "You've got some white stuff all over ya."

"Flour," Ray replied, "I was trying to lighten my feathers some. Felt I was too dark, so I'm trying it out to see how I like it."

"Jasus, Mary and Joseph," said Luke as he looked at his cell phone and discovered he had 23 missed calls. 1 new number. At that moment the phone rang again.

"Hello, sir," he answered wincing in anticipation of the yelling he was expecting.

"Burn the Star Wars collection, and activate the 'Lifers,' at O'Hare. Then meet me back at the hotel where we can decide if you gonna continue in your current occupation." Biy-Em's voice was calm. Too calm. He disconnected before Luke could offer any kind of explanation.

He walked up to the twins, tightened the coat arms that bound their hands and said, "See ya, fellas. I'm off ta burn your Star Wars collection." With that, he activated his rainbow transport and left Ray and the twins behind.

~~~

In the Tom Bradley terminal at LAX, weary travelers sleep fitfully at airport gates. They all share the same dream of a singing coyote, lost passports, and interminable airplane taxis.

In Arthur's mom's basement in El Cajon a fire rages. The smell of melting plastic fills the air. Luke watches with delight as

Luke Skywalker and Obi Wan Kenobi meld into one. "Use the Force, Luke," he yells at the burning mass. Then he laughs and laughs, until he cries. It hasn't been a good day.

In Fullerton, identical twins are bound and despondent. They try to comfort each other by quoting their favorite passages from Piers Anthony novels. It isn't working. They embark on a philosophical discussion on what it might be like to be good guys.

In Chicago, the Lifers are congregating. Obesity will never be the same.

26.
WHAT-EVER

Monday, Week 3

When Amber woke, Nikki was writing furiously in her journal chronicling the very eventful happenings of the day prior. They exchanged good mornings, but their hearts weren't really in it. How good a morning can it be when you wake up at LAX?

"Any startling revelations about the whole passport/identity thing?" Amber asked.

"Not really," Nikki answered, "to be perfectly honest I just wrote five paragraphs bitching about LA traffic. God I hate it here. Every time I'm in LA I always swear I'll never come back, but somehow I always end up back here."

"Very productive, Nik."

"Whatever."

Lefty groaned. It was going to be one of *those* days.

"I'm going to walk around and scout out gates and lounges with televisions. Do you want to come?" Amber asked.

"No, I'll stay here and finish this."

"I was talking to Lefty."

"Whatever."

~~~

Luke was on probation. The only reason he hadn't been fired was because the day prior Demi Devi Dai had convinced Biy-Em that the two of them (Demi and Biy-Em) needed to get away from the rigmarole. She convinced him that a day at the Chopra Center for Wellbeing in La Jolla was just what the Goddess ordered. It was a tinge self-serving as it had been a life-long dream of hers to go there, but in the end was beneficial for both of them. After a Chakra cleansing, an Aura steam bath, a guided meditation, a psychic healing and a bale of wheat grass, Biy-Em felt remarkably refreshed (if not a little gassy). If he could have gotten Ray to stop pestering him, the day would have been perfect.

As it was, that morning Luke found him rather mellow and

in fact pleasant, which was infinitely disconcerting.

Demi had only added one bracelet to her collection, and at least that one he could understand. It was a souvenir from the Chopra center, and the embossed word was "Wellness."

They were meeting for breakfast outside of the hotel on the grass. Biy-Em wanted to be "in nature." Luke had room service before going down, he couldn't imagine what culinary treasures Demi had in store, and he didn't want to find out the hard way.

When he arrived at the little picnic scene he was almost knocked back by the putrid smell which aggressively penetrated his nostrils. "Top o'the morning," he said, tearing up a little from the smell, "I think perhaps we should find another spot. This one seems to have been recently fertilized."

Demi burped. "Sorry," she replied in a whisper, "that's me. I had my toxins purged yesterday, and it takes a few days to complete and what you smell are the toxins evacuating my being. It's a very healing, and deeply spiritual experience, you should really try it some time."

Luke thought what he should try is buying a gas mask for these meetings. Surely even Love Canal didn't have this many toxins.

"So, Big Man," he said, "What's on the agenda?"

"Shhhhhh," Demi cautioned. "He's meditating. "

"Ahhh," Luke whispered back, "I understand." He didn't.

Thirty long minutes later Biy-Em emerged from his meditative state. "Namaste," he said to Luke.

"Uh, Namaste," Luke said back which really sounded quite funny with his puzzled Irish lilt.

"So, sir, are we headin' to Chicago?"

"Oh, me can't fly for tree days."

Entirely sure he did not want to know why, Luke asked anyway.

"Me aura. It need to dry out for tree days before me can expose it to all that human energy that generated when tree-hundred people all sitting in a small space together."

"OK," replied Luke, "so what shall we do?"

"We wait."

"We wait." Luke echoed. "For?"

"For the path to unfold, mon. Relax. Smell da flowers."

Not wanting to smell anything, Luke stood and yelled over his shoulder, "I'll be in the bar, when the plan is revealed, look for me there."

~~~

Amber returned carrying a Starbucks cup.

"Holy Fuck," Nikki screamed, "How did you get that?"

"I guess I can order coffee."

Nikki got tears in her eyes, "Three weeks and never once did we have you try to order it."

"Your obsession babe, not mine. Here you go, Venti low-fat, two-Splenda latte."

"I love you," Nikki whimpered, put the coffee to her nose, took a big sniff, and smiled. She put the cup to her lips, tilted it gently back, and the second the dreamy elixir hit her tongue the cup disappeared. She broke down in tears.

"I'm sorry," Amber tried to comfort her, "I'm so sorry. I didn't know. I wouldn't have brought it. I'm sorry."

Nikki licked a little drip of errant foam off her lip and issued a deep sigh. "It's ok, you tried. I'm ok."

"I found a couple of television spots," Amber tried to sound perky, which really wasn't a personality trait she possessed, so it came off kind of forced. "I think the best place to go is the first class lounge for British Airways. There was a bunch of TV's, so we should be able to get one of them tuned to Oprah."

"Do you think we'll get to meet Oprah?" Nikki asked.

"I don't know, Nik, anything is possible. It'll help if Jake and Melia are actually there and didn't just get a message to her somehow."

"We're leaving familiar territory, Am. I've been to Chicago a couple of times, and I love it, but there's not really any history there. No past to visit for clues. Well, I went there with Kassen once, but I don't think—"

"NO KASSEN."

"Right, no Kassen. No Kassen. I might miss him a little."

"No Kassen. Besides, this can't all be about the past. We did the past. We even went to the past and had fries, maybe now is the part of the journey where you look ahead, or at a minimum start to make sense of it. At some point the pieces in the puzzle need to start to fit."

Nikki looked at her cell phone, it was 8:33AM. "I guess Oprah's on at 9:00AM?"

"Could be, stations are different down here so I don't really know. We should head over anyway, we can't miss it."

"K," Nikki replied with zero energy or enthusiasm. She

picked up her pillowcase luggage and slung it over her shoulders. "Do you remember Hobo Kelly?" she asked Amber as they started to walk toward British Airways.

"Huh, uh."

"She was on TV when I was a kid. She was this androgynous Hobo thing…nice role model. And she had these huge plastic glasses, and at the end of the show she'd say kid's names. I always wanted her to say my name, but no little kids were named Nicole then, so she never did. Anyway, I feel like Hobo Kelly. I'd kill for a rollie bag, a laptop case and a latte. Even a Vasa airport water would be comforting."

"It's just a tough day, my friend. You don't look like Hobo Kelly."

"You don't even know that."

"OK, Nik, I'm doing my best here."

"Do you think Hobo Kelly is part of this?"

"I doubt it."

"I think she was Irish, and that guy that was trying to steal my eyes was Irish."

"If she was a part of it, I think Lefty would have a song about it."

Lefty, sick of the way the day had gone thus far, decided to get into the discussion, riffing the hook from U2's *Vertigo* Lefty sang, "Hobo, hobo. I know bum named Kelly-oh."

"OK, now do you think Hobo Kelly is a part of this?" Nikki asked Amber matter-of-factly.

"Nikki?"

"I know … enough with the Hobo Kelly."

Amber looked at Lefty, "You know you really are quite funny. You should participate more."

Lefty gave a coyote shrug.

They had reached the British Airways first class lounge, and breezed right in.

Airport lounge workers are only slightly more friendly than airport gate agents, which does not say a lot about their demeanor. They are like the bouncers who work at trendy clubs. The kind of place you can only get it if you are A. on the list, B. a celebrity, or C. A hot 20-something girl showing cleavage and thigh.

Nikki traveled a lot for business, and even when she was perfectly entitled to use the lounge, she felt like the lounge wardens interrogated her as though she were trying to pull a fast one. As if one hour of free diet Coke and use of a couch was going to break them.

She'd never been to the BA lounge; it was quite an upgrade from the United lounges she was used to.

They lugged all their belongings to an open couch which was facing a blaring television currently showing *Average Joe*. Amber tried to change the channel, but *Average Joe* was on every station. That was one of few reality shows that Nikki hadn't watched faithfully.

"Is this that Bachelor show?"

"No, it's *Average Joe*. It's kinda lame."

"But *The Bachelor* isn't lame?"

"No."

"What's the difference?"

"Well, it's on NBC for one thing, and NBC hasn't really had much reality TV success, except for *The Apprentice*, which I never got into. Anyway, this is good because I think *Oprah* is on NBC."

Amber felt a little bit exhausted by Nikki's knowledge of reality TV, but at least it made her happy and after the coffee debacle, she'd deal with reality TV babble.

"My top five reality shows are, *Amazing Race, Survivor, Big Brother, American Idol* and *The Bachelor* … I loved *The Mole*, but they only had two and then they did *Celebrity Mole* and that was stupid."

"I've never seen any of them."

"Wow," Nikki replied, "that's almost staggering."

Oprah wasn't on at 9:00AM unfortunately, and the trio sat through two more episodes of *Average Joe* before *Oprah* came on.

"Who does she pick?" Amber asked.

"I don't know. I *really* didn't watch this one."

"Well, that kinda sucks."

"Ahhhh, you're hooked baby."

They were interrupted by the *Oprah* music. It was 11:00AM. Oprah's on.

"They lost their eyes, yet discovered their vision," Oprah's voice intoned, "Omphaloskepsis. You'll be amazed at what they see. Next."

"I'm not hooked," Amber said.

Oprah's audience clapped and screamed. The audience was filled with preppy looking 30-something women. Probably single. There were two men. Probably gay. On Oprah's stage were a dozen people, and a half a dozen various animals. They immediately spotted Jake and Melia, and Xhu Shu the Asian man from the earlier show.

"Hooked," Nikki whispered.

Oprah began, "Meditation has long been heralded as the most effective, and widely practiced spiritual aid there is. Many believe that meditation is as important as eating or breathing. It frees the mind, instills peace and a sense of well-being. It brings quiet to our very noisy lives. But does it matter what your focal point is? Well, today we're talking about omphaloskepsis which is a very fancy word for the contemplation of one's navel. This relatively recent practice is said to induce a hypnotic reverie, but can it help the blind see?"

A camera scanned the audience where many of the 30-somethings were self-consciously checking their belly button piercings.

"We are connected to our mothers through the navel. We receive nourishment, and oxygen – for nine months it literally is life support. But is it also the cosmic portal which delivers your soul? Those who practice omphaloskepsis regularly think so, and they are not one bit surprised to learn that people who have lost their eyes can see through this practice. Today, you'll hear their stories and find out just what they've seen since they lost their vision."

The next ten minutes of the show told the remarkable story of how all six people, including Oprah's recently de-eyed Seeker, Gayle, had all lost their eyes in a similar fashion. This part of the show made Nikki extremely uncomfortable, since she knew her eyes were on the short list for acquisition.

For forty minutes after that, there was a lot of navel staring on the stage. When the gazers felt that they had sufficient vision to communicate, they would start relating what it is that they saw. Xhu Shu spoke about the animals, of course. It was rather impressive when he described in detail the six animals currently on the stage. "Unbelievable," came Oprah's booming voice.

"Jeez, other people's visions are boring," Amber yawned.

"Do my visions bore you?"

"Well, not really. Sometimes. Depends on the relevance, and considering the current circumstances, I don't find them boring. More disconcerting than anything."

"And do my dreams bore you? When I write them down and e-mail them to you, because I think they are fascinating."

"Sometimes they are, Nik, but usually it's more interesting to you than to me. And they're *long*!"

"My subconscious fascinates me."

"I know."

"This really *is* boring. I hope to God we're not going to Chicago to navel-gaze on *Oprah*. I don't need to sit in a tin tube for four hours to do that. I can do it here in the lovely British Airways lounge."

"I think this is almost over, should we look for a flight? We can probably catch a one o'clock." Amber was getting restless.

"Let's wait until it's over. See if she says what's on tomorrow."

She did. Oprah held up Nikki's old-battered-worn-torn-1984-first edition of *Jitterbug Perfume*.

The girls said, "Oh my God," in unison.

"We have a new book club book!" Oprah enthused. "Tom Robbins' *Jitterbug Perfume*. We have a copy for everybody in our studio audience. I love love love this book. Get ready for the read of your life, because you've never experienced anything like it."

"That was unexpected," said Amber.

"Maybe I'm gonna become a show consultant for Oprah. She seems to like my stuff." Nikki said as they gathered their belongings in preparation for the next leg of their journey.

~~~

Led by Lefty, Amber and Nikki caught a shuttle bus out of the International terminal, which is technically terminal 3.5, to the United Terminal which was 7. They really could have walked it, but it was LA and LA is dangerous. How many cities have a 'Nudes, Nudes, Nudes' two blocks from Terminal 1? (Not that 'Nudes, Nudes, Nudes' was dangerous, but its location nearby spoke volumes about the area.)

Nikki and Amber went to the departures monitor. There was a 1:47PM flight non-stop to Chicago.

"That flight isn't going to get us in until around 8:00PM Chicago time," Nikki said expressing concern. "It'll be dark, and we don't know where we're going."

Amber looked at her, dumbfounded. Then waited for it to sink in. It took a while.

"What?" Nikki asked irritated.

"It'll be dark no matter what time we get in."

"Shit. I really needed that coffee."

Once again they loaded up like pack mules and marched toward security. "No games this time," Amber said.

"I know. God, it's too bad we aren't getting mileage credit for these flights. This Chicago flight would bump me up to Premier status."

Without incident they cleared security, boarded the flight, grabbed two seats in first class and settled in. This leg of the journey was by far the most intimidating. Following instincts on blind faith to Disneyland was one thing, but going to a barely known city half-way across the country was quite another.

The flight attendants went through their rigmarole, teaching grown adults how to fasten their seatbelts, scolding frequent flyers who were talking during the review of the safety information card, and reminding those with little self-control that tampering with or disabling the lavatory smoke detector was against Federal Aviation regulations.

"For today's in-flight entertainment," the flight attendant perkily pronounced, "We are having and Rob and Amberathon! We'll be showing the last episode of *Survivor All Stars*, the last episode of the *Amazing Race 7*, and Rob and Amber's wedding. And we're going to get that started right away so you won't miss a minute of it! We've got a nice headwind today, so we should be a bit late and that should just about do it!"

"Who are Rob and Amber?" Amber asked.

"Really?" Nikki asked back.

"Yeah, really, I don't know who they are."

"No, I mean, really do you want to know?"

"It's that or *Hemisphere's* magazine and the *Sky Mall*."

"Amber was on *Survivor Outback*, and Rob was on *Survivor Marquesas*. Neither of them won, but they were both very popular so they got to come back on *Survivor All Stars*. Rob is very bright and a great game player – don't let his accent fool you. He and Amber formed an alliance, and then they fell in love, and then they got engaged, and then after that, as a couple they went on the *Amazing Race* together. And then they got married on national television."

"Good overview, thanks."

"No problem. I'm going to Omphaloskepitate."

"Did you just make that up?"

"Yeah, I needed it to be a verb."

Amber put on her headphones, and Nikki contemplated her navel. Lefty mentally updated his resume.

27.
Lose Weight Now!

Nikki followed the light emanating from her belly button and found herself standing in the parking lot of her old Laguna Beach apartment building, where she shared a small room with her mother for a brief period in the late 80's. It was not a good time in her life. It was a great apartment with the most spectacular, unobstructed view of the Pacific Ocean that anyone could hope for. The living room had a sliding glass door that faced the ocean, and many sunsets were watched from the couch or the kitchen counter bar stools.

Parked in one of the parking spaces was Nikki's 2001 BMW, as dirty as it had been the day she had last seen it almost three weeks ago. If she still had her list, she would have put "Go to car wash," on it.

Nikki approached the car and tried the doors, but it was locked. She decided to try the apartment to see if the keys were somehow miraculously there. Entering through the sliding glass door, she looked around and saw that inside the apartment, everything was different. None of the living room furniture was her mother's; in fact it was all easily recognizable as Kassen's. But that wasn't the only difference – where the kitchen was supposed to be was a very large shower with sunken tub with glass walls all around. 'No privacy there,' she thought. Next to it, where the kitchen nook should have been, was a small bare space that had a single shelf on the wall. There were five framed photographs on the shelf.

Since it was the middle of a weekday, she felt certain that Kassen wouldn't be there, and she would be able to peruse the apartment at her leisure. She had just made her way toward the photos for closer inspection, when she heard Kassen's voice. He *was* home and on the phone, a portable phone. His voice was growing louder.

As she attempted to back out of the apartment, he came walking out of the bedroom.

"Knock, knock," she said embarrassed by her discovery in

his apartment.

He held up a finger indicating she should wait and told the person on the other end of the conversation that he would call them back in ten minutes. He wouldn't, but it was his trademark line. Looking at him she felt all the familiar weakness that had plagued her for ten years. Her resolve from the previous week had shattered, and she wanted to do nothing more than to crawl up inside of him and absorb as much of his essence as she could.

"Uh," Nikki stammered once he was off the phone, "do you have my car key by any chance?"

He walked to a spot near the sliding glass door and picked up a ring of keys off of the floor. The BMW key slid easily off of his key ring, he then walked up behind Nikki and enveloped her in a hug from behind. He kissed her on the shoulder and slid the key into her hand. With both his hands free, he ran them down her back and grabbed her ass.

Nikki gasped and turned quickly around, "Well, thanks," she said. "I gotta go." He walked with her back up the stairs to the parking lot.

Standing next to the car, he hugged her again and looked into her eyes. He had this one look, and whenever he looked at her that way she melted. He was looking at her that way (and she melted).

"We should just do it," he said.

"Do what?"

"You know."

"No, I don't know. Get married?"

He smiled, a Cheshire Cat smile, followed up by a double eyebrow raise.

Throughout their ten year history there were times, albeit brief, that Kassen was truly enamored of Nikki. Fleeting moments, off-handed comments about their future, a look of pure love in his eyes. They were very confusing times for her because there was just enough in those moments to cause her to cling to hope for a future together, despite all (vast) evidence to the contrary. She always let the moments pass without calling him out, because she knew on a very deep level that they weren't real, that he was just caught up in a moment. However, on this day, after the last few weeks she'd had, she decided not to let him slither out of it, and to act as if what he was telling her was real.

"We could get married?" she asked coyly, "Where?"

"Sonoma," he answered.

"What would our wedding song be?"

"Stevie Wonder, *As*."

"I want to pick out my own ring," she said. "I want it custom made, diamonds and platinum."

His smile dropped.

"Could we get married right away? I don't need a big wedding, and in fact forget Sonoma, we can get married in Vegas and do the ring later. Then we could have a party in Sonoma."

His eyes showed fear.

"What?" Nikki asked.

"I can't marry you," he said.

"Why?"

He put his arm around her and led her back down the stairs and into the apartment, to the wall that held the photos. He stood on a scale that Nikki had not noticed earlier, with his hand covering up the face of the person in the fourth picture. Each photo was of a woman, (none of them Nikki) and under each was an envelope containing a letter. The postmarks varied, Pittsburgh and Dallas were visible to Nikki.

"Why are you covering that picture?"

"Because Karen is coming next week, and she doesn't like it when I talk about her to you."

Nikki thought she didn't like it much either, but let the comment slide. She was getting pissed, and in her anger getting her resolve back.

"So, you can't marry me because Karen is coming next week?"

"Right," he said as if it were the most logical thing in the world.

Nikki took all the pictures and letters off the wall, took them to the shower, threw them in, turned on the water and —

~~~

Intense turbulence shook Nikki out of her vision before she had a chance to destroy Kassen's photos. She grabbed on to the armrests and started pulling up, which was what she always did in turbulence. This convinced her that she was doing her part in keeping the plane up in the air. Hey, she's a team player. There's no "I" in plane crash. Amber, sitting in the window seat, was so engrossed in *Amazing Race* she hardly noticed the bumpy aircraft. She looked over at a petrified Nikki, moved the headphone off of her right ear and waited to see if Nikki had been talking.

205

"Kassen is a part of this."

"No Kassen."

"I know, Amber, but he's *part* of this."

"Nik, maybe you shouldn't be omphalosketicamabobizing while we're in the air."

"Good word," Nikki smiled, "But I've seen Rob and Amber's wedding, I know the ending."

"OK," said Amber skeptically, "I'm going back in. Rob and Amber just got to little Havana."

Amber put her headphone back over the exposed ear, and Nikki said, "Hooked."

"I heard that," she said loudly.

Nikki massaged her neck for a few minutes. She hadn't realized how long she'd been in navel-gaze position (which wasn't all that comfortable. Try it. I'll wait. See? Next time try it in an airplane seat). Even with condensed versions of *Survivor* and *Amazing Race*, a minimum of a couple of hours had to have passed. She hated not having a clock. She never did on flights because she always used her cell phone, but usually she could catch a glimpse of the time on the watch of somebody around her. Then the challenge was trying to figure out what time zone it was set to, a particular challenge and almost futile exercise on international flights.

Once her neck was sufficiently worse off than it had been before she started, Nikki returned to her navel, which could really use a pair of tweezers she noted and mentally added it to the list that no longer existed. She didn't know what to expect going back in, but she assumed that a new vision would begin entirely. However, she was right back in Laguna Beach and somehow knew it was the next day.

Alone, she stood fully clothed inside the shower. The photos were nowhere in sight. She was fiddling with the showerhead, but it seemed to have its own volition and was dancing all over the place. She turned on the water and it only came out in a trickle, until the showerhead pointed itself outside of the shower, and then it went on full blast soaking the nearby carpet. Nikki readjusted the showerhead, and was seriously scolding it when Kassen walked in the room.

"Wanna get in?" she asked coyly. (Oh, Nikki Nikki ....wherefore art thou sense?)

Kassen entered the shower, also fully clothed, and they both struggled to find a little bit of moisture from the errant showerhead. They finally got a slight trickle, and began to somewhat enjoy the shower when Nikki heard a noise.

"What's that?" she asked, alarmed.

"Oh, my mother is here emptying the dishwasher. My parents want me to go to church with them." Then he opened the shower door and called out (though where the kitchen was in all of this, Nikki had no idea) "Hey mom, I've got a girl in here."

They got out of the shower, and donned matching black t-shirts with towels wrapped around their waists. With their slightly damp hair, they sat down on the couch. Kassen's mother walked up to Nikki, put out her hand for Nikki to shake and said, "What's your name again?"

"Nikki," she answered. "We met several years ago very briefly."

She sat down on the couch next to them, looked at Nikki and said, "Kassen calls me sometimes and I can hear in his voice when he's met someone special." She approved of Nikki, "Your smile says you are happy and your eyes show love, but you are also worried."

"We've been together off and on for ten years. It has been very difficult." Nikki truly had given up all hope, and Kassen's mother knew it.

And then Mrs. Kyle said a very strange thing, "Do you think Kassen is going to die on the 12th too?"

"What?" Nikki gasped.

"Do you think he is going to die on the 12th as well?"

"No," Nikki was emphatic. She looked to Kassen's father who had entered the room. "Do you believe he's going to die on the 12th?"

"Yes, if his mother says it's true, it is." Kassen's father replied far too pragmatically for Nikki's taste. And then the scene went completely black and there was no more.

When she opened her eyes, she saw that Rob and Amber's wedding had begun. TV Amber was at Spring Training getting a painting signed by Boston Red Sox players as a wedding gift for Rob. Airplane Amber was completely engrossed in the show, and actually had tears in her eyes. Nikki smiled. She pulled out her journal and began to write down the memories of her vision. When she finished with that she started to sketch out a plan for when they arrived in Chicago. All that idle time at LAX, and never once did they think to try to find out where Oprah's studio was.

The aircraft began its decent as Rob and Amber became man and wife. The flight attendants were walking around asking everybody to return their seat tables and tray backs to their forward and upright positions. The always flamboyant Matthew walked by, reached over Nikki and put Amber's tray table up. "Anything I can get you girls before we land?" he asked, gaily.

Nikki froze and started pulling up on her armrests again. Apparently, this was an all-purpose security inducer. Amber replied, "No thank you," and returned her headphones to the seat pocket in front of her. Her ears were melded to her head.

Matthew winked and walked away, and Nikki still grasping the armrests became very agitated. "Do you know who that was??"

"Somebody who can see us?" Amber replied, still a little choked up over the wedding and not really giving the magnitude of the situation her full attention.

"*THAT* was the flight attendant from the Korean air flight. He's part of this. I bet he works with those half-witted twins."

"You think everybody is a part of this. Earlier you thought Hobo Kerry was a part of this."

"Kelly. And that flight attendant *is* part of this. Remember we saw him at Orange County airport too? After the time share thing?"

"Well," said Amber practically, "I guess that means we're going to the right place."

The flight landed smoothly, and there was no further sign of Matthew even in the buh-bye line, so Nikki stopped fixating on him, and started to focus on the fact that they had landed in Chicago with no plan.

They trammed and walked and escalated down to baggage claim without speaking. They were exhausted, spent and out of ideas. It was just too much work constantly trying to figure out what the next step should be. When Nikki did finally speak, she said, "You know that song *Vertigo*? Well, it says uno, dos, tres, catorce. Which in the Spanish I know means, one, two, three, fourteen. That really bugs me. Four is cuatro. Do you think in Spain Spanish catorce is four? Or do you think U2 really meant to go from three to fourteen?"

Amber patted Nikki on the head. "What must it be like in there?"

"Busy. Very very busy," Nikki replied.

Baggage claim was packed. It was 8:00PM and it looked like Disneyland on a summer day. People were everywhere. Many of them wore buttons that said, "Lose weight now, ask me how. Herbalife."

The travel-tired trio threaded tenuously through the tedious throng. Weaving in and out of people who were just milling about, standing in places that clearly should have been pathways. They didn't appear to have any real purpose except standing there. Professional millers. Most of the millers also were also coincidentally, Herbalifers.

Several baggage carousels away, Amber could see Howard's green head sticking out above the crowd. She waved to him, and tapped Nikki on the shoulder so she could see him as well. He bowed his head to them, and then indicated with a head tic the deep purple sky outside. They watched it as it turned to a dark dusk. Poor Lefty didn't see any of it, and was currently fighting to get his tail back from a Herbalife miller who thought it was a good place to stand.

"Guess he caught an earlier flight," said Amber.

"I'm just glad we know we're supposed to be here. Though where we go from here, remains a mystery. Maybe if we could get to Howard..." but when they looked again Howard was gone.

"Sneaky bastard," said Amber.

A bus pulled up outside, and the millers began to move en masse. Unable to break from the crowd, Nikki, Amber and Lefty were pushed forward, out the doors of the airport and on to the waiting bus, without any further discussion. Even if one of them had broken free, the other two were entrenched. Amber thought this must be what it felt like to be a piece of seaweed, always being carried along to wherever the ocean demanded.

They were shoved toward the back of the bus, and people began filling the aisle so again they had no opportunity for escape. Once the bus was filled beyond capacity, the driver turned it toward its unrevealed destination. Matthew's voice came over the loudspeaker. Nikki was sure it was Matthew, though she couldn't see him. Amber was a tinge worried it was him; the only saving grace was the knowledge that Howard was in the area code. Not that they had his phone number, but she felt a psychic 911 would probably reach him.

"Good evening Herbalifers!" Matthew yelled.

They cheered.

"I'm Matthew!"

"Hi, Matthew," they yelled. What was this, a freakin' AA meeting?

"I'm going to be your guide for the next three days, and I am just super super excited! Lose weight now," he yelled.

"Ask me how," they responded.

"I need a ruling," Nikki said to Amber, "is this better or worse than Amway?"

"It's a tie."

"We have such a neat treat for you tomorrow. I'll give you a hint … one woman, one name, one magazine, one TV show, billions of dollars. Who can guess? Don't be shy."

A nervous Herbalifer raised her hand and asked "Oprah?"

"Ding, ding, ding, you are correct! Oprah's on and we're going to be on Oprah!"

The crowd went wild.

"Well, that sorted itself out," said Amber to Nikki.

"Yeah, I'm thrilled," Nikki said sarcastically.

Matthew gave out the meeting time and location for the next day's Oprahfest, and promised all aboard three "really, just really, fabulous days in the Windy – Winfrey – city!"

After many rousing choruses of the "Lose weight now, ask me how" chant, the bus finally pulled into the House of Blues hotel parking lot, and eager Lifers bolted off the bus and to the long line at registration. Nikki, Amber and Lefty wearily followed, prepared to camp out in the hotel lobby provided that this was one of the times that they couldn't be seen. Otherwise they were fucked.

"I miss the British Airways lounge," Nikki whined as she settled on a very funky looking and exceptionally uncomfortable couch in the lobby. As she was drifting off to sleep, she said to Amber, "I have a lot to tell you tomorrow."

28.
Terms of Endearment

When Luke went down to breakfast he found Biy-Em sitting alone in the restaurant. No Ray, no Demi Devi Dai, no twins. He heaved a gigantic sigh of relief.

"Mornin' boss," he said.

"Ya mon. Matthew call. He got da Seeker at the House of Blues hotel. Dey goin' to Oprah today."

"That's bad."

"No mon, it's good. Matthew got the Seeker. You not listening?"

"No, sir. It's good that Matthew knows where she is, it's bad that they are going to Oprah."

"You worry too much, mon."

"And where is Ms. Dai this morning?"

"Me give her the day off. She smell. Me couldn't take it today. Got a headache. From all dat spiritual shit."

"So, then you are ready to go to Chicago sir?"

"No, me tole you yesterday, me aura too sensitive right now."

"Right. Shall I go then, sir?"

"Soon come."

"What?"

"Soon come. No need to fly to Chicago, Seeker comin' back here."

"You're sure?"

"Ya mon, Howard leff for Chicago and me read his notes. She comin' back to Disney."

"Howard's in Chicago?"

"Me tole you that."

Biy-Em was having a particularly effusive Patios day, Luke noticed.

"I'll be in the bar, should you be changin' your mind about Chicago."

~~~

Nikki's cell phone alarm clock went off at 7:00AM. The bus to Oprah was leaving at 8:00AM and they didn't want to take the chance on missing it. Several Herbalifers were already milling about the lobby with coffee and cigarettes, the smell of both permeating the building. It was an olfactory orgasm for Nikki.

She wondered why they had gotten up so early. They were already dressed, didn't need to shower, couldn't brush their teeth, had no need to pee, and wouldn't be having any breakfast.

"Let's go outside," Amber suggested, "Check out the new sky in the daylight."

"Ha," Nikki said.

It was as beautiful a day as it could be with sky the color of dark dusk. Things were definitely more visible than they had been. It was a bit windy, not remarkably so, just a few light wisps of wind. The second Nikki stepped outside she instantly felt an allergy flare up. Her eyes started watering, and her nose started itching and she could see bits of something floating through the air.

"Jesus," she exclaimed, "You can actually *see* the pollen."

"I don't think it's pollen, Nik, not the right season."

"OK, there is allergy-producing debris in the air, it's abundant, and it's mobile. I'm going back inside."

She left Amber and Lefty standing out in front of the bus. When the Lifers started to converge on her, at about 7:45AM, she chose the lesser of the two evils and joined Amber and Lefty, who had already boarded the bus.

Matthew must have been assigned to another bus, because the tour guide on their morning bus was as lifeless as a jellyfish on a sand dune. Ironically, he sort of looked like a jellyfish as well. Very pale skin streaked with red lines. Eerie. He talked like Ben Stein, with absolutely no excitement or inflection in his voice whatsoever.

"There's the Water Tower," he said offering no further information about it. "There's Sears Tower."

"And here are Harpo studios. You won't all be getting into the taping as there is limited capacity." (It's really imperative to read this with the Ben Stein voice, it makes it like ten times more boring.) "Exit the bus, walk to your left thirty feet and wait in the line. There is no smoking allowed. Should you be chosen to attend the taping, you will be escorted to the audience seats. If not, you will be taken to a satellite location to watch a taping of the taping. This is bus number 5. We will meet back here at 2:30PM, no food is served so I hope you brought a snack." At that, 31 heads dropped into their backpacks, purses and fanny packs, located and then quickly popped Herbalife tablets. Nobody told them there wouldn't be food. Jelly man continued, "I count 33 heads and a coyote, and we won't leave here until we have 33 heads and a coyote. As a courtesy to your fellow travelers, please be on time."

They all disembarked and followed Jelly Man's instructions to the letter. Nikki stood stock still, he face frozen in allergy position, "I think I'm finally going to sneeze," she told Amber. And they stood there and waited.

In an ah-choo sequence she got in an "ah", and then another "ah" and then she heard "choo."

"God bless you," Amber said.

"I didn't sneeze."

"But I heard it."

"The sneeze you hear may be your own."

"I didn't sneeze," Amber assured her.

"Did you make a sneeze sound?"

"I was trying to be supportive."

"Yeah, it was a nice thought. But please don't do it again."

Shortly after that, they ran into Matthew. Matthew with a clipboard, a list and a whistle. He was checking in audience members. In the interest of fairness, Herbalife had given actual audience seats to their highest producers. He looked Amber and Nikki up and down, shook his head and said, "Sorry, not on the list."

"We didn't even tell you our names," said Amber.

"Honey, you don't need to tell me your names. I know who you are and you are not on the list."

"Our friends are inside. Could one of us go in and look for them?" Nikki asked.

"Sweetie, that's the oldest trick in the book. What do you think this is, Studio 54? It's freakin' Oprah, baby and you aren't on the list, so move along to the satellite screening, I'm sure you'll adore it. And sunshine, everyone can see you here, so don't think you can try the invisible thing."

"OK," said Amber under her breath to Nikki, "He *is* part of this, and if he throws one more term of endearment at us, I might deck him."

They walked away dejected and followed a group of mildly milling Lifers to the satellite screening area. Which was a *zoo*! And not just a zoo in the sense that it was madness, but there were animals scattered throughout the room.

"God," Nikki giggled, "Are they waiting for a flood?" Another 70's Flashback Phrase, which was a question generally posed to people whose Toughskins jeans were inches too short.

The room was the size and shape of a hotel ballroom. There was a large screen and a podium in front, and folding chairs arranged in rows. All the folding chairs were filled, and studio employees were quickly trying to put more out for the remaining crowd, which was vast. Everybody was talking at once, Oprah staff members were running around trying to corral and organize. The show the day prior had gotten a lot of attention, and as a result of that demand for seats to the current show was greater than expected. Exultant Tom Robbins fans gathered to show support to their idol, delighted that *Jitterbug Perfume* was experiencing a resurgence, and yet a little protective of the gem they had kept so close to them for all these years.

Then there were the underachieving crop of Herbalifers, and several more eyeless people with their partners and animals. The Robbins fans were easily the most aggressive of the group, one even came dressed in a Pan (the God) costume. They spoke of beets and bees, they pondered the laws of immortality, they quoted particularly sublime passages. They were excited into a frenzy of Robbins delight that they hadn't felt since the publication of *Fierce Invalids Home from Hot Climates*.

Nikki, Amber and Lefty bumped through the crowd with no real purpose. Their only goal was to try to get word to Jake and Melia. They asked a couple of different people, who looked busy and were carrying clipboards, for help. However, they turned out to be Robbins fans taking surveys about who the crowd's favorite Robbins characters were, and why.

"I don't even think I could pick a favorite," Nikki said as she pondered the options.

"Nik, focus."

"Right," she saw a man unfolding a chair and assumed he was staff. It turned out to be Jake. "Jake," she screamed, "What are you doing?"

Amber ran up and hugged him, "Where's Melia, how is she? We saw you on the show yesterday. She looks good, but seems a little down. Is she OK?"

"Amber," Jake replied, "Calm down she's fine. We were expecting you two. Oh, sorry Quentin, you three. Melia's with Oprah and Gayle and the animals. Can you believe this craziness? Oprah says she's never had this many people show up on one day. Listen, I'll see if I can get you back there but it's just as chaotic, so I'm not sure if I can. If I don't come back for you before the show starts, wait here. If anything at all happens, we have a room at the Swissotel. Meet us there. There's a lot to talk about." And then he was gone.

"Maybe there *is* going to be flood, because he was like a hurricane," Amber commented.

"So we wait," Nikki said.

"So we wait," Amber echoed.

They didn't wait long. There still weren't enough seats for all the guests, and the standing people further contributed to the general disarray. There was so much going on in the room, hardly anybody noticed when Oprah approached the podium. Suddenly the room went dead silent, and then there was a bray of a donkey, an errant giggle, and then silence again.

"Wow," said Oprah, "Wow."

The crowd was practically apoplectic with excitement, and burst into banshee-like screams.

When the screaming finally got to a manageable level, Oprah began again, "Thank you all so much for coming. I understand we have two complete Tom Robbins fan clubs here."

Another interruption of applause, screams and whistles, and one lone voice which yelled, "Robbins Fan Club Cleveland 182. Woot."

"Wow," said Oprah again, "Unbelievable. We also have more omphaloskepsis converts, and an Herbalife convention."

More applause, but less enthusiastic and a weak "Lose weight now, ask me how" chant.

"We have a great show today," she continued, "Just to give us a little taste of the treat you're in store for with *Jitterbug Perfume*, we've got a Greek God expert in the house, who will give us the inside track on Pan! And, direct from the French Quarter, perfume maker Jani Colo. Enjoy the show!"

"That was nice of her to stop in," said Nikki, "I wonder if that's something she normally does."

Amber shrugged. The din in the screening room had picked up again. In one corner an eyeless person was agitated by an omphaloskepstic episode, screaming that she'd had a vision that everybody in the room was going to die. This in turn agitated those closest to her, who started making for the doors. The doors were blocked by the donkey who had just taken a massive (and smelly) dump on the carpet. The icing on the cake came when a heated debate between the two Robbins Fan Club presidents came to blows over who was the Tom Robbins character "Most likely to date Dick

Cheney." (The correct answer to that, in case you are wondering, is none of the above.)

Nikki grabbed Amber by the hand, and tapped Lefty on the bum indicating he should follow. They went out a side door and Nikki said, "We can stay in the chaos, or walk out. I say we walk out." And they did.

When they got outside, they looked up at the sky and saw that two new stars had joined Nikki's previous three.

"I guess you get stars when you figure shit out by yourself," said Amber.

They were quiet for a moment, absorbing the silence.

"Jesus, I just kept thinking, there is no point to this chaos. And you know, there's always that choice. We can stay in the chaos and learn, or we can walk out and learn. We don't need to inflict all that drama onto ourselves."

"So where to now? Not the bus?"

"No, I think we should go to the Swissotel and wait for them. I do wish I'd gotten to meet Oprah though. She looks good in person doesn't she? Really skinny."

"I don't suppose you know where we're going?" asked Amber. "We should ask somebody."

"No," Nikki replied quickly, "I don't want anybody around here to know where we're going. Sweetie, baby, honey, Matthew gives me the creeps. I don't want him having any clues. I've stayed at the Swissotel before, it's on the water. My guess is, we walk straight for a couple of miles, and figure it out when we bump into Lake Michigan."

They bumped straight into Wacker Drive which led, shockingly without incident, to the Swissotel. Two stars and a no U-turn journey, their day was looking up.

~~~

Matthew's day was looking down. He had spent a good part of it settling disputes between disgruntled Herbalifers whose sales figures had purportedly been misrepresented. When he finally got everybody calmed down, and the show had begun taping he walked into the screening room. He was reading from his clipboard, not paying attention, and stepped in the large pile of donkey doo. "Piss and chips," he yelled, dropped his clipboard and put his hands dramatically on his hips.

After an aborted mission to clean his shoes (he decided to

toss them in the garbage instead), he returned to his real task which was to locate and detain Nikki, Amber and Lefty. He searched the screening room to no avail. In a complete panic, he ran out the door, this time he slipped on the donkey doo and landed face first, lower-half inside, upper-half outside the building, scraping his nose on the asphalt. He laid there and cried for ten minutes, without a single offer of assistance from the ingrates in the screening room.

As he walked back toward the bathroom to wash up he yelled into the crowd, "Most of you wouldn't even be here if it wasn't for me!"

He was universally shushed. Blood from his nose, mingled with donkey feces, mingled with tears, mingled with dread of the report he was about to make to Biy-Em. It all made him extraordinarily nauseous. He should have stuck with hairdressing.

~~~

While Nikki, Amber and Lefty sat in the hotel lobby waiting for Jake and Melia, Nikki recounted for Amber and Lefty the two visions she had the previous day. She didn't expect any input from Lefty, but she felt it was important that he knew what was going on.

"What's the date, anyway?"

"Who knows?" Amber replied.

"All those notes I took, I never wrote the date down. I guess we just need to figure out what the last date we remember was, and add the number of days we've been at this."

"Do you know how many days we've been at this?"

"Oh," Nikki paused, "no."

After about an hour and much discussion on what the potential date was when the light went away, and a calculation of days since then from Nikki's notebook, they finally determined that it was almost probably the 6th of October.

"Let me just check my cell phone calendar to see if we're right," said Nikki.

Amber gave her another one of those looks. For such a bright girl, she could at times overcomplicate things. Once Nikki had confirmed, via the magic of Nokia, that it was absolutely the 6th of October, she blushed and said, "I guess I don't get a star for that one."

"I guess not."

"It was good to know we could do it, though, you know. Figure out the date without a calendar."

"Yeah," said Amber with sarcasm, "good to know."

"Amber, I know you what you are going to say, but I have to be back in San Francisco by the 12th, that means we have less than 6 days, and most of one day will be lost with travel time. I have to get to him. Even if he's not really going to die, whatever it is, I'm a part of it."

Amber didn't say anything, because Jake, Melia and Pilar walked into the hotel lobby.

~~~

In a studio parking lot, long after dark, 31 heads sitting on a bus are still waiting for two heads and a coyote. It will be a long wait.

At the House of Blues hotel, a gay flight attendant/tour coordinator takes seventeen showers, and still thinks he smells like poop.

In Anaheim, a 7 ½ foot-tall black man blow dries his aura.

At the Swissotel, four friends stay up late into the night catching each other up on a very busy seven days. Two of them savor a precious American Spirit on the balcony and plan the next stage of their journey.

A donkey drinks Pepto Bismal, a coyote sings songs in his head – unable to select just the right tune for the next leg, and a big green man makes long distance calls to a very satisfied, formerly crabby, waitress.

29.
Vicarious Butterflies

Wednesday, Week 4

Nikki was the first one awake the next day, in actual fact she'd hardly slept at all. She had become fixated on Kassen's death date and couldn't reconcile it to anything other than the fact that she was given the date so she could change the outcome. She alone had the power to save his life.

While the others slept, she gathered up all her belongings and Amber's and put them by the door, impatiently waiting for the others to awaken.

Lefty followed her around the room with his eyes, but he didn't move from his spot on the floor. He knew the difficult days were yet to come, that the brush with the twins and the close calls with Matthew, Biy-Em and the others were mere irritants. She had a bigger battle to fight, and he wasn't sure she was properly armed. Every Kassen thought weakened and diverted her. *That* was the purpose of the vision, but it was not his place to tell her that. She had to put the puzzle together on her own.

She looked over at him, and saw compassion in his large coyote eyes. She mistook it for concern about Kassen, which only made her want to get to the airport that much sooner. There was nothing he could do, the visions came from the other side and his only ability to counteract them was through love and support, and truly he had grown to love her.

It was 6:15AM. She had to wake up Amber. They had to get back to San Francisco.

Before she made it to the bedside, Melia woke up. She whispered, "Nikki, don't wake her." How had she known? "Lead me outside, we'll talk."

Pilar followed them out on the balcony, and Nikki looked out at the dusk colored sky, which could have passed for dawn. The five stars twinkled, celebrating her success thus far.

"I lost my eyes before I could earn any stars. I can't do anything on my own now, all my victories are shared. You are strong, powerful. You'll get through this and when you do, the sky will be filled with stars lighting up the sky, and a moon shining brightly. And it will be for you. The moon and the stars are yours for the taking. You can have it all, just put the pieces of the puzzle together and look at the beautiful picture you've created."

"That doesn't make any sense to me. Nothing does. The only solid thing I have is that Kassen may be in trouble."

"This isn't about Kassen."

"But he's part of this, and it seems like a bigger part than I realized."

"He's only part of it, because he's part of you. This is about you," Pilar's soothing voice joined the conversation.

"I've made up my mind, and I'm going back to San Francisco today. I'll put the rest of the puzzle together after that."

"You can't complete a puzzle without all the pieces. Besides, you have an appointment today," Melia spoke again.

"I do?" Nikki asked skeptically.

"Yes, with Oprah."

"I don't want to go back to that madness, there was nothing for me there."

"There's no taping today. She wants to meet you. You'll have some time with her today, just the two of you. She may help you get some clarity."

"Oh my God! I'm going to meet Oprah wearing a bra top that squishes my boobs together and that I've been wearing for three weeks straight? That sucks. Does Amber know?"

"No, we forgot to mention it last night. You'll see Oprah in a few hours, and your time will be brief so think about what you want to ask her."

"It is why you came to Chicago," Pilar added.

~~~

Standing at the American Airlines counter at Orange County Airport, the last of Biy-Em's spiritual buzz was killed.

"Me 7 ½ feet tall, woman," he told the gate agent, "me can't fly coach."

"I'm sorry sir, but First Class has checked in full."

Demi stood behind him munching on a Daikon stalk. Luke was leaning under the counter, with his arms crossed, extremely uptight about the fact that they lost two days over Biy-Em's drying aura. Ray, wearing glove, rubber bracelet, and white powder sat quietly on the Big Man's shoulder. He actually knew that this was one of those times he should be quiet.

"Here are your boarding passes, sir. Seats 17AB and C. It's a bulkhead aisle, the best I can do. Do you have a carrier for your pet?"

"What?"

"A carrier for the bird, sir? It needs to be in a federally regulated animal carrier, and checked into our pressurized luggage compartment."

"No," Biy-Em replied, "Me don't."

"We're happy to provide one for you at a cost of $125.00 plus the pet on board fee of $50.00 , a security fee of $9.99, and a fuel surcharge of $2.00."

Luke was very thankful he couldn't be seen at the moment, because he was laughing his ass off. In fact, he was laughing so hard he had to walk away. While he was gone Biy-Em asked the gate agent, "Is it to late to get a special meal for the little one?" he asked.

"I can request it sir, what would you like?"

"You got them Spaghetti-O's?"

"Yes sir, I've noted it. The flight is delayed by two hours; we'll be boarding at 11:30AM with a noon departure. Thank you and have a nice day. Next in line," she yelled before he had an opportunity to ask any more questions.

He packed Ray up into his little birdie cage, and whispered conspiratorially to him, "Dem Spaghetti-O's a little revenge for you mon. Luke hate dem." He gave the cage to a baggage handler, rounded up Demi and Luke and they walked toward their departure gate.

~~~

Nikki was ecstatic. "You don't understand," she kept telling the over-crowded room, "Oprah is my idol."

"We understand, Nikki, you've told us twelve times," said Amber.

"I have butterflies!"

"And I have butterflies for you," Amber answered again. "But Nik, it's close quarters in here and you have enough energy bouncing around the room to beat us all down. Let's relax. Do you have your questions ready?"

"Yeah, I made a list. You know what else guys? We need to make another list too. All the stuff we still have pending, you know. Like getting the eyes back, and I think the Disneyland thing is still unresolved, and I'm not sure if the ring I got from my old house means anything, and you know, all that kind of stuff."

Jake was well used to this type of manic behavior from Melia, he got up, grabbed Nikki's notebook, handed it to her and told her, "Start writing it all down, OK? Leave space under each item you come up with. When you're done with the list, after the meeting with Oprah we'll talk about where it all fits, OK?"

"OK," Nikki said, and was blissfully quiet for a good thirty minutes while she wrote.

~~~

"American Airlines announces the further delay of flight 374 to Chicago's O'Hare airport. Our estimated time of departure is 1:30PM, with boarding at 1:00PM. However, this can change at any time, so please don't leave the gate area."

~~~

At noon, Nikki, Amber, Lefty, Jake, Melia and Pilar left the Swissotel and walked back to Harpo Studios where Oprah had offices. Nikki's butterflies were performing their own rendition of STOMP in her stomach. They arrived twenty minutes before the scheduled meeting time and waited in Oprah's plush lounge.

"It's not like I watch the show all the time, you know. In fact, I've only watched it recently since this all started. I'm not a groupie. I just admire her so much. You know? She's so powerful and she does so much good in the world."

They knew. They knew because she kept saying it. Even the unflappable Pilar grew annoyed. When the clock chimed 1:00PM, everybody breathed a huge sigh of relief. Thirty seconds later an Oprah staff member came for Nikki. "She's ready for you," she said.

And Nikki, without Amber or Lefty, went to the most important interview of her life.

Oprah greeted her warmly, hugged her and said, "Welcome, welcome." Her toucan was perched on a desk chair, and Gayle sat on a couch. She appeared to be naval gazing. There were two comfortable looking overstuffed chairs, with a coffee table in the middle with a huge book on top of it. Oprah took one chair, and indicated for Nikki to take the other.

"Gayle lost her eyes last week," said Oprah. "We haven't separated since. You should never part from your Waker."

Nikki hadn't spoken a word, and for the rest of her life she would always remember that her first words to Oprah were, "Well if I'm not supposed to part from my Waker, why isn't she here?"

"Relax, she's ten feet away, and your animal is right outside the door."

"Oh, my God. I'm so sorry, that was so rude. I'm really honored to meet you. You changed my life. Really, I wouldn't be the person I am today if it wasn't for an episode of your show that had Marianne Williamson on it about twelve years ago. Not that the person I am today is so great, or has it all figured out or anything. But sometimes I give decent advice, I never really follow it for myself of course, but others do. Sometimes."

Oprah sat there, calm. "Do you know how many times you put yourself down in that last paragraph?"

"I'm a little nervous."

"I understand. Listen, I want to tell you a few things. First," she leaned over and opened the big book on the table, "You and Kassen have worked it out. See," she pointed, "right there." She closed the book quickly. The only word Nikki had seen was *reciprocal*.

"You mean we're a couple now?"

"You've worked it out. It's mutual, there's no need to give it another thought. What you need to focus on is what's been happening since you lost your light."

"Didn't everybody lose the light?" Nikki asked.

"No. It's different for everybody."

"But everybody loses their eyes, and everybody has animals."

"In your view of things, yes."

"I don't get it. You have a toucan."

"What if I told you that I have a toucan because you have a coyote?"

"I'd be confused."

"What significance does the coyote have for you?" Oprah asked.

"Well, a lot of different things. A Joni Mitchell song for one. The trickster, animal medicine, he gets in his own way, has to learn the hard way all too often. One time I was listening to a live version of Joni Mitchell's *Coyote* that I'd never heard before, and I looked out my window and there was a real coyote running through my backyard. In broad daylight. Later that night, I learned that I had been betrayed, tricked, by two people I really trusted. Somehow I was prepared though, because the coyote had warned me. I guess I developed an affinity for the coyote at that point that's sort of stuck with me."

"Right, the coyote is a part of you."

"And what about the coffee?"

"It's a weakness you see in yourself. Addictions to things, people."

"And what about this?" Nikki held up her little silver ring.

"Something precious to you, that was lost," Oprah replied plainly. "What else did you lose at that time you lost the ring?"

"My innocence. My self-confidence. My youth. My world."

"Right," Oprah answered, "and the pieces in the puzzle start to connect. Your journey will become introspective, that's why so many of you lose your eyes in your version, because you, Nikki, over think things. You see something, take it as a sign, and you grab a hold of it and don't let it go. That can suffocate. Without the extra stimulus you can focus."

"But I haven't lost my eyes." Nikki reminded Oprah.

"And let's hope you don't."

"And what about you," she asked Oprah, "why are you here?"

"You view me as a powerful person with answers, but I'm also a part of you, and guess what? You are a powerful person with answers as well."

"I'm certainly a person with questions." Nikki once again discounted herself.

Nikki thought for a moment, "So nothing here is really random. Well, except my Hobo Kelly comment, that was probably random. But all that I've discovered is connected, and I am the connecting points. The joints. The Disney bone's connected to the Nikki bone, right?"

"Right."

"And what about Amber?"

"What about Amber?" Oprah echoed.

"Well, I get that she's here because she's a part of me. But if this is all about me, why can't we separate?"

"Every Seeker gets a Waker and vice versa. Amber's journey is yet to come, though she is a Waker with you, she can – and probably will be – a Seeker next. You may or may not be her Waker. There are few clear cut rules. But know that your journey is laying the foundation for Amber's and she is gathering her own arsenal for what's ahead of her."

"Like the whales?"

"Exactly."

"Now, before you go, I have one last thing to tell you. Your adversaries are extremists from various walks of life. The best example you had of them was the Science Fiction twins, right? These people are so limited in their views and life experience because all their attention and energy is spent on their obsession. This singular focus is what ultimately causes their failure. Keep an open mind, always. Consider all circumstances presented to you, not just the easy ones, not just the ones that hold your interest. If you fixate on one thing, you will slow down, and they will catch you. The Eye Stealer's fixation is *you*."

And with that Oprah stood up, opened the door, gave Nikki a hug and sent her on her way. Nikki, who was disappointed over the abrupt parting, stumbled over Lefty who really was waiting right outside the door for her. She was definitely more confused than ever.

~~~

American flight 374 was ultimately cancelled due to a "mechanical." All remaining passengers ('cuz some just got pissed and went to another airline) were booked on American 477 which departed on time at 2:56PM and was scheduled to arrive into O'Hare at 8:45PM. They had lost another day, and last report from Matthew indicated they had no leads as to where the trio was.

Biy-Em was stuck in a center seat a row ahead of Luke and Demi. Since the flight cancellation had occurred his "special" meal plan for Luke had been foiled, therefore the only adequate revenge in Ray's honor was for Luke to sit next to Demi for the entire four hour flight. She had been burping daikon intermittently most of the day. The smell was so intensely fart like, that every time Biy-Em thought about it, he chuckled to himself.

Unbeknownst to anybody but him, Ray was currently stuck on a baggage carousel in El Paso, Texas.

~~~

After the Oprah adventure, Nikki was quiet, relaying very little of her conversation to the group. The six of them left the studio and walked down to the Lake to decompress and talk about next steps. The four humans sat on a bench with the two animals resting quietly at their feet.

"What next?" asked Amber.

Lefty stood up, "Ahem," he said, and then launched into song. It was a difficult decision, but ultimately he rejected both *My Eyes Adored You*, and *Double Vision* in favor of the musical pep talk inherent in his final choice. "It's the, eye of the tiger it's the thrill of the fight. Rising up to the challenge of our rivals. And the last known survivor stalks his prey in the night and he's watching us all with the eye, of the tiger."

"I have to retrieve the eyes," Nikki said plainly.

"Are you sure?" Melia asked.

"I'm sure, I'm sure sure. I knew it before he even sang it."

"How are we going to find the eyes?" Amber asked.

"Everything is connected, there's not a person we met, a thing we saw or a discovery we made that isn't somehow linked to all of this. We have to go back to San Francisco. That man in the wheelchair, the one in the park," Nikki said, "He knows."

There was a new confidence and power in Nikki. She always knew her power, and trusted her intuition, be generally belittled it because she was always so concerned that somebody would contradict her, discount her. She hated being discounted, it was something that Kassen did with great regularity and it was one of their greatest problems. Well, that, his lying, the other women and his inability to commit.

"Is the car at the airport?" Amber asked.

"Yes," Jake answered.

They were all quiet again for a few minutes, pondering the enormity of the next step. If, in fact, the eyes could be retrieved, Melia and others could potentially get their vision back. That was on the positive side. On the negative side, the retrieval of the eyes would put Nikki, Amber and Lefty directly in the eye of the storm. The lion's (or tiger's) den. Oh My.

"OK," said Melia, "this feels right. Jake and I are going to go back and let Oprah know what we're doing. She's been apprehensive since Gayle lost her eyes, so it's important we keep her apprised. You three go back to the hotel and wait for us. We can stay at the airport tonight to make sure we get on the first flight in the morning."

"When you get to the hotel," Jake said, "Go to room 612. That's Xiu Shu's room. Tell him what we are going to do, but ask him please not to tell the others who have lost their eyes. The fewer people who know about this, the better. We don't want to tip off the Eye Stealer or unnecessarily get hopes up. Tell him to stay here. If we

226

get the eyes back, Melia and I will bring them back to Chicago, if it's feasible."

"Sure," said Amber. "We'll see you at the hotel later."

~~~

At 9:45PM Biy-Em, Demi and Luke were met by Matthew in baggage claim. Everybody was so tired and cranky that they completely forgot to look for Ray, who was still circling in El Paso. They climbed onto Matthew's now empty tour bus and left the airport.

At 9:47PM, Nikki, Amber, Lefty, Jake, Melia and Pilar arrived at O'Hare in one of Oprah's limos. As they passed a tour bus, Nikki shivered and knew they just passed Matthew. She smiled. "Buh-Bye, sweetie," she said. They checked the departure monitor and found a 6:05AM non-stop to San Francisco on American, and then went in search of the Admirals Club to try to catch some sleep.

30.
The Aura! The Aura

Biy-Em woke with a fuzzy aura. It felt sort of like a hangover, but rather than the hangover feeling being in his head or stomach, he felt it in the energy force that surrounded his entire body. The air around him hurt.

"Flew knew shouldn't do," he said to himself, puzzled by the words that came out of his mouth. He was quite certain that wasn't how the sentence formed in his head.

A shower was impossible, the thought of the water pelting his aura was excruciating. He dressed quickly, called the others in their rooms, and told them to meet him in the lobby. Well, he didn't say that exactly, it sounded more like this, "Elevator, see you later." Somehow they all got the point.

Demi was the first to arrive, rubber bracelet bedecked, and daikon odor perfumed. She touched Biy-Em on the arm, and before she could utter "Goddess Bless" he screamed.

"Aura, horra'," he explained. She didn't get it.

When Matthew and Luke arrived, and the four of them were all together, Biy-Em finally realized that Ray was missing.

"Ray, hey, where does he lay?" he asked.

Luke and Matthew exchanged concerned glances.

"Sir," Luke ventured bravely, "Perhaps it's not the best time to be playin' with words."

"Howard, coward, made my speech flowered."

"Are you sure?" Luke asked.

Biy-Em ignored him. "Ray, hey, where does he lay?" he asked, more agitated than before.

Luke explained to Matthew that Ray had been checked as baggage at Orange County airport, and they had obviously forgotten to claim him at O'Hare the night before.

"Not a biggie," said Matthew, "I'll just take the bus up to O'Hare and check with the lost luggage people. I'm airline folk, we deal with this kind of thing all the time. Besides, a few of the Herbalifers are leaving early and I need to see them off anyway."

"Hey, pray, no harm done Ray."

"Of course, Big Man," Matthew said, and patted Biy-Em on the shoulder. Biy-Em screamed.

"Jeez," said Matthew, "Homophobia!" and walked away in a huff.

"Now what?" asked Luke.

Biy-Em looked as though he were about to utter another rhyme, so Luke put his hand up to stop him. Biy-Em screamed again. Luke had inadvertently touched his aura.

"I think his aura might be infected," said Demi. "He really shouldn't have flown. We should get him to a shaman."

"Shaman famine," Biy-Em whined. They didn't get it.

"We need to get to Oprah," Luke said trying to get something productive happening. "I don't think they are taping today so we may have a wee problem gettin' in ta her. Sir, nod if you think we three should go to Oprah."

Biy-Em nodded, and then he groaned. Nodding hurt. It was going to be a long long day.

~~~

Nikki and Melia sat in seats together across the aisle from Jake and Amber. It was nice to have different company, and Nikki and Melia had a great conversation about nothing related to their current circumstances. They really didn't know each other well, so they spent time getting caught up on their personal histories.

Lefty and Pilar were apart from the group, at the rear of the plane in the galley, deep in conversation. If Nikki had known Lefty was speaking, she probably would have tried to find a way to eavesdrop, but she was so diverted from everything she had almost forgotten him.

Jake and Amber watched a *Big Brother* 5 reunion show. Amber was hooked, whether she would admit it or not.

A couple of hours into the flight Nikki and Melia decided to try a little omphaloskepsis to see if they had the same vision. The vision didn't fade until they started their decent into SFO. Though neither of them spoke it out loud, they both knew they had seen the same thing. Nikki touched Melia's arm encouragingly. Melia returned the encouragement; it was all up to Nikki.

~~~

Biy-Em, Luke and Demi were standing outside of Oprah's studios trying to devise a plan when Biy-Em's cell phone rang.

"Hello, bellow mellow yellow," he said and shook his head at himself, which of course, hurt. He didn't need this today.

"Uh, it's Matthew, and I'm at the airport and it seems as though somehow Ray has ended up in El Paso, Texas."

"Texas? Hex us!" Biy-Em replied. Nobody got it.

"Boss, could I please speak to Luke?"

Biy-Em wordlessly (thankfully) handed the phone to Luke, who listened to Matthew intently while holding his hand over his mouth to hide the wide grin that blossomed when he heard of Ray's plight. He hung up the phone and cleared his throat to try to stop the laughter from coming out.

"Seems that when our first flight was cancelled, little Ray was put on a flight to Dallas, where he ended up on the wrong conveyer belt and went to El Paso instead of O'Hare. They have him on the next flight out of El Paso and Matthew is waiting for his arrival." Luke fake coughed. "He is well, just a little dizzy and dehydrated but is in good spirits overall. Matthew spoke with him briefly."

The idea of an airline employee holding a phone up to Ray's ear almost caused Luke to completely lose it. He had to excuse himself and walked around the corner to have a good chuckle over the whole situation.

"Ray, OK, Emi-Day."

"Ank-thay oddess-Gay," replied Demi utilizing her Pig Latin skills.

"Oye Vey," said Luke returning in time to hear their absurd exchange.

With Ray accounted for, they went back to the business of discussing entry into Harpo Studios. There was a sign on the door that indicated that the offices were closed for the day, and would re-open the following day. They couldn't afford to lose any more time, but they were out of leads.

"Howard, coward! Knows where they showered," Biy-Em contributed.

"Sure and he does, boss, but it's not likely he'll tell us."

"I watched some Oprah shows before," ventured Demi, "I don't have a television, of course, but at the Goddess sanctuary they do and sometimes they would record episodes and play them for us at gatherings. There was a wonderful vegan chef once, and another inspirational episode on the power of prayer."

Demi stopped talking and stared blankly at nothing in particular. Luke thought perhaps there was a point to the story but failed to comprehend it. Perhaps she was suggesting they pray. He wasn't against the notion, per se, but wasn't quite sure that particular Big Man would be interested in furthering Luke's evil quest.

"Ms. Dai?" he said.

"Yes?" she answered as if she had completely forgotten she had just been speaking.

"You were speaking of Oprah."

"Oh, my Goddess, yes. I just wanted to say a little prayer. Whenever I can, I pray, and I said the word prayer and it reminded me to pray, so I did."

He lost her again. Silence and another blank stare.

"Pray, pray another day. Away today we've make to hay," Biy-Em announced. They sorta got it.

"At the end of the Oprah show, they give the name of the hotel where guests of the show stay. I remember that part because I wanted to call the man who wrote the book on the –"

Luke interrupted before she burst into spontaneous prayer again, "Which hotel was it, Ms. Dai?"

"I don't know," she said.

Luke actually pulled his own hair in frustration. The woman was maddening.

"But I thought we could catch a re-run," she finally finished. She *did* have a point, and it was surprisingly lucid.

Biy-Em looked at Luke smiling his approval, "Smart tart, but smelly fart."

~~~

Amber's white Rabbit was just where Jake and Melia had left it a few days earlier. It was cramped quarters with the four adults, two animals and myriad stuffed pillowcases. While Nikki rifled through hers looking for a CD, Amber drove them out of the airport and up the 101.

Nikki pulled the Alanis Morissette case out, and though she wasn't in the mood for Alanis, they only had four choices, and it was the first one she grabbed. She opened the case, and let out a squeal of delight, which scared the bejesus out of the rest of the car's occupants. Sitting inside of the Alanis Morissette *Supposed Former Infatuation Junkie* CD case was Pearl Jam's *No Code*.

"*No Code*," she screamed with glee, "*No Code*."

"Nik," Amber said half-wishing she could vote Nikki out of the car, "what the fuck are you talking about?"

"Alanis isn't in the Alanis CD case, Pearl Jam *No Code* is in the Alanis CD case," she turned around to look at Jake, "We have Pearl Jam!"

Even Jake thought Nikki was a little more excited than the situation warranted and he *loved* Pearl Jam. However, once Nikki put the CD into the player, and cranked up the volume, everybody felt a little bit better. A little bit lighter. It was the perfect respite from the non-stop clamor in their brains. Nikki replayed *Hail, Hail* four times in a row, and was going for number five when Amber shot her a, 'if you touch that button you will lose your hand' look.

They listened to Pearl Jam all the way to the Haight, and by the time they arrived, the mood in the group was universally giddy. They joked and laughed as they trudged up the stairs to Jake and Melia's apartment, and nobody even made a comment when they discovered the sixteen Pottery Barn catalogs in the mail.

~~~

Biy-Em, Luke and Demi Devi Dai had returned to the House of Blues hotel and sat in Biy-Em's room flipping through the channels searching for an *Oprah* rerun. It wasn't long before they found one, which ironically was about aura cleansing. Biy-Em and Luke were watching intently, entirely focused on the episode lest they should miss the hotel name and have to watch another.

Demi had pulled a sage wand out of her bag of tricks, and was currently using it in an attempt to set Biy-Em's speech back to rights. Under her breath she was chanting. Luke couldn't be sure but he thought she was repeating "Smart, tart, smelly fart" over and over as she tapped Biy-Em with the wand. He winced at every touch. He was still quite sensitive.

At the precise moment that Oprah's voice said, "Guests of the Oprah Winfrey show stay at the—" she was interrupted by Biy-Em's cell phone ringing. It startled them all, which caused Demi to scream and drop the lit sage wand onto Biy-Em's shoulder, which made him scream in pain, which made Luke scream in frustration because they'd missed the name of the hotel.

Luke grabbed the phone and answered it, "WHAT?" he screamed.

His end of the conversation sounded something like this.
"Right."

"Of course."

"I see."

"Today?"

"Of course."

"I'll let Dr. Seuss know," he said and hung up.

"Tease me, tease me, that don't please me," Biy-Em said.

"Sir, perhaps you shouldn't speak," Luke was stalling. The news was bad.

"What askew with Matthew, hoo hoo?" Biy-Em hit himself in the head in disgust and then he screamed from the pain.

"Uh, good news and bad news. The good news is that Ray will land in an hour's time. More good news, he found the Seeker and the Waker, and they are with another pair."

There was silence while Luke waited for a rhyming reply; there wasn't one so he continued. He said it really fast, like ripping off a Band-Aid, "Theygotonaflightatsixoclockthismorningandarecurre ntlyinsanfrancisco."

"Excuse me, don't refuse me, I don't think I heard. This thing you are saying, is Matthew assured?"

"Yes, sir," Luke replied, sullen, "He bumped into one of the early departing Lifers at the airport, they were standing by for the flight and couldn't get on and saw the six of them walk right past and board the plane."

Biy-Em looked at the clock, it was 3:00PM, and another day was wasted. "Fuck a duck," Biy-Em uttered. Everybody got it.

Demi's sage wanding went into overdrive.

~~~

Jake and Melia's apartment was very quiet. Everybody felt varying degrees of surreal, and like intruders in someone else's home. Nobody was quite sure what to do, and all at once the four humans began mundane tasks. Nikki rearranged the contents of her pillow case while Amber straightened the cushions on the couch. Jake organized the Pottery Barn catalogs in chronological order, and Melia felt her way to the bedroom to make her bed. They craved normality in any form it could take. The task ahead was big, filled with hope, yet teeming with danger. They knew how to begin, and yet once it was begun there was no turning back, so they delayed.

Since there wasn't much mundane to keep them occupied, they quickly made their way back in the living room and sat on the neatly arranged couch next to a perfect stack of Pottery Barn catalogs and a recently re-organized pillow case.

Lefty broke the silence with a reprise of *Eye of the Tiger*.

"We know, Left," said Nikki.

He looked at her with a 'well, what's the hold up?' look.

"You try it," she said, and then looked back at the group.

"Maybe we should go see Riley," Jake suggested.

If Melia could see, she and Nikki would have exchanged glances. As it was they moved their heads in each other's direction.

"What?" asked Amber, "Do you two know something you haven't told us?"

"Not really," Melia answered. "It's just dangerous, Nikki could lose her eyes, and I'm just not sure it's worth it."

"How about this," Jake suggested, "We'll talk to Riley today, and we'll come back here and discuss it. We won't make a final decision about the eyes until tomorrow."

"The problem is," Nikki interjected, "We don't know where the bad guys are. They could be in Southern Cal, they could be here. They could be in Chicago for all we know. That Matthew guy was there, so they obviously knew where we were."

"Well, that's good then," Amber said, "they are probably in Chicago which means we should go today. Let's do the damn thing."

"I might puke," Nikki took a deep breathe then said "OK, let's go see Riley."

~~~

Luke, Demi and Biy-Em were in a cab on the way to O'Hare. By the time they arrived, Ray would be in from El Paso and the five of them could decide what to do. The one advantage they currently had was that Luke could rainbow back to his apartment if commercial air wasn't going to get them back in time. The disadvantage to that was a trip of that length could leave him disoriented for several days and potentially do more harm than good. In truth, it was probably already too late.

~~~

Golden Gate Park was quiet. Though it was mid-afternoon, the dark sky gave the park a particularly ominous feel. The air bristled with energy that could only be described as electrified truth. Melia got goosebumps, and Nikki immediately saw light. She grabbed Melia by the hand and started pulling her in the direction of the light, "Can you see it?" she asked.

"No, but I can feel it," Melia answered.

Jake, Amber and the animals took off after the other two who were now at a full sprint toward an unknown destination.

Lefty stopped to howl, a sound that made everybody shiver including Pilar. Riley answered the call by wheeling himself toward the running group. He was bathed in light, glowing really. He looked like he had just wheeled his way through a nuclear reactor. It was eerie.

"Greetings, all! Pilar, Quentin," he nodded to the animals. "Jake, Melia, how are you doing dear? Much eye pain?"

"No, Riley, I'm fine," she said quietly.

"Amber, hello, and Nikki, glad to see you still have your eyes."

"Thanks, me too," she answered.

"Well," he said, "I see the five stars so you are making good progress. It won't be long now. What brings you here?"

"OK, I need to ask," it was Nikki, "does everybody else see that he is glowing, or is it just me?"

"They all do," Riley answered, "it's my time of the month." Glances of puzzlement were exchanged.

"So," Riley said again, "You are here because ...?"

"We think Nikki is supposed to get the eyes back," Jake answered, "And we were thinking that somehow you were a part of this and could give us some direction."

"Yes," Riley answered.

"So," Amber said, "Maybe you could tell us where the eyes are."

"They know," Riley indicated Nikki and Melia with a head tic.

"You know?" Jake asked Melia incredulous.

"They're in Dublin," Nikki said.

"Ireland?" Jake and Amber said in unison.

"California," answered Melia, "At the eye stealer's apartment."

"Why didn't you say anything?" it was Amber now.

Melia and Nikki shrugged.

"The problem is we don't know where exactly. We can see the apartment building, and the surrounding area, but we don't know the street or the exact apartment number, right Melia?" They still hadn't discussed it so Nikki was making some assumptions.

"Right," Melia answered. "The building is older. Tan

stucco, there's a big water stain on the side of the building and his apartment is across from the water-stained wall. The door is painted green, but I can't see the number."

Nikki took up the description, "There's a large terra cotta flower pot outside the door, and there are tulips in it that are somehow in un-seasonal bloom. Across from his building there is a grassy knoll, and then a pathway that leads to a park."

"A grassy knoll?" asked Amber.

"Not *that* grassy knoll."

"I know, but it's just so dramatic, so you. Do you even know what a knoll is?"

"Whatever, Amber, it seemed knoll-like. You want to play semantics? There is a grassy mound, does that make it easier to find?" Nikki was pissed and yelling.

"I was just teasing, Nik, you don't have to get all huffy."

Jake looked to Riley, smiled apologetically and said, "Can you help us find the eye stealer's apartment, Riley?"

"Well of course, I can. He's my son."

~~~

At O'Hare airport a freak storm moves in causing the cancellation of all outbound flights and the diversion of all inbound. Biy-Em suspects Howard as the culprit, but his rhyme is so convoluted, nobody understands him. Luke activates the rainbow.

In Cleveland, Ray, incredulous, is once again spinning around a baggage carousel.

In San Francisco, Nikki sits in bed in the Haight apartment, shivering. She doesn't know if it's from Riley's light, or from his story.

31.
In the Pink

Nikki was the last one up. She decided to forgo any mention of coffee, it was redundant, pointless and a little bit pathetic. Lefty and Pilar were lying by the front door. Jake and Amber were watching *The Apprentice*, Melia was watching her navel.

"Well," Nikki announced, "Everything here seems to be in order. I guess I'll go back to bed."

No response from the humans. Lefty rose and walked over to her, putting his head under her hand for a pat. "I think I need the pat, Lefty," she said as she lay down on the floor and placed Lefty's paw on her head. "That's better."

"Oh, you're up," Amber finally noticed.

On the television, Bill Rancic (winner: *The Apprentice* season one, and terribly bad golfer) entered the board room.

"Hey," Nikki got very animated, "That guy hit me in the head with a golf ball at a celebrity tournament. He still owes me a pair of sunglasses."

"If you ever need them again," said Jake, "I'll buy you a pair."

"Yeah," Nikki said and plopped down on the couch between Jake and Amber. "What time is it?"

"8:15," Amber answered.

"What's she doing?" Nikki asked with a nod in Melia's direction.

"She's watching a re-run of Riley's story," Jake replied.

"You can do that?"

Jake shrugged, "You're the one who came up with this stuff."

"That was some trippy shit last night, I can't believe that the dude who is after me cut off his own father's legs."

"Hey, he's short and he was pissed," Jake defended him irreverently.

Amber chimed in, "Do you think The Doors *The End* was playing on the stereo when he did it?"

Nikki joined the fray, "Father, I want to cut your legs off."

"Can you imagine afterward?" asked Jake, "When he tried to duct tape them on to his shoes?"

"He really got a leg up on dear old dad that time," said Amber.

Jake groaned, Nikki giggled. It wasn't a bit funny, none of it. It was just one of those things that was so incomprehensible that they had to joke about it to keep from becoming paralyzed by the fear.

"And what the hell was up with the marmalade? I didn't understand –" Jake was interrupted by Melia.

"STOP!" she yelled, "It's not funny. Riley almost died, and lost his son in the process. How can you make jokes about it? Maybe you'd like to tell some funny stories about when I lost my eyes? What a ball!"

The three looked sheepish. Duly reprimanded. They really hadn't meant any harm.

"We need to go. The longer we delay the more opposition we'll have. Hopefully we won't have any 'funny' stories to tell about Nikki when we get home."

"Sorry, Lia," Nikki said, "We were just scared and blowing off steam."

"We really didn't mean to be insensitive," Amber added.

"Let's just go."

~~~

Luke's Rainbow dropped him (literally) in his apartment at 4:30AM, landing him a bump on the head which rendered him slightly unconscious. He lay on the kitchen floor which was actually convenient since the eyeballs were in the refrigerator. By 7:30AM he regained a degree of consciousness. Actually, he was fully conscious but was suffering the after effects of a four-hour rainbow ride. This consisted of a constant swirl of color and total distortion of vision. Everything looked like *Fear and Loathing in Las Vegas*, on extra acid. He had zero depth perception.

It would be hours before he would be fully recuperated. One time he had taken the rainbow to Jamaica. He was out for three full days that trip, though he long suspected that Biy-Em had fed him some mushroom tea which was the real culprit. Regardless, he was stuck now. All he could do was hope that the Seeker didn't arrive before his strength returned.

He scooted on his stomach out into the front room and hoisted himself up onto the couch. He closed his eyes and saw Jelly Belly's. Not the good flavors either, the gross ones like Grass, Ear Wax and Vomit. The colors melded, they lullabied, he fell back to sleep and dreamed of Easter eggs.

~~~

At 9:59AM, Jake, Melia, Nikki, Amber, Lefty and Pilar stood on the grassy knoll in Dublin.

"Huh," said Amber, "It really is a knoll."

Nikki rolled her eyes. Her skin prickled, she looked around. She could feel Howard's presence. 'I'm starting to get good at this shit,' she thought. Howard's dark form, in lotus position, could be seen perched on top of the apartment building. He nodded and did his usual open arm welcome gesture. Nikki pointed him out to the group.

"I guess we know which apartment it is," said Jake who had relayed to Melia what they were all looking at.

"So, we go?" Nikki asked.

"We go," replied Amber.

"Only the Seeker can go," said Pilar.

"What?" Amber was taken aback. "We can't send her in there alone."

"Only the Seeker can go," Pilar repeated.

"Well, Lefty will go with her then," Jake suggested.

"*Only* the Seeker," Pilar was adamant.

"Fuck," said Nikki. "So *I* go."

She took a good long look around in case it was the last time she saw any of it. "I wish I could see the sun one more time, or the moon," she said as she hugged every member of her party. She walked down off of the knoll and turned back to the group, taking them all in.

"We'll have a celebratory American Spirit when you get back," Jake said by way of encouragement.

She turned around and began climbing the stairs to the apartment. "Jesus Christ," she muttered.

When she got to the top of the stairs she was breathless, more from nerves than exertion. Her heart was racing. The first thing she noticed was the terra cotta pot sitting next to the door. But there were no tulips in it, merely dirt. It made her nervous; it made her doubt the vision. But Howard was there, and Riley had given them pretty explicit directions so surely she must be in the right place.

Her hand went to the doorknob and turned it, knowing it would open without a key. Luke was directly in front of her, sleeping on the couch. She froze. It was like the statue game all over again, only this time there was no *Star Wars* wannabe controlling her. She counted to fifty in her mind to calm herself, and get her breath under control. He was sleeping, there was a chance she could retrieve the eyes and be gone before he woke up. A chance. A small chance. A chance the size of Rhode Island, compared to Alaskan sized failure.

Once she was calm enough, she walked into the apartment, finally grateful for her lack of shoes. She paused again. Every step she took sounded like an earthquake in her mind. Fortunately, the apartment was small and the kitchen just past the sleeping form of Luke. She would be able to keep an eye on him while she retrieved the eyes. She thought maybe there was a lame pun in there somewhere.

The refrigerator stood before her. Looming, ominous, stainless steel; it was a very nice fridge for an apartment. She reached out to open the door, but stopped herself. She needed a container, preferably a cooler that she could put ice in to maintain the eyes so that they could still be re-inserted. Most of them had to get on a flight to Chicago.

Looking around the kitchen she didn't see anything usable, so she decided to try the hall closet. Feeling much more confident since she'd been in the apartment ten minutes and Luke was still asleep, she opened the closet door. There was nothing in the closet but a bucket and a mop and an illustrated book about herbs, oh and a bright blue Coleman cooler. She high-fived herself, it looked silly but it felt good.

She threw a kitchen towel on the floor so that the cooler wouldn't make any noise when she set it down. She opened it up, took another deep breath, checked the couch and went for the freezer. There was a lovely assortment of Blue Ice, so she chose a few and lined the bottom of the cooler. Then she started laughing at herself – quietly of course. She had everything ready, but hadn't ever bothered to check to see if the eyes were even there. She had taken it on – ready? – blind faith.

She took another deep breath, put her hand on the refrigerator door handle and pulled it open. A screaming, piercing alarm went off.

~~~

"Holy Shit," cried Amber, "What is that?"
"She found the eyes," said Pilar, calm as always.

"We're supposed to just stand here?" demanded Jake.

"She'll figure it out, Jake," it was Melia now, "She has to."

From behind the group, Howard spoke. He was currently using sort of a Jerry Garcia laid-back-hippie kind of voice, sort of Tommy Chong-ish (Dave? Dave's not here.) The whole group jumped about three feet when they heard his voice. "She'll be fine, man. She knows what to do." He handed a lit joint to Jake with a hand that was currently missing a middle finger. Then he sat back down in his lotus position, began omphaloskepsis, and waited just like the rest of them.

Jake tossed the joint aside. He had enough paranoia for one day.

~~~

It was noon in Chicago, and Matthew, Demi Devi Dai, Biy-Em and Ray were finally boarding their flight to San Francisco. The weather had cleared, and flights started departing at 7:00AM. Once again, they had to go through the rigmarole of locating Ray and then awaiting his arrival.

When he finally arrived, Ray looked like shit. Many of his feathers still contained the flour that he used to lighten them, however, in the spots his mouth could reach it was more of a sticky residue. Apparently, nobody had thought to feed him so he had been living the last two days on flour remains. His white glove was covered in his own poo. The yellow rubber bracelet was remarkably unscathed.

He wasn't speaking to anybody. Even Biy-Em's rhymes couldn't get a reaction out of him, and he tried.

"Ray, hey, had a bad day?" Tenderly.

"Ray, no way, da airline will pay." Indignant.

"Ray, ole', just one flight today." Conciliatory.

It was clear there was no raising the little bird's spirits, so Biy-Em gave up. He did insist, however, (through the translation services of non-rhyming Matthew) that the airline allow Ray to be carried in the cabin. They reluctantly capitulated.

When Demi pulled out a stalk of daikon to munch on, Biy-Em grabbed it out of her hand and threw it into the trash. "De organic make me panic, four hours too long for your lil' poop song."

Matthew looked around. With Biy-Em's rhyming, and Ray's sulking, and Demi's – everything – he was, just this one time, the most normal person in the group. That tickled him pink. (Just

243

a light shade of pink, not the magenta sort, not hot pink, a light cool pink. In fact, he might prefer to be tickled another color. Maybe lime green. 'I'm tickled lime green,' he said to himself. He didn't think it worked so he went back to being pink. Once he was pink again he realized all the color coding of his tickleness certainly eliminated him from the most normal person in the group category. That made him blue. Not royal blue, but a -)

When they were all comfortably seated, with their seatbelts securely fastened, Demi blurted out, "Omni Suites."

Biy-Em gave her his most bewildered look, when Matthew chimed in, "That's where the Oprah guests stay."

"Too late my dear, for us to hear, it brings no cheer when we were so near!"

Matthew put on his headphones, feeling very very pink again.

~~~

Nikki, hand still on the refrigerator door, turned slowly around to find Luke standing at the kitchen entrance. He was, however, not standing still. He was listing back and forth, and was reaching for something in his pocket. Nikki panicked thinking he was getting a gun, and ducked behind the refrigerator door.

"Wow," Nikki said aloud not meaning to be antagonistic, but she was surprised, "You're shorter in person."

Luke pulled out his remote keychain, the alarm sound was sending waves of nausea through his very sensitive body and he wanted the noise to stop. Nikki peeked around the corner in time to see Luke hold up the remote, point it toward the refrigerator and push, which caused him to immediately disappear. The alarm was still screaming. He had inadvertently activated the rainbow transport.

"That was easy," Nikki said to herself and turned back to her task of locating the eyeballs. They were in the crisper. Forty-two Ziploc freezer bags, each clearly labeled in bright blue Sharpie with the name of victim and date of acquisition.

"Cool," she said and gently started transporting eyeballs from the crisper to the cooler. It started to make her a little bit nauseous and she burped. When she looked up from the burp, Luke was back but more wobbly than ever. This time he managed the correct button and the alarm stopped ringing.

"Jesus, that's a relief," she said, feeling a little more confident than she had realistically deserved to be. She threw the last of the eyeballs into the cooler, less gently than before sensing her time was running out.

Luke swaggered toward her, doing a John Wayne kind of thing, only not on purpose. She picked up the cooler which she hadn't managed to get the lid on. Luke stopped swaggering and pulled a baggie out of his pocket, and while he was trying to unzip it, Nikki kicked him as hard as she possibly could right between the legs.

"That's for Riley," she said as she grabbed the cooler lid and bolted to the door.

Luke moaned, but managed to stumble after her. After all, how much damage could a slipper sock do? Nikki was first out the door, and as she passed the terra cotta pot, red and yellow tulips sprang into bloom. She stopped to look at them for a moment, and heard the shouts of her crew on the knoll. They were jumping up and down and yelling something, but she couldn't hear.

Luke appeared in the doorway, so Nikki went running down the stairs. He tried to yell stop, which would have temporarily frozen her in her tracks, but all he got out was the "Sttttttttttttttttttt tttttttttttttttttttttttttttt." When he put his hand out to grab the railing of the stairs, his depth perception miscued and he missed, causing him to plummet down the stairs. He flew past Nikki and was on the ground, really unconscious this time, by the time she hit the last stair. She ran right past him and to the celebratory group on the grassy knoll.

She put down the cooler, put her hands on her knees and tried to catch her breath. She looked up at Amber, and said between breaths, "I gotta be honest," breath, "that was a little," breath, "anti-climatic."

Lefty said "Ahem," and the sky lightened, and while they were looking up the North Star blazed into view. Howard gave Nikki a thumbs up, as Lefty began to sing, *Supercalifragilisticexpialido cious.*

32.
Eye, Yeye, Yeye

After five hours of waiting for Ray, four hours of flying and two hours in Friday afternoon traffic, Biy-Em, Demi Devi Dai, Matthew and Ray finally pulled into the parking lot of Luke's apartment. Ray still wasn't speaking, Demi wasn't farting, Matthew was still in the pink, and Biy-Em's speech had returned to normal. He surmised it was an Illinois (pronounced Illionoise) affliction. Overall, things were looking up.

When they arrived at Luke's building, they found Luke sprawled unconscious at the bottom of the stairs. Ray started to laugh, which Biy-Em took as an encouraging sign. He lifted Luke to his shoulders, carried him up the stairs and tossed him (not gently) on the couch. Luke started to stir.

Biy-Em went to the kitchen. He knew what had happened, but needed to see it to believe it. When they started chasing this Seeker, he never could have imagined she would cause so much trouble. No one, *no one*, had ever retrieved all the eyes before. And yet, when he opened the crisper, he clearly saw that there was not a cornea to be had.

"Wake him up," he yelled to Matthew.

~~~

Melia was blinking a lot. They had followed Riley's instructions to the letter, and Nikki was meticulously recording every step of the process so that explicit directions could be taken to Chicago with the rest of the eyes.

First they had to dig through the cooler to find Melia's eyes. Nikki let Jake do that, she was pretty much eyed out. Then they had to be allowed to warm up a bit. Enough so that they would not cause a brain freeze when inserted, but not so much that they would begin to lose their potency. According to Riley, this was a delicate balance and it was better to err on the side of brain freeze caution. He suggested fifteen minutes of thaw.

While the thaw was occurring, the recipient had to do all possible to create natural moisture. It was recommended that they continually massage the eye sockets to produce tears. The eyes needed a warm moist area to reattach. This, of course, was in the absence of saline solution which would be an acceptable substitute. Nikki spent most of her documentation time with her lip curled in disgust and a slight gurgle in her tummy.

There was absolutely no way to tell the left eyeball from the right eyeball, this could only be determined once the eyes were inserted. Once both eyes were back in and the period of blinking had passed, the recipient would either look normal, or like the character at the beginning of Dr. Seuss's *I Had Trouble Getting to Solla Sollew.* (Page 9, each eye is going in an opposite direction. Can you get the book out? No, I know, not everybody has it readily available.)

The popping in of the eyes was really the easiest part. Again, Jake was given the honors. He really had no doubt which was Melia's left and right eye. He knew every inch of her, including the color inflections in her eyes. Since he couldn't wash his hands, he used the Ziploc as a glove of sorts. He found Melia's right eye, held her socket open with his fingers, and dropped the eyeball in. Nikki gagged. He repeated with the left eye, and the blinking began.

"It would be good if you could cry," said Amber. So Melia blinked and concentrated on sad thoughts, and Jake and Nikki went out for a smoke.

By the time they had finished smoking, the blinking was far less spasmodic. Melia was sitting on the couch, feeling dizzy, like the feeling when you get a new pair of glasses or contact lenses. Amber sat next to her and held her hands. Tears were streaming down her face, but now they were tears of joy.

"Amber," she touched Amber's face, "Is that a key print on your face?"

They *all* began crying happy tears, Pilar included – Lefty misted up – and then laughed simultaneously, they'd gotten used to the key print on Amber's face, so to see it through fresh eyes (literally) brought the hilarity of it back.

"I can't believe it worked," said Nikki. "I'm in complete awe right now."

Melia rose, walked up to Nikki and gave her a huge hug. "Thank you," she said.

"Just doin' my job, ma'am," she felt uncomfortable with the praise. In actual fact, retrieving the eyes had one of the easier aspects of the whole adventure.

"Nik," Melia said seriously, "Nobody else could have done it."

"Anybody could have done it, it was—"

"It was your task, and you were successful. Don't discount it. Celebrate! I told you that you were powerful, are you starting to believe?"

"All I did was open a refrigerator –"

"Nicole," said Amber, always particularly serious when she used her whole name, "It was dangerous, it was important, and you did it."

"I did," was the only reply Nikki could give.

~~~

Luke, meanwhile, was given a glass of water and three Advil. His head had bumps in two places, and there were bruises all over his body. He was getting zero sympathy. Quite the contrary, Ray was haranguing him endlessly, Demi was trying to get him to let go of all his negative energy, and Biy-Em was interrogating him. Matthew was giving himself a pedicure.

"She jus' walk in here and take da eyes?"

"Yes, I told ya sir. I was discombobulated from the Rainbow. Sure and you remember the time I came to Jamaica and I was out for three days?"

"Mon, you drank mushroom tea."

Luke shook his head, which really really hurt.

"So, where dey go now, mon? We need to get de eyes back before dey make it back to dey owners. We gonna have a Seeker epidemic we can't handle if we don't get dis taken care of."

"I don't know, sir."

"How you don't know?"

"I was unconscious."

"Ya mon, me know. You see the flower pot? She bring out the friendship and love flowers. Make me sick. She almost done. We don't stop her and dis game is over, we lose."

"I'm aware, sir."

Matthew yawned, a deep loud yawn. "I'm bored," he said, "Anybody want microwave popcorn?"

~~~

"So, what next?" Amber asked.

"Jake and I need to get the eyes to Chicago as quickly as possible. I think we'll try to take a red-eye tonight. A red eye. My eyes will be red," she grinned.

"I'd like to try to see Kassen," Nikki mumbled.

Lefty put the kibosh on that idea with his current little ditty.

"So," Amber said, "No Kassen. You still have three days, Nik. We're going to Disneyland."

"That we are, I guess" she answered. "You don't suppose that anybody's cats will be trying to steal any tongues, like Lefty's song says, do you? The eyes were one thing, but if I see any cut out tongues, I *will* barf."

"I don't think so," Jake answered, "I guess we should head to the airport."

"I'm so friggin' sick of the airport," said Nikki. "Do you want to drive to Anaheim, Amber?"

"If we take the car, Jake and Melia won't have transportation when they get back."

"True, but we may not have transport down there anyway. Who knows if the Datsun will still be there? Besides, we absolutely have to be back up here on Monday, it's the 12th. You have to at least give me that. What do you two think?"

"Yeah, sure, you can drive there. It's, what? A six hour drive, right?" Melia asked.

"Yes," Jake answered, "Just make sure you watch *Oprah* on Monday. We'll get a message to you somehow on the show, if we can. That way you'll know what we're doing."

"OK, good plan. We'll drop you at the airport on our way down south. And hey, good news. We're all already packed."

Nikki made big fuss about making sure that they keep the eyes with them at all times. She had re-copied the instructions on her rapidly dwindling paper, folded them up and personally placed them in Melia's pocket. She was like a new mother doting on her forty-one pairs of twins. No one dared tease her, she had earned the right.

"I put Xui's eyes right on top, Lia. You can do his right at the hotel and then get the rest to Oprah. Gayle's are there too. Have we forgotten anything?"

"I think we've covered every possible base," said Amber, "Let's hit it."

~~~

At San Jose airport, Biy-Em, Demi, Luke and Matthew are

waiting for the 7:18PM flight to Orange County. Ray flies south for his sanity. His baggage carousel days are over.

At San Francisco airport, Jake, Melia and Pilar wait for the 11:45PM to O'Hare. It's starting to be a commute for them.

On the 101 South, Nikki screams "Road Trip" while Amber puts the Doors in the CD player. It's not the same without Beef Jerky, Denny's coffee or cigarettes, but they're in the spirit of it anyway.

In Anaheim, Howard celebrates his significant lead with Lucy, his new significant other.

33.
Riders Aren't the Norm

There were throngs of people standing outside Disneyland waiting for it to open. Admissions were purchased, strollers were positioned, fanny packs were brimming and zipped, matching Hawaiian print shirts were pressed. At $46.00 per child admission and $56.00 per adult, the crowd was eager to get in and get their money's worth. The smell of popping popcorn began to drift over the crowd, and a large colorful bunch of Mickey Mouse balloons came into view. It was almost time.

"I'm kind of excited," Nikki told Amber, "I love Disneyland."

Amber issued a half-hearted agreement, she didn't really love Disneyland. She was more of a Six Flags kind of girl.

"I wonder what we're supposed to be doing here," Nikki said.

"No idea. There aren't any Mary Poppins attractions, are there?"

"No, but I keep thinking about, the lyrics. Do you think one powerful word could cause a life altering experience?"

"Who knows? So what are we going to do when we get in there?"

"I'd like to ride Indiana Jones, personally."

"You think we're going to ride rides?"

"Maybe. I mean, until we know what we're here to do we may as well enjoy it, right?"

"It's your thing, Nik. I'm just the wake up call."

"Look, the gates are opening. Let's go."

They entered the park with the masses, bumping into very white men lathered in sunscreen (still visible in gelatinous blobs), and very large women, already harried, surrounded by six children clamoring about various topics ranging from their hunger, which ride to go on first, and when they can get back to the hotel to play Nintendo. Hostile teenagers mingled with Japanese shutter-bugs (zoom, click, click, zoom) mingled with doting grandparents.

Disneyland, California: the pot where humanity comes to melt.

The sky, now medium dusk, cast a sinister aspect over what was supposed to be a very happy place. Upon entering the park, Nikki and Amber felt an immediate change in atmosphere. The air was oppressive, hot, everything felt claustrophobic, like there wasn't enough oxygen allotted for all the people

They walked down Main Street passing the lockers and the camera shop. Amber looked to her right and saw a makeshift kiosk with WWJD stenciled haphazardly on a cardboard sign. Old Tom and Chuckie Rightwing stood inside. Madge was pacing in front, getting right up behind passers-by yelling, "What would Jesus do?" and "Invited Christ to live in your heart yet?" Amber tried to distract Nikki, but it was too late. Nikki saw them as well. They crossed to the left, picked up their pace and kept walking.

They made a left at the Enchanted Tiki Room and as they passed the Jungle Cruise they both saw Biy-Em standing in line. Next to him was Matthew. "Hail, hail, the gang's all here," said Nikki. They picked it up to a light jog.

By the time they reached Indiana Jones, the line had already reached the 45-minute-wait-from-this-point, point. The Burke family was in line ahead of them. They knew they were the Burke family because they all wore matching t-shirts with "Burke Family" printed on the back. On the front were the family member's first names. Little Jenny already had to pee, and Tommy was bored.

"I can't believe the line is already this long," said Amber.

Nikki was distracted. "You know why getting the eyes seemed anti-climatic?" The Queen of the non-sequitur.

"Because it wasn't the climax?"

"Exactly. *This* is the climax. Jeez, I can't believe this line is already this long."

They were quiet for a while, absorbed in the Burke Family show. Lefty was amazed. He couldn't believe that people would pay $56.00 to stand in line for 45 minutes to experience a 3-minute ride. He was especially puzzled by the Burke children who really didn't seem like they wanted to be there at all. A group of Chinese got in line behind them evaporating any personal space that may have previously existed. They kept bumping into the trio, and Lefty's tail was stepped on several times. It was a very long 45 minutes.

The light (not literally) finally dawned at the end of the tunnel. They could see the Jeeps pulling up, and the eager line-waiters filing into them, and immediately filing back out. The Jeeps were pulling away empty. Nikki overheard one "rider" say, "That was great! Can we go again?" She was puzzled.

This kept happening, the Jeep would pull up, and the riders would walk on and then right back off. Not one jeep departed with a rider in it. Finally it was Nikki and Amber's turn. They got into the Jeep, with Lefty trailing behind, sat down and waited. Nothing happened. The Jeep didn't move. A Disney cast member approached the car, pulled out a Walkie Talkie and said, "We have a problem with car 427." A sign was posted outside that the ride was broken down. The Burke family parents were ecstatic that they'd gotten to ride before the breakdown, but the Chinese were bitterly disappointed.

Amber and Nikki continued to sit in the car waiting for it to move. Three ride engineers approached the car, and started to tinker under the hood. They were perplexed. After about twenty minutes, Amber grew restless so they exited the vehicle. The Jeep immediately took off, and the ride was re-opened.

"Uh, that was fucked," said Nikki. "How the hell am I supposed to figure this out? What does that mean?"

"Think about it, Nik," Amber thought she had figured it out while they were sitting in the stalled car.

"We got in line, waited our turn, but nothing happened at the end. The rules changed while we were in the line. Nobody actually got to ride the ride."

"And?"

"And, some of the people acted like they actually had ridden, and claimed they had fun."

"Right."

"So, they are just going through the motions?"

Amber shrugged, "Maybe."

"OK, I want to try Space Mountain. The exit is not in the same spot as the entrance like it is here."

"Sure," said Amber. What the hell? This wasn't *her* microcosm.

Wanting to avoid the Jungle Cruise ride lest less than savory characters were still queued there, they veered in the direction of New Orleans Square. Nikki was amazed that she still knew her way around. As they approached the Blue Bayou restaurant they saw Howard leaning against the building and approached him.

"Hey," Nikki said.

He patted Lefty on the head, and they seemed to have a little telepathic mini chat. Today Howard spoke in an East Indian accent, "Well hello there little Seeker, little Waker. Exciting, day? Yes? Just waiting for my girlfriend."

"Swell," said Amber.

"Uh, anything we should know Howard?"

Howard dropped all accents, and said in the plainest most serious voice he could muster, "As long as you are in the park, you are safe. If they get you out of the park before you are done, you're toast."

"And how will we know when we are done?" asked Amber.

Howard reverted to his East Indian accent and said, "Thank you, come again." That was all they were going to get, which was more than they really expected. They continued on their way, avoiding Main Street altogether, but got caught in a little bit of pedestrian traffic when they ran into Belle from *Beauty and the Beast* taking photos with shy would-be princesses.

"No wonder we all think we get to live the fairy tale," said Nikki, "It's crammed into our psyches from the time we are old enough to watch a DVD."

They passed Star Tours, and stopped in front of Honey I Shrunk the Audience, presented by Kodak. They stopped for a good reason. In front of the theatre was Ray, the Raven, flying through the air. On the ground below him was a Mickey Mouse ears hat (upside down) with a couple of quarters in it. It was a bad hat choice for coin collection as it was completely imbalanced and every few minutes Ray had to fly down and straighten it. Next to the hat was a sign that said, "Heck no, bring back EO." The word "hell" had been crossed out, and was replaced with the word "Heck." It was Disney after all.

Ray, in full flour powder, was flying through the air singing, *We Are Here to Change Your World*. (The EO anthem.)

"Oh my," said Nikki. And they continued walking toward Space Mountain, where the wait from their point was currently 60 minutes.

"OK," she looked at Amber once they were firmly entrenched in line between a French couple, and four young men with many tattoos and horrible body odor. "Who are we missing?"

"Well, the Eye Stealer for one. Hopefully he's not here."

"Yeah, hopefully he's dead. Those two weird *Dungeons and Dragons* guys from Fullerton, we haven't seen them."

"Right, and that chick from the colon cleansing place."

"Is that everybody?"

"OK, the bird, the black dude, the Christian guy, the time share people, and Honey, Sweetie, Baby Matthew are all here. We're missing the twins, the hippie chick, and the eye stealer. I think that's everybody."

"And Kassen. We don't really know which side Kassen is on."

"I'm pretty sure, Nik, that Kassen is on Kassen's side."

"OK, so we just keep our eyes out for them and stay away from them until I figure out why we're here, which must somehow have something to do with not getting to ride the rides even though we're waiting to ride them, then do something and then figure out what happens next. We're screwed."

"Wow," said Amber, "Really screwed."

Lefty burst into a little refrain of *Supercalifragilisticexpialidocious.*

They were screwed.

~~~

Space Mountain was no different than Indiana Jones. They were escorted onto the ride, and immediately escorted off. That time they had to walk quite a distance to reach the exit. They experienced the same thing at Splash Mountain, Pirates of the Caribbean, and Haunted Mansion. They had been at the park close to seven hours, most of it spent in line, and they hadn't ridden one ride.

"We'd better hit small world," suggested Amber.

"If that's the one ride we actually get to go on, I'm going to be really pissed."

After they were escorted on and off the boat at small world, they spotted Luke the Eye Stealer and Demi the colon cleanser. The twins and Kassen were the only ones missing, and Kassen was iffy. They bolted into Toon Town and sat on a bench in front of Roger Rabbit's Car Toon Spin with a Mexican grandmother who was holding an infant. Nikki's cell phone said 5:07PM. Toon Town felt hotter than the rest of the park.

"Grandparents get shafted at Disneyland," Nikki said, "They have to walk around all day and they don't get to do anything but wait."

"Kind of like us," Amber remarked.

"I've been thinking, and this day has reminded me a lot of our first week back home. Your class going up and down the step, going through the motions, but not really doing the work, you know? And my neighbors with their nightly block party, just sitting there staring at the grass with nothing to talk about."

Amber followed the line of thinking, but didn't see the point.

"So my point is that if people are just going through the

257

motions of life, then they aren't really experiencing it. And that in some way, we put restrictions on ourselves that keep us from getting to ... ride the ride, I guess. Does this make sense?"

"Everybody is asleep, and they forgot to set the alarm clock?"

"Yeah!"

The woman sitting on the bench with them was radiantly happy. Beaming love at her grandchild, who was beaming that love right back at her grandmother. "Yo no duermo," she said, then more slowly in English, "I am not asleep. I am awake, alive. This baby reveal my purpose and my passions. *She* was my alarm clock."

The woman stood, cradling the infant carefully. Once she was settled, she turned back toward Nikki and Amber, and lifted up the black Ray-Ban sunglasses she was wearing. Her eye sockets were empty. She turned and walked away.

Nikki didn't miss a beat, "So, our purpose is our alarm clock?"

"Sounds right, and until it is discovered we are not awake."

"Which is why you are a Waker, Amber. Because you not only know your purpose and your passions, but you help people realize theirs!" Nikki was animated.

She continued, "The thing is, though, that we can be derailed. Right? Like, like that Christian guy. He's only passionate about one thing, and because he's so narrow in his life view, he only experiences the life that's available to him in that small space. And that keeps him asleep. And it's not just this extremist stuff, but being focused on the wrong things or the wrong people. Like me, with Kassen. Or my obsession with being the exception all the time. I've always wanted the impossible because somehow that would set me apart. But by definition, I could never have the impossible, but my desire for it kept me from achieving what *was* possible. Is that plausible?"

"Good Morning," replied Amber, "Did you have a good sleep?"

"Fuckin-A," Nikki answered, and a seventh star popped into the night sky. "Shit, there's the leprechaun dude, and he was looking up when the star popped. We have to get out of here."

They started to run, "Can we go to the Whale ride, Nik?" Amber asked as they ducked behind Minnie's house to avoid being seen.

~~~

Luke picked up his cell phone and dialed Biy-Em's number. "She got the seventh star," he said.

"I and I seen it."

"We're runnin' outta time."

"Me know," Biy-Em was despondent.

"We need Ray, he has to fly around the park and locate her. Is he still on EO protest?"

"Ya mon."

"We need him," Luke was pleading.

"You better tell him, mon. And you better be nice about it, because he mad mad mad at you."

"It's not my fault he was lost luggage."

"What can I tell you, mon? He irrational. He thinks he Michael Jackson. Me get the others and meet you by the kid shrinking ting."

"I'll see you there, sir," and Luke disconnected. "Jasus, Mary and Joseph."

34.
Ding Dong, the Fairy Tale's Dead

Still Saturday, Week 4

Storybook Land Canal Boats were closed. They close at dusk. It had been dusk all day.

"I need to dump the fairy tales, Amber. Storybook Land is closed."

They both looked up at the sky expecting to see another star, or a little lightening. Anything to indicate they were on the right track. Instead, they saw Ray who had begun circling above their heads. He made a loud caw sound, followed by a "Heeeee."

"Shit," cried Amber and then Ray let one fly. The bird droppings landed on Nikki's shoulder. She looked at Lefty, because she knew Amber knew better, "Don't you dare laugh."

He hummed. *Supercalifragilisticexpialidocious.* (I'd like to just stop for a moment, reader, and tell you that Word can actually spell check the word Supercalifragilisticexpialidocious. Try it. I'll wait. Cool, huh?)

Two minutes later everything wasn't so expialidocious. While Nikki was trying to remove the bird poo from her arm – by wiping it on a nearby railing, which was really rather awkward and not particularly productive – Amber continued to watch the sky to follow the direction of the raven. Ray circled, seven times in all. Each circle over the heads of Nikki and Amber caused a star to blink out. After the third star, Amber called out, "Nik, look up. You better see this."

Nikki looked up and watched as the fourth star blinked out of existence. She looked at Lefty, who didn't look pleased, "Can he do this?" she asked. He didn't reply.

The last star to go was the North Star and once it was gone, so was the dusk. The sky went completely black, like the first day. Lefty let out a very loud, very mournful cry.

"Amber," Nikki called out in the dark, "Can you come here please?"

Amber followed her voice, and they stood together in the blackness. Amber put her hand on Nikki's shoulder, directly on the remainder of the bird shit. She emitted a little scream and wiped her hand on her Hello Kitty pillowcase. "Gross," she whined.

"Lefty," Nikki called out, "What are we supposed to do?"

Lefty joined the girls but didn't speak.

"Dude, this is really not the time to let me figure things out on my own. We have trouble here."

Lefty remained silent.

"OK, Amber, we need to move. Hold my hand, uh, your other hand please. Lefty stay close to us, please."

Their eyes were beginning to adjust. They could make out shapes.

"Dammit, I can't believe we are clear on this side of the park. We almost couldn't be any further from the exit."

"You can't leave anyway, Nik, you remember what Howard said. In fact, that's probably why this happened. They are trying to get us to leave."

"OK, you're right. Fantasyland is close by. Let's go there, we can hang out in Sleeping Beauty's castle and regroup, at least we'll be out of sight."

Disney in the pitch black was disquieting, menacing. Other people started to pass them by, seemingly oblivious to the darkness. But the people they saw were different than earlier in the day. There was a man in a red kilt; he passed so closely they could smell him. He smelled evil. They kept on and bumped into a couple of young men who were having a fist fight and yelling horrible things at each other. Nikki and Amber were almost brought into the fray. A group of vagrants were setting up a cardboard house, a lone prostitute walked Main Street and a small mob of frat boys unleashed an extreme hell week on some young pledges near King Arthur's Carousel.

Disneyland was suddenly a very *un*happy place.

They ducked into the small passageway in Sleeping Beauty's castle. Unfortunately, it was just a passageway and there was no where to hide for any length of time.

"Amber," Nikki's voice shook and she was panting, "I have no idea what to do. Tell me what to do."

Amber took Nikki's hands in her own and just stood there, psychically willing all her strength to enter Nikki. "I don't know, my friend," she answered. "But I believe in you, and we will figure this out. We've been at this too long. Failure is not an option."

A man standing outside the entryway lit a cigar. The sudden flash of orange light caught their attention and they peeked out of the castle in time to see every person in the vicinity scatter.

Nikki whispered, "That can't be good."

They ducked back out of view. "I don't want to alarm you," Amber whispered, "but I think that was the black dude."

"I know, I –"

Nikki was interrupted by a young girl's voice calling out in the darkness, "Mommy. Mommy."

They peered out again, the cigar smoking man was still there, and several feet away they recognized little Jenny Burke. Jenny was blonde, with huge blue eyes, and the most innocent face a child could have. There she was, standing alone in the middle of the blackness, crying out for her mother. Her fear broke Nikki's heart, and she knew she needed to help.

Before she could say anything to Amber, the cigar smoking man, who actually *was* Biy-Em, started chasing after Jenny. Nikki didn't think twice, and bolted out of the castle after them, cutting across a patch of grass, reaching Jenny before Biy-Em could.

The Big Man started to laugh, "You so predictable, Seeker." He pulled out a gun, licked it, and started menacingly toward Nikki. The gun, however, was pointed at Jenny. Amber and Lefty had almost reached the group, when Nikki yelled for Jenny to run and they took off. Lefty jumped onto Biy-Em's back. This had no effect other than to trip him up for mere seconds. They were separated from the Seeker. This was not supposed to happen!

Lefty slid down Biy-Em's back, as Biy-Em lumbered off in the direction of the Seeker and the little girl. He was quickly joined by his motley crew; Luke, Demi, Matthew, and Ray. His frantic, and somewhat threatening, phone call to the Crystal Cathedral had paid off, and he rested somewhat secure in the knowledge that the Bible Belters were strategically placed on Main Street. It was impossible for her to leave the park without his knowing it, and no way she could get out without an escort.

Little Jenny ran her heart out while Nikki yelled, "Call 911," to everybody she saw. It was obviously getting close to parade time. People were gathering on the sidewalks creating barriers to their quick passing. Rather than bumping through the crowds, Nikki pulled Jenny into a store where they tried to catch their breath.

Nikki went behind a counter and reached for a telephone. Disney storekeepers were on her in an instant, keeping her from the phone. "Call 911," she kept saying but nobody would oblige. She took Jenny's hand again and led her into the connecting store, which was, oddly, a bath products store. There was a big claw foot tub sitting in the middle of the room. Hanging above the tub, on very thick cables, was a Nordic Track elliptical machine and on top of that was a telephone.

"Christ," Nikki muttered as she crawled into the tub, and hoisted herself up on to the elliptical. Her balance was extraordinarily precarious. Her legs going back and forth on the machine, she looked down to check on Jenny before she made the call. Jenny was gone. No where to be seen.

"Shit," she yelled, and picked up the phone. It was a dial phone, not a push button and wavering in the air above the claw foot tub, she dialed 9 – 1 – 1. The call didn't go through. She disconnected and tried again. The second time she got a recording, "You've reached emergency services. All our agents our busy at this time. If you'd like to hold please press one now." Nikki had no one to press. "Otherwise, please leave your name and number at the tone and one of our emergency service specialists will return your call within 24-48 hours."

She slammed the phone down and began her precarious climb back down elliptical mountain, and when she reached the tub she muttered, "Christ," again. This time her mutter was answered. Chuckie Rightwing stood in the store's front entrance, bible in hand. "You called for Christ?" he asked.

Nikki looked back at the doorway which connected to the store she had just come from. Madge was in that doorway, pacing back and forth with her hands behind her back. She stopped, waved a finger at Nikki and said, "What would Jesus do?"

Her last option was the door toward the rear which connected to a different store on the other side, but she knew that if she checked that exit, Old Tom would be there. and facing him was not an option.

She paused and to reflect on her circumstance. She was standing in a claw foot tub, completely blocked in by Jesus freaks. 'Good summary,' she thought.

Acting quickly she kneeled on the edge of the tub and cried out, "I need redemption. I want to ask Jesus to live in my heart. Please save me."

Chuckie was at her side in a flash, being far more fervent and far less suspicious than the other two who held their places at the doors. He kneeled beside the tub, and bowed his head. As soon as his head was down, she hit it as hard as she possibly could on the edge of the tub, then vaulted off of his back and ran out the building. She ran right into Luke, and with such force, that once again she knocked him flat on his back.

"You know," she said to him, "This is my favorite view of

you." She stepped directly on his crotch and ran off. He wanted to grab her leg, he really did, but he just couldn't move his hands away from his throbbing groin (and just to point out, not throbbing in a trashy romance novel way).

With no sign of Lefty or Amber, Nikki kept pushing her way through the parade of parade gatherers, keeping her eyes peeled for people she recognized, both good and bad. When she thought she saw Matthew across the street she ducked behind a tall man. She looked up and saw that she was standing behind Mr. Burke. Nikki tapped him on the shoulder and held her finger to her lips and whispered to him, "I had Jenny. I tried to call 911, but while I was dialing she was taken from me. A 7 ½-foot-tall black man with tattoos all over him was after her. I don't know where she is, I'm sorry."

Mrs. Burke ran up to Mr. Burke; she was ashen. He quickly relayed what Nikki just told him and she perked up, "I know where she is," she said. The other three Burke children were huddled at end of Main Street at the statue in the center of the circle, and once they were collected, the six of them went in the direction of Indiana Jones.

When they got to Tarzan's Treehouse, Mrs. Burke ran up to the top, and appeared at the edge holding Jenny in her arms. Biy-Em was around the corner. Nikki had walked right into his trap. She instantly saw him and ducked back to Main Street. Even though it was close to the exit, there were so many people there she thought it would be easier to get lost in the massive crowds. All the Boot Camp classes in the world could not have prepared her for the aerobic adventure she had embarked on.

She stumbled into Matthew who quickly gave chase, then brushed right past Luke while Biy-Em brought up the rear. The hippie girl was missing and there was no sign of the cretins for Christ, so she kept running. Main Street had gotten even more chaotic. There was still no sign of Lefty and Amber. She needed a minute to catch her breath and think.

The prostitute started doing a strip tease in the middle of the street, the frat boys showed up and were offering beer bong shots to children waiting to see the parade. Just a few people down from them, the man in the red-kilt stole a woman's purse and began to run away. Fights broke out on every street corner, everybody was yelling, screaming, and in the case of children, crying. There was anger, tension, confusion, pain, sorrow, regret, disdain; it was Madnesspalooza.

Nikki stopped right where she was; she put her head down and stared into her belly. In that one moment she found complete peace and silence.

While eyes were buried in her navel, Chuckie approached and knocked her flat to the ground.

He yelled for back up, and Luke ran to the sound of his voice while fumbling for a Ziploc bag inside his coat pocket. Nikki wasn't having it.

She lifted her head and cried out, "I am Nicole the Great. I brought out the stars, I retrieved the eyes. I walked out of the chaos. I gave Oprah show ideas. I can do this."

Lefty's howl pierced the cacophony, he wasn't far away.

Luke was getting closer, but Chuckie had decided to pray for her soul and when he shut his eyes, she punched him in the general vicinity of his kidney. She didn't actually know where the kidney was, but she aimed for organs. It did the trick, and he toppled off of her.

And then, on impulse, she looked up at the sky and yelled, "Supercalifragilisticexpialidocious." The whole park was suddenly flooded with light, the sky was still dark (it was really night time) but the stars and the moon came out! The moon was three-quarters full. Nikki looked down the street and saw Amber and Lefty running her direction. The man in the red kilt returned the purse, the prostitute looked embarrassed and put on her clothes.

"Super-fucking-califragilisticexpialidocious," Nikki yelled again with joy. The speaker above her head started to crackle, she heard Christina Aguilera's voice whisper "Don't look at me," and then music began to play, and Christina's voice rang throughout the park. Everybody stopped what they were doing and began to sing along.

Every day is so wonderful
Then suddenly, it's hard to breathe
Now and then, I get insecure
From all the pain, I'm so ashamed

All around her people were putting down their things, and grabbing the hand of the person standing next to them. A Japanese tourist held hands with a frat boy, who held hands with Demi Devi Dai, and still everybody sang.

I am beautiful no matter what they say
Words can't bring me down

I am beautiful in every single way
Yes, words can't bring me down
So don't you bring me down today

Luke held hands with a French woman, who held hands with the Mexican grandmother, who held hands with Madge (poor sweet Grandmother). And everybody swayed to the music.

To all your friends, you're delirious
So consumed in all your doom
Trying hard to fill the emptiness
The pieces gone, left the puzzle undone
Is that the way it is

Nikki held hands with Chuckie, who held hands with a biker chick, who held hands with Lucy and everybody looked each other in the eyes and sang.

You are beautiful no matter what they say
Words can't bring you down
You are beautiful in every single way
Yes, words can't bring you down
Don't you bring me down today...

Right there, on Main Street USA, in that moment, it really was the happiest place on earth. Biy-Em held hands with Mrs. Burke, who held hands with the red kilt guy.

No matter what we do
No matter what we say
We're the song inside the tune
Full of beautiful mistakes
And everywhere we go
The sun will always shine
And tomorrow we might wake on the other side

Howard held hands with sunscreen blob guy, who held hands with Old Tom, who held Lefty by the tail, who had a paw on Amber's foot, who was holding hands with a teenager whose acne was just coming in.

'Cause we are beautiful no matter what they say

Yes, words won't bring us down, no
We are beautiful in every single way
Yes, words can't bring us down
So don't you bring me down today

When the song ended, Ray let out a gleeful "Heeeeeee," everybody laughed and clapped. Some even hugged goodbye, and the crowd dispersed. Nikki ran down Main Street toward Lefty and Amber. She had tears streaming down her face. It was over. The light was back, and everybody was beautiful and she was caught up in the emotion of the moment. She hugged Amber, and then sat down on the ground next to Lefty and rubbed her face in his fur. Her happy tears turned a little bit sad as she had a brief flash of the future, but she pushed it away, savoring the moment of her victory and knowing that she couldn't have done it without him.

Amber saw Biy-Em approach Howard, who was standing with his arm around Luke. Biy-Em held out his hand to Howard, who shook it and said, "Congratulations, Mon. Good game." Amber decided to keep that little observation to herself.

When Lefty had enough of being loved on, he issued an abrupt and a little choked up, "Ahem."

"Dude, I thought we were done with this," Nikki whined.

"It's time to go home," he spoke quietly.

"Let's go home," Amber said.

"Can we ride the Matterhorn first?" Nikki pleaded.

~~~

At Club 33 there is a big after party. Everybody is there. Howard is the man of the evening. People keep buying him tequila shots. It takes a lot to get him drunk. Later he'll be bloated from all the salt. Lucy is never far from his side. It turns out, you *can* get alcohol at Disneyland.

Biy-Em is not as depressed as he could be. It was a good round. Luke is on the dance floor with Demi Devi Dai, Chuckie Rightwing is in the corner discussing the bible with Ray.

Madge and Old Tom are trying to convince Matthew to change his evil ways and take a wife. They don't really get how gay Matthew is. They think he has a choice in the matter. They are ignorant, but beautiful of course, no matter what I say.

35.
Road Trip!

After four rides on the Matterhorn, (really this time, no waiting and immediately being escorted out) Lefty, Nikki and Amber spent the night in the parking lot in the Rabbit. The day dawned dusk. Whatever had happened the night before, the world was not yet set entirely to rights. There was a task yet to be accomplished.

They pulled out of the Disney parking lot early in the morning and made excellent time back to the Bay Area. Their spirits were buoyed, and all three of them sang along to Sublime's *40oz to Freedom* for the bulk of the trip. It was the best day they had in a long time.

Not having slept well the two previous evenings, once they arrived at the Haight apartment they went to bed and slept all the way through until morning.

36.
No Regrets, Coyote

Monday, Week 4

The intense version of Nikki woke early that morning. A whole day of relaxation was a little too much for her, and she was raring to go. The Kassen factor had been ignored as long as it could and today would be the day that it was dealt with.

The first words out of her mouth to Amber were, "It's the 12th."

"OK," Amber replied sleepily.

"I have to get to Kassen."

"What time is it?"

"7:08AM."

"OK, Nik, we have all day. Anyway, we have to be here to watch Oprah at 9:00AM so why don't you go back to sleep."

"I can't. Besides, what if Kassen dies before 9:00AM? Then I'll be sorry, won't I?"

"I'm sorry, now," Amber murmured.

"What?"

"Nothing."

~~~

"It's an eye popping miracle, on the next Oprah," the television blared. Amber was sitting on the couch, Nikki was pacing and Lefty was nosing through a catalog. Pottery Barn. A new one. Nikki bit her nails.

"Welcome to a live edition of Oprah," she started. "We have a show so fabulous, it just couldn't wait." Gayle was standing next to Oprah, peering at the audience. "Gayle, along with several others featured on my show over the last few weeks, has had her eyes restored. Jake and Melia Oneiric are here to tell the tale of the dramatic recovery and subsequent replacement of several pairs of eyes. Stay tuned."

Jake and Melia appeared on the screen, they were holding a sign that said, "WE'RE STAYING HERE." As soon as Nikki saw it, she powered off the television and said, "Let's go."

"Where are we going?" Amber asked.

"Kassen's office, I just want to see that he's OK."

~~~

After several U-turns, and one wrong way trip down a one way street, the white Rabbit finally pulled in front of Kassen's real estate office on Lombard Street.

"Now what?" Amber asked.

"Now, we wait," Nikki answered.

"We don't even know if he's here."

"I know, I have to get into their garage, and I can see if his car is in there." Nikki looked at her cell phone to check the time, "Huh, my cell phone battery is down a bar. Looks like things are starting to return to normal." The sky was still dusk, and the seven stars were still visible. "How's our gas?"

"The same."

"Just stay here for a minute. I'm going to see if I can get into the garage."

Before Nikki could get out, a car pulled up from out of the garage. It was a black BMW, and Kassen was driving. An Asian woman sat in the passenger seat.

"Follow them," Nikki told Amber.

They spent the entire day following Kassen and his myriad attractive female colleagues around the city. From his office, to various buildings, to lunch, back to the office, to another building, and then finally back to the office where he spent the bulk of the afternoon.

"Surveillance is boring," Amber commented, "And we are starting to use up gas. I'm not really sure what your plan is, Nik."

"My plan is to make sure Kassen isn't dead by the end of the day."

"Maybe you should warn him, or something? Just go in the office and tell him you had a premonition."

Nikki thought about it. "No …. No …. No. That's not … I'll know when. I'll know what to do."

Kassen left his office at 5:38PM. He went to the gym where he stayed until 7:19PM. By 7:45PM he was sitting at Aqua restaurant with a brunette, having dinner. At 10:10PM, they left the restaurant in separate cars. Nikki hoped he was going home. Alone.

They continued to follow. He reached his house at 10:41PM. 1 hour and 19 minutes left of the day Kassen was maybe going to die.

He sat in his garage for a few minutes. He was talking on the phone. At 10:50PM he opened his front door.

Nikki got out of the car, and said to Amber, "I'll be back in an hour and ten minutes." At 10:52PM she knocked on Kassen's door.

~~~

Amber motioned for Lefty to join her in the front seat. "This day has been mind-numbing," she said. "What do you want to bet she'll end up spending the night with him?"

Lefty answered, "If she does, then she'll have failed."

Amber was surprised by the response, not by what Lefty said, but the fact that he answered.

"So, all this *was* about Kassen?"

"No. This was about Nikki. The things she has forgotten about herself. But every Seeker gets a test in the end, and Kassen is her test."

"Should we take a walk?" Amber asked, really enjoying the non-singing version of Lefty.

"Certainly," he answered, and they walked and talked.

~~~

Kassen had barely set his keys down on his desk when he heard the knock at the door. He smiled, thinking his date had changed her mind about spending the night. When he opened the door and saw Nikki, he was surprised. Mostly because she had never once found his house without directions.

"Nikki," he said, "Nikki, Nikki, Nik?"

"Hi."

"I just got home."

"I know."

He was still wearing his suit and tie. They were standing in his tiny entryway. He invited her up, and they climbed the stairs to the second level. The kitchen-living room-dining room-entertainment room, level. He loosened his tie. It was awkward. They felt like strangers. And Nikki suddenly knew what Oprah meant about reciprocity.

Kassen finally reached out to hug her. She hugged him back and felt it again. Indifference.

"I just got home," he said.

273

"You mentioned that."

"What are you doing here, Nik?"

She told him about the vision. They climbed the second set of stairs to his bedroom. It was 11:02PM. He went to the bathroom, changed out of his suit and into sweats and a t-shirt. He brushed his teeth. He peed. It was 11:11PM.

"Do you want to take a shower, Nik? I can give you something to sleep in?"

"I'm not sleeping here, K. I'm leaving at midnight."

He went to his bed. It was a new bed, one she hadn't seen. A California King, with a dark green 700-thread count Egyptian cotton duvet. Nikki wondered how many women had already slept in that bed. He lay down, his head resting on a pillow with a cream colored sham. Maybe it was off white, maybe it was ecru. He motioned Nikki over, and she lay down next to him. He spooned her and kissed her on the shoulder. 'It would be so easy,' she thought.

And then she did that thing that she did. Started off in the middle of a conversation. He never knew what hit him. "Oprah said that what we feel for each other is reciprocal, which I knew was impossible because I know you don't love me."

He grinded against her, he had an erection. He rubbed her arm. "You know we always get into trouble when you watch Oprah. Kiss me," he said, very sexy. Very tempting. They never kissed anymore.

"I didn't watch Oprah, Kassen. I *met* Oprah. She told me that what we feel is reciprocal. I finally feel it too. It's indifference. All these years I've loved you and you've been indifferent to me."

"Nikki," he whined, he ran his hand down her leg, "Why do we have to talk about this right now? Let's just have fun." If they had been on the phone, he would have hung up on her and taken the phone off the hook. For now, seduction was his best option.

He moved her hand to his erect penis, she pulled it back. She turned to face him. She looked at his face, into his green eyes. "You're so beautiful," she said. She closed her eyes, a tear spilled out of her left eye.

"I always knew, you know. Even though I hoped for something different, I knew the truth deep down. We've had an unspoken agreement that a time would come where we would both walk away, and mean it. All those times we thought we meant it, all those times we both said we're done for good, and yet we always came back to each other."

He issued a deep sigh. He was getting frustrated. It was

11:29PM. Thirty-one minutes. Thirty-one minutes left with the man she loved for ten years.

"I kept hanging on. Because I loved you, because I was afraid I'd never meet anybody who could take your place, because a lot of the time you were better than nothing. But a lot of the time, nothing was better than you."

"Why are you here?" he yelled.

"I told you."

"It's just another one of your manipulations, Nik. I'm obviously not going to die, so you can go."

"You're going to die to me," she was crying in earnest now, indifference replaced with futility. "The thing is Kassen, that as much as I loved you I was always happier when you weren't a part of my life. Not calling when you said you were going to call. Not making plans to see me, not kissing me. Always telling me about the other women in your life. It was long, slow, torture. Year after year I tolerated more crap from you. All your stupid rules. 'Don't talk about this, don't ask me that, I am not having this conversation.' The sex even started to go. No kissing, no affection, no terms of endearment. Year after year it went by the wayside, until the very minimal amount I got from you became normal. Accepted. Never tolerable, though. Having you in my life was like driving a monster truck over eggshells. You convinced me that I didn't deserve more, and you kept me hooked.

"We could never be to each other what we had the potential to be. Nobody loves falling in love with potential as much as I do. And because we never reached it, I had a constant drive and longing that kept me stuck here far longer than I should have been. I learned in ten years, what I knew in ten months."

He stood up and walked to the dresser. He started arranging piles of coins. Nikki sat on the edge of the bed, her head bowed, tears streaming down her face. He didn't even get her a Kleenex. It was 11:42PM. 18 minutes. She started to panic. Could she really walk out?

"It's late, Nik," he said.

"I'm leaving soon," she sniffled. "Will you hug me please?"

He held her. Not for long, though. He never did. She cried onto his shoulder, (consciously aware that she was living the expression). He dropped his arms, but she held the hug. Alone. When she looked up there was a mascara smear on his t-shirt. The mascara smear that had been on her cheek for four weeks was finally gone. 'Good,' she thought, 'I hope it stains.'

She went into the bathroom, blew her nose and dried her tears. She squinted into the dark mirror; her face looked strange without the mascara. She'd gotten used to it. Like everything else. We adapt. Nikki wondered how many women had stood in this bathroom. It no longer mattered.

11:50PM. She took him by the hand, and led him down the first set of stairs. He hated holding hands, she did it on purpose. She looked around his apartment one last time. There were threads of her all over the apartment, a book, a CD, a photograph, an inside joke. She was woven into his tapestry, and when she departed it would not unravel. It was just a part of the scenery. As if it had always been there. Normal.

Nikki listened to a clock tick. She hadn't noticed it before. Her last minutes with Kassen and she had nothing to say. It was time to escape, the minutes slugged by. 11:53PM. He stacked paper into piles on the desk. He looked up at her, gave her sort of a "Well?" look. An impatient look.

Five minutes.

Four.

Three.

Two.

11:59PM. Kassen would live on earth, and she prayed as she walked down the stairs, he would never be resurrected to her. She felt strong.

Midnight. She hugged him again.

"I'm glad you lived," she said.

"Me too."

He gave her a quick, dispassionate, indifferent even, peck on the lips and said, "I'll call you tomorrow."

"Kassen?"

"Yeah, Nik?"

"I never want to be a person who goes to bed early in Vegas." Queen of the non-sequitur.

"What does that mean?"

"No regrets, Coyote. Rest in peace."

She walked down the last few steps to the waiting Rabbit. Her face beamed a broad smile.

37.
Nikki's Final Journal Entry

I'm almost out of paper, one more sheet and there won't be another inch of writing space. I spent most of the morning reading through my notes. Amber is reading a law book; things are returning to "normal" whatever normal means. It's odd how fluid normal is, it seems like it should really be a baseline and everything other than it is something else, but it's not the case. We're still at Jake and Melia's. We're going home tonight. It's going to be weird. It should feel normal but it won't for a few days. Normal is fluid.

The sky is a bit lighter today, there were some *Friends* re-runs on television, my cell phone is ready to die. Amber says that "hopefully" we'll have enough gas to get home. Still no coffee, though. That sucks. Lefty is sprawled on the couch. He looks exhausted.

I want to summarize this past month. Put the final piece in the puzzle, stand back and look at the finished product. Throw some Modge Podge on it and glue it all in place so that I will never forget what it looked like. But even now as I ponder, the puzzle pieces are changing shape and already some of the pieces I thought were important don't fit. Kassen doesn't fit. I obliterated his piece, cremated it, then scattered the ashes. There's a big hole in the puzzle where he used to be, I wonder if I will ever find a piece to fit there.

There are so many obvious clues, the edge pieces. Quick to identify, quick to assemble. Everybody is beautiful, everyone is loveable, every person is who they are supposed to be. The top edge is finished. We need to know ourselves, to believe in ourselves, recover our lost innocence. The bottom of the edge is done. We have to look within, right side complete. We have to overcome our detractors, the edge is whole.

The complexities lie in trying to figure out what the rest of it means. Is it all important, or is it a mind fuck to try to assign a lesson to every occurrence? A moral to each story?

I know that before this all began, I had lost track of some of my identity. As a child, I was creative with a wild imagination and a thirst for discovery. It's all still there, but I had lost the innocence that had connected me to that part of myself. I know that I got it back when I visited my youth. When I found the passport and the ring.

I think that I've always been so attached to Disneyland because it reminded me of that child who I was. But in a way I think I made Disney a benchmark ... every day should be the Happiest Day on Earth. Every story should have a happy ending, every girl is a Princess and Prince Charming is just around the corner, puckered up and waiting to plant the kiss that will serve as the first moment of happily ever after. But that's not life. There is no fairy Godmother to come and transform everything. It all comes from within, and as long as we look outside of ourselves, we will be disappointed. We will wait in the line, but we will never ride the rides.

The fairy tale is disempowering. The fairy tale is dead. I need to want what's possible.

I've been living in my past and condemning my future. Holding myself accountable for all the mistakes that I've made, remaining attached to outmoded ideals, and people. I've kept myself out of the present, which is just another form of denial really. Another excuse for failure.

I guess one of the best things I've gotten out of all of this is a belief in my power, in my abilities. I constantly sell myself short because I'm trying to cover up for my bitchiness and my inadequacies. But if Oprah, the most powerful woman I can think of, can benefit from my ideas, then I think I may just have a little something to offer the world.

I'm really almost out of paper.

I'm ready. I'm ready to reconnect with the goofy kid who played Lady in the Cupboard. I'm ready to let go of the past. I'm ready to be powerful without apologizing. I'm ready to dump the fairy tale. I'm ready to yearn for the possible. I'm ready to love a man who can (and will) love me back. I'm ready to complete my puzzle. I'm ready to see, I'm ready to wake. But most of all, I'm ready for a non-fat, Venti, two Splenda latte.

~~~

At 7:00PM, the sky returned entirely to normal. The moon shone brightly in the sky, and stars appeared like they rarely did in the city. Nikki could still pick out her seven. They would always be special to her.

They loaded up the Rabbit with their meager possessions. A

shower was starting to sound good, stomachs were displaying the first signs of appetite return, and bladder sensors were springing into action. They still didn't have any cash, though, so getting home presented a new challenge.

Amber got into the driver's seat, and Nikki popped her seat forward so that Lefty could jump in the back. He looked up at her with his big eyes, very much the same as when she first saw him. He said "Ahem."

"Oh God," said Nikki, "We *have* to be done!"

And then he sang ... "Na na na na," he was very choked up. Each "Na" sounded more like a croak. A tear slid down Nikki's cheek. "Na na na na." Nikki looked to Amber, who had also welled up. "Hey, hey, hey, Goodbye."

Amber got out of the car and walked over to the passenger side. She and Nikki both sat on the ground next to Lefty. "Nooooo," Nikki cried, "Not yet, I'm not ready."

Lefty kept singing, "Na na na na, na na na na, Hey hey hey, Goodbye."

They sat for a long time, Nikki and Amber hugging and petting Lefty and crying. Finally, he stood up. He knocked his do-rag off of his head with his paw, and pushed it toward Nikki with his nose. "So you'll have something to remember me by," he told her.

She was sobbing, "How could I ever forget you?"

"Everybody," he said, "Na na na na. Na na na na. Hey hey hey, goodbye."

And they all sang, through choked up throats, as Lefty turned and walked down the street. Every step he took he faded a little bit more until he had disappeared completely. Even after he was gone they could hear his voice, singing goodbye.

It was a long sad drive home.

38.
Home

Nikki's cell phone alarm clock rang at 7:30AM. She hit the snooze button. At 7:40AM it went off again. She turned it off and powered the phone on. The phone emitted a single beep. One new voice mail message.

She grabbed her pillow, intent on covering her head. The pillowcase was missing, which startled her enough to fully awaken her. Sitting straight up and bed and looking around the room, she saw the case on the floor next to her. "Huh," she said to herself. She turned on the light on her bedside table, then dialed her voice mail box. You have one new message, sent yesterday at 11:23PM. Kassen. As soon as she heard his voice she pressed three to delete.

She stood up, stretched and yawned loudly. The CD's strewn all over her floor and bed made her laugh. She picked them all up and put them away on her way to the kitchen. Gratefully, she managed to wrangle two scoops of coffee out of the near empty bag and started her coffee brewing. She returned to her bedroom and looked out the blinds. It was dark and cold looking outside. Windy. There was a diet Coke can in the middle of her front yard. "Trash day," she said to herself.

From the closet she grabbed a sweat shirt, threw it on and opened her front door. She moved her trash cans and recycling to the curb.

When she walked back into the house, the smell of coffee permeated the air. "Ahhhh," she sighed a happy contented coffee sigh, and went back into the kitchen. She took her *Happy Bunny* "Hey you made me throw up a little," mug out of the cupboard and poured the coffee. The smell made her mouth water. She took a sip, and said to herself "Nectar of the Gods." It was her morning ritual.

She went back into the bedroom, went pee for a really long time and then stepped onto the scale. 118.5. Fuckin' A.

Everything was so incredibly normal, and yet she was filled with a sense of abnormality. She went into her office and powered up her laptop. While it was booting up she noticed her Desert Island

CD list. She tore it up and threw it into the recycle bin. She took another sip of coffee and logged into her computer.

Another sip of coffee. It never tasted so good. She went back to the recycle bin and pulled out her CD list. She taped it back together. You never know.

She picked up the phone and dialed Amber.

"Hey," she said.

"Good morning," Amber replied.

"Have you had your coffee yet?"

"I've been up for hours, just getting ready to leave for school."

"Kassen left me a voice mail."

"And?"

"And, I don't know. I deleted it without listening to it."

"Good girl," Amber was pleased.

"Amber?"

"Yeah, Nik?"

"Was it all a dream?"

Afterward

The game had ended. It was a good round. The basement was littered with game debris, character sheets, notes and snack wrappers. Arthur and Lancelot sat on the couch surrounded by their brothers and sisters. The family played *Dungeons and Dragons* for years, but over time they grew bored and decided to create their own worlds. The Twins had both written and acted as Game Masters for their latest adventure.

"Good game, everyone," Arthur said.

Guinevere was particularly pleased with herself, since she had created the winning character, Nikki. With her twin sister, Igraine, as her partner, she knew from the start they had an unfair advantage. It wasn't often they got to play on the same team.

Morgana, their younger sister, had played Demi Devi Dai. Though the truth, infinitely stranger than fiction, was that Morgana was far more extreme than Demi and way more gassy. She was currently meditating on her loss.

Mordred was sulking in the corner. He too was on the losing side. He thought Biy-Em was a strong enough character, but he wished he had partnered with Bors instead of Gawain. Bors had created Howard, and Gawain had been Luke.

"I don't think you could have won without Oprah," said Mordred to Guinevere. "It's not fair that you were allowed to bring in real-life people."

"Arthur and Lancelot let us, and as the Game Masters if they allow it then it's fair. Besides, we had her on our character sheets from the beginning." Igraine defended her sister, whose idea Oprah had been.

Tristan was cleaning up empty Mountain Dew cans and Snickers candy bar wrappers. "I just don't see why we can't clean up as we go," he whined. He had been Matthew.

Percival sat in a corner, thanking Jesus for his close knit family. And though his part in the game had been small, he was happy that he had gotten to spread the world of the Lord through his three characters, Chuckie, Madge and Old Tom.

"That part about burning the Star Wars collection, Mordred, was brutal," said Lancelot. "You can't even joke about that stuff.

Next game, there will be no destroying of valuable action figure collections." He added after a bit more thought, "Or comic books."

Riley, their father, rolled down the ramp that led from the room upstairs. "Sounds like you're done kids."

"We are dad," answered Percival, "it was a good game,"

After the Afterward
(or before any of it, depending on how you want to look at it)

In ancient Greece, Aesop sits on the steps of the Parthenon with his son, Willie. He had just finished telling him the very long tale of the Seeker and the Waker.

"So, son," Aesop asks, "What do you think the moral of the story is?"

"The dishonest, if they act honestly, get no credit?" Aesop's son quotes from a previous lesson. He isn't all that bright.

"No."

"It is easy to be brave from a safe distance?"

"No. Son, you're not trying."

"Ah, I know ... every tale is not to be believed."

"No."

"Our mere anticipations of life outrun its realities?"

"Closer," Aesop says, adjusting his toga.

"Necessity is the mother of invention."

"I have a headache," Aesop mutters.

A raven flies overhead. A far away echo of "Hoooo" can be heard.

"Dad, is there really a Jesus?"

"Not yet, son."

The End

Acknowledgements

Thank you to those who inspire me ....

Holly – Who really put Nayonaise in my refrigerator
Nina – Who inspired me in ways that shall remain unspoken, and
was the first to finish reading the first draft
Mom and Daddy – For giving me a love of music at an early age,
which has apparently stayed with me forever, because two of my top
five records of all time are from my childhood
Celexa – whose side effects include vivid dreaming
Rachael – For reminding me to keep my ass small and my dreams
big
Shelley – The Hallmark Phenomenon (and sneeze support, and
myriad other observations)
Tricia – For laughter and memories since 1974 (do *you* remember
those fries?)
Valerie – For always, *always* "getting it"
Heidi – For unwavering honesty and support
Kent – Shanghai, Coyote
Karl – Are you talking about me?
Eddie – for mad editing skills and encouragement
Michael – for even more editing, and some wicked art
My friends – for EVERYTHING

Fan Club:
Oprah – For awakening goodness in humanity
Tom Robbins – For every word you've ever written (except "The",
I can't really give credit for "The" so for all the words you've ever
written with the exception of "The")
Christopher Moore – Who is not only an amazing author, but a
great person, who spends time with his readers everyday. (And to
the Divi of the Fruit Bat Boardello, thank you for your friendship,
tremendous support and advice along the way.)
Mark Burnett and the rest of the reality TV gurus – what can I say? I
love it!
Joni Mitchell, Eddie Vedder and the rest of the brilliant musicians in

the world – I'm doing that Wayne's World not worthy thingy. You'd think as a writer I could some up with some words, but that's what springs to mind when I think of music.

Tom – There's so many things I'd like to – Sorry! An unexpected error has occurred.

Practically speaking:

Karen Townsend, my editor, thank you for believing in my book!

And to my fellow Bizarro authors, thank you for paving the way

Music:

When I first submitted this novel for publication it had a soundtrack 22 songs long. And then I learned about Copyright Permissions. Changes were made.

I am grateful for the permission I was granted to use lyrics from the following artists:

Na Na Hey Hey Kiss Him Goodbye
Words and Music by GARY DE CARLO, DALE FRASHUER AND
PAUL LEKA

About the Author

NICOLE DEL SESTO lives in Northern California. She likes peanut butter, the color grey and googling herself. She gets very crabby when she's hungry.

For more random information about Nicole, please visit her on MySpace www.myspace.com/nicoledelsesto

This is her first novel. She sincerely hopes you liked it.

Join the Army of the 12 Nikki's at www.allencompassingtrip.com

About the Artist

MICHAEL SHIRLEY lives in Melbourne, Australia and has always wanted to write one of these bios but is feeling rather awkward now that he is doing so. He would like to ink comic books or write movies for a living, preferably both, but also thinks doing more book covers would be cool. You can meet him online at www.myspace.com/rogue_elephant, see more artwork at http://rogue-elephant.deviantart.com or contact him at bingopyjama@gmail.com.

Coming Soon:

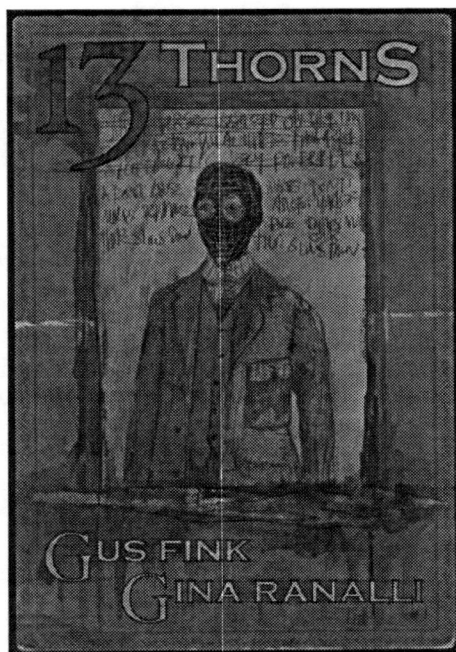

13 Thorns by Gina Ranalli and Gus Fink

13 tales of twisted, bizarro horror, from author Gina Ranalli and outsider artist Gus Fink. With Ranalli at the helm, and illustrated with drawings in Fink's unique style, fans of both of their work will want to see this, as well as anyone interested in a dark walk on the wild side.

Table of Contents

$13.00, 1-933929-13-8

www.afterbirthbooks.com

Coming Soon:

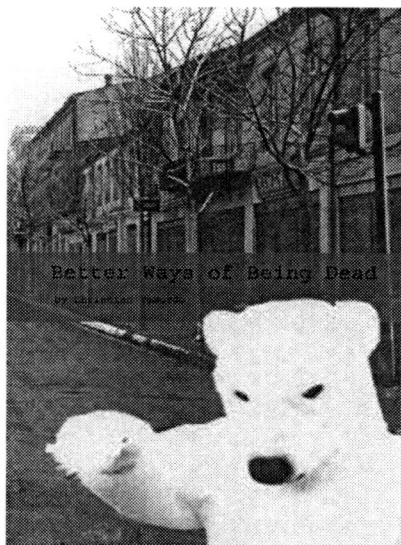

Better Ways of Being Dead by Christian TeBordo
Advanced Recomposition. He only needs one more elective, any
elective. However, in this class, the students have to keep one
palm down on the table at all times, and listen to lectures about a
panda who speaks Chinese. Surely there must be a better way to
get health insurance to cover his chronic congenital dermatitis…

The Cocoon of Terror by Jason Earls
Zelian Kurveg is an artist. One of the greatest in the world. But
he also has no conscience and is willing to take extreme liberties
with any living creature. He is on a mission to collect corpses—
decapitated corpses—for his masterpiece, "The Cocoon of
Terror."

And watch for:
Super Cell Anemia by Duncan Barlow
Wall of Kiss by Gina Ranalli
Help! A Bear is Eating Me! by Mykle Hansen

www.afterbirthbooks.com

Available Now from Afterbirth Books:

Suicide Girls in the Afterlife by **Gina Ranalli**
After Pogue commits suicide, she unexpectedly finds herself an unwilling "guest" at a hotel in the Afterlife, where she meets a group of bizarre characters, including a goth Satan, a hippie Jesus, and an alien-human hybrid. From the author of *Chemical Gardens*.
    "*Suicide Girls in the Afterlife* is weird and fun and hauntingly bittersweet. I read it in one evening and enjoyed it very much."
—Brian Keene, author of *The Rising* and *The Conqueror Worms*
$8.95, 100 pgs

Tales from the Vinegar Wasteland by **Ray Fracalossy**
One part surrealist farce, one part psychotic hallucination, this story begins with a visit from a friend who has been slowly losing his face. Other events include visiting a house with a non-existing room, purchasing photos of things that never happened, and attempting to read the book *What You'll Never Finish*.
$13.95, 220 pgs.

Chemical Gardens by **Gina Ranalli**
It's a night like any other for punk rock band Green is the Enemy.But things don't go exactly as planned. An 8.5 earthquake sends them to The Underground, hidden beneath the streets of Seattle, and it is here that the band finds themselves trapped and somehow vastly…changed. How will they escape this bizarre subterranean nightmare?.
$12.95, 188 pgs.

Deity (The Almighty's Adventures on Earth and Beyond) by **Vic Mudd**
Here's the first thing you should know about God: he doesn't like to be called "God." And he isn't crazy about churches, crucifixes or having his own pronoun capitalized. But once he decides to play all-American boy to help him decide if the human race is worth saving, he finds himself at a crossroads and discovers that his "typical" family is far from typical and the world at large is crazier than even He ever imagined.
$11.95, 168 pgs.

It Came from Below the Belt by Bradley Sands, *$12.95, 204 pgs.*

Pocket Full of Loose Razorblades by John Edward Lawson, $12.95, 190 pgs.

Find these and other Afterbirth titles on our website, through the Bizarro Books outlet (see order form on back page), at shocklines.com or Amazon.com, or ask your bookseller to order for you.

www.afterbirthbooks.com

What is Bizarro?

Is Bizarro a new thing?

Bizarro isn't really a new genre. Just a new term. For decades, people have been going into bookstores and video stores looking for the weird stuff. To them, "weird stuff" is a genre, just like horror or science fiction. But it has never been given an official name before. Until now.

What makes a book or film Bizarro?

Basically, if an audience enjoys a book or film primarily because of its weirdness, then it is Bizarro. Weirdness might not be the work's only appealing quality, but it is the major one.

Why bother labeling this at all?

It's all about the audience. A lot of people love this type of work but have difficulty finding it. They don't even know what to call it. Well, by creating the Bizarro genre this just makes it easier for readers to find Bizarro books and films. It also makes marketing to the Bizarro audience a bit easier.

Where can I buy Bizarro books?

Due to the underground anti-mainstream nature of the books, you'll most likely have to buy them through online retailers, such as amazon.com, shocklines. com, projectpulp.com, or genremall.com. You can get them from the websites of Bizarro publishers, such as Afterbirth Books, Eraserhead Press, or Raw Dog Screaming Press. Or ask your local bookseller to special order them! Let bookstores know this is the kind of thing you want to see more of on their shelves. Someday we hope you'll find a section labelled "Bizarro" alongside the sections for science fiction, fantasy, or horror.

Come visit us at www. MondoBizarroForum.net

The Bizarro Starter Kit
from Bizarro Books

(A cooperative venture of Eraserhead Press, Raw Dog Screaming Press, and Afterbirth Books)

There's a new genre rising from the underground. Its name: BIZARRO. For years, readers have been asking for a category of fiction dedicated to the weird, crazy, cult side of storytelling that has become a staple in the film industry (with directors such as David Lynch, Takashi Miike, Tim Burton, and Lloyd Kaufman) but has been largely ignored in the literary world, until now.

The Bizarro Starter Kit features short novels and stories by ten of the leading authors in the bizarro genre: D. Harlan Wilson, Carlton Mellick III, Jeremy Robert Johnson, Kevin L Donihe, Gina Ranalli, Andre Duza, Vincent W. Sakowski, Steve Beard, John Edward Lawson and Bruce Taylor.

$10.00, 236 pages

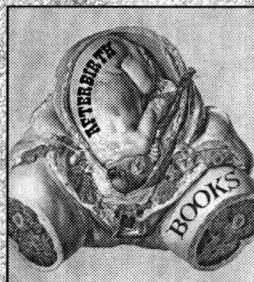

BB-001 "The Kafka Effekt" D. Harlan Wilson - A collection of forty-four irreal short stories loosely written in the vein of Franz Kafka, with more than a pinch of William S. Burroughs sprinkled on top. **211 pages $14**

BB-002 "Satan Burger" Carlton Mellick III - The cult novel that put Carlton Mellick III on the map ... Six punks get jobs at a fast food restaurant owned by the devil in a city violently overpopulated by surreal alien cultures. **236 pages $14**

BB-003 "Some Things Are Better Left Unplugged" Vincent Sakwoski - Join The Man and his Nemesis, the obese tabby, for a nightmare roller coaster ride into this postmodern fantasy. **152 pages $10**

BB-004 "Shall We Gather At the Garden?" Kevin L Donihe - Donihe's Debut novel. Midgets take over the world, The Church of Lionel Richie vs. The Church of the Byrds, plant porn and more! **244 pages $14**

BB-005 "Razor Wire Pubic Hair" Carlton Mellick III - A genderless humandildo is purchased by a razor dominatrix and brought into her nightmarish world of bizarre sex and mutilation. **176 pages $11**

BB-006 "Stranger on the Loose" D. Harlan Wilson - The fiction of Wilson's 2nd collection is planted in the soil of normalcy, but what grows out of that soil is a dark, witty, otherworldly jungle... **228 pages $14**

BB-007 "The Baby Jesus Butt Plug" Carlton Mellick III - Using clones of the Baby Jesus for anal sex will be the hip sex fetish of the future. **92 pages $10**

BB-008 "Fishyfleshed" Carlton Mellick III - The world of the past is an illogical flatland lacking in dimension and color, a sick-scape of crispy squid people wandering the desert for no apparent reason. **260 pages $14**

BB-009 **"Dead Bitch Army"** Andre Duza - Step into a world filled with racist teenagers, cannibals, 100 warped Uncle Sams, automobiles with razor-sharp teeth, living graffiti, and a pissed-off zombie bitch out for revenge. **344 pages** **$16**

BB-010 **"The Menstruating Mall"** Carlton Mellick III *"The Breakfast Club* meets *Chopping Mall* as directed by David Lynch." - Brian Keene **212 pages** **$12**

BB-011 **"Angel Dust Apocalypse"** Jeremy Robert Johnson - Meth-heads, man-made monsters, and murderous Neo-Nazis. "Seriously amazing short stories..." - Chuck Palahniuk, author of *Fight Club* **184 pages** **$11**

BB-012 **"Ocean of Lard"** Kevin L Donihe / Carlton Mellick III - A parody of those old Choose Your Own Adventure kid's books about some very odd pirates sailing on a sea made of animal fat. **176 pages** **$12**

BB-013 **"Last Burn in Hell"** John Edward Lawson - From his lurid angst-affair with a lesbian music diva to his ascendance as unlikely pop icon the one constant for Kenrick Brimley, official state prison gigolo, is he's got no clue what he's doing. **172 pages** **$14**

BB-014 **"Tangerinephant"** Kevin Dole 2 - TV-obsessed aliens have abducted Michael Tangerinephant in this bizarro combination of science fiction, satire, and surrealism. **164 pages** **$11**

BB-015 **"Foop!"** Chris Genoa - Strange happenings are going on at Dactyl, Inc, the world's first and only time travel tourism company.
"A surreal pie in the face!" - Christopher Moore **300 pages** **$14**

BB-016 **"Spider Pie"** Alyssa Sturgill - A one-way trip down a rabbit hole inhabited by sexual deviants and friendly monsters, fairytale beginnings and hideous endings. **104 pages** **$11**

BB-017 **"The Unauthorized Woman"** Efrem Emerson - Enter the world of the inner freak, a landscape populated by the pre-dead and morticioners, by cockroaches and 300-lb robots. **104 pages $11**

BB-018 **"Fugue XXIX"** Forrest Aguirre - Tales from the fringe of speculative literary fiction where innovative minds dream up the future's uncharted territories while mining forgotten treasures of the past. **220 pages $16**

BB-019 **"Pocket Full of Loose Razorblades"** John Edward Lawson - A collection of dark bizarro stories. From a giant rectum to a foot-fungus factory to a girl with a biforked tongue. **190 pages $13**

BB-020 **"Punk Land"** Carlton Mellick III - In the punk version of Heaven, the anarchist utopia is threatened by corporate fascism and only Goblin, Mortician's sperm, and a blue-mohawked female assassin named Shark Girl can stop them. **284 pages $15**

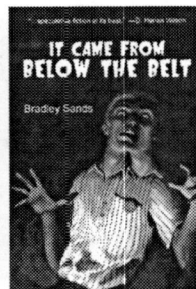

BB-021 **"Pseudo-City"** D. Harlan Wilson - Pseudo-City exposes what waits in the bathroom stall, under the manhole cover and in the corporate boardroom, all in a way that can only be described as mind-bogglingly irreal. **220 pages $16**

BB-022 **"Kafka's Uncle and Other Strange Tales"** Bruce Taylor - Anslenot and his giant tarantula (tormentor? fri-end?) wander a desecrated world in this novel and collection of stories from Mr. Magic Realism Himself. **348 pages $17**

BB-023 **"Sex and Death In Television Town"** Carlton Mellick III - In the old west, a gang of hermaphrodite gunslingers take refuge from a demon plague in Telos: a town where its citizens have televisions instead of heads. **184 pages $12**

BB-024 **"It Came From Below The Belt"** Bradley Sands - What can Grover Goldstein do when his severed, sentient penis forces him to return to high school and help it win the presidential election? **204 pages $13**

BB-025 **"Sick: An Anthology of Illness"** **John Lawson, editor** - These Sick stories are horrendous and hilarious dissections of creative minds on the scalpel's edge. **296 pages $16**

BB-026 **"Tempting Disaster"** **John Lawson, editor** - A shocking and alluring anthology from the fringe that examines our culture's obsession with taboos. **260 pages $16**

BB-027 **"Siren Promised"** **Jeremy Robert Johnson** - Nominated for the Bram Stoker Award. A potent mix of bad drugs, bad dreams, brutal bad guys, and surreal/incredible art by Alan M. Clark. **190 pages $13**

BB-028 **"Chemical Gardens"** **Gina Ranalli** - Ro and punk band *Green is the Enemy* find Kreepkins, a surfer-dude warlock, a vengeful demon, and a Metal Priestess in their way as they try to escape an underground nightmare. **188 pages $13**

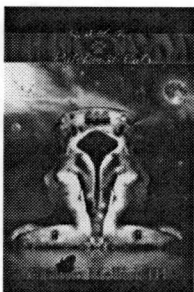

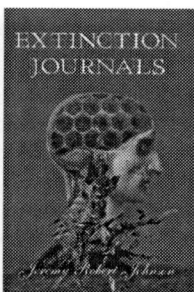

BB-029 **"Jesus Freaks"** **Andre Duza** For God so loved the world that he gave his only two begotten sons... and a few million zombies. **400 pages $16**

BB-030 **"Grape City"** **Kevin L. Donihe** - More Donihe-style comedic bizarro about a demon named Charles who is forced to work a minimum wage job on Earth after Hell goes out of business. **108 pages $10**

BB-031"Sea of the Patchwork Cats" **Carlton Mellick III** - A quiet dreamlike tale set in the ashes of the human race. For Mellick enthusiasts who also adore *The Twilight Zone*. **112 pages $10**

BB-032 **"Extinction Journals"** **Jeremy Robert Johnson** **104 pages** - An uncanny voyage across a newly nuclear America where one man must confront the problems associated with loneliness, insane dieties, radiation, love, and an ever-evolving cockroach suit with a mind of its own. **104 pages $10**

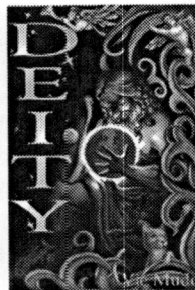

BB-033 "Meat Puppet Cabaret" Steve Beard At last! The secret connection between Jack the Ripper and Princess Diana's death revealed! **240 pages $16 / $30**

BB-034 "The Greatest Fucking Moment in Sports" Kevin L. Donihe - In the tradition of the surreal anti-sitcom *Get A Life* comes a tale of triumph and agape love from the master of comedic bizarro. **108 pages $10**

BB-035 "The Troublesome Amputee" John Edward Lawson - Disturbing verse from a man who truly believes nothing is sacred and intends to prove it. **104 pages $9**

BB-036 "Deity" Vic Mudd God (who doesn't like to be called "God") comes down to a typical, suburban, Ohio family for a little vacation—but it doesn't turn out to be as relaxing as He had hoped it would be... **168 pages $12**

BB-037 "The Haunted Vagina" Carlton Mellick III - It's difficult to love a woman whose vagina is a gateway to the world of the dead. **132 pages $10**

BB-038 "Tales from the Vinegar Wasteland" Ray Fracalossy - Witness: a man is slowly losing his face, a neighbor who periodically screams out for no apparent reason, and a house with a room that doesn't actually exist. **240 pages $14**

BB-039 "Suicide Girls in the Afterlife" Gina Ranalli - After Pogue commits suicide, she unexpectedly finds herself an unwilling "guest" at a hotel in the Afterlife, where she meets a group of bizarre characters, including a goth Satan, a hippie Jesus, and an alien-human hybrid. **100 pages $9**

BB-040 "And Your Point Is?" Steve Aylett - In this follow-up to LINT multiple authors provide critical commentary and essays about Jeff Lint's mind-bending literature. **104 pages $11**

BB-041 "Not Quite One of the Boys" Vincent Sakowski -While drug-dealer Maxi drinks with Dante in purgatory, God and Satan play a little tri-level chess and do a little bargaining over his business partner, Vinnie, who is still left on earth. **220 pages $14**

COMING SOON:

"Misadventures in a Thumbnail Universe" by Vincent Sakowski

"House of Houses" by Kevin Donihe

"War Slut" by Carlton Mellick III

ORDER FORM

TITLES	QTY	PRICE	TOTAL
	Shipping costs (see below)		
	TOTAL		

Please make checks and moneyorders payable to ROSE O'KEEFE / BIZARRO BOOKS in U.S. funds only. Please don't send bad checks! Allow 2-6 weeks for delivery. International orders may take longer. If you'd like to pay online via PAYPAL.COM, send payments to publisher@eraserheadpress.com.

SHIPPING: US ORDERS - $2 for the first book, $1 for each additional book. For priority shipping, add an additional $4. INT'L ORDERS - $5 for the first book, $3 for each additional book. Add an additional $5 per book for global priority shipping.

Send payment to:

BIZARRO BOOKS
C/O Rose O'Keefe
205 NE Bryant
Portland, OR 97211

Address

City   State   Zip

Email   Phone

9 781933 929125

ORDER FORM

TITLES	QTY	PRICE	TOTAL
Shipping costs (see below)			
TOTAL			

Please make checks and moneyorders payable to ROSE O'KEEFE / BIZARRO BOOKS in U.S. funds only. Please don't send bad checks! Allow 2-6 weeks for delivery. International orders may take longer. If you'd like to pay online via PAYPAL.COM, send payments to publisher@eraserheadpress.com.

SHIPPING: US ORDERS - $2 for the first book, $1 for each additional book. For priority shipping, add an additional $4. INT'L ORDERS - $5 for the first book, $3 for each additional book. Add an additional $5 per book for global priority shipping.

Send payment to:

BIZARRO BOOKS
C/O Rose O'Keefe
205 NE Bryant
Portland, OR 97211

Address

City   State   Zip

Email   Phone

Printed in the United States
95246LV00002B/93/A

9 781933 929125

ORDER FORM

TITLES	QTY	PRICE	TOTAL
Shipping costs (see below)			
TOTAL			

Please make checks and moneyorders payable to ROSE O'KEEFE / BIZARRO BOOKS in U.S. funds only. Please don't send bad checks! Allow 2-6 weeks for delivery. International orders may take longer. If you'd like to pay online via PAYPAL.COM, send payments to publisher@eraserheadpress.com.

SHIPPING: US ORDERS - $2 for the first book, $1 for each additional book. For priority shipping, add an additional $4. INT'L ORDERS - $5 for the first book, $3 for each additional book. Add an additional $5 per book for global priority shipping.

Send payment to:

BIZARRO BOOKS
C/O Rose O'Keefe
205 NE Bryant
Portland, OR 97211

Address		
City	State	Zip
Email	Phone	

Printed in the United States
95246LV00002B/93/A

9 781933 929125